# JATI'S WAGER

## WIND TIDE BOOK 2

### BY: JONATHAN NEVAIR

This is a work of fiction. Similarities to real people, places, or events are entirely coincidental.

**JATI'S WAGER**

First edition. August 18th 2021.
Copyright © 2021 Jonathan Nevair.
Written by Jonathan Nevair.
Cover design © 2021 Jessica Moon and Chad Moon.
Cover art © 2021 Zishan Liu
Editing by Susan Floyd.
Formatting by Mandy Russell.
Published by Shadow Spark Publishing
www.shadowsparkpub.com

**Content warning:** death of parent (mentioned), death of mentor, verbal abuse, graphic violence and death, blood, homelessness, trauma, guilt, kidnapping (mentioned).

*For those who live beyond the pale and walk a path
only they can see.*

# AUTHOR'S NOTE

The Wind Tide series is inspired by ancient Greek sources. *Goodbye to the Sun* (Book 1) takes its themes and tragic plotline from the Greek play, *Antigone*, written by the playwright Sophocles. *Jati's Wager* (Book 2) follows suit but turns to another source: the myths of the Trojan War. As with any book in this series, there is no need to be familiar with Greek sources before reading the novel.

The Wind Tide trilogy is constructed so that each book can be enjoyed without having read those that come before or after it. If you choose to start with *Jati's Wager*, you'll travel the Sagittarius Arm on an action-packed and philosophical adventure, enjoying a classic heist plot set in a distant portion of the Milky Way galaxy. If you like consistency and order, it is best to start at the beginning with Book 1, *Goodbye to the Sun*. I recommend it. But the choice is yours and should be up to no one but you.

Jati would agree, I assure you that.

# TABLE OF CONTENTS

| | |
|---|---|
| THE STORY SO FAR | x |
| PROLOGUE | xiv |
| ONE | 1 |
| TWO | 12 |
| THREE | 15 |
| FOUR | 25 |
| FIVE | 33 |
| SIX | 35 |
| SEVEN | 44 |
| EIGHT | 51 |
| NINE | 53 |
| TEN | 67 |
| ELEVEN | 78 |
| TWELVE | 80 |
| THIRTEEN | 98 |
| FOURTEEN | 108 |
| FIFTEEN | 123 |
| SIXTEEN | 126 |
| SEVENTEEN | 142 |

| | |
|---|---|
| EIGHTEEN | 164 |
| NINETEEN | 185 |
| TWENTY | 188 |
| TWENTY-ONE | 206 |
| TWENTY-TWO | 227 |
| TWENTY-THREE | 236 |
| TWENTY-FOUR | 241 |
| TWENTY-FIVE | 255 |
| TWENTY-SIX | 264 |
| TWENTY-SEVEN | 267 |
| TWENTY-EIGHT | 277 |
| TWENTY-NINE | 287 |
| THIRTY | 308 |
| THIRTY-ONE | 327 |
| THIRTY-TWO | 329 |
| THIRTY-THREE | 338 |
| THIRTY-FIVE | 348 |
| THIRTY-SIX | 378 |
| THIRTY-SEVEN | 387 |
| THIRTY-EIGHT | 396 |
| THIRTY-NINE | 407 |
| FORTY | 418 |

# THE STORY SO FAR...

The Wind Tide series begins in a remote star system on the desert planet, Kol 2. Razor, a Mote whose people live as outcasts, infiltrates and pilots a flight pod coming out of orbit. Her human cargo: an ambassador from the prosperous and powerful empire of Garassia, Keen Draden. A simple ransom transaction as part of a larger assault by the Motes on their local oppressors, the Targitians, turns into a disaster. The Targitians refuse to negotiate and instead try to dispose of Keen, making an opportunistic political play against their rivals in the energy business. Their city's defenses decimate the attacking Motes. The pod takes fire and crashes in the dunes, leaving Razor and Keen to negotiate terms. Razor agrees to lead the ambassador safely to her people and get him off-world to the planet Heroon where he hopes to reconcile with an estranged and (until the arrival of a recent letter) unknown daughter named Reynaria. In return, Keen will help support and fund a large militia for the Motes to take down the Targitians.

Chased by the infamous bounty hunter Pox, familiar to Keen from his days as a Legion soldier in the Patent War, he and Razor eventually escape Kol 2. The two find themselves on the *Carmora*, a ship captained by Keen's old war friend, the gunrunner and freedom fighter, Jati. To Keen's surprise, Jati knows Reynaria. Keen learns that his daughter leads the resistance on Heroon. Her rebels fight with Targitian backing against their planetary colonizers, the Garassians (Keen's own political culture and home world).

During a short stop at the moon base, Tarkassi 9, Keen has a personal revelation that inspires him to pursue sobriety and take responsibility for his dubious and selfish actions as a privileged citizen in the Sagittarius Arm. The *Carmora* comes under attack by Pox, who has managed to follow them from Kol 2. Evading capture, the three arrive at the orbit port off Heroon. When the *Carmora* drops out of FTL they are greeted with a shocking surprise: the planet is now controlled by Reynaria's faction. Razor and Keen attempt a daring escape from Jati's ship in a pod before it is boarded. Unsuccessful and captured by Pox's ship, they descend to the planet where Keen and Razor are placed in the hands of Reynaria's high priest. The group travel by boat along a river through the rainforest into the planet's hidden interior.

On arrival at Reynaria's secluded temple, Razor and Keen confront the construction site of a future city that will house "believers" after Heroon is eco-shaped into desert for wind (following a theocratic program mirroring that of the Targitians on Kol 2). Razor is sent to a work camp and Keen is thrown into a temple prison cell. Both come to personal realizations about their past and present lives and take what each decides are appropriate routes to a desirable future. Keen, manipulated psychologically in his cell and affected by PTSD, allies himself with Reynaria, thinking it to be the right decision. Razor puts her trust in Jati, who is also in the labor camp organizing a clandestine last-ditch effort to take down Reynaria's regime. During her escape attempt and rendezvous with Jati, Razor makes the difficult choice to sacrifice her freedom to ensure Jati can get out and lead a counterinsurgency in a surprise attack on the temple.

Keen kills Pox in a duel after the bounty hunter is caught attempting to sell secret information about Targitian wind energy design to the Garassians. Victorious, Keen is now the leader of Reynaria's military forces, and he confronts Razor in her temple prison cell with terms to re-negotiate their relationship. He offers what he thinks are personal and political outcomes to her benefit. Razor refuses, declaring his proposal to exchange the re-location of her people for the lives of her two children held by the Targitians to be an impossible moral choice.

Keen accidentally finds a box of letters his lover intended to send him that Reynaria never dispatched and his plans unravel, revealing a thread of deception, lies, and treachery pointing back to his child. He realizes that Reynaria manufactured the timing of one letter from his (now dead) lover that reached him, triggering a deceptive plot and sparking his trip to Heroon.

Reynaria, en route to meet a delegation of Targitians at the temple's landing pad, is unaware she is walking into a trap. Keen recognizes that the arriving delegation's pod is not from Targite and attempts to get to her before it is too late. His parent, Aradus, who heads the Garassian Council, arrives in the pod disguised as a Targitian and murders his granddaughter unknowingly. Aradus expresses no regret when informed by Keen of Reynaria's identity and declares his grandchild an illegitimate disgrace.

Jati arrives on the scene after a successful takeover of Reynaria's weakened faction at the temple. Aradus demands Keen leave with him and insists that he tell his story to the Garassian Council to ruin the reputation of their rivals, the Targitians. A broken Keen realizes the only option left to make good on his errors of judgment and the misleading lies of his child is to sacrifice his own life. That act of martyrdom will save Razor's people, prevent Aradus and the Garassian Council from usurping their rivals, the Targitians, and avoid further exploitation and abuse of power in the Arm. Keen relies on Razor to shoot him in front of his parent, and she is presented with a difficult, life-altering choice. Without knowing Keen's motivations, she reacts to his "false" threat to reveal the Motes hidden location on Kol 2 by shooting him with a blaster, thus saving her people and protecting others from exploitation and oppression in the Arm. Razor's choice comes with a hard price, but one she is willing to pay: spending the rest of her life in Targite prison.

Nine years have passed since the storyline in *Goodbye to the Sun* ended. Keen's role in the larger narrative of the Wind Tide series is over but Razor's continues, sentenced as she is to life in prison under the city of Targite on Kol 2. Her life, and the account she will write of her time with Keen while serving her sentence, extends beyond the timeframe of what follows...

# PROLOGUE

Jati didn't like stowaways. They'd let anyone join the crew of the *Carmora* so long as you looked them straight in the eye when asking to come aboard. If you needed to get the hell out of wherever you were from or had gotten to, for whatever reason, you could hitch a ride in exchange for honest work. They might dump you off at the first orbit port with a fistful of credit chips if you were a problem, but they'd trade you the work for a ride.

Stowaways tried to bypass a moral agreement as freeloaders. That wasn't how the new Arm worked. The one Jati and the People's Army were fighting for was built on a new value system. No longer would entire planets labor under exploitative monopolies to make life in other star systems worlds of luxury and privilege. In the wake of Jati's liberation forces, an autonomous federation of independent planetary nations took shape. Two territories remained before they'd have the Garassians on their knees. The fateful end of economic tyranny and political corruption would soon be mere lines in the annals of a bygone age.

But when Ailo appeared in the nav room on the *Carmora* struggling against the ship engineer's forceful grip, the chronicler's hand slipped. The pen's ink blotted over what would have otherwise been a swift epilogue to a tragic yet successful narrative of justice triumphant.

Fate's refrain was a reminder. Epochs die hard, and rarely do they go peacefully...

# ONE

Ship: *Carmora*, P-Frigate
Location: Tarkassi sector, Outer Rim
Year: 3058, Second Span

"The little rat was in the cargo hold," the burly engineer said to the captain who stood in front of a holo-field of the local star group. "Enjoying the freezestock produce from Quitreen." The machinist glowered at Ailo as she resisted his brutish grip. "Washing it down with a bottle of kartan." His eyes narrowed. "From the case set aside for the trade drop on Heroon. The *good* vintage."

Ailo tugged harder.

"Quit it, you freeloader," he said, pulling back. "You're caught."

Ailo sneered, revealing deep crimson stains on her bared teeth. She didn't know what kartan was, but it went down easy and emboldened her nerve.

*"Don't be so angry, Ai. Calm down, will you? There's nowhere to go. They have you."*

Shut up, Gerib. I know what I'm doing.

*"We're trapped on a ship in FTL."*

It's not about that. They don't get to own me.

Gerib sighed, his long exhale swirling in the shared space of Ailo's internal monologue. She smiled. Her longtime imaginary friend had no choice but to sit back and let this play out.

*"Alright, but it's going to make the situation worse."*

*For him, maybe.*

Ailo stomped on the engineer's shin. He yelped in pain. She took advantage of the surprise jolt to break his grip on her smaller, teenage wrist by twisting its weak point between the fingers and thumb. The machinist bent over to grab his leg, and Ailo, cocky from a belly full of kartan, homed in on his head.

"Ai, no. It'll make things more..."

Ailo sprung. Her right hand and the remaining fingers of her left wrapped around the engineer's neck. She drove a knee up into his nose. "Gor scum!"

The machinist teetered. She sent a kick to his ribs that laid him out on the floor, groaning.

"Well, old tot, I don't like to see anyone use violence unless it's in the cause of justice. But in your case..."

Ailo spun, fists clenched, ready for the next attack. The captain stood, arms folded, with a smirk on their face. They were huge.

"I don't think you can take them, Ai."

Ailo had learned to read people on the cold and oxygen-deprived streets of Tarkassi 9. She and Gerib classified everyone who passed through the forgotten outpost at the edge of the Arm using a self-invented ranking system.

"They're a NoGo, '8 pointer', Ai. Physique, scars... the eyes don't show any uncertainty. They almost seem amused."

Ailo nodded to Gerib inside her head.

"I like the hair though."

Ailo did too. The lavender-dyed hair, tied in a long ponytail, fell to the middle of the captain's back. Their chin and cheekbones had the strength of rock slabs tossed together by a giant's hands. Green eyes simmered against flax colored skin. The face, hatched with wrinkles, spoke of life at late middle-age. Underneath a deep blue tank top, their bulky muscles had lost none of their inner strength despite the wear and tear of time and experience. Ailo's eyes went to the red design on their bulging forearm.

"Legion tattoo, Ai. All bets off. Talk time or run."

Ailo stood, panting. Her scrawny physique couldn't match someone that size, not without the element of surprise. As scrappy as she was, her presence didn't physically intimidate enemies. This situation was a non-starter. She eyed the portal.

Through the door stood freedom, temporarily. She might make it into the ship's labyrinth but then what? Duck into the venting system? That only worked if they didn't know you were on board. It was time to talk.

"Not a good idea, old tot," the captain said and nodded at the door.

"I'm not a tot. I'm sixteen." Ailo brushed sweaty scarlet bangs out of her blue eyes. "And that doesn't make sense. Tots aren't old."

The captain smiled. Heavy crow's feet creased the golden skin around their eyes. The gesture softened the atmosphere in the nav room. "It's a figure of speech, Firecracker. But in this case, it does fall short of logic." They shut off the holo-screen with a wave of their paw-like hand. "So what are you then, besides a stowaway?"

Ailo glanced out the windowpane overlooking the docking bay. A group of workers milled about stacking cargo and making repairs to flight pods. A second portal, opposite the one the engineer dragged her through, led to stairs descending to the tarmac. If she slipped out and evaded the crew she might gain access to the ship's internal passageways. A spacecraft this size had to have enough random supplies lying about for her to scavenge until they dropped out of FTL to arrive wherever they were heading. Ailo had no idea where that might be and she didn't care, so long as it was light years from Tarkassi 9.

She'd be a hunted stowaway for the duration of the trip. But hiding and stealing were what she and Gerib did best. They called it survival.

"*No chance, Ai.*"

*Shut up, Gerib. I'm thinking.*

"You picked the wrong ship if you're trying to get away

from trouble." The captain smiled. "That's exactly where we're heading."

"Guess I'll be right at home then," Ailo said. She added a mocking smile as punctuation.

"Where'd you learn to fight like that?" The captain raised their fists and shifted their legs, mimicking her fighting stance with surprising accuracy. Ailo had never seen hands so large and strong in her life.

*Be careful, Ai. I wouldn't tell them anything.*

"None of your business."

Solazi would be proud of her for that leg combination. The old war vet turned proprietor of the Tip of the Beyond taught her how to work larger opponents down to her height through strategic body targets. Each impact forced them to involuntarily bend forward or back, exposing vital points. The tactical sequences were far more effective than struggling to reach up or extend an arm or leg that would lessen the potential force and damage and leave you open to a counterattack. Too bad she wouldn't be able to tell the bartender about it. Solazi was dead going on three months now. The Cough, the bane the veteran's body carried through exposure to the malignant Reaper gas on Yaqit in the Patent War, finally got the better of them.

"You move well." The captain let go of the ready position and relaxed. "Someone taught you tactics fit to scale. And did a good job of it."

The engineer grunted and rose to a knee. His eyes went from the pool of red dripping to the floor from his broken nose to Ailo. She flipped him the bird and smirked.

"Damn vagrants," he muttered between bloody sniffs.

"We're good, Viz," the captain said. "Go down to the med room and have Arira plug that nose."

The machinist pinched his nostrils and with his head leaning back, started towards the portal.

Ailo feinted a punch as he passed. The engineer flinched.

*"You're not making this any better, Ai."*

*Gotta make life fun, Gerib. No matter the cost.*

The motto served Ailo and her imaginary friend well for the last eight years alone on the depressing streets of the isolated moon base. Now they were off that shit hole. And where were they going? Ailo thought they were on the road to freedom, headed out into the big wide world of the Sag-Arm. Instead, they were going to the brig.

"Well, you've gotten yourself into a good old-fashioned dilemma." The captain walked to a control panel below the panorama glass and adjusted a dial. "And I don't approve of stowaways."

Ailo stole a peek out the window. At the end of a row of flight pods, a K-speeder leaned against a stack of cargo shells. The thugs on the moon base used these to patrol the streets. Its flashy orange and blue custom paint job beamed against the otherwise dreary landscape of the bay.

*"Ai, you're not thinking what I think you're thinking, are you?"*

*I am.*

"You've never driven one."

How hard could it be? She'd watched the patrollers work the small hoverbikes for years. She'd been chased by them. And caught, twice. Other than a red push-button ignition, Ailo wasn't sure of the control switches on the grips. She knew the twisting handle on the right side throttled the engine.

"I could use an extra hand in the mess and a runner down there," the captain thumbed a hand towards the window, indicating the docking bay. "You work, you get a ride. And food. Pretty good deal, kiddo."

"My name is Ailo-té," she said, including the suffix to express her gender identity. Even in a tense situation like this, it wasn't unusual. If you offered someone your name for the first time in the Arm, you did it on social instinct. Plus, she wanted to put a halt to the captain's inane monikers. "Stop calling me a kid. I'm sixteen."

*I think...*

The captain nodded. "Good for you, Firecracker. I like

your style." A finger pointed at her in mock blaster fashion. "Welcome aboard, Ailo the stowaway from Tarkassi 9. You're on the *Carmora*, by the way. And my name is Jati-tō."

*"Jati-tō? Ai, I think you were wrong about this ship."*

Ailo thought back to their argument at the shuttle hub off Tarkassi 9. Two spacecraft were in port: the *Carmora* and a nondescript freighter. The weapons systems on the *Carmora's* hull gleamed in the hazy light of Tarkassi, the nearby gas giant. A classic combat vessel from the Patent War, it had been through an impressive refit job. Ailo liked the ship. A little of herself ran in its battered and bruised yet militant exterior.

Gerib disagreed. What else was new? Gerib always disagreed, as if he existed solely for that purpose. He argued for the freighter. Better to take a vessel with more cargo and fewer passengers. Less chance of being seen. And discovered. Plus, weapons meant defense. That pointed to conflict.

Ailo overrode him. She chose the *Carmora*, betting on a cargo runner with no allegiance to either side in the Tide War. Plus, Solazi always said they didn't make ships like that anymore. If something went wrong in space, you'd want to be on an old P-class frigate. Those spacecraft could handle anything.

And so Ailo ducked through security on the orbit hub, diverted to the maintenance area, and got into a cargo stack heading for the frigate. Easy peasy. If she'd known it'd be a breeze, she would've done it months ago.

The captain leaned back against the control panel and rubbed their chin in a contrived gesture. "Now, let's see... tonight is Heroonese noodles and swamp boar medallions if I'm not mistaken. It'll be delicious, so long as Viz can still smell well enough to season it with that nose you smashed. It's his family's recipe."

*"Ai, food... real food. We could eat and not have to hide."*

*No Gerib. They'll hand us off to Child Services as soon as we make port. Plus, I don't want anyone's help.*

Ailo thumbed the lucky Rim wedge in her pocket. The

one she'd never spend.

"It sounds like a job offer, Ai."

*It's a trick. Just another liar out for themselves like all the others.*

"Not if this is 'Jati'."

*It's not. Look at them, Gerib. Jati's a general. The leader of the People's Army. The one who broke the Monopoly and Hamut Alliance. This one looks plain broke.*

"We'll call it a wash with Viz, no apology needed." The captain waved a hand. "I can tell you're eager to move on from T9. That standard-issue orange jumper's seen a lot of action... getting a bit small on you." They turned back to the window to observe the activity below. "Can't say I blame you. Been like that for far too long out here... at the Tip of the Beyond." They turned to face her and smiled.

*Ai... they know.*

Ailo back-stepped towards the door to the docking bay.

"Ai, no. If this is Jati and we're on a PA ship..."

Ailo dashed to the portal. Out of the corner of her eye, the captain reached for the control board to lock the exit. Her arm extended and she touched the screen on the wall. The door opened.

"Code yellow, folks." The captain's voice bounced around the docking bay as Ailo dove through and onto the staircase balcony. "A bottle of kartan to whoever can catch her. No harm please but watch yourselves. She's feisty. Viz is down in the med room getting patched up after Round 1."

A lanky crew member in oil-stained blue overalls threw down their tools at the nearest pod and cranked their head around, searching. They spotted Ailo. With her crimson hair and orange jumper, she made for an easy mark. The person ran for the staircase. Several other maintenance workers stopped repairing a flight pod and made their way across the tarmac.

"Trapped Ai. I told you."

Ai stole a glance back through the windowpane. Stone slab cheeks pushed upward in a smile. They winked at her.

*What is it with them?*

Footsteps rattled the staircase cage. The worker, their skin a sandy beige, climbed the steps. Spiky yellow hair bobbed up and down. They took them two at a time, their violet eyes intent on nabbing her and the bottle of kartan.

Ailo peered over the banister. The tarmac under the balcony lay fifteen feet below.

"It's too high."

Who cares?

She jumped over the railing. And landed hard.

Her ankle twisted and something popped. Adrenaline pumped through her veins and overrode the pain. She sprinted towards a set of parked pods. By the third stride, she was hobbling. Every step got more difficult as the ankle gave in to the injury and refused to take the weight of her leg.

Three crew members approached from across the tarmac, running faster now that they'd spotted the source of the commotion.

"Over here!" One of them pointed in Ailo's direction. The lead runner unholstered a small taser at their hip and aimed it at her.

"Watch out, Ai."

On it.

Tasers were nothing. Ailo learned how to evade their electro-darts by the time she was twelve years old running snatch and grabs with the other street kids. All you needed was to...

Ailo's calf on her injured leg went numb as the dart nicked her flesh. She stumbled and fell onto the floor of the docking bay. Her cheek smashed against the unforgiving tarmac. Searing pain shot down her face as the skin peeled away.

She shuffled across the ground, but the ankle had lost the fight against injury. With the added shock from the taser, the leg wouldn't respond.

"Ai, the hazmat alarm. To the left!"

Ailo lifted her bloodied cheek and turned. A body's

length away at waist height, the red and white stripes of an emergency panel stood out on the ship's white wall.

She bent her good leg, dug her heel in, and pushed off and up, lunging for the lever. The two remaining fingers and thumb of her left hand grabbed the handle. She pulled.

Sirens blared. Air rushed around her. Her lungs seized, desperate to inhale oxygen as hangar jets purged the existing atmosphere and replaced it with sterilized emergency air from the reserve tanks. She choked in the temporary vacuum. The room spun and her eyeballs pulled into her skull. A misty haze filled her vision as the two temperature currents collided. Oxygen returned and she collapsed, inhaling large gulps. The spinning room stabilized and the pressure rebalanced.

"Now what, Ai?"

*I think you know...*

Ailo edged her way down the wall towards the far side of the bay under cover of the mist.

"She's here somewhere," a voice yelled over the blaring sirens. Her pursuers were close, no more than ten feet away in the fog.

Ailo pushed on as quietly as possible. She made out the bulbous bows of the flight pods as she edged along the wall. She counted three. That meant it should be...

"You are a determined little maniac, you know that Ai?"

She managed an interior smile through the pain in her ankle.

*Come on, Gerib. You're loving this. Don't deny it.*

"And where do you intend to get to in a flying speeder inside a docking bay?"

*That's the future, Gerib.*

"Yeah, like two minutes from now."

*For me, that's a lifetime.*

An orange and blue glow tinged the mist ahead. Ai edged over and the K-speeder emerged into view. The sirens stopped. Someone had deactivated the emergency shutdown.

"O.K. Firecracker, you've made your point." The captain's voice sounded over the loudspeaker. "I'm impressed. It's been entertaining, but enough's enough. Come on out. We'll call it a truce. You can have all the swamp boar you want."

Ailo pulled up and, balancing on one leg, got up and onto the K-speeder's seat. She pushed the ignition button. The motor revved to life. The engine's roar boomed off the walls of the docking bay like a furious monster bellowing from deep in a cave.

*Whoa.*

Someone had dropped some serious Arm-credits to turn the rider into one special, supercharged custom machine. She fiddled with the switches on the handles and the bike bucked forward.

*"Ai, you'll get us killed."*

She twisted the throttle. They shot up and away.

*"Ai!"*

The speeder broke through the layer of lingering mist and rose into the clear air of the docking bay. Ailo leaned the steering column to the right and zoomed across the interior.

The windowpane with the captain approached dead ahead.

*"Ai, slow down."*

She pushed a button next to the throttle. The speeder bucked and almost sent her over the handlebars.

*"Ai..."*

She tried another one and the speeder accelerated.

The captain's eyes went wide.

*"Ai!"*

A line of buttons on the left handle caught her eye.

*"Push something!"*

"I can't..." She couldn't reach a red switch made for an index finger. She didn't have one. Her hand slid over the grip to push it with her ring finger, but without support the bike tipped left and almost flipped. She couldn't let go, but she couldn't hang on, not unless she slowed down. And fast.

*"We're accelerating, Ai. This isn't good!"*

Her sweaty bangs lifted off her forehead and joined the rest of her blazing cherry hair blowing back in the headwind. Through the glass pane, the ship's captain stood with their arms folded, an expression of impatience on their face.

"Foot pedal. On the left. Push it." The captain's voice remained calm.

Ailo's toes touched the lever under the foot slip. She pushed. Stinging pain surged up her leg. Nothing moved. Whatever she injured in the fall from the balcony wasn't responding and the taser shot had numbed the muscles.

"Push it," the captain repeated.

Ailo's eyes went wide. Her stomach dropped and with it went her cockiness and attitude. She shook her head as the window neared.

The captain's expression shifted, realizing this wasn't a refusal but communication of futility. They dove to the ground.

Ailo shut her eyes. It didn't help. The speeder struck the glass and her world shattered.

# TWO

This day was a long time coming. It would've arrived sooner had I not been doing my best to manage the chaotic turmoil of Ai's internal dynamics. But there are only so many places I can focus my attention at once. Plugging cracks in the dam of memory while working to stave off the self-destructive necessities of emergency responders is a full-time job. And I'm on overtime.

Ailo's existential nihilism and reckless abandon are bred from hardship. She's survived admirably considering what she's endured. I challenge anyone to persevere on a destitute moon base without parental supervision from the age of eight. That's a feat unto itself. To find shelter — and not just physical but also psychological (that's where I come in, by the way) - food and safety day in and day out takes guts. And tenacity. Not to mention determination.

Ai has no shortage of those three. Add the fact that she's developed a street-wise attitude, found mentors (and held on to them, at least until they passed on to a better place), and maintained a set of personal goals despite watching the world ignore you from the farthest outpost of human civilization in the Sag-Arm.

Let's get one thing clear right at the start. I am not a crutch. I'm a functioning part of Ai's psyche. Myself, her emergency responders (they don't have names, only I do), the exiles attached to traumatic memories, and her own inner 'self' are all healthy parts of her mind's mechanics. We are *all* Ailo. We're not coping mechanisms. Whoever touts that belief is a liar and is fooling themselves as much as anyone else.

Nothing about this internal psychological system is unique. For reasons related to Ai's early childhood experiences, she's managed to pull me up from the depths and make me explicit. I am, literally, a voice in her head. But I am *her*, a sub-personality keeping a central personality and 'self' protected and safe while building intrinsic trust.

Now here is what makes this extraordinary: I'm an imaginary friend. We've developed a social relationship. I've become a companion to a lonely, isolated child. That is unique. Don't get me wrong. It's not all fun and games. We bicker and fight like dogs. But at the end of the day, we are a team. I keep her company as a parentless street kid, working with her to survive from one day to the next. But I serve to protect and shield Ai from internal exiles whose wounds can return to consciousness, triggering emergency responders and leading to destructive or harmful behavior to herself and others. So, I make decisions about how much, when, and if, a memory can resurface. I don't always succeed, but I try.

'Ailo' the teenager has fought insurmountable odds for years. When she's ready for full leadership of her internal system, I can take a backseat and get some much-needed rest. But I'll always be there. She may dump me as an imaginary friend and reach a point where she doesn't need or want me as an explicit internal manager. If that happens, I'll fall back into the hidden depths with other psychological family members. But I'm still on the clock. Managers don't stop working. Ever.

For now, I'm fine as a voice in her head. I prefer it this way. It's easier to speak with her while also giving myself some creative agency. And there's no shortage of entertainment. We have a good time together.

My responsibility to protect Ai is my priority and essential purpose. She isn't ready to confront the reservoir of memory on the other side of the dam. Not yet. Look at what happened on the *Carmora*.

Subtle and indirect references to her internal exiles trickled over the rim. The responders were sent scrambling and Ai responded in the extreme. Resistance as self-preservation, violence as protection, nihilism as a shield from crushing disappointment of dreaming of the future... these lead to broken noses and rebellious rides into a headwind of shattering glass. I do have to hand it to her; she knows how to make an entrance. And an exit.

The water on the other side of that dam is rising. At some point soon, I'm going to have to figure out how to release some of it in manageable doses. Otherwise, it's going to crack and emit a flood of memories too powerful to control. If that happens, the psychological deluge will drown us all.

# THREE

Hissing. A brief silence. Splashing. Like a call and response, the two answered one another in a steady rhythm. Ailo took her time in the darkness, listening. Some were slow and bubbling, others fast and fleeting. One erupted far off on the edge of her mind, another so close she could reach out and touch it.

"*Ai...*"

A familiar voice: Gerib. Further than the most distant hisses and splashes.

"*Ai... are you there?*"

She moaned a soft reply.

"*Ai, open your eyes.*"

Gerib's voice grew closer as if he was gliding nearer through the dark.

*Shhh... I'm listening.*

"*Ai, you're back.*"

"What?" Her voice came out raspy and weak. The words tinged her mind with a reminder: lips and a mouth. She swallowed and coalesced back into physicality.

"The subject's awake."

Ailo's brow furled, revealing the full sensation of her face. The voice didn't sound 'alive.'

"Who is that?"

Again, the pattern of hissing and the splashing.

"Semi-lucid. Under two minutes for 100% consciousness."

"*Ai, open your eyes.*"

"Leave me alone, Gerib. Stop telling me what to do."

Ailo raised her eyebrows. They pulled the skin on her eyelids upward and out of the blackness came fluttering light and visual information.

"Subject is online."

A wall with a blurry, rotating object appeared about ten feet away. Waves of dizziness forced her to close her eyes. Was she spinning? She drew a deep breath and her equilibrium settled.

*Let's try that again.*

She opened her eyes. It came into focus — a fan. She knew those well from back home.

*"This isn't home, Ai. Not by the look of it."*

She studied the ceiling from her prone position. Soft and greenish in hue, it appeared almost fake, like something from a dream.

A circular white orb floated over her head. Several colored lights blinked along the sphere. It tracked down her chest and back up to her face.

"Vitals are stable."

"Will you shut up? And while you're at it, go away."

Ailo's bed folded inward and rose, lifting her into a semi-seated position.

"Preparing for integration," the orb said.

The ceiling passed by and met the corner of a wall. The bed contracted further and the mysterious noises revealed themselves. Out a wide rectangular panorama window, a series of moors, craggy and pitch black, ran in undulating waves into the distance. No trees marred their barren beauty. Low grey clouds hugged the land a few hundred feet overhead. On various rises and behind hidden valleys, steaming water plumed up in the air and dropped back to crash on the ground.

A few hundred feet from the window a geyser shot a massive jet of water upward. It penetrated the low cloud cover and disappeared in the dense atmosphere. Ailo waited with anticipation. How high did it go?

Water broke through the pillowed curtain as the plume

succumbed to gravity and plummeted back to the planet's surface. The force of impact against the rocky outcrops around the fissure rattled the panorama window.

Ailo smiled.

*It's wonderful, Gerib.*

"It is."

Tarkassi 9 had nothing on this place. That synthetic world of bleak and drab architecture was like living inside a design lobotomy. A worn and tired landscape created by forced poverty and neglect, not to mention the detritus. This place sang with a personality all its own. And the scale... easily the largest open space she'd ever seen. The central market square on T9 could be crossed in under a minute. It would take hours, maybe days to trek to the horizon through the window pane. She wanted to run to the farthest rise and discover what lay beyond it.

*Where are we, Gerib?*

"I have no idea, but we're alive, Ai."

*Yeah, whatever.*

Ailo focused on the small white orb hovering near her face. "Where are we?"

"You are on Ffossk." The voice came from her right. A stout person walked through a portal and hand-signed 'té,' indicating her gender presentation as female. She wore a single thick braid on the top of an otherwise shaved head. Her hair, a rich violet, fell on skin the color of red clay. The weave reached to her waist where she cradled it as if it were a child. A deep blue bodysuit fit tight against her stocky physique. Ailo guessed her to be in her late-twenties and about as tall as she: five feet when on tippy toes.

"How are you feeling?" She asked and waved the orb away. It beeped three times and floated through the portal. The stranger smiled and turned to the view out the window. "I bet you've never seen anything like that before?"

Ailo's mind warmed up and remembered. The Carmora. The nav room. The mechanic and the captain. And the speeder...

The person turned and rested a hand on the edge of the bed. "My name is Arira-té," she said, repeating the suffix with her formal, verbal introduction. "I was on the ship with you." She winked one of her green eyes.

*She acts like the captain... Jati.*

*"The suit, Ai. I think they're all part of the People's Army."*

One of the larger geysers erupted. The water launched into the clouds. She counted.

*One, two, three, four, five...*

It smacked down onto a rocky ledge, sound waves rattling the window. Water ran down the craggy outcropping and settled in a deep pool. Black grass on the hillside reflected off its surface. It shimmered in the breeze, an invisible hand running over onyx turf.

"I was fixing up a broken nose when you had your accident." She raised an eyebrow and fiddled with her violet braid.

"Huh?" Ailo hadn't heard a word.

"The broken nose you gave Viz-ti. Remember anything about that?"

She remembered what she did to him, that was for sure.

"Am I O.K.?"

"That depends."

"On what?"

"What that means to you."

*"Ai, she's avoiding telling you something."*

*Yeah Gerib, I get it.*

"Do me a favor, Ailo. Wiggle your toes for me."

Ailo moved her feet. They shuffled under the sheets.

"Good."

"Now bend your knees a bit. Slowly, please."

Two bumps rose like newly formed hills under a white curtain.

"Excellent. I think you'll be as good as new." Arira patted her leg. "You're lucky the general acted quickly."

*General?*

*"Ai... Jati."*

"You mean Jati?" Ailo asked.

"That's right. They saved your life," she said and fiddled with a ring on her index finger, twisting it. As pitch as Ffossk's landscape and shaped as nothing more than a simple band, it fit the tone of the view out the window. "You needed proper medical attention beyond what we had on the ship. You were in bad shape." Arira's fingers twisted the ring a few rotations. "We dropped out of FTL early and diverted to Ffossk." Arira turned towards the geysers erupting outside. "At great cost," she whispered.

*"What does she mean?"*

*I don't know, Gerib. But clearly, we're going to have to work it off.*

"When can I leave?"

Arira turned. "You need a few more days to recover. We've kept your muscles busy with electro-signaling to avoid any atrophy."

"Any what?"

"To keep them active and strong. I'd like to see you using them yourself." Arira pulled on Ailo's toe playfully. "I bet you'd enjoy exploring those hillsides." She gestured out the window. "It'd be good for your legs, especially the re-built ankle."

"Re-built?"

"You've got some synthetic bones in there now. Other than a few scars around the foot and shin you'll never know the difference." Arira sat down on the stool next to the bed. "And new ribs on this side as well." She poked Ailo's midsection. One of your lungs collapsed, but the general wasn't joking when they said you were feisty. You bounced back well."

Ailo lifted her arm and touched her face. Everything felt normal. She ran a hand over her head. The familiar shoulder-length bob sifted through her fingers on one side. But the other... "Where's my hair?"

"One side had to be shaved. I needed to perform some cosmetic work on a cheek and one of your ears. You took a lot of glass in there, despite the anti-cut shards. Quite the little daredevil." Arira winked.

"I'm not little."

"Right, forgot. You're sixteen. According to you."

"I *am* sixteen."

Arira nodded.

*"What do you think she means, Ai?"*

*I don't know.*

"There were no medical records for you in the database." Arira raised an eyebrow. "I couldn't get your wrist chip to scan either."

Ailo shrugged. No one ever could. At least not the authorities. She'd been booked twice on T9 and sent to the detention center, and both times they had to manually enter her info.

Arira's eyes stared at her face.

"Do I look different?"

The doctor handed her a small mirror from the bedside table.

Ailo faced her image. Except for the new haircut and a scar on her forehead, everything looked in one piece.

"That one cut was difficult," Arira said. "I did my best but it was deep and rugged. You'll have it as a reminder to be more careful."

*"I like it, Ai. It gives you some personality."*

Ai smiled internally. *I like it too. And the hair.*

The geyser, the large one next to the small lake, went off again. Ailo watched the water disappear in the clouds.

*One, two, three, four, five...*

It fell back and splashed on the rocks.

"I had to cut you out of your clothes after you crashed. But we've got plenty of things for you to wear. I already put some in the closet." Arira nodded towards the wardrobe across the room.

Ai's stomach dropped.

*"Ai, the Rim wedge."*

"Where's my money?"

"The coin? It's in the drawer."

"Give it to me."

"No one is going to take it, I promise."

"It's mine. I want it." Ailo shifted herself up.

Arira's eyes went wide. "O.K. stay put." She retrieved the Rim wedge from the drawer and brought it to the bedside. Ailo snatched it from her hand. On one side lay the familiar icon of a blazing star, the symbol for the rogue currency used as anarchic exchange on the Outer Rim. Ailo flipped the half-moon carbolite chip over. Hatched into the hard steel were the two initials she'd carved seven years earlier. She closed her palm around it.

"Ailo, I'd like to ask you something." Arira's russet-colored hand stroked her long braid.

*"Be careful, Ai."*

"Your oxygen level runs low. It's one of the reasons we had to get you here fast. I assume it's from the moon base. I know that Tarkassi 9 has a minimum atmosphere."

Ailo avoided Arira's gaze and focused on the geysers out the window.

"But your fingers." Arira took a seat next to the bed. "The ring and pinky don't show signs of circulation restriction. So it's not likely those other two were lost because of…"

"I don't want to talk about it." Ailo glared at Arira. "Go away."

"I didn't mean to pry. I was asking for medical…"

"Go away!"

Arira rose. "O.K. Ailo. I'm sorry, I didn't mean—"

"Don't be sorry for me! I don't need pity."

"I understand."

"No, you don't." Ailo burned a hole through the panorama window.

*"Ai, calm down. She's trying to help."*

*Shut up, Gerib. How many times do I have to tell you? I don't need anyone's help.*

Ailo shifted her legs and pushed off with her arms.

*"Ai, what are you doing?"*

*I'm leaving.*

"Ailo, please stay in bed," Arira said.

"Shut up, and don't tell me…"

The wave of anger and anxiety drifted away like the rush of water from a geyser. Her arms stopped pushing. She eased back into the bed.

"How's that?" Arira asked.

"What did you do to me?" The tranquility and numbness reminded her of the time she'd gotten into the cargo box trying to stowaway from Tarkassi 9, the first time. She ended up in a zero-gee space at the orbit port until caught on the pre-departure scan. But instead of physical weightlessness, this time it was psychological.

"Something to relax you. Believe it or not, Ailo, as a doctor I care about you. I care about all my patients. I care about the well-being of everyone. Even our so-called 'enemies'."

"Aren't you at war?"

"You might call it that. Often those who are not involved choose the term. I see it differently. We are fighting for something we believe is right. Fighting for something that should not be withheld or denied to anyone. When those who oppose it stand in our way, that makes it a war."

An unusual sensation, somewhere closer to her mind than her body, emerged. With the drugs quelling her resistance she didn't mind engaging in an extended conversation.

*How can she care for people who oppose her?*

*"Ai, if you have a question you should ask her."*

"What?" Arira asked. "You look as if you want to speak."

Ailo opened her mouth, then closed it. "How… forget it."

"What?"

"How can you care for people who are your enemy?"

"I don't believe in hate. And I don't like anger." Arira walked to the window. "I was angry, for a time…" Her voice trailed off. "For too long."

Ailo fought the drug.

"I won't tell you anything." The words were so hard to say with any backbone.

"I'm not asking you to answer anything else, Ailo. I promise. That's your personal information. I'm sor..." Arira caught herself. "O.K.?"

*"Ai, she seems sincere. I like her."*

*She's okay.*

"So now what?" Ailo asked.

"You take it easy for a few days. We'll get you up and moving about and you can explore the hillsides. Ffossk is far from the current conflict. We use it as a recovery station for those injured in our struggle. And," Arira smirked, "there's nothing out there for miles and miles, Ailo. So don't go trying for Round 2 of the stowaway's adventure."

Ailo smiled, not so much in reply but more at the thought of miles and miles of open land. The drugs made it easy for once.

"But as for what happens then," Arira said, "that's between you and Jati."

"So they're the leader of the People's Army?"

"Indeed. Were you expecting them to be different?"

Ailo nodded.

Arira sat down again next to Ailo's bed. "That's why they're the leader of the People's Army. Because they are different. If they were like familiar leaders and generals, nothing would change."

"Where are they?"

"They're off fighting for what is right."

"But they were with us on the Carmora?"

Arira nodded. "They were, yes."

*"Ailo... I get the feeling we're about to get hit with something. Brace yourself."*

"What aren't you telling me?" Ailo didn't do small talk. And she hated to dance, whether with legs or words.

"A lot has changed, Ailo. We were winning our fight for justice. But there's a new problem. The Tide is shifting. It's starting to ebb."

"That doesn't make sense. A few days and now you're losing?"

"Two months, Ailo."

# FOUR

Ailo spread out wide across the onyx spindles of grass and stared up at the low-lying clouds. A nearby geyser belched.

An uncontrollable giggle intruded on her heavy breathing. She'd run until her legs gave out and collapsed on a hillside about a mile from the rehab facility.

"Having fun, are we?"

Ailo smiled.

*Wait. Not yet.*

"Yes, I know Ai. You've been doing this for three days."

"Now!"

A loud smack interrupted her panting as geothermic water hit rock. It splashed up into the air and doused her body. She spat it away from her lips and wiped her face.

Running and exploring for three days in utter joy. Arira let her loose without care. No lecture, no rules, no 'don'ts.' The doctor showed her the path down from the rehab facility, gave her a snack pack, and a call button in case she needed help.

Ailo returned each day at dusk, drenched and exhausted. Arira would sit with her while she stuffed food down her throat. The doctor would finger her braid and ask questions about her ankle, her breathing, and whatnot. Ailo would nod and grunt with a mouth full of dinner. Everything was fine. It was better than fine. She was free.

Her senses were like a sponge soaking in Ffossk's topography and climate. Back on T9 they worked practically, occupied with the task of survival and opportunity. Now? She didn't need to focus on food and shelter or be on guard for surprises.

Seeing became looking. Hearing became listening. For the first time, she experienced the joys of security and leisure. The wilds of Ffossk, the black hills, endless and rolling, lured her to run with long strides. She scrutinized the planet's colors, a mix of waving ebony grass and rocks of nuanced greys and stark whites, with a close eye. Curious hands traced over rock surfaces. Steaming pools, heated by geothermal waters glowed azure and emitted pungent natural perfumes. The vivid blue against the pitch night grass and ivory rocks introduced contrasts unknown while cloistered in the cold, bleak synthetic prison of Tarkassi 9.

A roar interrupted her revelry.

Ailo rolled her head in the sound's direction, soft blades of black grass brushing her cheek.

"What was that, Ai?"

A second bellow echoed against the rocks, louder and closer.

"Ai?"

*Not sure.*

She stood and faced back towards the tiny rehab building in the distance. Nothing but spouting geysers and steam rose over the hills.

The roar repeated and a figure on a K-speeder popped into view from a hidden valley. They were tearing ass over Ffossk's ragged terrain. The vehicle zoomed a few feet off the ground, snaking its way up and down the black contoured hills. Each time it came up a rise, the howl of the engine boomed across the landscape.

The rider disappeared behind another sweeping mound.

Ailo smiled.

When it popped into view again, one hill away, she made out the vivid yellow and blue of the K-speeder's body under the figure's large frame. Lavender hair blew in the wind.

*Jati.*

The bike vanished down the last rise. Ailo's ears caught the distinct cry of the engine accelerating.

*"Um, Ai, maybe we should..."*

*Vroooom!* The speeder whizzed over Ai no more than ten feet overhead. She dove to the grass and turned to watch it pass.

Jati leaned to the left and arced the speeder back around in a rising turn. They hugged the underside of the cloud cover a few hundred feet off the ground. The speeder came around behind a large geyser spouting a stream of water.

Ailo's eyes went wide.

*I want on that thing.*

*"After the first time? Are you serious?"*

Ailo ran to the next crest to watch Jati approach. The yellow and blue speeder dove down over a steep rock ledge and zipped over a steaming turquoise pool, cutting a v-trail over the surface with its clean air discharge. Jati accelerated and red sparks blew out of the dual exhaust tubes. Ai covered her ears.

*"Ai, look!"*

The speeder bolted and reached the horizon in mere seconds.

*"I've never seen anything go that fast."*

*Me neither.* Ai smirked and uncovered her ears.

Jati banked left and aimed the speeder on a direct course for Ailo on the hill. She watched as they neared, a wide smile visible below green eyes and flowing lavender hair.

With a turn of their wrist, the K-speeder decelerated and coasted over the last few hills. Jati took one hand off the handlebars and ran it through their hair. The bike disappeared under the last dip.

The general emerged up the rise and glided the bike to a halt about twenty feet from Ailo. It hovered a few feet off the ground, idling low. Jati revved it up in neutral and Ailo had to cover her ears again. They winked and hit the kill switch. The last rev of the engine echoed off the surrounding hills and escaped into the distance. A tripod leg system extended from the lower body and the speeder settled down on the grass.

Jati swung off the seat and reached into a saddlebag. They turned and threw a package at Ailo.

"Welcome back to the world of the living, Firecracker."

"What's this?" Ailo held up the bag.

"You never did get to try Viz's swamp boar medallions." Jati pulled out another larger bundle and walked up the hill.

Ailo opened the bag. A warm savory wave hit her nostrils.

*Ai, how strange it smells.*

*I know, it's so...* Ailo's mind told her stomach to prepare for a pleasant experience.

She reached in to grab one.

"Not yet, old tot."

"I told you, I'm not a tot." She stopped with a boar medallion halfway out of the bag.

"That's right. You're going to have to give me a bit of time with that one. It comes naturally to me. I've been saying it for almost sixty years." Jati opened their satchel as they approached and pulled out a bottle. "Got some other things to go with those medallions. We're going to have a picnic."

"A what?"

Jati stopped. They cocked their head. "Picnic?"

Ailo shook her head.

"Well, old..." Jati raised their eyebrows and laughed. "Well, this will be your first. It's an outdoor meal. Usually not a fancy one, either. Just the kind where you bring some food, sit and talk."

*Great, talking. I should've guessed.*

*"Ai, Maybe it will be no big deal."*

Ailo wasn't so sure.

"So..." Jati nodded towards the speeder. "I guess you noticed it's all back in one piece."

Ailo dug her shoe into the black grass. "Yeah, sorry."

"Apology accepted, kiddo." Jati winked and plopped onto the ground. They unpacked a blanket and some glasses and other items.

"You're not going to make me pay for it?"

Jati unfurled a large woven blanket with striated bars of yellow and red and nudged onto it. They raised a hand and gestured for her to sit.

Ailo plopped down and Jati handed her a plate and utensils.

"You can pay me with some wisdom," they said.

"Huh?"

"Tell me what you've been thinking since you woke up."

Jati poured a dark liquid into her glass and laid out various greens and fruits. "That's Cantinool tea, by the way," they said, handing her the glass. "Made from the nectar of trees. The food is spiced with Marmish, which is from the same source but gives off a spicy and tangy flavor."

Ailo lifted the glass to her nose and inhaled. A rich and complex scent, more intense than the medallions, triggered a memory flash: someone handing her a small cup of steaming liquid. She remembered it being so large she had to grab it with both hands.

*My parent...*

*"Ai, you need to answer Jati."*

Ailo snapped back to Ffossk and the picnic.

Jati lay on their side and leaned on an elbow. "What do you think of Ffossk?"

Ailo gazed at the rugged yet beautiful landscape alive with geothermal activity. "I love it."

"Is it the landscape you love, or is it the freedom to explore it?"

*"Ai, that's an interesting question."*

*It is.*

Ailo sipped the tea. A savory nuttiness ran over her tongue and triggered another memory. An image of Tarkassi 9 bubbled up to her conscious mind: sitting at a small table in a cramped kitchen. A person humming a simple melody.

*My parent.*

*"Ai, Jati..."*

"Interesting question, isn't it?" Jati popped a medallion

into their mouth and winked.

"You're weird."

Jati laughed. "Thanks, kiddo."

Ailo sighed. She would have to live with the 'kiddos'. But the 'old tot' thing was not negotiable.

"I'll take it as a compliment," they added. "Normal is both boring and dangerous."

"Dangerous?"

"Oh, yes." Jati reached over and put some greens and fruits on her plate next to a few medallions. They gestured for her to eat. "Normal is one group's idea of the way things *should* be. And it creates a way that things *shouldn't* be. That's where we get into problems."

Ailo popped a medallion in her mouth and instantly wanted to eat everything on her plate.

"You like it, huh? Thought you would." Jati smiled before continuing. "Weird, on the other hand, is only a criticism from a position of normal. For me weird means… individual. Unique. Maybe even, ironically, freedom from being normal. Which brings us back to my question, Firecracker. And your 'payment'." They nodded over at the K-speeder.

"Both." Ailo popped another medallion in her mouth and chewed. Easy peasy. Conversation over and payment rendered.

Jati nodded. "Agree. However…"

*Here we go…*

"Ai, be patient. They're just asking for you to talk."

*They're asking me to think.*

"Is that so bad?"

Ailo thought back to the conversation she'd had with Arira the first day when she woke up after the accident. She'd enjoyed their exchange.

"I asked you for some wisdom. I want to hear about what you've learned after what you've been through. And what you've learned out here." Jati gestured at the hills and rocky cliffs. "Explain why you chose to answer 'both' and not one or the other."

Ailo's insides rattled.

*"Ai, are you O.K.?"*

Her mouth opened but she froze.

*"Ai, what's the matter?"*

She pinched a bit of the blanket's fabric between her fingers and rubbed it back and forth. "What kind of blanket is this?"

"It's made of bereese."

"Bereese?"

"It's the hair of a common animal, about the size of the speeder. From Heroon."

"Heroon? Where the headquarters are for the People's Army?"

"That's right, kiddo. And where this food you're eating comes from too. Been in the *Carmora's* freezestock hold for half a year. I know you remember *that* place." Jati winked.

Ailo stuffed another medallion in her mouth. Her eyes sunk to her plate, embarrassed.

Jati knocked back their Cantinool tea and sat up into a folded leg position. "You take your time on that answer. But I do expect you to give it to me at some point. For now, think a bit on what you can do here compared to back on Tarkassi 9."

"Why?"

"Because it'll give you a sense of who I am and what the People's Army is fighting for."

"Who do you think I am?"

*"Ai, I don't know if that's appropriate."*

*Shut up, Gerib.*

Jati smiled. "No idea. Which brings me to another point. Arira said…"

A sonic boom blew over the hillside sending the food and drink tumbling over the grass. The blanket folded over and the K-speeder rattled and almost tipped.

Jati rose to their feet, facing back in the direction of the rehab facility.

"What was that?" Ailo stood and wiped food off her shirt

and pants.

"Arira, everything O.K. over there?" Jati spoke into their wrist com. No reply came. "Arira? You O.K.?"

"There's smoke." Ailo pointed at the horizon to the left of the rehab facility.

"Do you have a call button?" Jati asked.

Ailo nodded and reached in her pocket. She handed it to Jati.

They tried it and waited. Nothing.

Jati picked up the satchel and tossed it to Ailo. "Pack up that stuff, quick." They went to the speeder and climbed on.

Ailo grabbed the glasses and plates of spilled food off the black grass and stuffed the bereese blanket into the bag.

"Come on." They nodded for her to get on the speeder behind them.

*"Back on the speeder, great."*

Ailo got on, ignoring Gerib. Two handles popped up from the speeder's body behind Jati's hips. Ailo gripped them with each hand.

"Foot slips, kiddo."

Her feet probed around, hitting Jati's calves until she found the second set of foot slips and slid them in. The system latched and secured her ankles.

Jati fired up the engine. "Hold on, old tot." The speeder bolted forward and up into the sky.

Ailo screamed at Jati, but the supercharged engine's roar drowned out her retort.

# FIVE

Don't forget that for Ai things like K-speeders and older folks who live risky lives are wonders that inspire admiration. Especially if you've lived somewhere like T9, where the most exciting people are also the most dangerous. Jati's mixture of a hazardous occupation and cavalier attitude was rooted in decency and justice and presented a new kind of alluring for Ailo. Even with her history of consistent deceit from others on the moon base that bred mistrust, Jati's kindness held a strong attraction.

Ai was hesitant and rightly so. It meant taking a risk and not in physical form.

Ai is tough. *Real* tough, physically. The vulnerability of the bodily type she can handle. Back on the moon base it resulted in bouts of post-incident self-reproach for making a poor decision or acting on necessity. I would do my best to ease those sessions and second-guessings, but not too much. You see, back on T9, our circumstances required us to avoid regret. You couldn't carry a heavy psychological burden on top of the stress of day-to-day survival.

Ffossk's dynamic presented a different relationship. Even in a short span of three days, we didn't need to carry the weight of unpredictability regarding food, shelter, and safety. And so I encouraged Ai to engage with Jati. To try a bit of vulnerability of the psychological and social kind. I was proud of her for taking a second step at the picnic (the first being her initial discourse with Arira from her bed upon waking). Sure, Ai avoided Jati's follow-up question. But I think even Jati knew to be patient with a response, both from what they read of Ailo's personality and because it was, to be honest, a rigorous question.

The irony is, I expected get some relief now that we were off Tarkassi 9. Sure enough, by the time we were on Jati's speeder racing back to the rehab facility a crack in the dam of memory began to open. I did my best to redirect Ai back to Jati's questions. That was my function. Now wasn't the time for those memories. And if that fissure to suppressed memory wasn't enough, my brilliant idea to encourage social experimentation was about to expand my job description. And eventually re-write it.

# SIX

Ailo leaned to the left as the K-speeder roared over the hillsides. Her garnet hair whipped back in the wind. Squinting against the wind, she saw the rehab center edging closer by the second. A plume of smoke rose a short way off in a valley obscuring a portion of the geyser-filled black hills.

She loved the K-speeder. You absorbed the traversed terrain so potently and viscerally. Without physical boundaries like on a pod or ship, space and the heights touched the senses. The temperature fluctuations hit your skin, falling and rising when gliding up and down the slopes. Hot and cool walls of air slammed into your face when you passed from land to water and back again.

"Hold on," Jati said.

They aimed the bike up, gaining altitude. Ailo's heart dropped into her stomach. She gripped the handles tighter. The geysers and hills grew smaller with each passing second. Ahead and above hung the dense and heavy grey cloud layer. Ailo didn't know much about atmospheres. T9's barren, rocky, and dusty clay-colored wasteland lay on the edge of the Arm as part of the vacuum of space. From what little she'd overheard and read on news feeds, atmospheric weather changed and moved. But these clouds appeared obstinate like they'd staked claim to the air above this land and had no intention of leaving.

"Is it always cloudy?" she yelled at Jati's ear.

They shook their head back and forth and said something she didn't catch.

"What?"

Jati rotated their head a quarter turn. "No, not always."

The cloud line approached.

"Sometimes it looks like this." Jati pushed an orange button on the left handle. The speeder bolted up and forward at double-speed like when they'd crossed the landscape before arriving for the picnic.

Ailo thanked the designers for the toe clasps because she almost lost her grip on the left handle with her two fingers and thumb.

"Ai, that orange button..."

*Yeah, that was the one I was trying to push inside the ship.*

"Good thing, you couldn't reach it or we would be..."

Before Gerib finished, Ailo's senses smacked her mind silent. The speeder penetrated the cloud layer. Everything went white. The bike rattled and shook about. Jati worked the handlebars to keep their heading true.

Ailo lost her orientation in the whiteout. Even with the pull of gravity, vertigo hit, and fear shot adrenaline through her veins. The clouds grew darker as they rose and the shaking more violent.

"Ai, try and breathe."

*I am. But it's like there's no oxygen.*

The K-speeder sputtered and bucked. Jati worked the gears with their feet, adjusting and responding.

*Gerib, I'm scared.*

"Ai, I want you to think about something you like. Something from back on T9. If you do..."

*Gerib. Look!*

The speeder broke out of the white void. A second planetary landscape spread as far as the eye could see. The clouds were now the ground and a clear, sea green sky illuminated the billowing surface with light from a radiant binary star.

In all directions ran a world of floating islands. Verdant and lush, each matched the size of the biggest cargo hauler she'd seen docked off Tarkassi 9. Most were bigger, scattered at random locations and altitudes like someone had tossed a bag of credit chips in zero-gee.

Massive, intricately branched trees and other greenery towered from the islands' surfaces. On their undersides, cubic habitations with circular windows dangled from the ends of exposed roots reaching down into the open air. Skywalks connected the various geometric buildings in each island's root system, creating underhanging, landless sky towns.

Ailo, confident and curious in the stable air, released a hand and tapped Jati's shoulder. "What is this place?"

"Ffossk archipelago. No time to visit now. Need to get back down. The rehab center's on the other side of that smoke. Didn't want anyone taking a shot at us." Jati banked hard right and aimed the bike back down towards the clouds. The speeder accelerated with the pull of gravity. "Hold on, kiddo. And take a deep breath. Low oxygen in the clouds. Higher above and below."

Ailo inhaled a full chest of air. They shot down and hit the cloud layer. Hot, low oxygen air slammed her in the face. Again the speeder rattled and shook. Jati shifted gears and pushed back and forth on the handlebars. Ailo closed her eyes to the white and waited.

Her ear popped and the suffocating atmosphere dissipated. Luminous light filled her shut eyelids. She inhaled and opened them. To the right a thousand feet below, the rehab facility stood in stark contrast to the natural landscape. In a nearby valley, a landing pad cut a square in the black grass. The wreckage of a transfer pod burned and billowed thick black smoke.

"Ai, this isn't good."

*No, it's not.*

Jati made a pass over the wreckage and banked left, heading towards the rehab facility. Two bodies came into view splayed out on the ground near the entrance. All the lights in the buildings you'd expect in daylight were extinguished.

*Something terrible has happened, Gerib.*

Jati descended and put the speeder down a short way from the rehab center, along a low rocky ridge next to the tarmac. They cut the engine quietly this time.

The snaps around Ailo's feet auto-released. She removed her hands from the grip bars and hopped off the speeder. Jati followed suit and reached into the saddlebag.

"Come here."

Ailo stepped closer.

Jati held a blaster in their hand and gestured for her to take it.

Her eyes went wide.

Jati took her right hand and put the blaster into it.

"You ever use one of these?"

"No," she whispered.

Jati wrapped her fingers around the handle and stood behind her, placing their right arm alongside her own. "This is the trigger."

She nodded.

"Other than that, for now, it's just the sights. You see these?" Their thumb went to the notch at the rear of the barrel and the single point at the front. "Line them up. Squeeze the trigger. Got it?"

"Yes."

Jati leaned their heavy torso into her back. She tipped forward and had to use the strength in her toes to stay standing. "You feel that? Like you are a little off-balance to the front?"

She nodded.

"That's what I want you to think in your head when you shoot. Don't do it, think it. Your mind will make your muscles compensate. This thing has a kick." Ailo's shoulders rotated as Jati's hands turned her around. Their green eyes were like emeralds.

"You stay here with the speeder." Jati went to the bike and retrieved another blaster and holstered it to one hip. Their belt had a slot for another on the other side, the one Ailo now held. The general reached into the bag and pulled out a small canister.

"See this?" They threw it to her.

She managed to catch it with her left hand.

"It's called Reaper gas. You pull this pin and toss it. It creates a wall of dense fumes that will hold in place for several minutes." They pointed to a narrow cleft in some rocks leading towards the rehab facility. "If something goes wrong, throw it that way. That's where I'm heading and it's the way to the rehab buildings. It's the same way trouble will come if something isn't right. Got it?"

Ailo nodded.

"Then you get on the speeder and go up through the clouds. Make for any one of those islands and tell them you were with me and what happened. You got all that?"

Ailo nodded.

"At least I don't have to tell you where the foot brake is this time, right?"

She tried to smile but her mouth wouldn't obey.

"This bike is a custom job and built to my specifications. But on this refurb I had our mechanic rearrange the handlebar controls in case someone else uses it. Although..." they gave her a stern look, "that should only be with my permission."

Ailo nodded.

"Come over here," Jati walked to the speeder and motioned her to follow them.

"You'll need the orange button to make it through the clouds. I'm sure you watched me use it. Can you hit it with your left hand and still hold on?"

"Yes." Ailo wasn't so sure but what choice did she have?

Jati winked. "Don't worry about the bucking and stalling. Your light; the engine can handle the push through the low oxygen without the issue we had." They slapped her on the arm. "O.K. kiddo, I'll be right..."

A massive explosion rang out. Jati looked over Ailo's head. She turned. A plume of red flame puffed into the sky over the rehab center. Jati pushed Ailo to the ground.

"Cover your head!"

Ailo folded her arms overhead and tucked her elbows by

her ears. Debris clanked and pattered as it impacted around them.

"Come on," Jati said.

A strong hand gripped her arm. They pulled her up to her feet and pushed her towards the ravine. She ran, the blaster held tight. The hum of an airborne vehicle intruded on the chaos. Jati's voice behind her yelled to run faster. She made it to the ravine as a ship whizzed overhead. A whoosh broke the silence and the K-speeder exploded in a blaze of fiery orange light, parts flying in all directions.

A burst of laser strikes pelted the ravine, sending rocks tumbling. Jati shoved her deeper into the chasm. Ailo turned and caught sight of a strange ship rising in the sky. Its features were sharp and threatening, its color midnight blue. Jati pulled her on through the rocky opening.

Ailo turned back. "Look," she said. "It's getting away."

Jati turned. They watched as the craft disappeared in the clouds.

The general's emerald eyes relaxed in disappointment.

"Come on."

She followed Jati through the ravine and up and out onto the familiar grounds of the rehab center. They crossed the trimmed black grass towards the entrance. A geyser erupted nearby but Ailo barely noticed.

"Stay here, kiddo." Jati gestured for her to stop. They walked on with their blaster drawn. Ailo knew the general's destination. The bodies. She followed.

*"Ai, no. They said to wait."*

*Shut up, Gerib.*

Jati knelt at the first body and shook their head. As Ailo approached they glared at her. "You sure you're ready for the world out here? It defends power with killing and murder. It's a brutal place. It's not fun and games." Jati's face softened. "This is the world that thinks itself 'normal'."

"I am. I want to help."

They held out their hand and gestured for Ailo to approach.

She walked forward.

*"Ai, grab their hand."*

*No, I can do this myself.*

*"Ai, take it. I think you will need it."*

Ailo's eyes connected with the body. Viz, his nose a bit bent from the break she'd given it, lay dead on the black grass. Three smoldering holes in his chest ran red with blood. Ailo's eyes filled with tears. "I didn't mean to..."

"This has nothing to do with you." Jati grabbed her hand and pulled her in close. She couldn't remember the last time she'd had someone's body near hers in comfort.

"Let me go," she whispered.

*"Ai, it's O.K."*

*I don't need anyone to comfort me.*

Jati rotated and she moved with them. She knew why. They were going to examine the other body.

"You can look if you want, but stay with me," they said.

Ailo lifted her head from inside their large bicep. The person she'd hit her with the taser on the *Carmora* lay before her on the ground. Their face was brutally shot up. She gasped.

"Good people lose their lives to fight for what's right, Ailo," Jati said. They released her from their arm and kneeled, facing her. "You see this?" They showed her the fading red laser tattoo on their forearm. "That's a Legion tattoo. I served in the Patent War. I've been a soldier most of my life. Not by choice, but by necessity."

They rose. "And right now, that's exactly what we have to do. We have to fight for what is right. And it means that sometimes you have to wait to grieve, or to even allow your feelings to affect you."

"I understand."

Jati nodded. "I'm sure you do. And this is one of those times. We need to make sure the others are O.K." They walked towards the entrance to the facility.

Ailo stood over Viz's body, oddly conflicted. Resentment and remorse vied for dominance.

*Maybe that's what it is to be a soldier.*

"Come on," Jati said.

Ailo caught up with them at the entrance. The building lay in shambles. Most of the equipment in the lobby had burn marks on screens and at outlets from shorting out. Bodies draped over chairs and lay on the floor in the central reception area.

"What happened? Are they unconscious?" she asked.

Jati walked to the nearest person, a middle-aged employee Ailo recognized as one of the orderlies. They bent down and examined the head and neck. "No, unfortunately not. They were gassed." Jati walked to a nearby com terminal and inspected the burns. "E-pulse."

Ailo didn't know what it meant but didn't ask. The way Jati said it made it sound like they didn't expect it.

They strode down the hall with determination. Ailo knew by their direction and earnest gait they were heading for the wing where Arira worked.

At Arira's office suite, Jati stopped in the doorway.

*"Ai, I don't know what that look is on their face."*

*Neither do I.*

Jati disappeared into the room. Ailo surreptitiously approached down the hallway. Something told her that unlike Viz and the other crew member outside the facility this experience would be different. She turned into the room, afraid of what she would find. Jati knelt on the floor next to the bed. In their hand, Ailo recognized the black ring from Arira's finger.

Ailo's eyes went to a small piece of paper on the white linens. Brown and circular, with words written in an unusual script, it stood in stark contrast to the clinical environment of the rehab center. The font, a deep red, ran in florid and fancy passages. At the end of the missive an odd symbol concluded the textual passage. Three arrows spread like fingers with a square around the feathers at the bottom. Something about it rang familiar.

*I know that symbol, Gerib.*

"I don't think so, Ai. It's similar to a lot of others, like Legion icons."

*No, Gerib, I've seen it before.*

"Can you read?" Jati whispered, without turning their attention from the ring.

"Yes."

They gestured to the note.

Ailo walked over and took it in her hands.

'You took my child from me. Now I've taken yours. This leaves you one choice.'

Ailo glanced at the general. Their eyes were despondent.

*"Ai, Jati is Arira's parent."*

Now that she considered it, a similarity to their features and demeanors manifested in her mind.

"Aradus," Jati said, staring at the ring.

"Yes, that's who signed it," Ai said, examining the handwritten signature, 'Aradus-ti.' "Are they someone on Ffossk?"

Jati shook their head. "He's far away. On Ceron."

"Ceron? Ai, that means the enemy is taking her to Garassia."

The full implication of the situation hit Ailo. The mark drew her eyes. "There's a symbol."

"Three arrows and a square?"

She nodded.

Jati's eyes narrowed. "Hekron."

# SEVEN

Jati contacted the *Carmora* and requested a second transfer pod descend from orbit to pick them up. The People's Army general acted aloof during the wait on Ffossk. It didn't bother Ailo; she needed time alone. She sat on the edge of her favorite geothermic pool and took a mental break from the day's events. Jati stood on a nearby hilltop overlooking one of the larger geysers, a lone figure motionless amidst the onyx grass. After what had unfolded since their arrival, Ffossk appeared more ominous and tragic than beautiful. Even so, the planet still held her captivated, especially the silty striations under the thermal waters that now drew her attention. How deep did they go?

After some time lost in reflection, she returned to the present to find the curving hill of black grass where Jati had stood empty of their presence.

A high, swirling whistle intruded on the symphony of spewing water, splashing, and hissing. She turned to see Jati waving her back towards the rehab buildings. They didn't say anything when she reached them. Instead, the general nodded and walked in the direction of the ravine leading to the tarmac. As the two crossed the lawn near the facility entrance doors, Ailo fought the urge to observe the bodies on the grass. She lost. To her surprise, they weren't there. When they reached the landing area she knew why. Jati had retrieved and readied them to be brought back to the *Carmora*.

Ailo spent the first half of the flight alone in silence, processing what she'd witnessed and experienced on Ffossk. Jati stood at the front, conversing with the two pilots in the cockpit. She tucked her knees to her chest in the window seat and watched the black hills, steaming waters, and geysers fall away.

The pod broke through the clouds into Ffossk's sea-green high atmosphere and she got another view of the archipelago. The forest islands hovered like shadowy silhouettes against the fading green light of the binary star. Now, at dusk, the lit circular windows of the under-cities dappled the sky above the clouds like far off chandeliers.

Jati turned from the cockpit and walked to the rear of the pod, their thick hands reaching from headrest to headrest down the aisle. They sat at a small com station. Ailo sneaked a peek back over the line of seats as the general flipped on a holofeed. Another PA general's bust appeared in virtual form over a desk in front of Jati's chair. Without a door for privacy, their conversation wouldn't be discreet.

Ailo hadn't seen Jati act or speak this way before. Embittered, emotional, and worried words came from their mouth during the conversation with the other general. When the remarks became heated, she caught the two pilots at the front of the pod exchanging worried glances.

From her seat a few rows from the conversation she gathered the following: Jati chose not to inform the civilian population in the sky archipelago on Ffossk of the attack and abduction. They didn't want news getting out of how close the enemy had gotten to the leader of the People's Army. As Ailo listened, she learned this wasn't the first time the person named Hekron had infiltrated a secure PA territory. According to the generals, suspicions could no longer be denied. Someone close to Jati was offering vital information to the Garassians. They'd lost two clandestine space operations to surprise counterstrikes. A third of the PA fleet had been destroyed in less than two months. To make matters worse, four PA-liberated star systems fell due to sabotaged diplomacy, triggering chain reactions both political and economical that threatened the core of their war effort. In short, the People's Army might lose a fight nine years in the making. One they'd been on the brink of winning a few short months earlier.

Ailo tried to wrap her head around one more piece of the puzzle. The incident with the speeder on the *Carmora* that sent her to the rehab facility connected to the crisis, yet she wasn't sure how or why. No fewer than three times did the other general (named Hirok-ti, she learned), make passing reference to Jati's "decision" to divert to Ffossk and how it cost them to miss a vital opportunity. His body language as he spoke expressed concern bordering on anger.

Jati defended their decision with vehemence. At General Hirok's reference to "the child," Jati glanced her way. Ailo ducked back under the seat hoping they didn't catch her eavesdropping. Butterflies swirled in her stomach and her mouth went dry.

*This is my fault, Gerib.*

"No, it's not Ai."

*If I hadn't run out of the nav room...*

"Ai, stop. You ran because you needed to at the time. Remember what Jati said, about wisdom? I think this is one of those moments."

*Don't lecture me, Gerib.*

"I'm not lecturing you. I'm asking you to think a moment. What have you learned from this experience?"

Ailo fidgeted in the seat. Her feet jittered and bobbed her legs up and down.

*I don't want to talk about it.*

"You know what, Ai? You said you aren't a tot. That means you're an adult. And if you are, you can't say things like 'I don't want to talk about it.' You have to face your problems and your fears. You can't have it both ways."

Ailo leaned her head against the window. They were crossing the exo-line. Below the pod, the sky islands of the archipelago dotted the blanket of clouds. In front and ahead stood the pitch void of space. Stars glittered in the distance.

"Ai, look where we are. It's amazing."

*It is.*

"You took a giant leap getting off T9. There were a lot of

*missteps before that. This was the first misstep in your new world."*

It was a big one.

"No, it was one with bigger consequences because now you're not on a tiny moon base. And you're not a tot. You're a young adult, in an adult world."

*Jati said it, Gerib. The world is brutal and violent. Good people die all the time.*

"I think they're right, Ai. But I'm pretty sure it's those circumstances that make for the world Jati wants. The one where there's no more fighting."

*What did I do though, Gerib? What did I prevent them from accomplishing?*

"You'll have to ask Jati."

Ailo sighed.

*I don't want to know.*

"No, I'm sure you don't. But that's part of growing up, I think. And like you said, you're not a tot."

Ailo looked back as General Hirok saluted and cut the transmission. Jati took out a small container from a pocket and popped something in their mouth before leaning back in the chair and staring up at the ceiling. Ailo unhooked her safety belt and walked astern.

"You should stay strapped in," they said, chewing on whatever they'd put in their mouth as she approached.

"What did I cause to happen?"

Jati swiveled the chair around to face her and swallowed. Their eyes narrowed, the crow's feet crinkling flaxen skin. "What do you mean?"

"I heard the other general. You diverted to Ffossk. From what? You missed an opportunity in the war and now you're going to lose. It's my fault."

"Oh, that." Jati smiled. Their expression didn't hold the same sanguine quality as earlier in the day. "You've got good ears, kiddo. But sometimes words mean more than the sounds we hear."

Ailo cocked her head in confusion.

"Let's go strap in over there." Jati walked to the passenger seats, picked a row, and settled into a window seat. They gestured for Ailo to sit beside them.

"Remember I told you I've been a soldier for most of my life?"

She nodded.

"Well, I'm pretty new at this general thing. Been doing it for about nine years. That might be a long time to you, but I didn't plan on ever being a general. I retired from being a soldier in the Legion for twenty years. I was thrown back into it because of unexpected circumstances and had to wing it." They chuckled. "I'm still winging it most of the time. And I jumped ranks. I didn't get a lot of leadership under my belt before I became general." They settled a bit more into the seat. "That means I make decisions with limited experience. Sometimes my choices save lives and sometimes they take them."

Ailo watched Jati's face tremble, their chiseled cheeks twitched.

"But..." Their emerald eyes pierced her own. "That decision, the one you are referring to wasn't one of those choices. It wasn't even a decision. You weren't going to make it if we didn't divert from our destination. Never mind where we were heading. What I realized, kiddo," they sat up a bit, growing more animated, "at the beginning of the Tide War is that I never stopped fighting. I may have put away my Legion reds after the Patent War, but for those twenty years as an ice and gun runner, I remained a soldier, fighting for what was right. To me, that meant human rights." Jati leaned back a bit. "I remember a close friend who accused me of having no 'side.' But I didn't see it that way. I was doing what I knew was right in my heart. I was helping people in need, regardless of politics or circumstances. Giving aid to people who didn't have the same privileges as others."

*Gerib, is Jati talking about me?*

*I think so.*

Ailo watched Jati gaze out the portal. The Carmora

grew larger as they approached its orbit track.

"They're all battles in the same war." Jati turned to her. "Sometimes the battle is for an entire culture, sometimes it's for one single life." They smiled. "If we focus or care about one and not the other, the Arm will never change."

Ailo traced her finger over the Rim wedge in her pocket, the one with 'K.D.' scratched on it. The person who'd given her that... did it count? The stack of wedges had saved her life.

An uncomfortable, yet inspiring current ran through her mind.

*"Ai, do it. Remember, you're an adult."*

*No, it's awkward.*

*"No, not at all. You're having a mature conversation. Ask them."*

"Is that what wisdom is?" Ailo's voice was a whisper.

"I guess you could call it that, Firecracker."

*"See, Ai?"*

*Hush, Gerib. You're distracting me.*

Jati turned to the portal. "If wisdom leads to compassion and a better world," they added.

"Arira said you were different. Now I know why."

"Did she now?" Jati smiled and stared out the window at the approaching ship

Ailo nodded, uncertain if Jati could see her from the corner of their eye.

"I want to help you get her back," she said.

"I'm not sure that's a good idea." Jati ran a hand through their lavender hair and wiped an eye.

"This is partly my fault. Plus, I..." Ailo stopped. The words wouldn't come out.

"It's O.K. Ai. Go ahead."

Ailo steeled herself and summoned her courage. "Plus, I liked Arira. She was kind to me. You both saved my life."

Jati nodded. "She's good at doing that. Did it for me too." They wiped their eye.

"So? Can I help?"

"It may be dangerous, kiddo. And you may not like how it ends."

"I'm not afraid. I've been fighting too, you know. For my whole life."

"I guess that makes us both soldiers, doesn't it?"

Over Jati's shoulder out the window, the Carmora hovered over the massive arc of Ffossk. Behind the curved blanket of white clouds an endless array of twinkling stars represented the galactic civilization in its entirety.

"I left T9 to see the Arm. To explore the world," she said.

"Is that why you left? Or was it to be free?" Jati turned.

"Both," Ailo said.

# EIGHT

I *could* push Ailo. It took a change of circumstance to make me realize that she'd grown up some without me noticing. Could I be the one keeping her stagnating in early adolescence? Look what happened on the pod flight back to the *Carmora*. I got testy (and a bit angry and frustrated, if I'm honest), and catharsis turned into a catalyst for progress. Normally managers are nudging their charges to be more confrontational. Ironically, I needed to step up and speak my mind to Ai. I wasn't doing my job to the best of my abilities because I had been unassertive.

I made a note to remember that what I earmarked as the 'right moments' to tackle big issues with Ailo aren't necessarily accurate or in our best interest. From now on I would step back from the controls and work more in response to what's happening. Not only was I being non-confrontational; I was being a control freak.

I'm still ready to die on one hill: Hekron. I won't budge on that one, at least not yet. It wasn't the right time when Ai read the letter from Aradus to Jati. Nor was the earlier memory flash with the Cantinool tea that opened a door to Ai's recall of her parent. The two are related. They're intertwined. It's a mess, and it's complicated. It is going to be painful. And to that, I say, "not yet." Not with everything else going on.

Ai's on to me, though. There's no fooling her after she sipped the tea. And then the symbol on the letter sealed it. It's a matter of time now. Where we're heading with the PA that dam is going to burst. I hope she's ready for it. If she keeps impressing me by taking risks rewarding her with the benefits and comforts of maturity (and not declaring them as 'gross' or merely 'annoying'), this may work out. If not...

I tabled all that once we were back on the *Carmora*. Ai attended her first funeral, a double. Viz and Tynti-té (the other crew person) were ceremoniously eulogized in the docking bay before being sent out into the void. Their capsules were aimed together, a pair of corpses, ironically towards Tarkassi. That's the farthest extremity of the Sag-Arm. Once they passed Ai's former home on the gas giant's tiny moon, they'd drift into uncharted cosmic territory. Nothing but the Great Beyond awaited. Others had gone before in that direction, alive but in cryosleep, generations prior at the height of the Second Span. But they were never heard from again. Those colony ships may still be traveling outward. Tynti and Viz are centuries behind them now and moving slower. But maybe someday they'll wash up on a cosmic shore into the hands of their ancestors. The future returning as the past.

Ai spent most of the funeral negotiating foreign etiquette and the formalities of a new ritual while maintaining her composure. We both noticed several of the crew staring with resentment. It may have been the incident with the speeder and its related consequences to the Tide War, or it may have been a tenuous association of her role in the deaths of their friends on Ffossk. Either way, it was enough to keep me busy. And don't forget where we were for the ceremony — the site of Ai's failed stunt with the speeder. That's a lot of layers piled up for an adolescent.

Afterward, alone in her small bunk on the *Carmora*, Ailo's wall collapsed. The layers of pent-up emotional guilt, shame, and self-reproach needed to be let out. This time I knew it wasn't my job to manage them. So, I remained silent. We'd done this so many times on T9.

I couldn't help but wonder why she didn't engage me to talk her down. She always had before, after the worst had passed. I sensed something different and new this time, as if maybe another might be poised to take my place.

# NINE

"Alright Firecracker, let's see what you got." Jati nodded, indicating she should attack.

Ailo eyed her opponent. They'd been introduced as JeJeto-tō. They were the lanky, spiky yellow-haired worker with violet eyes who tried to catch her on the staircase before the speeder accident. Suited up with protective gear for hand-to-hand combat training, they were barely recognizable other than the distinctive violet eyes glimmering against hints of deep copper skin. Thick padding covered most of their body, and like Ailo, they wore headgear and donned fighting gloves.

The helmet limited her range of vision and made her hands and feet slow and heavy. Jati insisted on it. She didn't understand why when JeJeto served as a target dummy.

Solazi's training sessions and their three rules of fighting came to mind. First, if time permits, size up your opponent. JeJeto was much taller but slim. Solazi's voice rang inside her head, "gauge their reach." Ailo stayed a good foot beyond what she assumed to be the farthest extension of JeJeto's legs. Second rule: know your surroundings. In this case, the setting and potential exploitation and/or hazards of accessible or nearby resources, be it walls, objects, etc. were irrelevant. They were in the training room on the ship, standing on a large square wooden platform. The scenario was spartan, distilled to a body-to-body situation.

"Come on, kid. I don't have all day," JeJeto said, feinting a step towards her in a mock attack. Ailo's feet responded by maintaining a safe distance. The last rule: a mind like water. "You hear but don't listen (cough). Taunts, demands, insults (cough)... they're all psychological weapons of the enemy. Don't acknowledge them because they aren't in charge. You are."

JeJeto acted impatient. She waited, letting it fester and gnaw at them. Violet eyes flashed at the digi-clock on the wall. Ailo sprung. She closed the gap with a lunging punch to JeJeto's face, but her fist fell at least a foot short. They responded by shifting back slightly, knowing it wouldn't reach its target. But it wasn't a punch. It was a distance gainer disguised as an attack. Ailo's other leg shifted with her twisting hip and she covered the remaining gap. JeJeto never saw the second punch. Her fist slammed into the pad on their stomach. They hunched over from the shot and she sent an elbow up under their descending chin.

Her opponent's head shot back.

"Call and response." Solazi's words rang in her mind as the chain reaction initiated, leading the larger opponent into her strikes. Ailo's right knee banged JeJeto's crotch and reversed their upward motion.

"Rrgghh!" They hunched over, head now at their waist.

She reached her right arm towards the ceiling and dropped her elbow to the back of their neck, letting her torso fall to the ground with it to add all the mass possible to the strike.

"Hold!" Jati's voice boomed.

Ailo stopped an inch before the nape of JeJeto's neck. She stumbled and fell back to the wooden floor, panting. JeJeto stood, hunched over, hands on their knees. They weren't happy. The low shot caused them pain, even with the protection.

Jati hopped up onto the platform. They walked to JeJeto and laid a hand on their shoulder. "Alright, JJ?"

"Yeah," their eyes went to Ailo. "Crafty," they grunted. "Reminds me of the way we used to scrap in Tinex." JeJeto straightened out and walked over to Ailo and offered her a hand. She took it and they heaved her up to her feet.

Ailo had heard of Tinex. Everyone in the Arm had. The

most famous prison – a lone orbital station in a desolate solar system and the place where the Garassians put dangerous offenders who threatened their rule.

"We're good, JJ. Thanks for playing victim," Jati said.

"Sure thing, boss." JeJeto winked at Ailo and gave her a friendly jab on the shoulder. "See ya, kid."

"I'm not a kid." *What is it with these people?*

"Be careful, JJ. Trust me. Best to back away." Jati smiled.

Their expression carried more of the spirit she'd sensed before the Garassians abducted Arira. Hopefully, Jati was less distraught.

JJ raised both hands and backed off the platform with a smile on their face. Several of their teeth were missing, giving them a rambunctious, almost mischievous appearance. "Catch you all at lunch." They walked out a side portal into the changing area.

"Solazi-tu taught you well."

"Ai, how could they...?"

*Not sure.*

In all her years on the moon base, Ailo had never heard of another Solazi; not to mention one that had formal training in martial arts. The General's use of Solazi's preferred suffix made the likelihood of a match even higher.

Jati's face had a smug expression. They raised an eyebrow. "T9 isn't a big place, kiddo. There's no one else on the moon base who could've taught you how to fight that way." Jati mimicked the combination she'd performed.

Their motions were formulaic with a rhythm and familiarity as if Jati had done it thousands of times.

"I've done that combination a thousand times," they said. "Classic first-line attack sequence."

Ailo took off her helmet.

"Not something I've ever used myself in a real situation, being a larger person," Jati said. "But for you, it's top-notch. Unless you sprout up in height it'll be a go-to in your arsenal you can count on for a long time."

"You knew Solazi-tu?"

Jati jumped into a fighting stance. They threw a few punches and did a surprisingly nimble spinning kick for someone almost sixty years old. "Tip of the Beyond. Had many a drink in that bar. Did you know they fought in the Patent War?"

Ailo nodded. "They didn't talk about it, though."

"No, I'm sure they didn't. But you heard about it all the time."

*"Do they mean the Cough, Ai?"*

*Yes.*

The day she showed up for a self-defense session at the Tip flashed into her mind. Per their usual agreement, Ailo had done some intel in exchange for a hand-to-hand combat lesson. Instead, she found Lorhas-ti, the stock person, sitting alone at the bar and drinking from two glasses side by side. When he looked at her with watery eyes, she knew something was wrong. Lorhas told her that the owner's remains were being sent back to Yaqit. They had family there. The Patent War veteran turned bar owner had never said anything about it.

Solazi had always kept their relationship formal and based on a fair and equitable exchange: information for fighting lessons. Ailo never got a free hand-out. The war vet avoided personal questions and didn't try to change her in any way. She appreciated that. Somehow Solazi perceived when she was most desperate and in need of support to push through particularly difficult periods on the streets. Ailo would spot the small red mark on the tinted violet glass outside the establishment indicating an intelligence assignment.

Once that ended, T9 had little else to offer. The establishment was strangely vacant without the persistent soundtrack of Solazi's cough and the new owner wasn't as tolerant of her presence. With a growing confidence, and a need to escape what she understood would be a dreary and short life, the wider world of the Arm beckoned.

"What's the matter?" Jati relaxed from their fighting position.

"Solazi's dead. It's why I left."

Jati sighed. "I know. A few months back." They turned to face a strange weapon on the wall of the room. "Solazi carried the Patent War until the end. We all do."

Jati walked over and put their hand on the weapon's shaft. Ailo had never seen anything like it. One end sprouted into three stems with barbs in decorative silver, and the other had a button and another extension with electronic components similar to a blaster.

Ailo crossed the platform and stood next to Jati. Below the horizontally mounted weapon, a small plaque rested engraved with a name, a motto, and a set of dates:

### Keen Draden-ti (3000-3049). 'Legion, to the End.'

*"Ai, that name...."*
*It's him, Gerib. But how?*
*"If Jati knew Solazi..."*
*Should I ask?*
*"You have to, Ai."*

"Was this a friend of yours?"

Jati broke out of their internal world. "A friend? Yes." They turned back to the weapon. "And a fellow fighter. This was his Talon Caster."

The famed Legion weapon. She'd heard mention of it but had never actually seen one.

*Keen Draden was a Legion soldier...*

"Did he die like Solazi?"

"In a way, yes." Jati stroked the handle of the weapon. "He fought a disease for a long time after the war, too. Of a different kind." The general gripped the shaft and pulled the weapon off the wall holding it parallel. "Remember I told you that sometimes a choice is made to save one person, and sometimes to save an entire culture?"

"Yes."

"Keen saved a culture by dying. But by doing it, he saved himself."

Ailo pictured the portly, long-haired, and bearded person who'd dropped the Rim wedges into her hand in Solazi's bar. Why did everyone who helped her end up dead? She'd always hoped to meet him again one day. It helped push her off Tarkassi 9.

A foolish and silly thought, at least now, but she'd pictured pulling out the Wedge that had been a talisman for survival on some alluring planet light years from T9 and watching his eyes go wide in realization.

Jati pushed the weapon's shaft back into its holder.

"He saved me too," Ailo said.

"Yes, kiddo. By making that sacrifice the Arm began to change. And I started fighting another war."

"No, I mean he saved my life. On T9."

Jati turned and cocked their head.

Ailo held out the Rim wedge from her pocket. She watched Jati's eyes register the initials scratched on the surface. Their face rose and green eyes stared at her.

"He gave me a stack of wedges when I was seven, in the Tip of the Beyond. Without them, I wouldn't have survived."

Jati's expression shifted and came alive. A radiance glowed in their eyes. The stone slabs of their face grew inspired. Like a mighty giant, they rose in size and height. The platform shrunk and the room cramped around them.

"One little tot on Tarkassi 9," they said.

"I'm *not* a tot."

Jati laid a lion's paw on her shoulder.

"No, Ailo. You're not. I know what you are."

"What am I?"

"You're the reason we're going to win this war."

Ailo stood next to the captain's chair on the bridge of the *Carmora*, mesmerized at the light radiating through the ship's wraparound window. Blue cosmic mist spiraled from a central point while flashing beams pulsed through the cut in space and time. Her body remained stationary but her eyes told a different story.

"So, this is what FTL speed looks like, Ai."

*Yeah. Faster than light.*

Ailo stared, almost hypnotized.

"Coming out in thirty seconds, General." The navigator, their slender neck and head visible over the top of their seat back, worked a board at the front window below and didn't turn when addressing Jati. Their long hair, divided into half green and half electric blue at the center of their crown, fell down their back over their uniform.

"Roger that, Tera," Jati said and turned to Ailo. "Get ready, kiddo. You're about to enter the heart of the People's Army. The place that started it all." They tapped the arm of their chair. "You might want to grab hold of this. I assume it's your first time coming out of FTL?"

Ailo gripped the chair with her two fingers and thumb.

*"Wow, Ai. I thought for sure you'd say you didn't need to hold anything."*

*Shut up, Gerib.*

"In five," the navigator announced.

"Remember when I told you to think 'lean in' with the blaster?"

"Yes."

"Well, do the opposite now. Think 'lean back'."

Ailo sent mental signals to her heels and imagined standing slightly back from straight.

The cosmic spiral expanded and reached the ship. To Ailo's eyes, the *Carmora* went from supersonic to stationary. The streaming light zipped past the window and they were back in 'normal' space.

Even though her body didn't react, her mind sent her lunging forward. She barely swayed because of Jati's advice.

"Not bad for your first jump. I'm impressed. Wouldn't you agree, Tera?"

The navigator turned to Ailo and smiled, gold eyes glinting against deep umber skin. "Absolutely," they said. Tera held up a hand, signing, 'ta-té' before returning to the view out the window. She looked to be in her early thirties and had a poise and grace of movement different from Jati and the others on the *Carmora*. Ailo made a mental note to keep in mind her gender fluidity. Tera might choose to self-express differently the next time they interacted.

To the navigator's right, a pilot with a violet topknot similar to Arira's worked a set of steering controls. She watched them rotate the parallel bar and bank the ship right.

"Ai, look."

She gasped.

A ring space station with a series of docking ports panned into view. The area around the hub buzzed with small transport pods leading to and from a fleet of massive star cruisers and destroyers. Ailo had never observed a station this size. The sublime scene rendered her mute.

"You're looking at General Hirok-ti's armada," Jati said. "He was on the holo-feed when we left Ffossk." They winked, indicating they'd known of her eavesdropping.

"This space station is your headquarters?"

Tera laughed from the nav chair.

*What's funny about that question?*

"Not sure, Ai."

"This is our central jump port hub," Jati said. "A lot of these ships can't descend through the atmosphere. This station is where they dock. We use transfer pods to enter and leave the planet."

"What planet?"

From down at the nav station Tera pointed right. The pilot at the steering controls banked the *Carmora* further to starboard. Ailo's mouth dropped.

"Welcome to Heroon," Jati said.

A planet at least twice the size of Ffossk broke into view in front of the ship. Ffossk was spectacular because of its unusual landscape on the surface, and floating islands above the cloud layer. But from space, it looked like a milky quartz sphere, uniform, and bland. The planet before her hovered like a jewel aglow in the night. A single large continent of intense green edged a world of blue. Purple spiraling clouds, some deep violet, flashed with light from violent storms.

"Is that water?"

"The blue?" Jati asked.

Ailo nodded.

"Yep. That's the Lantoon Ocean. It covers four-fifths of the planet. And the continent is Oneek. The one landmass of Heroon. This place has a long history of struggle, Ailo. And triumph, at great expense. Yet it remains a place of strange wonders and natural beauty."

"The Cantinools..." Ailo thought back to the picnic a few days earlier — the unique taste of Marmish on the food they'd barely eaten before things went wrong. She remembered the flavor. Even from space, it fit her first impression perfectly.

"That's right. You'll see them after we get to the capital, Gontook."

"We're going to Heroon?"

"Sure are."

"But," Ailo lowered her voice, "I thought Arira was on Ceron?"

"She is, but I'm heading to an important meeting to decide what to do."

"Don't you want to get her back now?"

Jati turned. She knew the look. Solazi had sometimes given it to her. It usually meant the imminence of a learning moment.

"That note got under your skin, didn't it, kiddo?"

"Of course."

"Made you want to go get Arira now and teach this Aradus, and his nephew Hekron a lesson, didn't it?

*Hekron is related to Aradus?* Ailo understood. The entire problem linked back to Garassia. The leak she overheard Jati and Hirok discuss, the sabotage and killings by Hekron.

And now the note from Aradus with Hekron's symbol.

"Firecracker?"

*"Ai, Jati is asking you a question."*

"Sake of the Arm, yes," she said.

Jati's eyes went wide at her use of an expletive. Tera and the pilot exchanged looks.

"What? I'm old enough to say whatever I want."

"Good for you, Ailo." Tera gave her a thumb's up. "Don't let anyone tell you otherwise."

Ailo shot Jati a precocious look as if to say, "See?"

Jati shook their head in futility.

"In any case, to get back to the note and its effect. Aradus is old, and as a result, wise. He is a master of diplomatic games. He's playing one now or trying to, with me. But I'm not letting him pull me in."

"But what about Arira?" Ailo spoke a bit too loud and both Tera and the person steering the ship turned.

Jati leaned over and gestured for Ailo to come closer.

"Sometimes to win a war you have to know when to fight and when to wait," they whispered. "Not retreat, but when to pounce. Now isn't that time. We're going to root out an internal problem first."

"But your child?" she whispered back.

"Arira is fine, for now. Think about it. What purpose does she serve Aradus right now?"

Ailo gazed into Jati's emerald eyes. They were wide with anticipation.

"To make you come to Garassit."

"Exactly. And I will. The People's Army will when *we* are ready." They raised their eyebrows. "And then we get to pounce."

Ailo smiled. She liked this type of thinking, it reminded her of the delicious sample taste of food during preparation, the precious anticipation of knowing that soon you'd enjoy the full meal. As rare as it was in her past.

"It's called strategy, kiddo. You need it to move beyond bare tactics. Tactics get the job done but they can also get you in trouble, or worse if you don't think about the when and why."

"The when and why?"

"Like the way you might wait and strike when someone checks the clock." Jati winked.

Ailo smiled.

*"They noticed that, Ai?"*

*I guess so.*

"Solazi started you down that road. We're going to work more on it, O.K.?"

Ailo's eyes went wide. She nodded with enthusiasm.

Jati leaned back and spoke in their usual manner and volume. "You're going to get to see Heroon. And those Cantinool trees."

"Are we docking at the spaceport?"

"Not the *Carmora*." Tera answered from the nav station. "We're going down directly."

Ailo watched as the ship aimed towards Heroon's atmosphere.

"This ship's old, Ailo," Tera said.

"Hey," Jati broke in. "Not *that* old..." They winked at Ailo.

"Older than you," Tera said, working the board and, without looking back added, "so it's gotta be old."

"Hah!" Ailo laughed.

Jati turned, their lavender hair flowing over their shoulders.

"Sorry."

"Don't worry," Tera said, waving a hand. "Don't let the general fool you, it's a compliment. This ships an..."

"Old P-Frigate," Ailo interrupted, finishing Tera's sentence.

The navigator turned, her green and blue hair spinning. "That's right," she said.

"If something goes wrong in space, it's the best ship you want to be in. Don't make them like this anymore." Ailo repeated the oft-spoken phrase from Solazi and knocked her two knuckles on the armrest of Jati's command seat.

Tera's gold eyes went to the captain. Jati's eyebrows bounced up and down.

"I like you, kid," Tera said.

Ailo went to respond and Jati raised their hand. "I'll tell them," they said to Ailo. "Later."


Heroon greeted the *Carmora* with heavy rain accompanied by intermittent flashes of lightning and thunder. Ailo watched the pilot, Pozix-té, steer the ship around volatile cloud formations. The *Carmora* was a big vessel to be in-atmosphere. Even so, the unstable air of Heroon's nightly storms shook and rattled the old P-Frigate.

Ailo sat in a crew seat on the bridge at the edge of the wraparound window next to Tera. Once or twice when the turbulence jolted her she glanced at Jati. They winked, their large hands resting on the armrests of the captain's chair. Jati acted nonplussed, so Ailo did her best to appear at ease.

Towering storm clouds flashed in and out of view. Every so often, a break in the thunderheads revealed dappled lights below, the first sign of the Heroonese culture on the tropical planet.

"Tera, is that a window to the east over the Lantoon?"

Ailo turned from the view. Jati pointed at the radar screen next to the navigator.

"Yep, Cap."

"You think you can shoot it and wrap around to come in low to the coast?"

"Sure, but it will add fifteen minutes onto our arrival."

"Will the weather hold?"

"For this old clunker?" Tera shot Ailo a humorous smirk. "Of course."

Pozix laughed from her seat at the steering station.

"Poz, take us out there, bearing east over the Lantoon Ocean," Jati instructed. "Tera send her the coordinates."

Tera raised an obsidian hand with a thumbs-up. She turned to Ailo.

"General must like you. You're getting the grand entrance."

Pozix eased the stick to the right and the *Carmora* banked and dove. The ship shot straight through a storm cloud.

"Hold on to your seat, kiddo," Jati said.

Ailo turned. The general grinned.

Rain pelted the ship. Unsteady air jostled them in their seats.

Nothing other than blackness lay out the window and the pattering of water hitting the hull.

"This your lane, Tera?" Jati asked, voice rattling in the turbulence. Again, as in the pod, they pulled out a small container, popped something in their mouth and chewed. "Looks more like a wall to me."

The ship reversed its turn and banked left.

"One little cell, Cap." Tera's gold eyes watched the board. "Coming out in three, two, one..."

The tempestuous invisibility broke. And so did Ailo's perspective.

Before her ran a rippling ocean, illuminated by the rosy light of a large moon low on the horizon. The moonlight edged the frothy caps of waves driven by the passing storm. They reminded her of the brushy pink accent make-up on people in the upscale district on T9. Two long beams of cold white light ran diagonally across the dark water's surface for miles.

"That's Ran." Jati's hand came to rest on her shoulder. They leaned over and pointed to the pocked rose sphere. "Heroon's largest moon, and always the first to rise."

*"Ai, I'm so glad we left T9."*

*Me too, Gerib.*

Something clicked inside of Ailo's cognitive faculties, her dimensional perception expanded like she'd moved out of a small, single-occupancy sleeper portal into the District mansion, the one extravagant and large-scale residence on the T9.

"*The universe is a big place, Ai. Isn't it?*"

*And full of surprises. This is why we left.*

Rose-tipped waves dappled and danced on the ocean's surface.

"Quite a sight, huh?" Jati said.

She nodded.

"Nice work, Tera," Jati added. "Now I know why you put us through that."

Tera's lips curved upward, pushing on her smooth umber cheeks.

"What are those two white lines?" Ailo pointed at the diagonal lights cast across the ocean.

"The twin moons. Harmon and Karpel. You can't see them because they're behind us. They used to be one rock but it fractured ages ago. They rotate all night, like this." Jati made a pattern of interconnected spherical motions with their hands.

"Will we get to see them?"

"Of course. They're up every night. One of the favorite pastimes in Gontook is to walk along the Cantinool boardwalk on the shoreline and watch the Twins 'dance'."

Ailo watched Jati's eyes. Something shifted when they referred to the moon as Twins.

"Are you alright?" she asked.

"*Ai, isn't that a bit forward?*"

*But they look upset.*

"Yes, kiddo." Jati put a hand on her shoulder to reassure her. "I was thinking about some old friends."

"Gontook on the H-line," Tera said. The navigator pulled her loose green and blue hair into a ponytail.

Jati gestured for Ailo to look out the window.

Over the edge of the moonlit sea, yellow and orange light speckled the horizon. A coastline of dappling lights spread out left and right as the seconds passed and they sped over the water towards the capital.

"Gontook, Firecracker. Welcome to Heroon."

# TEN

Of all the cultures to rise in the Arm's Third Span, the Heroonese most profoundly and consistently embraced spirituality. Many claimed it as a carryover from the settlers who reached the planet during the Fleeing. Heroon's first human inhabitants were diasporic pilgrims seeking refuge from the violence and turmoil of an intolerant, devolving epoch. The world they left behind at the end of the Second Span had been laden with worship and ritual, albeit twisted and corrupted by tyrannical hands from its more ethical origins. A preserved and coveted version, a sanctity of the original, traveled with the persecuted, providing security and reassurance as they escaped to an unknown.

But those who'd visited Heroon, breathed its air and trod its soil, said otherwise. It didn't matter what culture arrived on the planet's single continent; spiritual reverence was inevitable. There was a soul to Heroon. A vital life force whispered from hallowed ground. A latent hand guided the world of the living with an uneasy and mercurial personality. One that seduced and enthralled those who walked amidst its natural wonders. But it twisted and distorted marvel into malice.

By the time Ailo set foot on Heroon the abstract planetary current had been translated into a series of human religions and forms of spiritual worship. The recent intrusion of a foreign cult, introduced as an attempt to colonize and terraform the planet into a desert for wind energy, interrupted longstanding indigenous tradition. That outside spiritual zealotry fell when Jati's comrades, spun together into a web of moral conflict, set down their lives and futures to stop human exploitation and the annihilation of a planetary ecosystem. Their efforts sparked a new war for justice in the Arm and returned the Heroonese to open celebration of suppressed, homespun spiritual practices.

Ailo's ears first sensed evidence of the Heroonese religion. She stepped off the shuttle with Jati and Tera on the edge of Gontook's central district into a steamy and hot, cloudless morning. And heard nothing. The silence was deafening.

A youth, not much older than she, greeted them but didn't speak. They hand-signed their gender as 'ti.' His hair appeared like the clouds of Heroon from space — light violet and trimmed short against tanned, tawny skin. Ailo recognized the same loose-fitting patterned fabric on his shirt and shorts from the blanket Jati laid out during their brief picnic on Ffossk. She couldn't remember its name.

"*Bereese.*"

*Right, thanks Gerib.*

Ailo scrutinized her outfit. Dressed all in blue, with one red sleeve, anyone would recognize her as associated with the People's Army. That morning, when Jati told her to wear the junior volunteer uniform, they explained it as common for those interested in joining the PA to spend a month on Heroon.

The youth held a tray with steady, patient hands. He approached Jati and offered a bowl cast of hardened red clay. Jati's fingers reached in and pinched something. They applied a dab of dust to their left earlobe. The youngster's offer shifted to Tera who did the same.

Something about the navigator's presence that morning had shifted. Ailo couldn't pinpoint the source, but Tera expressed it in posture and gait. Maybe the formality of the holiday and the ritual made the crew member take on a different presentation than what she'd experienced in their previous interactions. Either way, Tera's body language had changed.

"*Ai, I think you're next.*"

Jati held a finger over their lips, indicating Ailo should be quiet and not speak.

She nodded. They gestured to the bowl and mimicked the motion of applying the dust to the earlobe.

The teen approached, his yellow eyes kind and innocent. He nodded at the bowl. Inside a coarse and unglazed exterior lay a pile of green powder flecked with yellows and blacks. The youth encouraged her with a nod. Ailo pinched the powder and put a bit on her earlobe. He smiled to the three of them, turned, and walked back to a small shaded hut at the edge of the shuttle station.

Jati and Tera moved towards the densely compacted buildings and narrow streets ahead. Tera turned and waved Ailo to follow.

"*This is odd, Ai.*"

*It's some kind of ritual.*

"*It's so quiet. I don't think anyone in the whole city is talking.*"

After a few steps forward, the vista opened to her right. Tiers of urban dwellings, the same color and texture of the bowl with the powder, descended a gradual hillside to the coast. Ailo got her first view of the Lantoon Ocean in daylight. Frothy white surf and clear, bright aqua water lined the city's shore a mile distant. Beyond the lagoons, it turned a rich and deep blue.

"*Ai…it's Ran.*"

To the right of the rising sun, at the sea's horizon, only a small upper lip of the pink sphere of Heroon's dominant moon remained visible.

Jati and Tera stood a few paces ahead, watching the moonset. When Ailo reached them, Jati again gestured for her to remain quiet.

"*There it goes, Ai. Another moment and it'll be gone.*"

Ailo watched as Ran vanished below the horizon.

*Dong! Dong! Dong!*

Ailo jumped as bells rang from all directions.

In the streets and the neighborhoods around them and down to the sea, signs of life emerged. Figures appeared on rooftops to tend to plants, set tables, and attend to domestic tasks. Small transport shuttles climbed into the sky from stations around the capital. Colorful banners rose on poles at the city's official-looking buildings. Within a minute, amidst the ringing of the bells, the city came alive.

"We arrived during the Ran cycle," Tera said, the first to speak. The navigator made a hand sign to Ailo indicating they were presenting as 'ti.'

"Ran cycle?" Ailo spoke, assuming it to be acceptable now.

"Once in the Heroonese yearly calendar there's a seventeen-day period when Ran remains above the horizon until after daylight," Tera said.

"Most of the year it sets shortly after Harmon and Karpel rise," Jati added.

"Is it a holiday?" Ailo asked.

"More of a special religious time," Jati said. "The Heroonese use it to reflect on their life and planet. No one speaks on each of the seventeen days until the moon sets in mid-morning as a way of turning inward."

The bells halted. The last chimes bounced off the city's walls, echoed, and fell away.

"The bells ring one-hundred and eight times," Tera said. "That's seventeen multiplied by eight, the days of the Ran cycle and the number of calendar months around it. Minus twenty-eight, the number of hours in a Heroon day."

"What is this?" Ailo pointed at her earlobe.

"It's ground jeekoo, a stone indigenous to Heroon," Jati said. "It's placed on the earlobe as a symbolic gesture of bringing the soul of the planet, its spirit, into the ears of your mind."

"The ears of your mind..." Ailo repeated the phrase out loud. Her eyes shifted towards the Lantoon Ocean where Ran had set.

"The Heroonese believe that if you listen intently during

the silences of the Ran cycle, the planet will speak to you," Jati added.

"'When the ears of the mind are open, silence reminds us how to listen.'" Tera spoke the words with a tone of prophecy.

"Ponder that one for a while, kiddo," Jati said and winked. "Come on," they gestured for Ailo and Tera to follow them and headed towards the nearby street. "Let's get something to eat before the meeting. I'm starving."

So much human activity. Ailo could barely see around the masses of people. The central square of the governing district, an open six-sided plaza, buzzed with late-morning activity. Diners sat at outdoor tables eating and drinking. Buyers and sellers haggled and argued over prices in crowded market stalls.

"Welcome to Gontook," Jati said. "The heart of the city. Stay close to us and take it *all* in, kiddo."

The next few minutes passed in a blur of wonder and excitement. Voices calling out, people bumping into her as she moved through the crowd, scents like none she'd ever inhaled... both inviting and repulsive. They passed a group of people bidding on something out of her view and a rank scent sent her hand over her mouth.

"Yuk!' She gagged. "What is that?"

"Gor. A reptilian/mammal hybrid. And I agree," Tera said, holding a hand over his mouth.

"Worthy of its curse," Jati added, crinkling their nose.

*"So that's where it comes from, Ai."*

Solazi had called more than one ornery patron at the Tip of the Beyond a "Gor scum."

More rabble and crowds followed. Ailo caught the melodic call of music, strange and alluring somewhere off to her left.

"This is my favorite breakfast spot." Jati pointed to a

small café on the southern side of the plaza.

A mishmash of tables lay set, scattered in a shaded grove of mid-sized trees. More patrons wore bereese fabric than at the other cafés. At those establishments, Ailo recognized trendy Arm fashions familiar from the lifestyle broadcast streams.

"Are those Cantinools?" Ailo pointed at the stand of trees growing amidst the tables and chairs.

"Oh, no. They're just Yonteese runners. They grow out of every crack around the coastline." Jati took a small cloth from their pocket and wiped the sweat from their forehead. "The one thing they're good for is shade. Their sap and even the leaves are poisonous. The Cantinools live in the interior, in the rainforests."

"And you won't mistake a Cantinool for a runner," Tera added. "You see that tower over there?" He pointed to a large building a few blocks beyond the square. A column with a spiraling narrative carved into dark wood rose on the roof. "*That's* a Cantinool trunk."

Ailo shaded her eyes to observe the column. It stood at least fifty feet tall and had to be almost ten feet wide.

"That one was carved over five hundred years ago, mid-Third Span," Tera said. "It commemorates the founding of Heroon and the fracturing of the moons."

Ailo dropped her eyes from the column to the building. A series of six straight sides formed its basic architecture, like the plaza.

*"Ai, look at the colors... of the stone."*

The building's large slabs were speckled with green, yellow, and black. The palette matched the powder she'd dipped her fingers into for the ritual when they arrived.

*Jeekoo stone, Gerib.*

Ailo's eyes went back to the spiraling Cantinool column. She couldn't make out much of anything, and the other sides weren't visible. "How are you supposed to see the sculptures that tell the story?"

Tera bent down and pointed to the middle of the column, his umber finger at Ailo's eye level. "Watch the surface where I'm pointing."

The details, almost indiscernible at this distance disappeared behind Tera's finger. Ailo waited. They appeared on the other side.

"It's moving," she said.

"That's right. It works on a solar mechanism and spins slowly. We can go up to the Temple roof to see it while Jati and the generals have their meeting."

Ailo turned to Jati. "We're not going with you?"

"Sorry, kiddo. Top brass only. Even secret agents like you aren't allowed." They winked.

Tera laughed.

*"Ai, what's wrong?"*

*I want to be there. At the meeting.*

*"Why? It's not your place."*

*It* is *my place. I'm partly at fault.*

*"Ai, this isn't about you, or even what you did. This is official PA business, about the war."*

Ailo eyed Jati. "But..."

"Non-starter, Firecracker." Jati held up a hand. Their gaze went across the open square. "There's Hirok, right on time."

Ailo recognized the person from the holo-feed on the pod, roughly Jati's age, with short-cropped black hair and the distinctive scar across his cheek. General Hirok approached a table in the grove and sat. He spotted Jati and nodded.

"O.K. secret agent," Jati said. Ailo sensed that they had picked up on her disappointment. "I'll catch up with you after the meeting. You and Tera have a few hours to enjoy Gontook after you get an early lunch." Jati turned to Tera. "You mind ordering and bringing me my usual before you two head out?"

"Not at all," Tera said.

"Make sure you pay, Tera."

"Of course. Same for General Hirok?"

Jati nodded. "Except no Marmish on his." They turned

to Ailo. "Lightweight," they whispered and headed to meet Hirok.

"Come on, Ailo. You'll like this," Tera said. "They have a great menu."

Ailo didn't follow.

*"Ai, what's the big deal?'*

*I don't want to be blamed for anything.*

"You won't, Jati's not like that."

*And what about the others?*

*What about them? Jati's in charge. Trust them. You need to relax.*

*Shut up, Gerib. I told you never to tell me that.*

"Ailo, what did I say about respecting the crew's instructions?" the navigator asked.

"Yeah, yeah." She followed Tera, reluctantly.

"Jati doesn't make me order and pay because they're a general," Tera said as they crossed through a set of tables and chairs. He brushed some green hair of out his eyes.

"They don't?"

As she and Tera joined the ordering line, Ailo eyed a set of display cases containing a variety of colorful pastries and fruit-based platters. Her stomach rumbled. She wanted one of all of them, especially a large bowl rimmed with crusty dough and filled with a creamy pink filling.

Tera shook his head. "They do it because otherwise we wouldn't have to pay."

"Why not?"

"Because they're Jati. Heroon is free because of them."

"So why pay?" Wasn't it a benefit considering what the general had done for the Heroonese people?

"Because it's the right thing to do, and it honors the people who work to make this food. They have mouths to feed and loved ones to support."

That did make sense.

"And because Jati isn't any different from anyone else."

"I think they are," Ailo said.

Tera's expression made it clear she'd picked up on her

defensiveness.

The navigator smiled. "They are special, in certain ways. Jati was raised by Garassian parents on Ortor, which is pretty unique. But they're like everyone else. We're all the same. All across the Arm."

"I wasn't the same as everyone else on Tarkassi 9."

"No, that's true. And wrong. And I'm sorry about that. It's all of our faults."

*What?*

Ailo took a small step back.

*"Ai, are you O.K.?"*

Ailo's mind reeled from the genuine remark. And that made it hurt. She eyed the pink cream pastry, not wanting to meet Tera's eyes.

"That's a Ran toolani," Tera said, changing the topic. "They're for the celebration cycle. You can only get them during the seventeen days each year."

"Can I try it?"

"Of course, it's a good way to start to learn about Heroon." Tera greeted the person behind the counter and ordered.

Ailo noted they had a 'té' icon on their apron for efficiency of communication when taking orders. Over the edge of the display case, on the back wall, red digi-letters glowed on the screen listing meal items. So many of the words had double letters.

"Tera," Ailo tugged on his arm, "why do so many words use double letters?"

"It's a distinctive feature of the Heroonese language. Those words weren't invented until after the settlers arrived here. Their original language was based on an adapted form of Contex from the Second Span. But Heroon developed a separate language too."

The person behind the counter smiled, following the conversation. Ailo liked her vibe. She wore a bereese apron, covered in various food powders and materials from working with her hands to prepare the items in the case. Violet hair sat tied up in a bun on her head. Tanned russet-colored forearms, lean and strong, bulged with visible veins.

"That's right," the server said, smiling. "Heroonese evolved from Contex. New vocabulary, but the same syntax." The server nodded at Tera, who signed 'ta-ti.'

"What does that word mean… 'syntax'?" Ailo asked and signed 'té.'

The baker shifted her gaze to Tera. He nodded and shrugged, as if to say, "Give it a shot."

"The structure of words and how they work to make meaning," she answered from behind the counter. "That came from Contex. But the vocabulary of the Heroonese language… the words with double letters, the planet gave those to us."

"Gave them to you?"

The baker nodded while packing up their order. "Our ancestors listened for the sound of what things were like in their minds and the words came to them. Everyone here speaks Neo-Contex like the rest of the Arm, but we also preserve an indigenous language. That's why your food and other things on this planet have names that appear and sound different."

"Like Cantinool. And Gontook," Ailo said.

"Exactly. I like your red hair by the way. It's so bright."

Ailo's eyes went wide and her cheeks flushed.

Tera leaned down. "Want to learn how to say 'thank you'? She'll be impressed."

Ailo nodded.

Tera whispered in her ear. More double letters.

"Muneet Dartool," Ailo said.

"Wow!" the baker said. "Ruleesi narpuulo."

"Is that 'you're welcome'?" Ailo asked.

She nodded and handed a bag to Tera. "I'll have the runner bring the tray to Jati and the other general. Theirs are on the house."

Tera opened his mouth but the server held up her hand before they could protest.

"Muneet Dartool," Tera said and scanned the thin credit square for their food.

"What's your name?" the server asked.

"Ailo-té."

"Nice to meet you, Ailo. I'm Rinyaro-té." She moved to a small jar on the counter and reached in. "Here." She handed her a small brown cube made of paper. "Have you visited the Cantinools yet?"

Ailo shook her head.

"Her first day on Heroon," Tera said.

"Well, that's Cantinool candy wrapped in Cantinool paper. Consider it a teaser for the real thing."

"Muneet Dar..."

*Gerib, I forget...*

"Dartool," the baker said and winked.

"Dartool," Ailo said, her cheeks growing warm again.

"Come on, Ailo," Tera said. "We've got plenty to do and see. We'll take our food to go and eat on the terrace overlooking the Lantoon Ocean."

Ailo waved to Rinyaro as they left.

"I'm impressed, Ailo," Tera said as they walked through the plaza. Ailo caught sight of Jati and Hirok engaged in conversation at the table. "Your pronunciation of Heroonese is good for a first-timer. You seem to like the customs of other cultures."

She did. But now she wasn't sure about something.

*Do I have a culture, Gerib?*

No response.

*Gerib?*

"Well, yes, Ai. *You're part of the Arm.*"

*But so is everyone. Where am I from?*

"*Tarkassi 9.*"

*No, I mean where are my parents...* Ailo halted.

Tera walked a few more paces and turned around. "You alright, Ailo?"

Ailo dropped the candy and ran.

# ELEVEN

Back to work. The emergency response team sent Ailo running. The crowds and streets flew past. Physical distance became ersatz for denial. Dashing off, hiding, violence — these were all tangible and external responses to crises that worked to protect Ailo.

Usually, a point arrives when the EMT unit packs up their gear and goes back to their stations to wait for the next alarm. That's when I return. Ai and I work through things, most often by talking around them delicately (well, pretty much *always* talking around them), and I help lower the vitals of her mind and help get life back to stable.

But I couldn't stop this train. Nor could I lower her vitals. Ailo's denial of access to Jati's meeting compounded the fear of confrontation, as well as her unknown familial identity and its associated lack of cultural belonging. Despite my best efforts, she wouldn't quit running. It took almost a half-hour to slow her down, and not before we passed through a series of walking/sprinting cycles was it purged from her system.

With enough distance and time, Ai slowed to a walk and wandered through Heroonese shopping districts and neighborhoods. She ignored the various peddlers and occasional con-artists marking an obvious tourist and pushed aside all attempts to pressure her to buy items, lure her into a "tour of the city," or worse. Tarkassi 9 taught her how to communicate her status as a 'non-starter' in street language. It didn't take learning how to say "no, thank you" in Heroonese to scream out silently through body gestures and eye expressions that she wasn't a willing mark.

After several minutes and my growing concern that we were lost in a strange city, I realized Ai's roaming had ended. Once her nomadic dislocation settled, she switched from reaction to action. And caught me unawares.

In the dense and foreign streets of Gontook, Ai made a decision.

We were running again. Not to escape a problem, but to head right into it.

# TWELVE

"Ai, you can't be serious?"

Ailo watched the entrance to the Assembly Building from the corner of the adjacent street. A mix of civilians and uniformed PA officials came and went. That made it easy. The grand staircase was the problem. Pairs of guards stood at the bottom flanking the steps and at the top on either side of the Cantinool portico leading into the two-storied hexagon structure.

She scanned the buildings around the Assembly. The distance between the roofs made a jump out of the question and the bulbous dome's ledge left no place for her to hook something to cross with a rope (which she didn't have). And getting that would mean a delay. She didn't have the time or patience.

"Ai, what is the plan?"

*We're going into that building. To Jati's meeting.*

"And then?"

*That's too far in the future.*

"Sake of the Arm, Ai!"

*Would you rather sit and eat lunch, looking at the Lantoon Ocean?*

"Yes, that sounds lovely."

*Sounds boring to me.*

A group of youngsters approached the steps. They all wore blue jumpsuits with a red armband: the youth volunteers. The same uniform she'd put on this morning.

*Here we go, Gerib.*

Ailo hurried across the arrivals/departure circle in front

of the steps. This would be easy. She'd latched on to public tours and fit in hundreds of times on T9, mostly for food at official events or to get around the moon base without having to pay. Once she'd even infiltrated a youth education group, which was pretty risky considering she wasn't in school and never had been. But it was worth it. She'd gotten to meet a visiting celebrity and ate so much she almost exploded.

The youth cadets acted uncomfortably with one another. She guessed they'd arrived on Heroon no more than hours earlier and hadn't yet formed social connections. Ailo slid right in at the back of the group. A stocky youth, a year or two younger than Ai with ice white skin and orange eyes turned around.

"Hey," Ailo said.

"Hi. Just get in?"

Ailo nodded as they climbed the steps. The youth turned back around to follow the others, satisfied that Ailo was part of the group. Now she needed to keep her head down. She'd learned over time on T9 to watch near the back of a social group. The people there were often the least confident or the least interested. Locate someone meek who would serve as a model for your behavior or find someone pulling up the rear out of disinterest and defiance. Ailo could make either work. She preferred the latter, from personal taste and her personality, but the former presented more security. Look like you are lacking in direction, like you need to be told what to do and where to go – that is the best way to get through closed doors and into exclusive areas.

"We'll be going to the orientation session first. It's on the second tier," an older cadet at the front said. They'd turned around and walked backwards up the steps. So, the leader in this group wasn't a rookie. That made it easier in terms of following and getting in, but more difficult because she would need to try and remain unnoticed. The last thing you want is someone in charge pulling out a list and you not being on it. Because then it's fast talk or flight time.

"First time on Heroon?" The orange-eyed newbie asked,

huffing the words as they walked up the steps. Pitch black hair cut high and tight in a style common on T9 before the breaking of the Alliance told Ailo the cadet's heritage: Hamut.

Ailo nodded in reply. The quiet routine worked best.

"Me too. My name's Artelia-tu-tō."

Ailo's mind, distracted with maintaining her discretion, caught the bigender suffix but missed the 'tō,' indicating their preferred gender pronoun at present as "they."

The youth waited.

*"Name, Ai. She's waiting."*

"Ailo-té," she said and brushed her scarlet bangs away from her eyes.

The youth smiled. "I'm from the Hamut station sequence, Xertari quadrant." Their head went up as they passed under the Cantinool columns. "And I'm a long way from home."

Ailo needed to lose this one. Otherwise, she would have to give out more information.

"Make a line everyone," the lead cadet said. "We need to go through security."

*"Ai, security?"*

Ailo bobbed her head left and right, peeking between the other rookies to try and look ahead. Before she had time to react her feet stepped over a yellow line. A large metal arch, running across the entire hall, passed overhead.

Ailo shut her eyes tight and waited for the alarm.

Nothing.

She sighed in relief. A general chip check for entry and exit. She never had an issue with them. If anything, she had to identify *herself.* The technology never worked.

"So where are you from?" The Hamut asked.

*"Ai, this one's going to out us..."*

"Hey!"

A hand landed on Ailo's shoulder. Her instincts tensed, ready to lash out in self-defense but she managed to turn as calmly as possible. The leader of their group faced her.

"You weren't with us when we left the shuttle port." The cadet looked to be about eighteen. A nameplate on their chest read, 'Pelta-ti.' A fancy ribbon and medal hung from one shoulder. By design, it appeared to be something given in recognition, or maybe a symbol of rank.

"No, I was running late," Ailo said. She used her best overly confident tone. "Nice pin. Is it a medal?" She took a chance and stroked her hand over the ribbon.

*"Flattery will get you everywhere, Ai."*
*Usually does.*

The other secret is to keep things moving, keep your side of the conversation proactive, and theirs reactive. Same as the fighting strategy that Solazi taught her. Call and response. The question about the medal like the first strike of a rhetorical fist.

"Oh, this?" He pulled the blue uniform an inch off his chest. "It means I'm a junior cadet leader. It's my third season."

"Hey, is it this way?" Artelia asked. The Hamut youth and the rest of the group were heading up the interior set of grand stairs to a second level where the hallway split in two directions.

"To the right, at the end of the hall past the Assembly chamber," the leader said over the rabble in the lobby.

"In the Assembly chamber?" The Hamut youth tripped into another cadet as they walked backwards up the step.

Ailo watched Pelta grow flustered. "I think I'm in the wrong group," she said to keep his head in two places at once.

"Wait at the top," he barked and turned back to Ailo.

"You're probably in Gontira-tō's group. They're meeting here in half an hour for the same orientation."

Ailo nodded. "Yeah, I thought I was early when I arrived... couldn't figure out why the guide at the shuttle station sent me running after your group."

Pelta's face settled.

*"Nice, Ai. Smooth as an orbit pattern."*
*I still got it, Gerib.*

"Head back outside." He pointed towards the entrance

they passed through. "You can sit on the steps and wait. They'll be here in a bit."

"Thanks." She waved and walked back. After a few steps, she turned. The cadet, on his way up the stairs, turned too.

Ailo smiled her best 'nice medal' smile. It worked. He blushed and hastily headed up the steps.

Ailo milled about the interior, invisible in the crowds of staffers and Heroonese civilian officials. Once the cadets were out of sight, she followed the directions the leader had given to his group. Except she wouldn't be going farther than the first room on the right.

Ailo sized up the guard at the top of the staircase. They stood in front of the Assembly Hall at ease.

"*Definitely gullible, Ai.*"

*Yeah, I'm thinking we do an 'Eyeball Twist.'*

"*For once we completely agree.*"

"Wrong portal," the guard said as Ailo approached. "You're the last door." They pointed to the end of the hall.

*Bored, even better.*

"Thanks," Ailo said. "I'm early for the next orientation. I think it starts in five minutes."

"You can wait down there. On the bench." The guard motioned with their head.

"Oh good, that's why I came up. It's scary what's going on down there."

The guard cocked their head. "What do you mean?"

"Someone ran inside, non-PA. He got to the line and the alarm went off. He freaked out. They had to taser him, but not before he did some damage. There's even blood. It's gross." Ailo acquiesced to playing the squeamish youth and offered her best expression blending thrill and disgust. "I think he's famous or something." She rolled her eyes per the tactical plan, shrugged, and walked down the hall.

At the bench, she sat. And waited.

*"Think they'll bite, Ai?"*

Ailo watched the guard. They leaned forward, trying to pick up the sounds over the low wall.

*Yep.*

Their head turned down the hall to Ailo.

She made as if absorbed in her wrist com, which she didn't have.

*Come on.*

*"They're not going to bite, Ai. You have any other bright ideas?"*

*Now it's my idea? You were 'all in.'*

Out of the corner of her eye, she caught movement. The guard moved to peer down the stairs.

Ailo hurried along the balcony wall, crouching low.

*"Hurry up, Ai."*

*Shut up, Gerib.*

She crossed and opened the portal and dashed through.

*"ID scan, Ai."*

The light panned from floor to ceiling.

*No alarm. Like always.*

*Made it.*

Ailo tip-toed down the low-lit hallway. It reminded her of the balcony level of the theater on T9. She didn't like recalling the image. A disgusting place and a haven for creeps.

An unfamiliar voice, deep and resonant, echoed through the open porticos and around the curving corner.

"We must strike now. We have no other choice."

She reached the edge of the first archway and peered into the chamber.

"One opportunity has been lost because of error in judgment. It does not please me to say this, General, but it was a costly mistake."

A steep view down rows of semi-circular tiered seating led to an open area like the performance stages on T9's broadcast channels. A tall figure with brown skin stood to the right side. Their white beard and angular features gave them a stately bearing. They wore the same uniform as Jati, but with a 'ti' icon on their chest.

"That is a subject of debate, General Galank." Jati stood in the center of the stage wielding a staff. The way they gripped it and the careful manner with which they kept it visible suggested it was ceremonial.

"General Galank, the decision is before us." The voice came from a person seated with four others at a table to the left. All wore the same uniforms. The generals. A holo-text over the table translated the speaker's words in live-time into readable text for visible access to the discussion. In the tiered rows below, several of the audience members' heads were aimed at the holo-text feed.

"Let us proceed with the decision of our present and future course of action," they said.

The other generals at the table nodded. Jati gestured with the staff indicating agreement.

"Very well," Galank said.

The holotext changed color. Ailo's eyes shot to Galank on stage. The general wore a small glowing pin on their shoulder lapel that matched the text. Jati's had one too. She understood. The device offered transcribed access to the debate, color-coded by speaker.

Ailo stepped in and found a spot against the back wall cast in shadow.

*"Ai, this is risky. Why are we here?"*

*Shhh... look.*

Ailo's eyes went to the grand and sweeping holo-mural of a cosmic landscape behind Jati. At points on the horizontal, three-dimensional rendering, stars twinkled in various colors. Icons, their meanings lost on Ailo, hovered over sectional grids.

*It's a war map, Gerib.*

*"You're right, Ai."*

It reminded her of the holo-field on the *Carmora*, the one Jati'd stood in front of when she'd first been caught stowing away, but bumped up to the scale of the Arm.

Her eyes tracked through dense star clusters dappling

the galaxy's arm. One small light at the far side twinkled at a great distance from the others: Tarkassi, the gas giant.

"Jati, you believe a coordinated strike with the main forces against Garassit to be a mistake?" the person at the table who'd spoken asked, interjecting a second time. They had a single topknot like Arira and similar russet skin.

"I consider it to be a disaster, strategically, General," Jati said. They took a step towards the assembly.

Ailo scanned the crowd. A sea of People's Army uniforms, their variations made explicit by sleeve colorings, separating the ranks. With a few exceptions, the age of attendees increased the closer the members sat to the stage. Rank structured the audience.

"For two months, we have been plagued by infidelity," Jati said to those assembled. "Somewhere in our ranks, perhaps in this very room, there is a mole." They swept the staff around for effect. "Whoever it is has caused us to tilt from swift and easy victory to a struggle to persist, and even survive."

Even at her distance, Jati's presence loomed. A natural orator, the entire room sat gripped by their words.

"We've lost a third of our fleet. A third!" They paced the stage. "Several systems have slipped out of our hands, losing a brief taste of liberation. And now, they've taken my child."

The Assembly gasped.

Jati nodded. "For those of you uninformed, Arira-té was abducted a week ago from our clandestine rehab facility on the surface layer of Ffossk. By none other than the assassin who does Aradus's bidding." Jati rested the bottom of the staff on the stage. "Hekron-ti."

Noise erupted from the assembly.

*Hekron, Gerib. Everyone seems to fear him.*

*"And for good reason..."*

"And what do you suggest we do?" Galank asked, standing to the right. The opposing general's words interjected into the rabble and quieted the assembly.

Jati aimed the staff back at the holo-mural. "Focus all

our efforts on rooting out this traitor. The Tide is shifting. Unless we can stop this leak, we may not be able to regain its current. The ebb of defeat looms large."

"So why not attack now?" Galank said, walking closer to Jati. "We must strike while we still have a fleet!" A large rabble rose in the seats supporting the general's suggestion.

"I'm surprised at you, General Galank. So easily you'll take the Garassian's bait?" Jati walked closer to the edge of the stage. "Have you not grown wise to the nefarious ways of Aradus? He's luring us in. He wants us to attack."

"And why not?" General Galank spread his arms wide. "If we waste our time trying to find a spy we may not have the power to fight the Garassians, not at the rate they're hitting us." Galank turned to the PA ranks. "For nine years we've been chipping away at star systems, shaving off the reach of economic monopolies. It's been a game of cat and mouse. We've gained ground, yes. And we've gained support in our fight. But now?" Galank turned to the generals sitting at the table.

Ailo's eyes followed. There were two vacant seats.

*Jati and this Galank...*

"*They are a committee, Ai.*"

*But Jati is the leader?*

"*I believe so, but knowing them, it is probably still a community of decision-makers.*"

"You can't take down Garassit without leaving our liberated territories vulnerable," Jati said. "And even then, to infiltrate the planet's exosphere with its advanced defenses? Even if it were possible, then what?"

Galank turned to Jati. "And then what?" Galank turned to the PA ranks in the audience. "Take the city. Destroy it."

Echoes of applause and support bounced off the domed ceiling.

"Destruction is not the goal of the People's Army," Jati said.

A different reaction overtook the applause from the tiers below Ailo's position. Something noble, almost idealist, resonated about Jati's words. They inspired, but she got the sense debate was about the present vs. the future. Still, Jati's response reminded her of the lessons they'd given her about strategy.

"You heard Aradus say the words yourself, here at the start of this war." Galank pointed down at the floor, indicating Heroon. "Now famous amongst our army; that he would not rest until your body was dragged before the palace gates of Garassit. That itself leaves little doubt that our one option is destruction."

Cheers rose from the assembly.

The general at the table who spoke earlier, the one with the topknot, raised a hand without turning. The room went silent.

Jati shook their head for all to see. "There are other ways to solve that problem, safer ways."

"And your child, Jati?" Galank said. "Do you not fear for your family? You said yourself how nefarious Aradus and his minions can be."

Jati pivoted to face Galank. "Do not speak to me about family."

"Maybe you are too close to this. Perhaps it would be better if..."

"I am not close enough!" Jati's staff hit the floor and echoed through the hall.

Energy radiated around the Assembly Hall with the threatening strength of one of Gontook's nightly storms. Jati's paw of a hand tightened around the shaft. "You dare to question the love I have for my child?" They pointed the staff at Galank. "My love for the People's Army?" Jati took a step toward Galank. "They are all my family!" Jati slammed the staff on the floor a second time.

The Assembly erupted in cheers. Galank stood his ground, but Ailo sensed cracks in his confidence. His eyes went to the sentries stationed at the door.

Jati nodded. "You forget what love means to me, General. My priority is always my family. Arira *or* the People's

Army."

A large portion of the Assembly cheered.

Jati waved a hand for the crowd to quiet.

"My love extends to everyone who suffers in the Arm."

Portions of the Assembly exploded in rowdy shouting and applause.

Ailo scanned the crowd. A sea of blue uniforms, placid moments earlier, swelled to life, churning with the current of pride. Through the shouting, she caught one of the older PA nearer to the stage shouting. "We were there with you at the beginning, Jati! We're with you now!" Shouts of "Jati!" echoed off the walls of the Assembly Hall.

Ailo's heart surged with newfound pride. She'd never been witness to such collective human spirit. Every part of her wanted to yell with them but knew she must be silent or give away her presence.

The general at the table, the one who'd stood earlier raised a hand to quiet the room.

Galank finally spoke. "You can muster an army's spirit, but there is more at play here, Jati."

"Let us be done with veiled accusations," Jati said, lowering their voice and speaking with an even tone. "I tire of your constant attempts to demonstrate to the rest of us that you should be in charge."

The Assembly gasped.

Ailo's eyes went wide. She hadn't expected Jati to strike with such subtle, direct force.

*I guess that's called 'pouncing,' Gerib.*

*"I guess so."*

"Fellow liberators," Jati stepped forward. "We are family." Jati glared at Galank to drive the point home. "We must always make sure we protect one another and support one another. Therefore, I believe that we must focus on turning inward to find which of us has decided to betray their own. This way we maintain the protection of those who are already liberated, who are now part of our family. A direct attack on the palace in their capital city? Far too risky and far too dangerous in our condition. Do not take Aradus's bait. That is how others have fallen in the past." Jati banged the staff on the floor three times and stepped back.

Many in the crowd cheered and applauded.

Galank walked to the center of the stage.

"There is too much risk, too much uncertainty as to whether we can even find this spy, this traitor, who gives our enemy vital information and peels away our defenses. Unless we strike now, we chance exposing the heart of our war for justice."

Galank waved to a staffer standing at attention next to the general's table. Ailo watched as the person went to a screen on the wall. The holo-mural zoomed in to a quadrant of the Sag-Arm.

"The Kusk meteor shower passes through Garassian space starting tomorrow."

Ailo watched as the holo-mural displayed a massive belt of asteroids moving through a solar system. One planet marked 'Ceron' glowed green.

"In ten days, it will be out of the quadrant. Until that time, Garassit is in strategic stasis. We have this time to prepare the fleet and to arrive at the tail end of the event. Even if they learn of our plans, they can't do much. The cosmic debris disrupts communications and the defenses around the planet. If we send in a lead armada, in this case, General Hirok..." Galank turned to the table.

Ailo recognized the general with black hair and ivory skin shifting in his seat next to the other three military leaders.

"We may be able to break the orbit line and ease the siege for the rest of the fleet. Either way, the Garassians themselves are trapped there for now. We have it on good intel that both Aradus and his nephew, Hekron, are back at the palace."

*Hekron...*

Galank watched as an animation of the entire PA fleet arrived out of FTL to lay siege to Garassit. He turned to the assembly and the generals.

"Let us strike, like the tail whipping around from the passing fire god whose name is given to the meteors foreshadowing our fury. Let us raze Garassit to smoldering ash and finish this war!"

There were cheers from a portion of the Assembly while others booed.

*"Ai, Jati may lose this debate."*

Jati held up the Cantinool staff and pointed it around the hall. "Do you remember why this war started? I was there, at the beginning. So was General Hirok." Jati aimed the staff at Hirok seated at the table. "A violent exploitation of entire cultures, a blatant disregard for their humanity. Domination and ignorance... the bedfellows of corruption and hegemony. Keen Draden started this war by seeing through that. By understanding it had to stop. All of it."

*I'm not so sure, Gerib.*

Ailo stepped forward into the light out of excitement and anticipation.

"Keen Draden?" Galank's voice carried a tone of disgust. "He was a washed-up alcoholic who found a path at the end of his road... after it was too late. The veteran was wooed into an illusion by a traitorous bastard child who was the spitting image of her grandparent. Evil incarnate. One is dead and the other can't die soon enough."

Jati shook their head.

"You miss the entire point, General. Didn't you learn anything after the Patent War? We are here now because we didn't grasp the value and power of mercy and forgiveness."

"You're a fool, Jati."

The Assembly gasped.

"You're a great warrior and a role model to inspire others to fight. You'd lead a group of pacifists into war and they'd fight for you. But it's time to let the ones who will be aggressive take action. Garassit must fall and it must fall now."

Shouts of support rose from the tiers of the hall.

"We'll end up right back where we began," Jati said, shaking their head. "Nothing will change until we change how we do things. It starts with how we treat those we liberate."

"Don't you mean conquer?"

Several in the hall shouted agreement.

"You disappoint me, comrades." Jati pointed the staff at those noisily supporting Galank. "The People's Army are not warmongers. 'Conquer'? Such words define the world we fight against. We must show compassion when victorious over those who stand against us." Jati's eyes cut a line to Galank. "That means not razing their city to the ground or decimating innocent lives. It means liberating those under their control, even on their home planet. Do we fight? Yes, we fight. Do we take lives? Yes, we take lives. But we do it for the cause of liberation. And we take the lives of those who stand in battle against us, reducing their reach and resources with strategic strikes. We liberate humanity from economic tyranny. Look at Heroon. Is this not what we want for the rest of the Arm?"

A rabble of support rose from the assembly.

"And what of the rotten core, Jati?" Galank stood a bit taller.

Ailo sensed a defining moment in their argument.

"What of Aradus and his nephew? And the Council?"

Jati twirled the staff. "When they are left with nothing else except their planet and its resources, they will know defeat. They will come to the table as equals."

"You would have them live?" Galank spoke to the Assembly more than Jati.

"If they did not stand against me. If they accepted defeat, yes."

"The future of our cause is at risk with such words." Galank turned to the Assembly behind the table of generals. "No, with such words it is doomed to fail."

The hall erupted in vocal support of Jati's challenger.

"It is the Legion way!" Those in the assembly hushed.

General Hirok stood, his chair crashing to the floor behind him. The impact echoed off the domed ceiling. Ailo watched as the person from the holo-feed on the pod spoke. His back remained to the Assembly, his words directed at Jati.

"I would stand with you should that happen, Jati. We are Legion, you and I. This is the code of honor and the path of righteousness. It is because we have strayed that we now find ourselves sailing in a moral tempest with a rudderless ship."

Galank didn't respond.

*"Ai, I get the feeling that he doesn't want to challenge Hirok."*

*I think you're right. He's more interested in Jati than the war.*

"Thank you, sibling," Jati said.

*Gerib, are they related?*

*"No, I think it is a figure of speech. A kind of 'family' amongst soldiers."*

"Come now, this is nothing but foolish idealism," Galank said. "To spare evil? To give a second chance to those who have done egregious wrongs to their fellow human beings?" Galank grew noisier and more enthused. "No one changes once they've been made to embrace wrongs. It's too seductive. You can't make them see the world is more than what they want."

"You're wrong!" Ailo screamed so loud her voice cracked. The words bounced through the hall. When they came to settle in silence all the noise from the others went with it.

*"Ai, what are you doing?"*

Ailo stood at the back, her chest heaving up and down.

A sea of heads turned, their eyes climbing the rising steps. A hundred eyes pierced her like needles.

"Is this the youth, General?" Galank pointed up at Ailo. "Is this the reason we are standing here in need of such desperate countermeasures?"

"It is," Jati said.

Ailo caught their gaze. She expected it to be stern, to

express disappointment or anger. Instead, Jati appeared happy to see her.

"Come down here, Firecracker."

All eyes were on her.

Jati waved her down. "Let her through," they said to those assembled.

*"Ai, go."*

Ailo snapped back from her self-induced shock and walked down through the tiers of seating to the stage. The generals at the table, and Galank too, all followed her with their eyes as she passed. Jati pulled her in, their massive arm resting on her shoulder. The faces of the leaders of the People's Army in the audience were a mixture of shock and anticipation.

"So, this is your poster child, Jati?" Galank asked.

"Be careful, Galank. There are some lines that I don't allow even my equals to cross."

Jati's arm strengthened on her shoulders and neckline, holding her close. Galank shrunk at the remark.

Jati leaned their mouth to Ailo's ear. "Do you mind if I mention where you are from?"

Ailo, too nervous to speak, shook her head.

"This is Ailo-té. She's from Tarkassi 9. You all don't need me to give you a history lesson on the moon base and its relationship to why we are fighting this war."

The Assembly nodded and muttered amongst themselves.

Ailo looked at Galank. His expression shifted. He appeared nervous as if his mocking strategy might now backfire.

*"Good, I hope it does, Ai."*

*Me too.*

"You want to know why I diverted to Ffossk, Galank?" Jati turned to the line of generals at the table. "Generals?" Jati pointed with the staff up into the tiers. "Assembly?" The Cantinool swept across the open air on the stage. "I was fighting the war."

Jati's grip tightened on Ailo's shoulder as they spoke the last word.

"That's right. I told Ailo this, and I will tell all of you as well. This war is being fought for humanity. Not for money, not for power, and certainly not for *revenge.*" Ailo knew from Galank's expression that Jati's glare challenged them on the last word.

"Our cause, our priority, is to save lives, not take them. That takes precedence."

The Assembly was silent.

"Even when it prolongs the conflict? When it prolongs further suffering... and loss of lives?" Galank's eyebrows rose in arrogance.

Jati held up the staff. It lay horizontal in their hand. "Two strategies. They lie at opposite ends." Jati dipped the staff. It swung down and up like a see-saw. "I have mine. You have yours."

"I call for a vote," Hirok said at the table.

"Seconded," Galank said and then walked and sat at his seat.

The heads of those in the Assembly lowered as they entered data on the polling system in front of their seats.

"Thank you, kiddo" Jati whispered.

"For what?"

"For reminding me why we're going to win the war."

A bell rang. All the faces in the assembly and at the general's table watched over Ailo's head. A click echoed and the hall exploded in voices and shouting. Galank smiled.

"What happened?" Ailo asked.

"Nothing unexpected," Jati said.

The generals were in a heated conversation at the table. Hirok's gestures made clear that he disagreed with the rest of them.

"Don't you want to turn and look?"

Jati's eyes narrowed. She watched their crow's feet tighten. "Remember our conversation about strategy?"

"Yes."

"You think they want me to look? You think they want to see my reaction?"

"Definitely."

"And that's exactly what I am not going to do." They winked.

Ailo's nervousness at being in front of all these people was overtaken by another, foreign sensation.

*"It's admiration, Ai."*

*What is?*

*"That feeling you're trying to describe."*

*Shut up, Gerib.*

"Now what?" Ailo whispered.

Jati nodded, indicating the generals.

Galank approached, a smug expression on his face.

"Go out to the Legion camps, General." Galank clasped his hands behind his back and walked across the floor with an air of performative arrogance. "Boost morale. That's what you're best at. You can serve this final push by staying alive so the PA troops have their 'role model' filling their hearts with courage as we crush the Garassians. You can watch the siege from here, under the safety of central command."

"You're making a terrible mistake, Galank. One that doesn't allow room for error or recovery."

"We've fought, chipping away at the fringes of Garassian power for too long. It's time to strike with the fist."

Jati dropped the Cantinool staff on the floor. The impact echoed off the dome ceiling. The assembly gasped. "A fist has no power without the arm behind it. You hit the Garassians now and you'll find out a hard truth. You've got nothing to bring power to your clenched fingers."

Jati led her by the hand out of the auditorium.

She glanced back. Galank walked over and picked up the staff.

"Idealists never survive reality," Galank said.

Jati stopped but didn't turn around.

"No, they don't. They fall to save the innocent."

# THIRTEEN

"Damn Aradus and his diplomatic sorcery!" Jati stormed out of the Assembly Building and down the flight of steps to the street.

Ailo trotted to keep up.

"And damn the foolish pride and arrogance of war!"

They barreled down the stairs. The PA officers and staffers on their way up parted like a boat's wake cutting through still water.

Ailo hoped to never be on the receiving end of Jati's anger.

"Jati!"

Lavender hair spun in the air. They turned.

Ailo swung around towards the voice. General Hirok hustled down the steps.

"This is insane," he said, flustered. "We don't have enough ships left to do this." His teeth were clenched tight in frustration. "And, I'm to be the front line." He pointed at his chest. "My armada will never last out there. They'll pick us off at the exo-edge like Gor in a swamp dam."

"Fools," Jati said and began moving. Ailo walked a pace behind the two generals as they made their way into the streets of Gontook.

"They've left me no choice," Jati said.

"You're going to let them do this?" Hirok hustled to keep up with Jati's pace.

Ailo agreed. This was so not like them. They'd let a war they'd fought, and led, for nine years fall in defeat?

Jati stopped. Hirok tripped over his feet and caught

himself. Ailo bumped into Jati's colleague.

"Sorry," she said.

"No, Hirok," Jati said, emerald eyes alive and sparkling, "I'm going to go against my own best advice."

"What does that mean?" Hirok asked.

"I'm going to do this myself."

Ailo smiled. That was more like it.

"You're going to defy the Assembly?"

"I'm going to save them from making a fatal mistake. And get Arira back while I'm at it."

"How? With the meteor shower, we're in a holding pattern." Hirok held out his hands wide in a gesture of futility. "We can't do anything."

"Meteors?" Jati dusted their chest as if wiping away a small fly. "Going to take more than that to keep me back. I've pushed back against worse." They grabbed Hirok's arm and led them away from the Assembly Hall. "Come on."

Ailo followed a pace behind, relieved that some of the 'usual' Jati returned. The two generals turned a corner and walked another block into a market street filled with vendor stalls and afternoon shoppers.

"You ready to do this with me, Hirok? I can't pull it off without you."

Hirok stopped.

Ailo halted a few paces back but stayed within earshot.

*"Can't these two decide if they want to walk or stop?"*

*Shhh, Gerib. I'm listening.*

"It means you'll be on the butcher's block if it goes wrong." Jati's eyebrows rose in earnest.

Hirok's gaze went to the street corner leading back to the Assembly Hall. "Why not?" He shrugged. "'To the end' and all that old-school justice stuff, right?"

*"Ai, that was the same slogan on Keen's plaque. 'To the End'."*

Gerib was right. The reference pointed to the Legion and the Patent War.

"Third time's a charm." Jati winked.

Hirok smiled, the jagged scar on his warm ivory cheek shifting. "Just like old times, eh?"

"That's the spirit, old tot." Jati swatted him on the shoulder.

"But Jati, if you can't get this done by the end of the Kusk shower, I'll have no choice but to attack with the rest of the fleet when it arrives."

"Deal." Jati rubbed their knuckles on Hirok's head.

He pushed their hand away. "Sake of the Arm." Hirok ran a hand around his crown, fixing his short-cut black hair.

"Thank you, old friend."

"You and I *were* even after the Reynaria coup, back at the start of this war. So now you're gonna owe me one." Hirok poked Jati's chest with a finger.

No one had been so causal with Jati before.

*They're old friends, Gerib.*

"Old veterans, Ai. Of two wars."

"And I intend to retire after this is over if I'm not dead," Hirok added. "So I'm going to think of something expensive and annoying when I cash this favor in. I want to be sitting on a comfortable pile of credits, doing nothing but savoring the peace of my last days."

"If we can pull this off," Jati said, "we'll save my Arira and the war. It will give us time to regroup. You've done enough in the Tide. Help me with this and you can step down with the assurance there won't be a need to worry about peace. It'll come. And it will stick around."

"Forget that. I want to see Aradus fall. Do you think I'm going to let you have all the glory? No way. I'll see this through until Garassit collapses. Then I'll retire."

"Alright, alright," Jati laughed. "Kartan on me. We'll drink from the golden wall atop the Garassian palace and watch the sunset over the Lorassian Sea."

"That's a plan. Now," Hirok declined an offer from a passing peddler selling fruit, "what's *our* plan?"

"Working on it. Make sure your crews are back on board their ships and the entire armada ready to depart in four days. Can you convince Galank and the other generals that you want to head out two days earlier?"

"Can do, old friend." Hirok slapped Jati's thick shoulder. "Unlike you, I haven't lost their ear."

"Good. Tell them you're going to break the jump in half to work on maneuvers in space."

Hirok nodded.

"In the meantime, I need one other favor."

"Name it."

"I need an A-Dodger." Jati's face made a jocular expression that Ailo read as making light of an extreme request.

"You've got to be kidding me? An A-Dodger? Is this for what I think it's for?"

Jati nodded and gave their old war buddy a charming smile.

"You're still crazy as ever," Hirok said.

"You know it." Jati smiled at Ailo and winked.

"I'm ready to retire after this." Hirok shook his head.

"Can you get me one?" Jati asked. "Yin Tarni-té is still running her crew out at the Pinolt Belt. That's about thirty hours FTL. It would get here just under the wire."

"And I suppose you want me to ask her to 'lend' us one?"

"You know she won't even look at me these days."

"That kartan better be good!" He pointed a finger at Jati.

"You're lucky on that front," Jati said. "This one got into some of it, but I was able to find her before it was gone." Jati nodded in Ailo's direction.

Her cheeks reddened.

"I'll get on it," General Hirok said. "I better do it right away. If Yin doesn't have one or if she refuses we're going to be tight to find another."

"Thanks, Hirok. When I'm back up in orbit on the *Carmora* I'll hail you. Probably three nights from now, right before you'll depart. Transfer over from the jump port on a pod to cover your tracks."

The old Legion veteran gave Jati a thumbs-up.

"And Hirok, come alone. We need to keep this airtight."

"You got that right."

*"Where do you think he got that scar, Ai?"*

*Probably in the Patent War. It looks old. Whatever it was had to be nasty.*

Ailo noticed the Hirok's eyes on her.

"You trust everyone around you, Jati?" he asked.

Ailo watched their reaction. They knew Hirok meant her.

"Absolutely. And don't worry about this one." Jati thumbed their hand towards Ailo. "She's coming with me."

Ailo eyes lit up.

*"Ai, where are we going?"*

*I don't know, but I hope we get to visit the rainforest.*

"I'm not sure I want to know how and why you ended up in our meeting, kiddo."

Ailo's cheeks grew hot.

"By the way," Jati's crow's feet crinkled as their eyes narrowed, "does Tera know where you are?"

Ailo wedged her shoe in between the cobblestones and tried to kick out a bit of dirt. She stole a peek at Jati. Their bulging forearms were crossed over their chest, expression impatient.

She acquiesced and shook her head.

"Didn't think so." They raised their wrist to their mouth. "Tera?"

"I can't find her anywhere, Cap." The navigator's voice sounded hurried. The rabble of crowds and traffic came through over the frequency in the background. "I've been all over the district. Sake of the Arm, she's got me worried."

"She's here with me."

"With you?"

"Yep. Decided to make an appearance and speak at the Assembly."

Hirok chuckled.

"What? That little..."

Jati gestured for her to speak.

*What do I say, Gerib?*

"You apologize."

*Why? This had nothing to do with Tera?*

"Because you ran off. And had him worried. He's been looking for you for an hour."

Jati's wrist loomed in front of her.

"Sorry, Tera." Ailo forced the words out, annoyed at having to say this in the presence of the two generals. She would rather have done it later, privately.

"You had me worried sick, Ailo," Tera said. "I'm glad you're alright."

A tinge stung in her belly. Her eyes welled up.

Jati noticed the effect of Tera's words and retracted their wrist. "Tera, meet me back at the shuttle in half an hour."

"Will do, Cap."

"And stop and grab some boar medallions and Marmish sides. I suspect someone's hungry." Jati winked.

Now she was embarrassed. Excited, and starved. But embarrassed.

"Tots," Tera said over the com.

Ailo's eyes shot at Jati. She opened her mouth but they cut the line before she could respond.

"Jati," Hirok said, his expression shifting. "How many others knew you diverted to Ffossk?"

Jati considered the question, counting on their fingers.

"You and the other generals... and my crew."

"And you trust them?"

"The generals?"

"I meant your crew."

"Of course. The only ones privy to that information are Tera-ta and Pozix-té. Only the bridge crew gets access to the *Carmora's* headings."

"Unless someone has you bugged."

Jati shook their head. "Low probability."

"But possible." Hirok raised an eyebrow. "That kind of information is invaluable. Could set someone up for life."

Jati sighed.

They appeared tired not with physical, but mental exhaustion. The mole was a constant frustration.

"Give me a minute." Hirok gestured to the restroom station, walked over and entered.

Ailo watched the market bustle. Fruits of all colors, long and short, wide and narrow, with oddly textured surfaces, sat or hung at stalls. Some were split open to entice buyers, revealing luscious interiors dripping with nectar.

"Firecracker, I need a favor." Jati waved her over. "First mission as a secret agent."

"Seriously?"

"Jokes aside, I need you to do something for me." They bent down and whispered in her ear.

Ailo nodded. "No problem." Now she had a job. She carried responsibility that would be a part of righting this wrong, both for herself and Jati. Getting Arira back would be a team effort, and she was on the team.

Hirok returned from the restroom.

"I need to hit that too," Jati said. "Damn meetings are always too long." They walked to the lavatory while Hirok and Ailo waited.


"Tea?" Hirok turned to Ailo as the three approached a vendor's stall selling iced Cantinool. "I imagine your throat must be parched after that performance back there." The scar on his face shifted as a faint smile curved his mouth upward.

"Ai, you're staring."

"Oh. Um... yes. Thank you."

Hirok made a series of gestures with his hands to the vendor.

"Right away," the merchant responded.

Ailo noticed the Heroonese tea maker wore an icon on his bereese shirt as a service industry worker and a blue identity mark on their neck indicated 'ti.' The additional design on his skin made it known he preferred to be approached with non-verbal communication.

The general accepted two teas and handed one to Ailo.

Condensation from the humid heat of the city wet Ailo's two fingers and thumb. The late afternoon remained as hot as mid-morning. Did Gontook ever cool down?

Jati performed a similar set of hand actions. The vendor retrieved their tea and moved his hands in a series of gestures. Jati responded with additional hand movements this time they were more animated.

"Here we go," Hirok muttered.

Ailo watched as both Jati and the vendor moved their hands.

*It's a conversation, Gerib. I saw someone do it once on T9.*

*"I think it's an argument."*

"Forget it, Jati," the vendor said and shook his head.

Jati laughed and nodded, halting their hand gestures. They took their tea off the counter.

"Were you talking?" Ailo asked.

"Yes," Jati said and took a sip. "I was trying to pay, but I lost. That's twice today."

"How do you know how to do that?"

"Everyone in the Legion was required to learn basic Neo-Contex signing," Hirok said, taking a sip on his Cantinool tea. "For us, it was both practical should we need to speak with someone this way, and also out of respect for those we served throughout the Arm."

"Still serve," Jati said and winked.

Hirok raised his glass.

*Another language, Gerib. I want to learn.*

"Ask Tera."

*I will.*

Hirok took a long sip. "Claw blade," he said placing his glass down. "Back in the Patent War. From a Hamut mercenary in a botched ambush at night. Got cornered against three of them."

Ailo cup was at her mouth, mid-sip. "Excuse me?" she said, lowering the glass.

"You've been eyeing the scar. That's where I got it."

"And a bunch more under his shirt, kiddo," Jati said and took a large gulp of their tea.

"If it wasn't for this one coming to my aid I would've been shredded." Hirok nodded towards Jati.

"You saved him?" Ailo asked.

"Unfortunately."

"Hah!" Hirok knocked back the rest of his tea. "Don't let them fool you. They've needed me. I rescued their ass with a barge full of weapons out in that rainforest twenty years later." Hirok gestured west, inland away from the Lantoon Ocean.

"Still do," Jati said and took Ailo's empty glass and placed it down with their own.

"Well, time to get going with my 'assignment,' Jati said as they started walking.

"What do you mean?" Hirok asked.

"To do what was asked of me by the other generals, of course. Heading into the interior to visit the troops and boost morale."

*"Ai, we're going into the rainforest!"*

*We'll get to see Cantinools.*

"Jati, you're not serious. It's not necessary. They were trying to save you some face."

"Oh no," Jati brushed a hand through their long lavender hair, "I can think of one soldier in particular in need of a morale boost."

"Where's that?" Hirok asked.

"Parshoo."

Hirok stopped walking. "You can't be serious."

Jati nodded. "I am."

"You're crazy. Nisi-té's a loose cannon."

"That's what I need. Plus, she's not doing anything else right now."

"Oh, I bet I know exactly what she's doing," Hirok said.

"Getting into trouble."
  Jati laughed.
  "I'll bet you're right."

# FOURTEEN

"Yep, as I expected." Jati pointed ahead.

Fifty feet down the dirt road, a rowdy crowd gathered to the side of a thatched roof cantina. On an elevated platform, a person barked back at the raucous group and dangled something over the edge of a railing above swampy water.

"Is that Nisi-té?" Ailo asked, remembering the name from Jati's conversation with Hirok.

"Yep."

*"Ai, is that a person she's holding?"*

*I think it might be, Gerib...*

"Jati, is she holding someone over the railing?"

"Yep," Jati answered as if it was the most normal thing in the world.

Ailo walked briskly to keep up. "Is that who we're here to see?"

"Yep."

Ailo wiped the sweat from her forehead.

They'd flown two hours in the small two-seater pod over dense rainforest and intermittent, scattered towns. Several times they passed over human-made precise hexagon lakes. The puffy lavender clouds above them, and even their ship as it crossed, made no reflection on the placid surfaces. Jati leaned over from the controls and fought the hum of the engine to tell her they were solar-infusion generators, the main source of energy for the planet's one continent.

Ailo shielded her eyes from the sun's intense rays and peered ahead on the road to the shaded cantina. Forget Gontook. The heat of the planet's interior offered a whole new kind of hot. Nushaba, the star giving light to Heroon, was a powerhouse. Jati had muttered its name under their breath as they exited the pod at the small and dusty clearing serving as a landing strip.

There was something else too, now that they were out of the city and its urban distractions. Ever since they'd landed a feeling lurked somewhere inside. Or was it around her in the air? Either way, Heroon made her anxious.

"You'll get used to it, Firecracker," Jati said, walking past her. The general nodded for her to follow them. "But never enough to forget it."

The cantina stood at the dead-end of the road, surrounded by dense rainforest and hugging a watery swamp. Ailo struggled to read the words engraved on a large plank of wood over the entrance. Judging by the amount of double letters, the foreign script had to be an indigenous language.

The sign, like the architecture around it, was carved of deep violet wood. Ailo's eyes followed the yellow grains running in elegant patterns like golden streams through a velvet forest. Her eyes circled the entire establishment. The crude panels of the bar, the tables, and seats, and posts all swirled with the delight and intensity of color compliments.

"Ai, it's got to be Cantinool."

*It is, and it's amazing up close. I want a piece.*

"Good idea. Let's grab one along the road on the way back to the pod."

"Welcome to Parshoo marsh, Firecracker." Jati didn't stop but walked in and made for the commotion.

Only a few patrons ignored the disturbance. They sat at the long bar like the fixtures at the Tip of the Beyond, their sole interest lost within the liquid in their glasses.

"Jati!" A shirtless old bartender with tanned tawny skin and thinning hair the same color as Heroon's clouds called from behind the bar.

"Nool a' Fenee, Scorpi-ti!" Jati barked back but kept walking. "She at it again?" they asked.

"What else is new, eh?" Scorpi said. He stopped wiping

the counter when he caught sight of Ailo.

"Hello," she said and waved.

The old bartender waved back. "Hello, little tot."

*Sake of the Arm!*

"Come on, kiddo." Jati waved her on without turning.

Ailo made her way around tables and chairs following Jati's path towards the crowd.

They stopped at the edge of the throng and focused on the dramatic situation on the platform. Ailo couldn't see much at her height within the crowd. She grabbed a nearby chair and stood on it.

"Just like her parent," Jati shook their head.

Ailo got her first good look at the person. She was tall. *Really* tall. The tallest human Ailo had ever seen. She would tower over Jati standing next to them.

*"Wow, Ai... check out her muscles."*

*Awesome.*

Ailo watched her arms and shoulders flex as she dangled the person by their legs. Two large triangular muscles angled down from her neck and disappeared under a yellow tank top. Her olive skin glistened with sweat. Atop her head, a large mess of thick black curls matched the strong eyebrows along her brow line. Below her cargo shorts, strands of muscles in her thighs were a powerful presence. As she stepped along the railing the muscles in her legs danced up and down.

*This person is so cool.*

"She's unleashed, General. Worse than last time," someone next to Jati said.

"Put her back in a cell, General. The jeekoo stone would do her good," another added.

Ailo watched as the person yelled and spit out a series of expletives at someone up front attempting to talk her out of dropping the person into the water.

A splash below the platform drew Ailo's eyes.

*"Ai, what was that?'*

*Something in the water, Gerib. I get the sense from the*

*mood here it's not friendly.*

Jati turned to Ailo. "Stay here." They pushed their way through. As the patrons recognized Jati, they made way and gave hearty pats on the general's back. A few even cheered.

"Nisi," Jati called when they reached the front of the crowd.

The person's fiery eyes turned towards Jati's voice.

"You hoping to add another month to your suspension?"

A wide grin grew on her face. To the side of one eye, a red laser tattoo of a radiant star glimmered. Ailo's smile of admiration doubled in size.

The crowd hushed down to a rabble.

"You'll miss out on the best part of the war if you drop them."

"He wouldn't 'kick teeno', Jati. Left the swamp boar machine and tried to run on me."

Jati shook their head. "Everyone knows you're the best, Nisi. Except for your parent."

"Don't you bring my parent into this..."

"You should listen to them," the person pleaded from over the railing as they flailed about. From her position on the chair, Ailo noticed their face flushed red as a gas giant from being upside down.

"Maybe I'll listen to the general and let you go," Nisi went to drop the person.

The crowd erupted in pleas to stop.

"Then no one gets to 'kick teeno', not unless they want to take on me!" She snarled at the crowd.

"I'm sure Scorpi agrees, Nisi," Jati said, making a calming gesture with their hands.

Nisi's eyes darted back across the cantina to the bar. "Scorpi?" she asked.

The entire crowd pivoted.

"Yeah, yeah, no 'teeno'," he said while wiping the counter. Ailo picked up on the indolent and tired tone, like this wasn't the first time.

Everyone turned back to the platform.

"You heard him, Nisi," Jati said. "No one 'kicks teeno' until you get back."

Nisi cocked her head, confused. "What do you mean 'get back?' You throwin' me in jeekoo stone?"

Jati shook their head. "Got a job for you."

"I'm suspended from active duty," Nisi said.

"This is special. Let the person..." Jati caught themselves. "Put the person back on the platform. Come down and talk with me over a Canti-ale. I think you're going to like what I've got to say. Plus, it's better than spending a month in the brig." Jati gave her a fake blaster shot.

Nisi let go of one leg.

"No!" The person screamed and flailed about. A monstrous growl came from below the platform. Water splashed up onto the railing.

"You're lucky I like fighting more than killing," she said to them. With one arm, Nisi lifted the person up and over the side.

Ailo's eyes went wide. *Amazing.*

Nisi dropped them on the platform and hopped down to where Jati stood.

The general raised their arm to reach Nisi's shoulders and put it around them. "Scorpi," Jati barked, "two Canti-ales and an iced C-tea." The crowd cheered. Jati reached up with their other arm, the one with the Legion tattoo, and rubbed their knuckles over Nisi's head, brushing around her black curls. Ailo noticed her temperature cool and the two walked back through the crowd.

Jati nodded for her to follow. The general chose a table near the bar and sat, guiding Nisi into the chair next to them. They pulled out a chair for Ailo.

Scorpi approached with the drinks on a tray. The old bartender had two rounds of Canti-ales with the Cantinool tea. He put a tall, iced glass of deep brown liquid in front of Ailo, and handed two Canti-ale bottles off to Jati and Nisi. They clanked them together and both knocked back the entire contents in one tilt and a few chugs.

"Ahhhh...." Nisi said while wiping the empty bottle across her sweaty forehead. Scorpi took the two empties. He placed the next two in front of them on the Cantinool table before walking back to the bar.

"Who's the kid?" Nisi nodded at Ailo.

"Ai..."

*Don't worry Gerib, I know my limits.*

A trace of a smirk resonated on Jati's mouth.

"What's so funny?" Nisi asked.

"You two have a lot in common." Jati turned to Ailo. "Ailo, meet Nisi-té." They turned to the soldier. "Nisi, meet Ailo-té, aka 'Firecracker'." They raised their eyebrows for emphasis on the nickname. "Ailo is a new addition to the *Carmora's* family. She's managed to hang around long enough and cause enough trouble that I've decided it's better to have her on my side than against it, wreaking havoc on life and limb... and K-speeders."

"Nice, kid." Nisi chuckled. She raised her bottle of Canti-ale and took a swig.

Jati's emerald eyes went to Ailo. "Nisi is something of an adopted child of mine. I fought with her parent, Lexar, in the Patent War." Jati gazed out over the marsh. "Not that far from here."

Nisi's expression darkened.

*"Ai, I think her parent is dead. You should say something."*

*What should I say?*

Ailo knew the confusion and nervousness on her face were apparent.

"Don't sweat it, kid," Nisi said, running a finger over the rim of her bottle. "My parent was Legion. She died with a Spirex Displacer in her hands, ripping off fifty rounds per second into a platoon of Hamut scum."

"Hold off on the 'kids', Nisi. Try 'Firecracker'. It'll save you from potential broken bones and bruises." Jati said. "And that war was a long time ago. The Hamuts are allies now."

"Yeah, whatever." Nisi scanned the cantina and took

another sip. "They driving you crazy with their 'Jati-isms' yet?"

Ailo smiled, too nervous to respond.

Jati tied their lavender hair back in a ponytail and flexed an arm at Nisi, playfully showing her their muscles. She squeezed it.

Her hand wrapped around most of the upper arm.

"I can almost make it around. You're losing mass, old tot."

Ailo laughed.

Nisi winked at her with the eye next to the star tattoo.

"How did you get so strong?" Ailo asked.

"You mean me?" Jati said.

"Hah! In your dreams." Nisi lifted her arm and curled it, her bicep forming a wrecking ball. "I'm Birevian. We're all like this."

"Birevian?"

"Ever hear of Birevia?"

Ailo shook her head.

Nisi glanced at Jati, eyebrows raised.

"Ailo jumped ship from Tarkassi 9. She's an explorer of the Arm now." Their emerald eyes softened and the crow's feet above their cheeks creased flaxen skin. "And a freedom fighter."

"Tarkassi 9? Woohoo, that's way out there. Edge of the Arm. That's the line in the sand. Don't blame you for jumping ship."

"Jumping *onto* a ship," Jati added. "Uninvited, I might add."

"Hah! Nice move," Nisi held out her bottle. Ailo knew from spending time in the Tip of the Beyond she wanted her to clink with her tea.

"Thanks," she said and hit Nisi's bottle.

"I'm going to regret putting the two of you together," Jati said and took a sip from their bottle.

Nisi rolled her eyes at Ailo.

"I saw that," Jati said.

Ailo laughed.

"So you've never heard of Birevia?" Nisi asked.

Ailo shook her head.

"It's way over on the other side of the Arm. One of the oldest systems. At least according to the fossil records. My whole planet is mountains. Big ones. No oceans. Just small lakes and rivers. My people are tough because our world makes us that way."

Ailo tried to imagine what a Birevian town must be like, with everyone the size of Nisi.

"Don't let her fool you Firecracker, Birevians are large, but Nisi is a workout fanatic. Takes after her parent. Lexar was just as big and strong."

"But you still beat her on the swamp box," Nisi said rocking her head back and forth with a sing-song tone.

Ailo could tell Jati had repeated it ad infinitum growing up.

"Care to go a round?" Nisi asked, nodding at an odd contraption in the corner of the cantina.

The mechanism, a kind of two-person combat device, sat sectioned off by a circle of sandbags from the rest of the cantina.

Jati sipped on their bottle like a performer overacting, ignoring her words.

Ailo thought it inviting. "I'll try it," she said.

Nisi pointed at Ailo, her eyes locked with Jati. "Sake, you weren't kidding. Like Harmon and Karpel the two of us."

Jati rolled their eyes.

"Can't stop finding yourself with more feisty children to care for, can you Jati?" Nisi took another swig "How is Arira anyway?"

Ailo's eyes went down to her tea.

Jati sighed.

"What?" Nisi asked.

"That's why I'm here," the general said.

"What's the matter? Is she sick?"

Jati shook their head. "Aradus got her."

"What?" Nisi slammed her bottle down on the table so hard it drew the attention of several patrons. She lowered her voice. "Where? How?"

"Ffossk."

"Son of a Gor hunter!" Nisi put a hand to her lips. "Sorry, kid."

Ailo shrugged. She'd heard worse on T9 in the Tip of the Beyond. Solazi wasn't exactly prudent in their choice of words.

"How long ago?" Nisi asked.

"A week."

"I'm sorry, Jati."

"Thanks, kiddo." They sipped their Canti-ale.

Ailo noted the phrase. She wasn't the first one with the moniker.

"Then you weren't pulling my leg back there about a job. I mean, we're going to get her back, right?"

"I'd rather not talk about it here."

Two sets of eyes — Jati and Nisi's — both scanned the cantina.

Nisi nodded. "Got it. You know I'm in. Anything for you and Arira."

"Going to be hot, Nisi."

"Just how I like it. Plus, I need a change of scenery. Getting kind of tired of staring at jeekoo stone. I'm sure you can relate."

*"Ai, what do you think that means?"*

*Not sure. Jati must have been in prison here too.*

"One thing," Nisi said in a low voice. "That half-dead, sadistic Gor scum didn't leave Garassit and do this himself, did he?"

"No, he's almost ninety." Jati's gazed to Nisi in earnest. "Our old pal did it for him."

"You can't be serious?"

Jati nodded.

"Hekron," Nisi said.

"We need to make the rounds and recruit a few others before the sit-down," Jati said.

Nisi raised an eyebrow as she kicked the dilapidated speeder to life. Black smoke belched out the dual exhausts as the engine rattled.

"Get that thing out of here!" Scorpi waved his bar towel from inside the cantina. "It stinks!"

Nisi ignored him. She settled on the bike and revved the engine. The machine looked like a toy underneath her burly frame. Somehow it kept hovering off the ground despite the giant riding it.

They'd sat for two more rounds of Canti-ales and verbal sparring in the cantina. Ailo enjoyed every minute, absorbed in the humorous banter and razzing between her two companions.

"You ever finish the refurb job on that classic K?" Nisi yelled over the engine she kept from stalling out with continuous twists on the throttle.

"Don't want to talk about it," Jati said over the engine's rattle.

Nisi turned to Ailo.

She knew her face said it all.

"Oh," Nisi said and mouthed the word, 'awkward.'

Jati leaned forward to examine the design plate on the side of the bike.

"Nice paint job. Appears to be thinning in spots." They ran a finger over the dusty silver frame.

"What?" Nisi pumped the throttle. "Can't hear you."

"There's a serial number underneath..."

"I can't hear you." Nisi shook her head and pointed at her ear. She revved the clunker louder and winked at Ailo. "See ya, kid!" Nisi switched into gear. The speeder shot down the road and into the air, the front handlebar and twin forks tilted up in a tireless wheelie.

Ailo waved dirt and dust away from her face. Jati

coughed and swatted at the air as Scorpi's curses in Heroonese echoed from inside the cantina.

"She is so cool," Ailo said when the dust cleared.

Jati, still coughing from Heroon's dust, started down the road. "The two of you will be the death of me."

Ailo skipped and hopped until she caught up with them.

"I mean she's so..." Ailo side-stepped next to Jati. "Can I bunk with her?"

"Absolutely not."

"Why?"

Jati's eyes connected with hers. "Because she is an adult and she's working."

"So am I." Ailo stopped and put her hands on her hips.

Jati ran a hand down their face. "Just do me a favor, OK? Don't accept any invitations from Nisi. If she wants you to do something with her, say 'Jati said I can't'."

"But why?"

"End of discussion, kiddo."

*I'm going to find a way to spend time with her, Gerib.*

*"Ai, be careful. Make sure you respect Jati. They've been forgiving thus far."*

"Come here," Jati waved her to follow them off the road onto a narrow dirt path leading into the rainforest. Their large frame passed through violet leaves and branches and vanished.

"Where are we going?"

"A shortcut."

Jati's voice faded with their distance.

"You wanted to see the Cantinools, right?" they called back.

Ailo ran in after them.

It only took a few hundred feet into the wilds of the Heroonese rainforest and Ailo entered another world. The road, the cantina, Gontook... even the war. It all fell away. Ailo stood in awe. It switched to dense and lush rainforest so quickly, like crossing an invisible threshold.

They'd stopped at a stand of Cantinools. Rising majestically around her, the prodigious trees rendered her speechless.

Jati didn't corrupt the silence with words. They let her take it all in.

Ailo touched the tight skin of the bark. Her two fingers slid over the smooth surface. Again, the uncanny sensation of Heroon tingled her inner core.

She wandered the grove, stopping to watch Nushaba's light flutter on the lower branches and purple plants on the forest floor. Light played on the veined leaves around her feet with hypnotizing rhythms. Jati reached up and pulled down a branch. They plucked off one of the perennially blooming flower cups and handed it to Ailo.

Ailo cradled it in a hand with talismanic wonder. She raised the orange and yellow cup to her nose and sniffed. The scent of Marmish, piquant and tangy, tingled her nostrils. But here in the wild, in its raw form, something earthy and visceral lingered in the Cantinool nectar. It pulled Ailo back in time. She knew almost nothing about the history of the Arm. She didn't need to; this was history primordial, a trigger hidden deep in human DNA. It told her one thing: Cantinool was *old*. It, or one of its close relatives elsewhere in the Arm, had been a companion in the human ecosystem for millennia.

The effect wasn't that different from the leavened bread she'd smelled back on T9. Bilky, the nightshift food processor for the civil services department, would give Ailo a loaf fresh out of the oven once a week. When she waited in the bakery and watched him work the processors and mix the dough, that yeasty scent had a similar impact. The scent carried an intrinsic link to humanity. An uncanny flood of abstract memories from those weeks at dawn in the bakery returned, her nostrils inhaling the sourish, fermenting mounds on the counter. The olfactory experience sent her over the threshold of some alluring and unreachable history.

Out here, in the natural landscape of Heroon, Ailo put together a greater understanding of humanity and its relationship to flora and fauna. The Cantinools, the clouds and rain, the dirt and the sea... she'd been living on the outside, at the fringe of a world politically and ecologically. And then it dawned on her: politics and ecology were both alluring and exciting... and also potentially threatening or even deadly. She felt pulled back to Ffossk, to its natural phenomena on land and in the sky, and also the presence of politics made manifest in bodies lying dead on black grass. And those abducted.

She lifted her nose from the flower cup. She'd traveled through a vast inner journey in the time it took to inhale and exhale the scent of a Cantinool's petals. But she'd returned with something that hadn't been there when she left — the memory of the note.

"Jati?"

"Mmmm." They were gazing up the trunk of a Cantinool, their large hand flat against the tree as if to feel its heartbeat.

"What did Aradus mean when he said you took his remaining child?"

Jati took their hand off the bark. "Aradus is Keen's parent." They kept gazing up to the canopy.

"Keen Draden's parent is Aradus?"

"Yes," Jati said and faced her, running both hands through their long hair. "It's amazing how one family is so central to so many problems in the Arm." Jati laughed and walked to a low branch before pulling a flower cup to their nose. "I'd never really thought about it. But the Dradens are connected to most everyone who has played, or is playing a role in the future of human civilization in the Arm."

Ailo watched Jati inhale deeply. "So that's why General Galank brought up Keen's child and her grandparent at the meeting. Because they are all related?"

"That's right." Jati released the branch. It rose back to its resting position, Nushaba's yellow light dappling its leaves.

"And Hekron?"

"Keen's cousin. Or, rather Keen *was* Hekron's cousin."

Ailo cast her eyes over the tropical rainforest. Tall Cantinools, young and old, intermingled among their fallen brethren, laid to rest and rot either from long years or storms that caused their premature end. The Cantinools were a family, the forest landscape evidence of their history of long life. And sometimes, early tragedy.

"Aradus thinks that I turned his child on him. That I'm responsible for making Keen a traitor to his people."

Ailo turned away from the vista of natural genealogy.

Jati fiddled with a small branch they'd picked up from the ground. They peeled off pieces of Cantinool bark and tossed them in the air to fall onto purple undergrowth.

"Did you?"

"Keen made his own decisions. I supported him however I could. That's what we did for each other in the Patent War. And that's what we did again when we ended up back together." Jati stopped peeling the branch and tossed it into the woods. "The problem with Aradus is that he had two children. One, his firstborn, died in the war and Aradus resented Keen for it."

"Why?"

Jati sighed. "It's complicated. Things get messy when you fall in love. Or when you're in love with a cause. There was blindness on all sides. But Keen's sibling, Reardon-ti, lost his life in a way different from what Aradus thinks. He believes Reardon died a hero saving his sibling. Only Keen and I knew what happened, at least the whole story. If Aradus learned the truth..."

"Wouldn't it be better to tell him, especially now?"

"He doesn't want to know, Ailo. Trust me. He's better off believing he died saving his younger sibling, a fallen hero."

This was Jati. The same person who spoke with compassion even for their enemies in the Assembly Hall. So much inside of Ailo screamed vengeance; that Aradus should experience the pain and sorrow he caused others.

"But was he a hero?" she asked.

"Who Keen?"

Ailo shook her head. "No, his sibling."

"Yes. And the storm passed for both of them. They each found peace."

Ailo watched Jati ruminate on the words.

"Are you a hero?"

"Huh?" Lavender hair flew around as Jati homed in on her with their green eyes. "Me, Firecracker?" They pointed at their cinder block chest. "No. I'm just a broken and shattered antique whose shards have been glued back together."

Ailo wasn't sure she understood.

"Heroes are young and determined. And pains in the asses." They poked her in the stomach. "They leave home to change the world. Crash other people's speeders and such."

Ailo smiled, the hot tinge of embarrassment in her cheeks.

"The thing about heroes, kiddo…" Jati put their arm around her and led them down the trail. "They give their lives for others. It's not about them anymore."

The way Jati said the last line suggested an end to the conversation.

"How do you like the Cantiools?" The general raised their head to the canopy as they walked back towards the landing area.

"They're amazing."

"Everyone needs to see them like this." Jati's head went back and forth around the grove of towering trunks.

"And thank you for…"

Ailo couldn't finish though she knew what she wanted to say.

*"Go on, Ai."*

*No. Another time.*

Jati kept walking, their arm around her shoulders. Heroon's rainforest, the animal and bird calls, and the rustling and crunching of leaves under their feet filled the silence.

"Ruleesi narpuulo, kiddo," Jati said and tugged her in tighter. "Ruleesi narpuulo."

# FIFTEEN

Talk about ups and downs. Let's start with the 'ups' to celebrate. Commitment to a cause. A clear and defined motivation with the potential to forge a path of purpose. And an almost explicit "thank you." To witness Ai manifest these in her actions and words — gratitude, trust, dedication, and a sense of belonging — served as reward considering the day began with requisite silence.

Ai's exclamation at the Assembly in defense of Jati didn't lead where I expected. As soon as her scream echoed through the chamber, I cringed with expectation; regressive behavior and an unsettling outcome were sure to follow. Little did I know that both she and Jati were more comfortable with their vulnerabilities than I realized. Who knows what mayhem would've ensued if I'd have been right. I'm glad I was wrong.

So many wonderful moments to acknowledge in Gontook. The philosophical awakening through the Ran cycle ritual of silence. Tera and the exchange with Rinyaro at the café about the Heroonese language. Sure, Ai slipped back into 'T9 mode' to sneak and cajole her way into the Assembly Hall, but the outcome of that event nullified the means to the end. Prudence dictates that I do not get ahead of myself or be fooled by one good morning. There's much work still to be done. But this was progress.

The best part was the subtle but powerful reward of Ai's efforts: an invitation from Jati to help retrieve Arira and play an essential role in their plans. Responsibility was offered and taken. I sensed a shift in Ai. I'm eager to watch where it leads.

And then we come to Nisi. How different mornings are from afternoons. By the time Nisi fired up her clunker and popped a wheelie, taking flight, the Emergency Response Team had her flagged. It didn't take a genius to realize that all of Ai's progress since she left T9 threatened to dissolve in the presence of the Birevian rogue. Ai *really* liked her and I know why. Nisi has the qualities of a positive role model but to get to them means living through a tempest of experiential and existential fury (*if* you survive). Jati had their hands full with her growing up, no doubt.

But that brought me small comfort. Judging from Jati's influence on Ai, I knew that somewhere underneath Nisi's gruff and raging exterior there hid a moral and sensitive person, unsure if the world would accept their weaknesses. Trust me, it's my job to know these things. Jati was spot on when they said Nisi and Ai had a lot in common.

Would I be satisfied with Ai ending up barely controllable by the strictures of military discipline and venting her leftover excess rage and competitive impulses through the encouraged use of force and violence? That's a moral question best left to germinate through her own experience. Philosophy is not my purview; it's Ai's responsibility to solve that ethical dilemma.

The good news is that Ai is accumulating a tangible and reliable set of guardians around her which means it eases some of her internal shieldings. Jati, of course, is the main mentor and protector. But others are gathering as well. Je-Jeto, her sparring partner in the dojo, offers something of a friendly older sibling rivalry. Ai is warming to Tera's teachings about language and cultural sensitivities. An alternative and expanding concept of family is opening up doors inside of her once assumed locked forever. Even the Cantinools and the natural world of Heroon are an intimate and personal connection offering her a sense of grounding.

But families aren't all warm and fuzzy, and once we got back to the *Carmora* that sobering reminder crashed the party. Jati's 'family' wasn't based on blood, but on political alliances and united social causes, and even dubious self-serving buy-ins. Translate sibling rivalries, parental favoritism, and backstabbing from a traditional family to a collection of people whose common bond is a commitment to the person who brought them together (or their wallet), and the potential for crisis and far-reaching consequences grows exponentially.

Like Jati said, the fist needs the arm. But in this case, the joints, muscles, and tendons of the supporting limb didn't fit as snugly together as they should. Assembled without all the nuts and bolts tightened and fitting properly would influence its aim, power, and speed. Luckily, Jati was there. They had a set of tools on hand and were wise enough not to let anything cross their desk without giving it the once-over. One loose screw is all it takes for an entire system to start towards collapse.

# SIXTEEN

Ailo stood at the bottom of the ramp and watched the transport pod land a few hundred feet from the *Carmora*. Dust swirled behind its dual exhausts, spiraling yellow clouds into the hot morning air. She held her hand up to block Nushaba's morning rays and squinted. Through the intense light and dust, the unmistakable hulking figure of Nisi hopped out. The soldier grabbed her gear from the shuttle's luggage compartment and tossed it a few feet away from the aircraft. She sparked a cantirillo and slung the large duffel over her shoulder.

Ailo received a typed message from Jati over the com in her room to wait on the landing strip for Nisi's arrival. Gontook was silent for the first ten minutes. Ran had lingered over the Lantoon Ocean. Not more than five minutes after Ran set Ailo's ears picked up the hum of the transfer pod approaching over Gontook's tiered cityscape, coming in low from the east out of the rainforest.

A voice reached her ears over the idling shuttle. Ailo caught sight of a head sticking out the cockpit window, shouting. Judging by the familiar hand gestures accompanying the Nisi's indiscernible words in retort she and the pilot were in a heated argument.

Ailo smiled. The soldier was a force.

Nisi kicked the side of the shuttle with a boot and walked towards the *Carmora*. The pilot leaned their head out of the cockpit window and yelled something back.

Nisi flipped them off as she walked through the swirling dust. The pod rose in the air, rotated its exhaust thrusters to face her, and took off towards Gontook. The soldier vanished in a storm of Heroonese dirt.

"It's like she scripts this stuff," JeJeto said, appearing next to Ailo. They smiled, the gap in their teeth adding flavor to the remark. The mechanic's beige skin deepened under Nushaba's rays.

Nisi emerged through the haze, her combat boots stomping with confidence in long strides. "Hey ya, Firecracker." She took a long draw on the cantirillo and blew out a cloud of smoke.

Ailo had never seen anyone inhale anything that held a spark. Everything on T9, like all artificial atmospheres, had to be electro-charged.

"JJ," Nisi said, nodding. "How long has it been, two years?"

"Just about," they said and reached out their hand, offering to take her bag. Nisi pulled them in and gave them a hearty pat on the back. She grabbed the cantirillo from between her lips and offered it.

They shook their head. "You know I don't touch low-grade bulk."

She shrugged and threw them her duffel bag. JeJeto caught it and nearly fell over.

"Birevians," the mechanic said and shook their head.

"Firecracker?" Nisi offered Ailo the cantirillo.

Ailo reached for it but JeJeto pulled back her hand. "Easy there, Ailo. I don't think that's a good idea." JeJeto turned to Nisi. "And you," they pointed. "I'm watching you. Jati's orders." They slung the duffel over their shoulder and almost tipped over.

Nisi pointed at her chest and mouthed the word, 'Me?'

"Yes, you," JeJeto said. "Don't be working to convert this one. She's doing well enough on her own. Sake of the Arm, can't imagine what would happen if you were in charge of her." Their mouth opened wide, revealing the signature 'JJ smile.'

"Never got those teeth fixed?" Nisi said.

"Nah, I like the look."

"You want me to knock out a few more?"

Ailo eyes went wide. *She punched out his teeth?*

"Minor disagreement, Ailo," JeJeto said, noticing her curiosity.

"Don't worry," Nisi said. "JJ and I are good. Aren't we?"

"So long as you still believe I was right."

Nisi jumped into a sparring stance, cantirillo squeezed between her lips.

*Gerib, what should I do?*

"Hah!" Nisi relaxed and pointed at Ailo. "Got you good."

Ailo smelled smoke. She turned to find JeJeto lighting a cantirillo and holding a semi-crushed pack with a few rolled brown paper leaves sticking out.

Nisi's hand went to the pocket on her chest, eyes wide.

"Still got it," JeJeto said to Ailo and winked as they puffed out smoke.

Nisi laughed. "Best fingers in the Arm." She held out her hand and JeJeto threw back the lifted pack.

"Gotta have them to get out of Tinex." JeJeto's eyebrows bounced up and down as they smiled.

*So they actually escaped from prison...*

"Wish I had your fingers," Nisi said. "Jeekoo stone's getting too familiar."

JeJeto laughed.

"Can you teach me how to do that?" Ai asked the mechanic.

*"Ai, the idea is not to have to steal things."*

*Shut up, Gerib.*

"I hear you're pretty good already," JJ said. They reached out and ruffled her hair.

"Quit it!" Ailo shoved their hand away. She hated when people did that.

Nisi coughed in a contrived manner.

Ailo turned. The burly solidier pointed at her ear. She reached up and her hand grabbed a cantirillo. "Whoa."

JeJeto snatched it back. "When you're eighteen you

can do whatever you want. Until then, don't let Nisi convince you otherwise." The mechanic's violet eyes narrowed.

"My K-speeder arrive?"

JeJeto gave a thumb's up. "Don't know why you're bringing that clunker along."

"Thought maybe you could work your charm on it."

JeJeto laughed. "Let me guess... not just the engine. But an identity facelift?"

Nisi winked her eye next to the star tattoo. She took a long pull on the cantirillo and tossed it into the Heroonese dirt, snubbing it out with her boot. "We rolling, or waiting on more?"

JeJeto nodded, indicating that Nisi should turn around. A second shuttle descended on the same spot where Nisi's had landed.

Ailo raised her hand to shield her eyes. A figure disembarked and eyed the *Carmora's* ramp.

*"Ai, they don't look like People's Army."*

*No, they don't.*

Dressed in a mishmash of subdued earthen colors, made up of pants, a shirt, and a vest of many pockets in a weathered but tough fabric, the person took their time walking toward the *Carmora*. Chin-length unkempt black hair blew in the breeze. Eye shields strapped tight reflected Nushaba's light.

The figure waved. Something about the gesture told Ailo it wasn't sincere.

"What a Gor hunter!" Nisi said. "He's on this job?"

"Jati wasn't kidding when they said it'd be hot," JeJeto said.

"Yeah, more like a scorcher," Nisi said. "He's not getting on this ship until we settle a few things."

"And what would that be?"

Ailo turned. Jati stood a few feet up the ramp, arms folded. They'd tied their lavender hair in a half-up, half-down twist and were sporting a set of small hoop earrings. Ailo liked the look. It added a rebellious spice to their usual personality recipe.

"He's on this job?" Nisi said, pointed an accusatory finger at the approaching person.

Jati nodded.

"You've got to be kidding, Cap." Nisi turned to face Jati. "You trust that money-grubbing mercenary?"

Ailo noted the change to a formal address. They were in work mode.

"We need him," Jati said.

"Why?" Nisi's hands went wide. "I can match that Hamut slime shot for shot."

*"Ai, a Hamut pirate. And clearly 'ti'."*

"No one flies like him," Jati said.

"I do!"

"You're good, kiddo. But not that good. And besides, I need you for something else."

Nisi gave Jati a glare that said, 'Explanation please.'

Jati shook their head. "Later. Plus, his mercenary days are over. He's stationed at the consulate here in Gontook now. Sits at a desk."

"All the more reason not to trust him," Nisi said. "Who knows which side he's on, for all we know he might be..."

"Well, well. This is turning into quite the reunion, isn't it?" The person put down his duffel and small backpack behind Nisi. He took off his sun shielders revealing orange eyes surrounded by bone-white skin.

Nisi's eyes were fixed on Jati. They stared back.

*"Ai, I think this is going to get ugly. Nisi isn't going to back down."*

Yes, she is.

*"How do you know."*

Ailo smiled. *Because it's Jati.*

"Been a long time, Nisi," the Hamut said. "I see you haven't solved your personal problems yet. Those muscles are bigger."

Nisi swung around. Her fist connected with this chin and sent him stumbling back.

"Enough!" Jati's voice boomed with authority.

Nisi stood, arm extended where it had finished the strike.

The Hamut pirate wiped the blood from his mouth and spat into the Heroon dirt. "Still can't knock me down, Birevian." He grinned through red-stained teeth.

"Both of you," Jati said, stepping down the ramp and placing their boulder-like presence between them. "I'm only going to say this once. We don't have time for your personal issues. I don't care about them. You two know the saying, don't you?" Jati glared from one to the other. "Or do I need to drag you by the ears up to the training room to read the sign?"

Nisi cast her eyes at her feet.

The Hamut grunted.

"I need you all at one-hundred percent," Jati said. "We have five days to do this and we need to pick up one more. And that itself will be a challenge."

"Boar," Jati pointed at the person. "You keep your words to a minimum. And show me you've still got the sharpest wings in the Arm. That's why I hired you."

He nodded.

"And you," Jati turned to Nisi. "You keep your head down and your temper in check. And save your strength. You're going to need it."

Nisi nodded. "I'm sorry, Jati."

Ailo noticed her use of the informal address.

"I don't have time for this crap, Nisi," they said. "Try me once more and you'll sit this out in *my cell* on this ship."

Head lowered, black curly hair falling on her shoulders, Nisi made a fist in response.

Jati walked back up the ramp, lavender hair flowing. "All of you get on board asap. We're going exo." They stopped at the top and turned. "We've got a long ride to get out to Cesix."

"Cesix?" the Hamut said and picked up his bag. "This *is* going to be a ride."

"There's nothing out there," JeJeto said.

"Exactly." Jati made a hand like a blaster and aimed a shot back at him.

Ailo hadn't heard of Cesix. She'd ask JeJeto or Tera as soon as possible.

"All of you, meet me in the nav room in an hour. And bring an open mind because this plan is going to need it." Jati turned and walked onto the *Carmora*.

Ailo watched as their lavender hair disappeared over the ramp's edge into the cargo hold.

"And leave those cantirillos on Heroon," Jati called back. "I need all of your heads on straight. We'll all smoke together when we're done and back safe. Hopefully, in one piece."

"I'll never make it, JJ. Not to Cesix," Nisi strode next to JeJeto in the open cargo bay of the *Carmora*.

Ailo followed a step behind, swaying back and forth to dodge the massive duffle bag swinging from JeJeto's shoulder. The mechanic pretended not to struggle but Nisi's gear overburdened their tall and lean body.

Boar trailed behind them, whistling.

"Not without gluing his lips shut," Nisi added.

JeJeto laughed. "Chill, Nisi. You're wound too tight. Even high on the 'nool."

"Hamuts," she muttered.

Ailo turned. The Hamut halted the taunting melody to smile and wink.

*I don't like him, Gerib.*

"Why, because Nisi doesn't?"

*Yeah, and he gives me the creeps.*

"What's that?" Nisi pointed at a stack of black and grey material at least twenty feet high. A group of crew members lifted boulders and shoveled rubble into containers next to the pile of inch-thick slabs.

"No idea," JeJeto said. "But I'm sure we'll find out at the briefing."

"Jati's cooking up something big. Might outdo the Slipstream Run on Karnex 5." Nisi slapped JeJeto on the shoulder.

They stumbled left from the blow and almost tipped over.

"You O.K. with that?"

"I got it." JeJeto shifted the bag. "And I'd rather not have a repeat of Karnex 5."

Ailo glanced back.

Boar waved his free hand.

*Ai, why do you keep looking at him?*

*Shut up, Gerib.*

"Who is that guy?" Ailo threw out the question hoping either JeJeto or Nisi would respond.

Nisi turned to JeJeto. They shook their head, refusing.

"Ailo." Tera's voice barely reached her over the activity in the hangar, the navigator's signature two-toned hair unmistakable across the bay. The navigator waved, gesturing her over.

"Guess you're out of here, kid," Nisi said.

"I'm not a kid," Ailo said. "What is it with all of you?"

"Woooooooo!" JeJeto swung around to walk backward and almost tipped over.

"Give me that," Nisi said. She grabbed the duffel bag and slung it over her shoulder.

JeJeto smiled, revealing the signature gap between their teeth. They held out a fist.

Ailo smacked it with her knuckles, the way the two did after they finished a sparring session.

"Ailo!" Tera called, hands on hips.

"What?" she turned and yelled back. Her voice echoed through the bay so loud everyone heard it and either stopped or slowed their work.

JeJeto nodded towards the navigator, still walking backward. "Ask Tera." They winked a golden eye before turning back to Nisi.

Ailo watched them walk away. Nisi gestured with her free hand and talked enthusiastically. JeJeto nodded and laughed. Another slap on the back sent JeJeto into a quick step to keep their balance.

A blast of heat cut through the air conditioning and pushed on her back. Turning, the open cargo doors reminded her that Heroon still lurked outside the ship. The planet wasn't ready to give up its hold on the *Carmora*. Something told her it had to do with this person, the Boar.

Ailo's eyes went to the side of the bay. Tera nodded at her impatiently.

"You got Outer Rim written all over you." Boar's voice carried into her ears as he passed by and turned around, walking backward. He shifted the bag to his other shoulder. Lines of blood trailed from his nostrils.

Ailo flipped him the bird.

Boar scoffed. "You'll fit right in." He turned around and resumed whistling, following Nisi and JeJeto.

Ailo faced back toward the bay doors and the blazing light of Nushaba. Fierce yellow rays hit the dusty tarmac outside the ship.

"What was that all about?"

Ailo turned. Tera approached.

The navigator signed 'ta-té'. She repeated the question in the form of body language — hands up in the air at her sides.

"Just a typical conversation where I come from," Ailo said.

Tera rolled her eyes. "I'm sure." The navigator gestured for Ailo to follow. "You're going to need to respect some rules on board this ship."

Ailo rolled her eyes but kept staring in the direction of the Hamut. "Who is that person?"

Tera's face held the same hesitation as Nisi when she deferred to JeJeto.

"He's a Hamut diplomat. His name is Darro Kin-tuk-ti."

"Diplomat? He looks like a soldier." Ailo watched the person walk towards the exit. "Like the Gor scum from the Alliance."

"Ailo!" Tera's grip was on her arm, turning her around. "Listen, the Hamut Alliance was part of the way things used to be in the Arm. That's behind us. Now I know Nisi says things." The navigator's gold eyes scanned the vicinity before continuing. "You have to understand, her parent was killed in the Patent War. Nisi holds a grudge."

"Well, she should. They treated us like crap on T9 too. When they even bothered to check on us."

Tera's face softened. "I don't doubt it. But we have to let go of things at some point. Or else we'll never make progress."

The recovery room on Ffossk flashed into her mind. Arira had said something similar.

*What was it, Gerib?*

"She was angry. But not any longer."

*Yes, that was it.*

"Ailo, are you listening?"

She nodded.

"Darro is called 'Boar.' It's his nickname from his mercenary days. Around the *Carmora* that's his identity, at least with this group. He's a diplomat on Heroon now, going on two months. He's moved on, past his anger."

Ailo cocked her head.

"That's right. You don't think the Hamuts were angry, too?" Tera raised her eyebrows. The navigator turned back towards Boar who was almost at the other end of the cargo bay. "Just steer clear of him. Especially when Nisi is around. The two of them have history and you don't want to get in the middle, physically or otherwise. Got it?"

Ailo nodded.

"Come on," Tera motioned towards a side portal. "I want to examine your ankle and ribs and see how they are doing."

"They're fine," Ailo said, following behind.

Tera ignored her and walked through the portal to a cylinder elevator. "How do you say 'thank you' in Heroonese?"

she asked, pressing the down button.

"Muneet Dartool." Ailo smiled precociously.

"I'm impressed."

The drop tube opened into a long corridor. Ailo hadn't been down to this level of the ship. Rooms with sophisticated medical equipment lined the halls. Most were empty. One had a middle-aged person sleeping in an upright shell with a series of tubes in their leg.

"Who is that?" Ailo said.

"Letios-ti, second engineer. He fell repairing one of the fusion towers a few days ago. Broke his leg pretty badly. Without Arira we had to take him into Gontook to get it set right. He's on a hyper-heal cycle. He'll be as good as new in a week."

Ailo thought of Arira. Her absence left a void in an important position on the *Carmora*.

"You were down here after the accident until we dropped out of FTL to Ffossk."

"I was?"

Tera nodded.

"Arira stayed with you the entire time. What she did to keep you stable until we got to Ffossk was extraordinary."

The K-speeder. She'd hoped to leave that incident behind. With so much going on she'd forgotten about it. Now the guilt and shame re-emerged. She still didn't know what opportunity had been missed by her bravado. More than ever she needed to work to help Jati fix this, for her conscience, and also to return what Jati and Arira had done for her.

"Aren't we going to the briefing with the others?"

Tera checked the time on her wrist band. "Depends... if we get through this exam in time."

Ailo's eyes lit up.

"And if you're fit enough for any job that Jati has for you."

"They said something to you?"

"*If* they have a job for you. None of us know what they've got planned yet. Hop up onto the table and let's check how you're healing up."

Ailo practically jumped up onto the exam platform.

Tera hit a series of switches at a small monitor station and a device about the size of a fist descended from the ceiling. The free-floating orb reminded her of the one she'd encountered in the recovery room on Ffossk.

*I hate these things.*

"Be patient, Ai. Especially if you want Jati to let you help."

Several lights blinked on the white sphere. It aimed a glowing eye at Ailo. A blue triangular field of light expanded, scanning from her hairline to her feet. Tera watched the readouts as they appeared. Ailo understood none of it. Long bars in rich colors stretched horizontally in a holo-field in front of Tera's monitor. Various numbered charts were synthesized into clinical readouts around a virtual skeleton of Ailo at a one-to-one scale.

Tera took a pair of thimble-tips off a holder attached to the side of the monitor and placed them on two onyx fingers. She waved the hand and layers grew on Ailo's virtual skeleton. Tendons and ligaments, organs, and even her nervous system, stacked in translucent layers within a three-dimensional holographic field.

Ailo's patience shortened.

"Relax, Ai."

*I want to get to the meeting.*

"Then let her finish."

"Blood pressure is going up." Tera's spoke to the holo-version of Ailo with an unmistakable tone of sarcasm.

"Sorry."

"Relax."

Tera spent several minutes reading the reports as the orb did a close-up scan of Ailo's ribs and ankle. "You've healed up well," she said.

The *Carmora* trembled. Ailo's stomach dipped.

"Did we just take off?"

Tera nodded. "Say goodbye to Heroon."

Ailo scanned the room for a window.

"Don't worry. We're going exo, but we'll hang around in orbit off the jump port tonight. You'll get to see the planet again before we FTL to Cesix."

The *Carmora* pitched and swayed as it aimed up and away from Heroon. It'd been such a short stay yet so much had happened.

"You'll get used to it."

"To what?"

"Coming and going like this," Tera spoke as she read the incoming data. "Stepping onto soft dirt and breathing humid air, then turning your back and watching an entire world fall away like a small pebble."

Ailo marveled at the thought, but felt tinged by a mild regret. The pathos in Tera's words sent something uncomfortable through her veins.

"If you stick around, the ship will become 'home' and all these planets like brief dreams," the navigator said.

Ailo watched Tera's lips curve into a smile.

"You like it on the *Carmora*?"

Tera nodded. "But I also like the dreams in between."

"Are they ever nightmares?"

Tera let out a small, but dramatic exhalation. "You've got some poetry in you, Ailo."

"What does that mean?"

Tera turned. "You've got a gift for language. You choose words well. I've noticed you use metaphors to good effect."

"I don't know what all that is." Ailo ran a hand through her hair, the shaved side a good bit beyond crimson fuzz and almost an inch long. The other side would need a bang trim soon.

"That's what makes it a gift," Tera said.

"Do you like languages?"

"I do. I studied Rhetoric and Linguistics before I joined the P.A. I specialized in the Radicals. Mostly from the Second Span. Contex fascinated me."

"Is that why you could explain Heroonese at the café

and its origins? And... 'syntax'?"

Tera nodded and turned her attention to Ailo's left arm on the holo-projection.

"How far is Cesix? The Boar said something about it being far away."

Tera laughed. "Boar," she said, making quotation marks with her hands. Ailo's virtual body rotated sideways at the motion of the thimbles.

"Ooops!" Tera twirled her fingers bringing the body image back to vertical. "Not 'The Boar'... just 'Boar'." She waved her hand and dragged Ailo's holo-arm closer. "Cesix will feel a lot like home to you. It's one of the most remote places in the Arm, like T9."

"What's out there?"

"I'm not sure. Nothing I've ever heard of."

"Then why are we going?"

"If you want to find out, stop asking questions and let me finish."

Tera studied a readout. She zoomed in on the layered projection of Ailo's left wrist. "Ailo, were you born on T9?"

"I think so." Something turned in Ailo's stomach.

*"Gerib..."*

*You're doing fine, Ai.*

"I'm not so sure," Tera said.

"What do you mean?"

Tera shut off the holo-screen and turned.

"You're not chipped."

"Of course I am. Everyone is."

Tera nodded in agreement. "As crazy as it sounds, there's no evidence you were ever Cored. There's no trace of rogue extraction either, or any other type of post-Core tampering."

Her eyes went to Ailo's left wrist. "It explains a lot."

*Gerib, what is she saying? I don't understand?*

*"Me neither, stay calm and listen."*

"What do you mean?" Ailo pulled her hand away.

"Do you have trouble getting through scans?"

"If you count being stopped sometimes and having to explain that my chip is messed up, yes."

"I don't think it's messed up."

"Well it must be, and it's annoying."

*"And helpful, too. Admit it, Ai. We get through places that we shouldn't."*

*Shut up, Gerib.*

"You told Arira your last name was 'Harrond' right?"

Ailo nodded.

"It's an odd pairing of names, though isn't it? 'Harrond and Ailo'. Harrond is so common, found all over the Arm. But your first name... I've never heard it before."

"Are we done?" Ailo slid off the table. "Shouldn't we get going?"

Tera checked the time and her eyes went wide.

"Sake of the Arm! We're going to be late." The navigator closed down the scanning system. "Come on, we've got to get up three levels and over to starboard." They hurried out the portal and into the hall.

*"Ai, I can't believe we're going to be at the meeting."*

*Of course, we are. Jati needs us.*

*"For what, we don't know. Don't get your hopes up, Ai. I don't think it's going to be something important."*

*You don't know that. And stop playing everything down. You know you do that all the time now, right?*

"No, I don't."

"You do!"

"What?" Tera stopped.

"Oh, sorry." Ailo's cheeks flushed. "I was talking to myself."

"Come on," Tera pulled her arm. They hustled down the corridor.

*Gerib, I don't understand. Why wasn't I chipped?*

*"Save it for later, Ai. After the meeting"*

As the elevator doors closed, Tera turned and said, "Well, Ailo. You're coming full circle today in your journey and time on the *Carmora*." They shot up in the tube.

"What do you mean?"

The curving door rotated open. Ailo followed Tera down a wide hallway. Several crew members created a path, moving aside to let them through and acting as if aware they were headed to an important meeting with the *Carmora's* captain.

Tera was going at a trot. "Come on, Ailo." She turned a corner and after another fifty paces or so they came to a T-junction. An insignia Ailo missed last time stood on the portal. Down the hall to the left, a wide transparent panel ran on the side with the door. Through it was the cargo bay where she'd fled from Jati and flown the K-speeder... back into the nav room via the window.

"Oh," Ailo said.

"Try not to make this a repeat of last time, O.K.?" The *Carmora's* navigator opened the portal.

# SEVENTEEN

"Sit over there, Ailo." Tera pointed to a chair next to Nisi. The soldier sat near the panorama window hunched forward, pushing and pulling an anti-gravity training ball between her open palms and the floor. Veined, olive-skinned forearms flexed as she pushed against the resistant electromagnetic static.

Tera walked to where Jati stood next to the holo-starfield. A full view of the Arm stretched over ten feet across. The *Carmora's* navigator whispered something in the captain's ear. Jati nodded.

On the opposite side of the room from Nisi sat Boar, his chair leaning back against the wall. His pale skin matched the cold light of the *Camora's* nav room. He winked at Ailo when their eyes met.

*Creep.*

Ailo shuffled through the chairs and sat next to Nisi.

"So you're in on this too?" JeJeto's head popped into view on the other side of Nisi's hulking frame. A quick rise of their eyebrows punctuated a gap-toothed smile. Her training partner's spiky yellow hair had been cleaned up since the welcome on the ship's ramp an hour earlier.

Ailo shrugged. She ran a hand through her asymmetrical hair.

"Your first op is gonna be a doozy," Nisi said and let go of her resistance to the ball. The orb shot up into her right hand. "You make it through this with the rest of us and..."

"Let's get started." Jati said from the front of the room.

The legs of Boar's chair plunked down and he straightened it.

"And what?" Ailo whispered to Nisi.

The soldier shook her head, indicating now wasn't the time, and motioned for Ailo to bring her attention to Jati. The *Carmora's* captain tied their long lavender hair back in a clean ponytail, their bulky frame stretched tight against the same deep blue fitted People's Army jumpsuit they'd had on at the Assembly.

"Well, well," Jati's eyes went around the room. "If we aren't the best damn looking group of rogue justice fighters in the Arm, I don't know who is." The opening remark elicited chuckles from those assembled.

Nisi shook her head and smiled, crinkling the star tattoo next to her eye. Ailo's tension eased.

*They're always optimistic, Gerib.*

"Always, but I'm not so sure if it's a good thing."

*Why?*

"Sometimes it can get you into trouble, remember what General Galank said?"

*'Idealists never survive reality.'*

"That's right."

*But Jati will.*

Jati waved a hand in a large arc. A square quadrant of the Arm expanded out to a view of a star system with four planets, the one closest to the sun labeled 'Ceron.' The PA general drew their fingers into their palm and the planet magnified.

"Most of you are more than familiar with Ceron. Home of the original Legion and the Third Span's energy monopoly superpower, Garassia. The planet's location in the Arm is ideal, despite the triennial barrage of Kusk meteors." Jati walked closer to the holo of the planet. "The Garassians rose to prominence as a central crossroads, a conduit for trade between ends of the Arm." Using a virtual stencil, they drew extensions in both directions from Ceron to the edges of the known areas of space. "From there, with the rise of economic might, Garassia's expansion through star system colonization and eco-shaping made its energy empire flourish. But at the cost of unforgivable abuse and exploitation." Jati erased the stencil marks and turned to the team. "And for too long. Nine years of fighting to stop it is also too long. And yet they persist." The general swiped a hand and another quadrant expanded off to the left in the Arm. "Other than the Targitians, the Council has had the longest run of hegemonic rule in the Third Span."

*Targitians?*

Ailo didn't know the word 'hegemonic' but she remembered the larger holo-version of the Arm in the Assembly Hall. This new quadrant lay in the direction of Tarkassi 9 and the moonbase she had called home.

"Kol 2... the start of a second run of fighting for justice and equality, leading right up to the present." Jati's crow's feet crinkled as the edges of their mouth rose. The smile held a tinge of pathos. "Kol 2 is where my own story of returning to official military status was sparked. And, I fear, it remains something to be reckoned with after the Garassians come to their senses." The PA general stared at the orbiting sphere with its rose-tinted atmosphere and two moons.

So the planet Kol 2 hosted the city of Targite. Ailo had overheard stories about the legendary city. It rose from the desert on the lone planet in the Altiron system; the Fins. There was talk on T9 in Solazi's bar about the mysterious, spiritually driven Targitians and their political power as an energy producer. Huge turbines amidst endless dunes. Arcane technology, unrivaled by even Garassia and its expansive energy empire. A planet of blue sand and Wind Tides... and supposedly, of a lost resistance. Ailo thought back to the drunken stories in The Tip of the Beyond; rebels described in ways both alluring and crude.

*The Motes.*

"Place is a nightmare," Nisi whispered to JeJeto. "Better to leave them alone with their wind god. Gives me the spooks."

JeJeto nodded in agreement.

"The last thing we need is another Reynaria," Nisi said.

An internal image threw open a set of memory doors. Ailo sat on the floor of a cramped, destitute kitchen. *Her kitchen on T9.* Someone bent down and handed her a cup of brown liquid.

*The smell... it's Cantinool.*

"Ai, you should..."

Ailo pushed an internal hand over Gerib's mouth. The image faded but she caught it and pulled the memory back.

*"They're rebels,"* a voice said.

*"No, Osil. They're Targite's toy to push out the Garassians. Look at how they treat the Motes. Now they want to try their hand at exo-colonization?"*

*"Reynaria's a true spirit, Teluv."*

*"No, Osil. You can't trust her..."*

Even with the blurry image, she knew the voice.

*It's my parent. Gerib...*

Tera cleared her throat a bit too dramatically.

Ailo snapped back to the nav room.

Jati returned from their drifting introspection and faced the team. "So here we are," they said. "And what we need to do is pull off the impossible."

Ailo scanned the room. Boar looked indifferent. Tera's face expressed concern. Nisi? She couldn't wait to begin.

"This plan the PA has of laying siege to the planet and the capital after the meteor shower is lunacy." Jati shook their head. "It's founded on impatience and a false sense of superiority."

"You don't think the PA can take them?" JeJeto asked.

The general shook their head. "You need three-to-one superiority to take anything that size. Anyone who studied martial strategy knows this, especially in the Legion." Jati sighed. "It'll never work. And it will mean pulling all of our defenses and resources away from the star systems we've taken. We'll be exposed and unable to recover when it goes wrong. And believe me, it will."

"So what's the score, Cap?" Nisi asked, squeezing

the exercise ball. Bursts of electromagnetic sparks sizzled around the sphere between her fingers. "We stalling Galank and doing a quick freeze? Or you want to pull a tooth?"

"The way you fly and shoot?" Boar asked. "A freeze is out on this scale. With your pace, we'd take half the time getting down to temp."

Nisi rose from her chair and made to head for Boar. Ailo reared back.

"You think you got a better shot, Gor scum?" Nisi's face flushed, her eyes wide. "Like that mess you made on Deritan 8?"

Boar waved her off. "No one could've made that shot and you know it. Doesn't matter. You've never had the finesse to freeze anything bigger than a laumper."

Nisi lurched forward but JeJeto had her by the arm.

"Sit down, Nisi!" Jati said. "That's an order. And you," they turned and pointed at Boar. "Do me a favor. Keep your opinions to yourself. I thought you were a diplomat now?" Jati's eyes went back to Nisi. "You two can duke it out on the machine at Parshoo marsh after this is over to settle your egos."

"Gladly," Nisi said, staring at Boar.

"Any time." Boar spread his arms wide to mock her. "Beinoo j'al Kootuk. Teeno ma'o koo."

Nisi laughed and sat back down. "You couldn't kick teeno with me if you tried."

Both Tera and JeJeto relaxed. Ailo decided to keep her chair a short way back from Nisi's in case of Round Two.

"Now, what's the score? That was the question, I believe, before the children started teasing one another." Jati winked at Ailo.

She noticed they were chewing on something again and must have popped it into their mouth during the commotion between Nisi and Boar.

"We're going in first and getting out before the PA even get there," Jati said. "We'll get Arira and flush out our traitor who's weakening the PA in the process. By the time the main fleet drops out of FTL after the Kusk shower, we'll have the identity of our mole and I can convince the generals it's worth pulling back. Without an internal threat, Galank loses his grip on the fleet. The rush to engage is over. We can push the Garassians into a corner by taking the remaining systems and forcing them to the table for peaceful negotiations." Jati aimed their gaze at Boar. "Without having to annihilate innocent lives."

*"Why did Jati look at Boar like that?"*

*No idea, Gerib.*

The comm on the nav board buzzed. Jati walked over and turned a knob on a flashing indicator. The memory of the captain's expression as the K-speeder barreled through open-air towards the window flashed into her mind.

Ailo shifted in her seat.

*"Yeah, that wasn't one of your best moments."*

*Shut up, Gerib.*

"What about the meteors?" JeJeto whispered to Nisi.

Nisi made a non-verbal response like she was equally puzzled.

"Go ahead, Poz," Jati said as they shut off the comm light.

"Ship's in the bay. He's on his way up. Should be there momentarily."

"Excellent." Jati went back over to the map.

Nisi and JeJeto shot each other looks. Boar appeared unaffected. Tera acted like she knew who Poz referred to and edged up to peer down into the bay from her seat.

"I don't need to stress the importance of what is about to be shared with all of you." Jati's face carried an earnestness that spread into the empty air of the room. "Since we're going to jump after this meeting we'll be going dark and will stay that way. No communications are authorized without my approval during drops from FTL. Understood?"

A bunch of nods and grunts rang from the team. Ailo nodded as well, more to be included than because she would need to follow the instructions.

"General, welcome aboard."

Ailo swung around. General Hirok entered. Everyone stood.

*"Ai, stand up too."*

*Why?*

*Do it.*

Ailo rose to her feet.

"At ease." Hirok waved a hand around the room. "Ailo." He said and nodded as he walked past to join Jati at the front by the holo-screen.

"Making friends in high places, huh?" Nisi whispered, leaning over.

Ailo shrugged.

"Kid's full of surprises, isn't she?" JeJeto said, in a low voice as Jati greeted their fellow Legion veteran. "This is going to be Old School."

Ailo glared at JeJeto.

"Sorry, kid. I keep…"

Nisi smacked them on the head. She gave Ailo an, 'I got your back' look.

"Now," Jati said. "Let's get to it."


Jati stood with General Hirok at the front of the nav room. Two rogue generals, against all odds and about to embark on a cause for justice, stood framed by a holo-map of the entire known extent and reach of human civilization. Ailo could almost imagine a future statue carved of Cantinool with the two of them in front of the Assembly Hall in Gontook.

"As you know, the Kusk meteor shower has begun." Jati addressed the room. All eyes were on them, waiting for the details of the mission. "It will keep both Garassit and the PA fleet on hold for another seven days. We've not had any correspondence or strikes against us since Ffossk."

"Actually," General Hirok said, "that's changed. This came in over my private fleet com-line this morning via exec hub."

Jati's eyes widened.

Hirok pulled out a small data bar. Jati nodded to Tera to take it. The navigator went to the control board by the panorama window and ran it in the system.

Ahead of the holo-starfield, a virtual version of the same parchment Ai read on Ffossk hovered in the air. Again, like last time a message and an insignia marked the paper.

Ailo gasped.

*Gerib...*

"Ai, is that?"

*It is.*

Nisi read the words aloud. "'My uncle and I will negotiate with Jati directly. No one else. Either they come to Garassit or they'll face the consequence, both political and personal.'" The soldier's thick neck flushed in anger. "That insignia," Nisi said, "...it looks like Hekron's — three arrows with a square at the bottom. But what's that below it?" She pointed at a small dot under the square where the arrows aligned.

"A new element," Jati said. "One with symbolism we all know too well."

"So it's Hekron?" Nisi asked.

Hirok nodded. "Same as the note left on Ffossk,"

*"Ai, I can't believe it."*

*Neither can I.*

Jati winked at Ailo.

"My guess is it's either a death mark," Hirok said. "Or, he's jumped in rank."

"More likely self-importance," JeJeto snarked.

Jati took a deep breath. "Well, now we know we need to do this and do it fast if we are going to get Arira back. Let's proceed. And thank you, Tera." Jati moved to the side so the team could view the holo-map of the Arm. "General Hirok, like me, understands the danger to our cause and the need to avert a potential strategic and tactical disaster. He is, therefore, taking a risk and joining our operation. Under the veil of practice maneuvers, his armada will leave early for Ceron. But rather than stop for target shooting, his fleet will proceed to the planet."

General Hirok nodded. "We'll drop out of FTL and stay back, clear of the asteroid storm. Our presence will be known to the Garassians. They'll rush to prepare for a strike."

Jati switched the holo-field to a close-up of Ceron with a mock-up of Hirok's armada at scale a few 100,000 miles back from the planet.

"You're not going to make Galank happy doing that," Boar said.

"We're hoping Kusk is as heavy as it was four cycles ago when it blocked transmission from the planet. Last time it was almost thirty hours at its peak. If we get it again, as it's predicted we should, then Galank will assume my armada is still on a layover a few parsecs from the Ortor system," Hirok said.

Boar laughed. "Risky. I like it."

Hirok's expression made clear that he too didn't care for General Galank.

"Now," Jati said, "we'll rendezvous with the armada at a safe distance from the Kusk shower."

Ailo recognized the *Carmora* as it blipped into the holographic. For a decent-sized P-Frigate, it was dwarfed in scale next to the battleships in the PA fleet.

"Nisi, JeJeto and Boar, you're the infiltration team. Along with me."

"Right, cap." Nisi high-fived JeJeto.

"What about me?" Ailo stood up. "I'm coming, aren't I?"

Nisi laughed.

"What?" Ailo said.

"Sit down, kid. Leave this to the professionals," Boar said.

Ailo lunged for Boar.

"Whoa!" A massive hand wrapped around her arm. "I like this one, Cap," Nisi said. "You weren't kidding about the two of us."

JeJeto laughed.

"Let me go!" Ailo struggled against Nisi's grip. "I'm not a kid. All of you, stop calling me that!"

*"Ai, relax. You're overreacting!"*

"Easy, Ailo," Tera said.

"It's O.K. Tera, have a seat." Jati motioned with one of their hands. "Firecracker."

Ailo turned to Jati.

*"Ai, relax."*

*I told you never to tell me that, Gerib.*

"I need you for something else, beforehand. Plus, you're already on the job, right?"

*"Do they mean what I think they mean, Ai?"*

*Yeah.*

Ailo relented and sat down. Nisi released her grip and smacked Ailo on the shoulder, buddy style.

"Right?" Jati asked.

Ailo nodded.

"Good. Now, you three are with me." Jati turned back to the holo-display. "We'll proceed through the Kusk shower to the non-orbiting moon, Yelo. General Hirok will accompany us." Ailo watched as the heads in the room spun around in confusion. "We'll dock planetside so we're out of range of any meteors and debris. Boar you're at the wheel."

"The wheel of what?" Nisi asked. "You can't fly into Kusk. It shuts down everything. Only the shield wall around the capital keeps it safe."

Jati nodded towards the window, indicating everyone should walk over. "Your answer's down there, thanks to General Hirok."

Ailo rose and followed the others.

"An A-Dodger," JeJeto said peering out the window.

Ailo leaned on the angular panel and gazed out and down. A sharp and sleek ship with a bulbous arrowhead sat parked in the middle of the bay. Two 'Y' wing formations protruded from the bow. Four circular engine boosters extended off its back like feathers at the end of a squat arrow's shaft.

"How old is that thing?" Nisi asked.

Jati shot her a look.

"What?" Nisi shrugged her massive shoulders. "I mean, the thing's a relic."

"The specialist is right," Hirok said. "The bird's old. Pre-Patent War."

"What's an A-Dodger?" Ailo whispered the question to JeJeto.

"Asteroid Dodger. A maneuvering ship. Turns sharper and faster than any other vessel in the Arm. That's a flexible tail with those boosters. Even the V-darts can't match it. They use them in the fields to drop miners on mineral-rich stones and ice."

"Fields?"

Boar scoffed at the question. "I was right, Outer Rim."

Ailo went into internal distress. Half of her wanted to lash out. The other half cowered in humiliation. Her body responded by opening her mouth and freezing.

"Back off, Boar. Not everyone's seen as much as you," JeJeto said. They put a hand on Ailo's shoulder. "Field — as in asteroid field."

*"JeJeto has your back, Ai."*

Ailo smiled in thanks.

Jati and Hirok's voices came down the line from the other end of the window. Ailo watched them talk animatedly on the other side of Nisi.

"You've got your work cut out for you Boar," Jati said. "See those frontal fins tips?"

Boar's eyes went to the ship. The Hamut's brows furled. "You're kidding?"

"Sorry, old tot. Pre-nav assist. You're going to have to take us in manually."

"Are you kidding me?" Nisi turned to Jati. "He'll kill us. It's suicide to fly into Kusk without assist. All those micro-meteors? This ain't like dodging A's."

"Boar," Jati peered past Nisi, ignoring her concern. "I need to know right now. Ego aside. Can you do it? No shame in it if you can't. Everything is going to rest on your ability to get us inside and onto Yelo."

Ailo watched Boar's face. His eyes went back to the A-Dodger. "What's the E-thrust on that, General?"

"It's a mod version of the Firewax drive," Hirok said. "Yin told me they use it in tight spots on the Pinolt Belt. It's got a low-to-high ratio of 250."

"Wow," Boar said.

Even Nisi's eyes got wide. Something in her expression slackened and relaxed.

Boar folded his arms and nodded. "With that power, I can get you in. So long as the bird can take a few dings here and there, we'll make it."

"A few dings," Nisi snarked, shaking her head.

"That's the spirit," Jati said. "Tera can work up a simulator program for you to play around in while we're in FTL."

"That would help."

Boar's remark came as a surprise. Ailo expected him to wave it off as unnecessary.

*"I guess this is that dangerous, Ai."*

Her stomach shifted.

*I guess so.*

"That's settled," Jati said and turned back to the holo-field of the Arm. Everyone returned to their seats.

"No bells and whistles," Hirok said. "No complicated approach here. A simple diversion on a grand scale."

"Everyone likes to overcomplicate things," Jati added. "They get all fancy using 'star slides' and 'yellow twists'. The general will tell you, in the Patent War that stuff always gave us trouble."

Hirok nodded.

"The best success we had was when we kept it simple," Jati said.

"Worked with the Hamuts," Hirok added. "No offense, Darro."

Boar put up an open hand in a gesture of peace. "None taken. When this is over, and we're sipping kartan, I'll tell you how we used to run circles around you in the rainforest."

Hirok nodded, his response solemn but respectful.

*Boar is strange, Gerib.*

"What do you mean?"

*It's like I hate him, but then he says or does things that make it hard to be angry at him.*

"Tera said he's forgiven himself and others about the war."

Ailo watched the Hamut soldier turned diplomat. His eyes caught her scrutinizing him. She turned her attention back to Jati at the front of the room.

"So now we're on the planetside of Yelo," Nisi said to Jati.

"You noticed the rubble and black diorite slab on your way in earlier, right?"

Nisi nodded.

"One of those pods out there is going to be covered in it. It'll pass for a large meteor. And we're going to drop in amidst the rest of the Kusk shower. You, me, JJ, and Boar. General Hirok will stay on the A-Dodger." Jati ran a cycle of the Kusk shower passing by Yelo on the holo-screen with a small dot on the moon's planetside indicating the ship. "We need to time it right so we drop in at the strongest cycle."

"Won't they pick up our signal?" Boar asked.

"Nope," Jati said and waited, a twinkle in their eye.

"Diorite," Tera said. "It'll block almost anything. That's brilliant."

"Thank you," Jati bowed. "Once we burn through we'll have to shut the power down. Too much of the material will fry off on entry and we'd get picked up by their atmospheric systems." Jati turned to the holo-display. Ailo watched as a pod fell in an arc towards the planet's surface. "Glider modification for in-atmosphere. We drop down offshore in the Lorassian Sea about a mile out. That's where you come in Nisi."

Nisi cocked her head. "Me?"

"You and Boar will work a manual rowing system on

either side of the pod to bring us in under the shield wall. I would do it with you but, I'm..." Jati sighed and focused their gaze on Boar but addressed their words to Nisi. "I'm sure you'll have to go easy so Boar can keep up and we don't spin in circles."

Nisi shot a furtive glance at Boar. "I'll be careful not to go too hard."

*Jati's clever, Gerib.*

*"Yes, they know everyone's weaknesses and strengths." Even their own...*

"I cannot emphasize the importance of this next piece of intel remaining confidential," Hirok said. Everyone nodded in earnest. "We've got someone on the inside. They've been giving us vital information for about a year now. I've arranged for a set of access codes, along with false chips, to be left at the entrance to one of the spring tunnels running underneath the palace."

"Tera, you'll need to prepare a set of wrist blockers using the diorite to cover our chips," Jati said. "It's never been tried before but I think it'll work."

"It should," Tera said. "I mean, hypothetically."

"Never liked hypotheticals," Nisi muttered to JeJeto.

"Me neither." They smiled their signature smile.

"Hopefully, we'll encounter minimal resistance," Jati said. "We'll split up. Boar will go with JeJeto and they'll locate data revealing where Arira is being held."

"How?" Nisi asked.

"That's JJ's department," Jati said. "It's why they're here." Jati nodded at the mechanic/pickpocket.

"'Problem Solver Extraordinaire'," JeJeto said, holding out their arms and nodding to imaginary applause.

"That's it?" Nisi asked.

Ailo had to admit it was vague.

"I got it, Nisi," JeJeto said, patting her on the shoulder. "I'm way ahead on this. Chill."

The soldier shook her head but acquiesced.

"Once you two get that intel, Boar will revert to diplomat. Being Hamut, and a long ally of the Council, you should be able to talk, and walk, your way into wherever they have her held, especially since your new diplomatic area is human rights violations..."

"Hah!" Nisi exclaimed.

"Since Boar's diplomatic area is human rights violations," Jati repeated, ignoring the snide outburst, "having him show up for an inspection of a political prisoner, even one held against formal war standards, shouldn't be too hard to pull off against a few sentinels."

"And if they don't abide, I'll do it the hard way," Boar said, leaning back in his chair.

Ailo caught Nisi rolling her eyes,

"I'm hanging back, I assume? Until Boar clears a path?" JeJeto asked.

Jati nodded. "You'll break her out with those fingers of yours, which shouldn't be difficult once the guards are out of the picture. Courtesy of a bit of 'Hamut diplomacy'. The nice or nasty kind."

Boar smirked. "JJ, you thinking it's gonna be a 'walk-away'?"

"Nah," JJ said. "With their security? More like a 'roll-over.'"

"Makes sense." Boar acted satisfied with the answer and settled back into his chair.

Ailo turned to Nisi, confused. The soldier made a face saying, 'Don't bother.'

"As for us," Jati looked at Nisi. "We're going to head for the comm-stack."

"To do what, exactly?" she asked.

"We'll unlock Aradus's account and get the identity of the traitor and copy the correspondences."

"We? I can't do that. And I know you can't. You can barely remember how to run the reboot program on this bird."

Tera laughed. Jati swung around in surprise.

"It's true," Tera said, raising her hands in a gesture of innocence.

"Cap, you're talking about the Core," JeJeto said. "The central system hub for the Council and the entire capital. You'd need someone expert in hacking at the highest level. And even that wouldn't be enough to get in."

Jati nodded and folded their arms across their chest. "You'd probably have to find the person who designed it. If only they were still around somewhere… living on the edge of the void in the Cesix sector."

Silence filled the room. Judging by General Hirok's expression even he hadn't yet heard this news.

"You can't mean?" It was Tera. Ailo watched as the navigator edged up in her seat. "But he's assumed dead. I mean… no one's seen him since a few years after the Patent War."

"No, almost no one has." Jati raised an eyebrow.

"Here comes a Jati-ism," Nisi said.

Jati swiped their hand and a quadrant came forward. A small sun glowed, alone in space. "This is going to be delicate. It's going to need a diplomat," Jati directed their attention to Boar, "and someone who knows what it's like to live far off… just shy of the Beyond."

Jati's eyes met Ailo's own.

"Me?"

"That's right, kiddo. I need you to help me convince Rence-ti to do this. I think you two will get along well and see eye-to-eye on several issues."

"He and I certainly won't," Boar said.

"Very true," Jati said. "And I need you to help him put the past behind him. Like you've done, Darro." Jati's eyes focused on Boar in earnest. "This is more important than flying that Dodger. We need him. Rence can set up a scrambler on the pod and most importantly, he can get into the com-stack. He built it. It's his baby."

"That's a tough sell," Boar said.

"I haven't been out there in a few years. And no one else knows he's there."

Tera's face lit up.

"You've visited Rence Tusolo?" Tera asked.

Jati nodded. "I've helped him. I know it's complicated." They returned their attention to Boar. "This means as much to me as getting back Arira. It's what this war is about."

"You're one of a kind, Jati," Boar said.

Ailo's admiration for the PA general grew. Her heart warmed.

"Hopefully not for long, but thank you, Darro."

"How much time will we need, Cap? At the Core?" Nisi asked while examining the holo-floor plan. "I'm guessing we're going to have to coordinate Arira and the hack and move fast to do this."

"Depends how out of touch with the latest tech Rence is... but he designed the original core processor so as long as he can bypass the virtual sentries added through updates it should be easy."

"If you can get the loon to do this," Nisi said. "And if he still has his wits."

"He'll do it. And he's not a loon. Without him, and the others, our entire war is without philosophy and understanding. The future of the Arm rests on the shoulders of the Radicals of the past."

*The Radicals? Gerib, that's the writers Tera studied.*

*"This is getting interesting, Ai."*

"We get the mole's name and the data and we get out," Jati said. "With Arira." Their eyes went to Boar, who nodded.

"What about the score?" Nisi asked.

No one responded.

"Hello? We're taking out Hekron, right?"

Jati shook their head indicating the negative.

"What?" This time it was Ailo.

All heads turned to her. The Assembly Hall on Heroon came back as an associative memory.

"He killed all those people on Ffossk. And more in other places too," she said.

*"Ai, be quiet. It's not your place."*

"Shut up, Gerib!" Ailo's eyes went wide as soon as she

said the words.

"Excuse me?" Tera half-turned in her chair. The expression on her face told Ailo she was working something out in her head. This was the second time she'd blurted something out in front of the navigator.

"Sorry." Ailo sunk into her seat.

"Who's Gerib?" Boar asked.

She spun her head to the Hamut. "No one."

"The kid's right," Nisi said, too pissed off to realize she'd use the term Ailo hated. "You can't expect us to go all the way there and not take him out. He's an assassin with no morals."

"And Aradus," JeJeto added. "They both need to get clipped."

Jati shook their head and walked to the panorama window. "How long have you been with me, JeJeto, seven years?"

"Eight."

"And Nisi? I practically raised you."

Nisi's body twitched as if an electric current ran through it.

"And you, kiddo?" Jati's eyes went to Ailo.

Ailo snapped to attention.

"Have you been listening to anything I've seen saying? Didn't you forget what happened in the Assembly Hall?"

Ailo lowered her gaze.

"If you want things to change you have to do things differently. You can't act accordingly and then ask for a new approach afterward." Jati walked over to the three of them. "You think I'm an idealist, Nisi?"

"Sometimes, Cap." The soldier muttered her response at low volume without making eye contact. But she said the words in earnest.

"The Arm needs more of them. And I'm counting on all of you to inspire them." Ailo felt Jati's eyes on her. "Especially you."

*What do they mean, Gerib?*

*"I don't know."*

Jati put a finger on Nisi's chin and raised it so their eyes met.

"No one dies by our hands, not unless they choose to stand against us. Agreed?"

Nisi nodded.

"Good," Jati turned and walked back to General Hirok at the front of the nav room. "But if anyone tries to stop us from getting to our objectives, and doing what's right, they're fair game."

Nisi smirked. "Legion to the end," she whispered to JeJeto, who nodded.

"Your pal Rence should drop a Trojan in the Core system when you're done," JeJeto said, loud enough for everyone to hear. "That thing's geothermally-sourced. I've heard about the energy that thing gives off. Full of hot air."

"Not the only one," Nisi mumbled.

JeJeto chuckled.

Jati shook their head. "We need the system online and running."

"And how are we going to get out in the middle of the meteor shower?" Nisi asked.

"Who said anything about getting out?"

"Huh?"

Jati smiled.

"We're going to dismantle the shield bubble. From the Core."

Everyone's heads went left and right, checking if anyone understood.

"I thought you were against destroying Garassit?" Boar asked.

"Oh, I am."

Hirok stepped forward. "As soon as it's down, I'll contact the Garassians and give them terms."

"They'll have no choice," Jati said. "They'll have to surrender or be decimated. It's an SPF. They'll have only minutes."

"What's an SPF?" Ailo asked Nisi.

"Single Point of Failure. No redundancy."

Ailo indicated she didn't understand.

"It's like the human heart," JeJeto said. "If it goes down, nothing else can step in to keep the blood pumping. Get it?"

Ailo nodded.

"But you'll all be there too." Tera said, concern in her voice. "If they delay you could get killed as well. It's too big a gamble."

"Gotta play the big stakes to take home the pot, kiddo," Jati said. "And this way we save the lives of all those in the other star systems by risking our own."

"You wager they'll cave, Jati?" Nisi asked.

"I'm 'all in' they will. Everyone at the table will fold." Jati swiped a hand, shutting off the holo-field of the Arm. "And besides, there's always Plan C."

"Plan C?" Tera asked at the front.

Hirok shook his head and laughed. "Like that time with Razor and Keen? Off Heroon at the jump port?"

Jati nodded. "Kartan helped on that one too, at least for Razor and me."

"And what exactly is Plan C?" JeJeto asked.

"Improvise something." Jati did a little dance.

Nisi shook her head.

"Are they serious?" Ailo asked her.

Nisi nodded. "Sometimes you gotta roll and work with what you got. Put too much reliance on a certain way of doing something and you lose the creative edge. That's how you get yourself killed."

JeJeto shifted in their seat.

"Happened to my parent," Nisi said in a low voice. Her hardened exterior softened. A different person sat next to Ailo, transformed into a fragile and vulnerable little child.

The soldier's aura refilled with militaristic energy and hubristic confidence, her psychological armor reforming. "If more generals were like Jati back then, she'd still be alive and we would've taken Heroon. Instead, we lost it to Hamut scum." Nisi's eyes darted to Boar before returning to the front of the room.

"But what about Hekron and Aradus, and their demand that you come in person?" Tera asked.

Jati's face shifted. They gazed at Hirok in earnest.

*Gerib, is something wrong?*

"I'm not sure."

"Screw them both," Jati said. "Screw all of them. If they choose to act dishonorably then so be it. It won't matter when we pull this off."

Hirok nodded in agreement.

Nisi pumped her fist and JeJeto put a beige hand on her shoulder, their gap-toothed smile wide.

"And if we don't?" Boar asked.

The spirited moment fizzled.

"Have that little confidence in yourself, Boar?" Nisi snarked.

"I'm a diplomat now, Birevian. I think about both sides and all outcomes. It's an advanced form of intelligence."

Jati stepped forward, their hand rising in a gesture to squelch the pugilistic argument before it ignited.

"If it fails, then General Hirok returns to his armada after Kusk clears the planet. He waits for the fleet to arrive and engages the Garassians under the direction of Galank and the others," Jati said.

"It won't fail," Hirok said. "My person on the ground is reliable. So long as you all do your jobs at each phase of the operation, we can pull this off. You're the best at what you do."

Everyone nodded and took pride in being in the room. Ailo didn't respond. She burned a hole in the floor between her feet.

*"Ai, you should act more appreciative."*

*I can't. I don't like thinking about what might happen.*

*"Have confidence in Jati. They know what they're doing."*

Ailo peeked up and caught Jati's gaze. Their eyes sizzled with anticipation, one eyebrow raised.

"It's all about strategy," Jati said and winked.

# EIGHTEEN

The *Carmora* rode the FTL waves with the cool ease of a ripple over still water. A furious tempest of space/time contradiction blew past the ship, but inside the crew worked with the low hum of well-oiled machinery. Everyone had jobs. People busied themselves applying diorite veneer to the pod, working on core chipband blockers, and flying in the simulator to prepare for an impossible run through the Kusk meteor shower.

All but Ailo. Even her sessions with JeJeto in the training room were put on hold. The sleight of hand expert was too busy shoveling rubble and moving slabs with Nisi or poring over plans of the Garassian palace with Boar.

Ailo swiped a finger with a holo-thimble through the air and pulled up the ship's broadcast database. She hugged a pillow to her chest, three fingers and thumb clasping it against her torso, and tucked her legs up onto the couch. The lounges on the ship felt like a dream world of comfort after living on the streets of T9. The *Carmora* might be an old P-Frigate, but it offered intimate and cozy places to unwind from long days of hard work.

The mood at mealtimes required improvement, however. Those brief social gatherings demonstrated an off-putting pattern of predictability. Banter about progress on prep work for the op veered into references to earlier missions. That led to reminiscing and razzing until Nisi or Boar directed a micro-aggression or explicit jab at one another. Verbal sparring and accusatory threats escalated until the two had to be separated (with Nisi held back by one, or two, people depending on the extent of her rage). Everyone dispersed or drifted into separate groups. The mood soured and never sweetened back up. Ailo had no idea of the core issue between the Birevian and Hamut, but their intensity made clear the sore festered still.

The lounge nearest her sleeping pod became a temporary home base while they made their way to Cesix. Tera, noticing her boredom the night before, set her up with a virtual Heroonese language program. It held her interest, but only for so long. And that's how she drifted into the searchable database and entered a request for information on the Radicals.

Her eyes went over the list of entries on the holo-screen. Short and to the point, that's what she wanted. She knew next to nothing about the Radicals and chose a summary presenting the basics. The tone made clear this production came from the center of the Arm, manufactured by a central media outlet with control over information and its dissemination.

The broadcast presented the Radicals as a brief threat to the existing power dynamic in the Arm. Their methods — propaganda spread via underground networks — preached an alternative political doctrine to the model used by the Garassian Council and nearly resulted in the destabilization of the Arm and a threat to the Council's central role in politics.

Their ideological current ran through progressive channels in universities first, picked up by ambitious young minds hungry for polemics and a different world than their parents and caretakers. Before long, it swept into labor groups, and on two planets in a profitable but tenuous star system it blossomed into local coups, one succeeding long enough to install a junta under the auspices of Radical-inspired revolutionaries. Their success inspired protests, strikes, and walkouts across the Arm that ended only when the Council had no other choice but to slam its iron fist and squash the resistance with military force.

Portrayed as idealists, the broadcast drove home the

idea that the Radicals concerned themselves with plants, animals, and atmospheres over the collective needs of humans in the Arm. Their outlook wouldn't 'help' humanity in the long term. But the kicker came right near the end: brief mention of Rence Tusolo. The name caught Ailo's attention.

The clip included a visual but no biography. A person, short and broad, with thick brown hair brushed back and falling to his shoulders stood in the holo-feed. A mustache and long goatee, speckled with gray (the one sign of age on him) and tied with a pendant, typical of well-to-do Garassians, framed his jaw. She guessed him to be about forty at the time of the image capture. His green eyes emitted an intensity similar to Jati's when they grew animated. Tusolo radiated intelligence, but not in the 'bookish' sense. Ailo imagined him doing physical labor and being inspired by the first-hand experience to create design improvements. The phrase that came to her mind was, 'practically-minded.'

What did Rence Tusolo have to do with the Radicals? Tera's mention that she studied the controversial group during her medical exam kindled Ailo's curiosity, but Jati's reveal that Rence would join the mission sparked the fire of interest. Something about the way everyone reacted to the announcement made Tusolo's story worth investigating.

Using the thimbles on her fingers, she typed in the air, entering his name into the database.

"Ai, are you sure this is a good idea?"

*No one said I couldn't.*

"But no one said you could, either."

*What's with you?*

"What do you mean, Ai?"

*"It's like you're trying to protect me from knowing things. Stop it. I'm not a kid."*

The start icon flashed. She selected it.

*Access denied. Please enter PA password.*

"You're not the only one." She tossed off the thimbles and got up.

"Where are we going?"

*To learn about Rence Tusolo.*

She took the elevator to the lab level. Using her ears, she followed the clanging she'd heard roaming the ship. The trail took her down the medical corridor and past the same room from a few days earlier with the person who'd broken his leg. Still in stasis in the liquid shell, she stopped and stared at him through the transparent wall. An eerie, naked figure floated in suspension, green fluid bubbling around their body. Tubes flowered from the chest like a flower in full bloom and connected to ports at the top of the chamber. The idea that she'd been in one of those after the speeder accident gave her the creeps.

"Sake of the Arm!" A crash came from a room further down the hall.

*There they are.*

Ailo passed the exam room where Tera had examined her before the team meeting on the other side of the corridor and reached the end of the hallway. She ducked through the portal where the sound originated. Tera sat, head aimed upwards, staring at the ceiling. A bent plate of diorite rocked back and forth on the floor at her feet.

"Hi, Tera."

"Ailo, I didn't know you were there." The navigator puffed her cheeks full of air and blew it out through a circle of her lips. "I'm sorry about my language. It's just... this isn't working." She held up a scanner used to read wrist chips.

"The diorite?"

"Yes." She placed the scanner on the counter. "What's up?"

"I had a question if you're not too busy."

Tera gestured at the chair next to hers. "Might as well take a break to cool off. You can help me shape this band to fit over that one." She nodded at the one on the floor.

Ailo picked it up and sat. She handed it to Tera.

"Thanks." The navigator placed it on the counter next to the scanner. "Hold this and I'll work the edges down with the grinder." She put a second curved piece of diorite into

Ailo's hand. About the size of an adult palm, not yet bent to fit a wrist, the material lay heavy in her hand despite being thin as a wafer.

With two fingers and her thumb, Ailo rotated it under the cool bulbs of the lab. Rather than reflecting light, the black material drew it in. Faint sparkles in the stone made it appear like a miniature stellar world, full of star systems.

"Ask me what you like," Tera said. "But I can't promise you I'll be able to answer to your satisfaction. I'm no Jati." She winked parodying the general and leaned in to work the edge of the slab in Ailo's hands.

"Tell me about Rence Tusolo."

Tera rose. "Wow. Wasn't expecting that."

"Why is everyone acting so shocked he might join us?"

Tera leaned in and sanded the corner of the slab in Ailo's hands. "Hold it tight."

Ailo used both hands to steady the diorite as the navigator worked to match the edges of the other band. Ailo guessed it doubled the thickness and blocked the chip from scanning.

"And what does he have to do with the Radicals?"

Tera stopped moving her hands. She straightened and placed the grinder on the counter. "Where did you hear about that?"

"I figured it out," Ailo said and winked like Jati.

"Right."

"It wasn't hard, considering how excited you got when Jati mentioned him in the meeting."

Tera's eyebrows went up.

"Plus, you said in the exam room that you studied the Radicals."

Tera nodded. "Very well. Do you know what a pariah is?"

Ailo shook her head.

"An outcast. For the general public in the Arm, and I imagine on most broadcasts..."

Ailo noticed Tera's pause. Did she know she had been trying to find information about him? She couldn't know.

The navigator had been down here working on the diorite.

"Rence Tusolo is associated with something terrible."

"I don't understand."

"Tusolo's from Garassit. He *was* considered the greatest scientific mind of his generation, responsible for discovering the single-cell organism that almost wiped out humanity at the end of the Second Span."

"You mean Urios?"

"So you know it?"

She'd seen it mentioned. The brief broadcast on Tusolo included it, but she'd skimmed over it. Ailo examined the diorite. It sat like a small galaxy in her hands.

Tera put out her hand, indicating she wanted the slab. Ailo handed it to her.

"It's interesting, isn't it? Were you thinking it's like a little universe viewed from space?"

"I was."

"Well, think of this," Tera held up the diorite, "as the Arm. A small airborne spore almost decimated humanity. Every star system in the Second Span."

"Tusolo discovered it?"

The navigator shook her head. "He figured out how to eradicate it. Urios is a human-specific problem. It lives in some atmospheres that share the other gasses needed for human habitation. Other flora and fauna are not troubled by it, but the spore is deadly when inhaled by our lungs."

"How did he do it?"

"By working on samples from uninhabitable worlds. In a lab on the planet, Urolo. It's an ecological and moral paradox, Ailo. These systems are fine without us, but if we want to join them, we have to interfere with their natural ecology. It means taking life away to make room for the expansion of our species. Urios did not intend to be the near-extinction of humanity in the Arm. Nor did it ask to be captured and taken to a lab, either."

"Urios," Ailo said picking up on the linguistic connection. "Where does the 'ios' come from?"

Tera shifted the slab to one hand and put the other on Ailo's knee. "Your skill with languages continuously impresses me. Here's a word for you. You'll like it. Ready?"

Ailo smiled in anticipation.

"Etymology. The origin of words. And their evolution."

"Like from Contex to Neo-Contex."

Tera nodded. "And on to Heroonese. Speaking of which, how far did you get?"

Ailo balked at the mention of the language program. "Not far." She thumbed her fingernails.

"That's alright. The instructor is pretty boring."

"Totally."

"I'll teach you myself. How about that?"

"Really?"

"Well, I imagine when this ends you'll be spending a lot of time on Heroon if you want to finish your cadet training." Tera handed her back the slab.

She took it but didn't say anything.

"What? I assume you'd like that, right?" Tera asked.

Ailo hadn't thought about it. She still abided by the, 'too far in the future' credo.

Tera picked up the grinder and bent down to work a corner of the diorite in Ailo's hands. "Ur is an obvious reference to the planet, as you astutely pointed out. 'Ios' is sourced from the Contex suffix for 'origin'."

Ailo observed the mini-cosmos in the stone like an omniscient god. "So it was Tusolo's way of acknowledging the Second Span and the near-disaster?"

"Very good. With that kind of deductive reasoning, you'll do well at the Academy," Tera shifted the slab in Ailo's hands to focus on another edge. "It was eulogistic."

"What does that mean?"

Tera stopped grinding. "Words for the dead. Made in praise." She spoke in a whisper and didn't look up.

"Tera?"

The navigator raised her head. Her gold eyes stood like dual suns against her umber skin.

"Where are you from?"

"I'm from Firex. Have you heard of it?"

Ailo nodded. One of the most affluent colonies in the Arm, with a reputation for cultural refinement and sophistication.

"What do you know about it?" The navigator asked.

"That the people there are all like you. Elegant."

"Ha!" Tera started grinding on the stone, shaking her head. "I should write that down for posterity."

Ailo cocked her head. Tera *was* elegant. She carried herself differently from the rest of the *Carmora's* crew. Her gait and gestures spoke in body language as if to express that she always had all the time in the world to do everything. It made sense that she hailed from a world known for its appreciation of economic comfort and 'high' living.

"Elegant," Tera muttered and ground the stone.

Ailo caught a trace of a smile on her face as the navigator worked the diorite.

"Is that where you learned so much? I mean, about languages?"

"No, I went to the Language Institute on Ortor. A cold world, and a perfect place to be for academic pursuits. No hills of black grass and geysers. Just endless tundra and bogs. Very few distractions from your studies. Except, well..." The navigator looked up and smiled. "I'll save that until you are a bit older."

"But why did you join the People's Army?"

Tera's face softened and she stopped working. "I went back home after my studies and found a different world than the one I left."

"What happened to Firex?"

"Nothing. It was what happened to me. My vision changed. A different reality lay before my eyes. Not the same as before I'd left for Ortor. And so, I walked away from that one to help shape a new one. And from there to here, talking to you." She winked like Jati.

"Did that make you a pariah?"

Tera lay her tools on her lap and ran both hands through her green and blue hair. "Well, to my parents at least."

"What about Rence Tusolo? How did he become a 'pariah'?"

"Do you know about the ships?" Tera re-started work on the edge of the slab.

"I've seen them on broadcasts. They carried citizens from the Second Span and fled, on great colony vessels, out of the Arm."

"And with them went a level of technology yet to be rediscovered. We still don't understand how they managed to create self-sufficient biospheres. Tusolo, however... well, I'm getting ahead of myself. About the Second Span – it took severe isolationist strategies to save the remaining portion of humanity. Few worlds were spared from its spread. From those few planets, a civilization rose again."

"And what about the Radicals? And Tusolo?"

"Hang on. History can't be told unchained." The navigator stopped working and bent back up, her gold eyes aimed at Ailo. "You need the links to meet." She took an onyx finger off the grinder and hooked it to one in her open hand. "Like this. Sit tight. We're almost there." Tera leaned back in, flung the electric blue side of her hair over her neck to the green half, and rotated the slab in Ailo's hands to a third corner. "So Tusolo discovered the solution to eradicate Urios in a lab on Urolo. It's near to T9. And therefore pretty far away from the rest of the Arm."

"Yeah, I know." Ailo had heard of it. As a prosperous outlying territory on the edge of Garassian space, it was common for departing ships from the affluent planet to stop on a layover at the small station off T9. People talked about dangerous things related to science happening there, and now she understood why. Urolo lay far enough from other systems to ensure its isolation should there be an accident.

Ailo wasn't surprised that Tarkassi 9, as a nearby neighbor, was discounted from concern.

*No one gave a crap about us out there.*

"Edge of the Arm," Ailo said. "Far away, in case there was an accident."

"Luckily, an accidental leak of Urios never happened," Tera said. "But... and here is your answer because now we have a chain... Tusolo figured out how to eradicate Urios-laden atmospheres on planets in habitable zones. That led to Garassia occupying new worlds. And they started to eco-shape them."

The links were working. A much more complicated picture, but a clearer one, formed in Ailo's mind.

"So now you end up with the reason for the Patent War. Tensions grew between the Garassians and the Hamuts, each vying for territories in the Arm. And here is how Rence Tusolo became a pariah. His discovery was made to safeguard the human species and promote settlement throughout the Arm, but others recognized its potential as a powerful weapon. And they used it... in reverse. It brought a quick end to the war."

"Is this how my friend Solazi got the Cough?"

Tera stopped working the diorite and rose. "You knew someone with the Cough?"

Ailo nodded. "They worked at a bar on T9." Tera's expression shifted. It wasn't legible. Ailo marked it as somewhere between pity and frustration. She'd observed similar body language on patrons at the Tip of the Beyond. Most of the time after they'd had too much to drink, especially Solazi's special, the Tarkassi Tail.

"No, that's not how your friend got the Cough," the navigator said. "Sorry, by the way. I know there is no recovery."

Ailo gazed at the diorite slab in her lap. She imagined a small capsule with Solazi's remains drifting through space inside the miniature world. Had the former soldier been sent adrift, like other veterans?

"But," Tera said, "after the Hamuts used their dangerous chemical weapon on Yaqit — the one that gave your friend the Cough — the Garassians retaliated with their own, based on Tusolo's research. It was called Serek. And with it, they destroyed the Hamut homeworld, Xerteej."

"Is that where Boar is from?" Ailo asked.

Now it was clear. Tera's expression was pity. "Yes. And what Tusolo envisioned as the future course of humanity through his discovery created a political paradox."

Ailo struggled to understand. "I don't follow."

"The Patents, Ailo. And the reason why you, out there on the edge of the Arm, lived on minimal energy cells. We could inhabit planets abundant with natural resources now, utilizing eco-synchronization technologies in non-damaging and non-dominating ways. But that's not what came to pass. Those worlds were made safe for humans and colonized in short order, but their existing ecologies were left unutilized. Every newly settled planetary society was at the mercy of outside energy producers to survive. On the surface, it appeared as a moral solution. Their planets remained pristine, but it meant they were controlled by others. They could not do what they wanted."

Ailo watched as Tera's demeanor shifted. Was this still a history lesson? The discussion felt real and political. Was Tera speaking as a voice of the People's Army?

"A non-proliferation treaty regulated all eco-shaping and energy-producing technology. It meant no one else could generate energy through technological innovations or by themselves. Only patented Garassian and Targitian designs were permissible to produce energy in the Arm. And the Hamuts, losers in the Patent War, were tasked with enforcing those Patents. I'm sure you had firsthand experience of that on T9."

She did and hadn't forgotten their brutish ways. And she knew their spacecraft well. When the Hamut Alliance made one of their infrequent inspection stops at T9, their Enforcer class Destroyers were visible in view panes on the moonbase. The menacing ships in orbit were like a school of predatory fish lurking on the edge of a reef.

The Hamuts were bullies. On T9 they had fun going to extremes with the vulnerable citizens who had no choice but to violate mandates in order to survive. Was Boar one of these?

"There were other worlds affected by the Patents, too, Ailo. Planets in unsettled systems were turned into energy-producing sites, their natural ecosystems destroyed. Gone. Wiped clean. Razed to the ground. The Garassians did this to make wind."

*The Wind Tides.*

"Have you seen them, Tera?"

"The Wind Tides? I have." The navigator's voice carried a new earnestness. "They're not exciting, Ailo. They're terrifying."

She'd heard stories of the Wind Tides. Raging currents crossing empty and cloudless planets comprised of windswept dunes.

"The Wind Tides are storms of tremendous size, the front wave crackles with orange lightning and swirling sand. The swell rises so high it almost leaves the atmosphere. Believe me, you don't want to be near one when it breaks."

Ailo's eyes went wide.

"And on one planet in particular, the government is as scary as the Tide Waves. Do you know of the Targitians?"

She'd viewed them on broadcasts. Black-robed figures, hooded and standing in vast and empty stone-tiled plazas. Images of them walking towards a sleek city of angular mirrors, like small mites approaching shards of broken glass. Epic in scale and sublime in their architectural simplicity, the structures broke the laws of time, appearing as the future set in the past.

"The Targitians are members of the Council too," Tera said. "But they have a secret technology. It's so powerful that they compete against Garassia without the need of exo-colonization."

"Is that Kol 2?"

Tera nodded. "Eco-shaped centuries earlier. But Targitian innovation surpassed that of those in the Second Span who first turned the planet from a lush world to a desert of currents. They invented turbines of mysterious design that capture wind and harness an unrivaled potential for energy cell production."

"What are they like?"

"Who? The Targitians?"

Ailo nodded.

"Much of their culture is guarded and kept private. They are strict worshippers and keep to themselves other than diplomatic responsibilities that take them to Ceron."

"It's a wind god. That's what Nisi said."

Tera nodded. "Kol 2's history is marred by an internal division, a civil war that fractured the indigenous culture. Much of that heritage faded when the Targitians assimilated the customs, religions, and languages of the eco-colonizers until they broke away and invented their own." Tera raised a slender finger. "By the way, the original language of Kol 2 is close to Contex. So close that if someone still spoke or read it they could glean the gist of a Contex text."

"But what about Rence Tusolo?"

"Yes, you're right. I've given you a history lesson rather than answered your question. And now I'm leaning towards a sermon. Jati accuses me of this all the time." She bounced her eyebrows. "I can't help it. My investment in our cause riles me up." Tera expression grew earnest. "But you must understand where Rence fits in all of this."

"I understand," Ailo said. "The chain."

"I deserved that one. Alright, back to Tusolo... he meant his discovery to promote human life and the expansion of civilization in the Arm. Instead, it led to its immoral destruction. Humans vanished in a single strike to the Hamut's homeworld. And it ended the Patent War."

"Wait. How?"

"Serek. It was used on Xerteej. Delivered as a weapon of annihilation."

"*Ai, was that what Tera meant when she talked about Boar? And his anger?*"

*I think so.*

So the Hamut too had no home.

"They twisted Rence's discovery into a brutal and callous weapon of mass destruction. He was demonized and scapegoated for his role in that process. Out of frustration and perhaps out of guilt, he sought escape. And that is when he found a new home with the Radicals. They were intellectuals, Ailo. They wanted to resurrect the work of Second Span writers and theorists touting ecological anarchy."

"What is anarchy? We got accused of it on T9 when we would riot."

"Well, it all depends on who you ask. But for the Radicals, it was less political and more ecological."

Ailo handed back the diorite slab. "I don't understand."

"I'll tell you more about that next time. For now, here is the thing you've been waiting for with Tusolo. After he declared himself one of the Radicals, he vanished."

"What?"

"Well, until a few days ago, I, like most other people in the Arm, assumed it meant he'd been 'removed' by the Garassian Council. They have a habit of carrying out secret operations to silence political opposition. You know who Aradus is, right?"

Ailo nodded. "Keen Draden's parent. A leader in Garassit."

"That's right. He's also Hekron's uncle."

Hekron. Something stirred inside her belly. That fire shifted from curiosity to anger.

"Aradus has a history of enjoying murder and assassination of rivals. And in the last decade or so, his nephew has become his favorite tool to carry out his desire. Hekron is an assassin, Ailo. A member of the Sicara, an elite group that carries out shadow killings in the Arm."

"And he took Arira."

Tera nodded. "Aradus needs her to get Jati to come to Garassit. She's most likely safe. For now... Let's hope."

Ailo thought back on the kind person who'd healed her and set her free in the wilds of Ffossk. Knowing her relationship to Jati and going through those events during her abduction created more hate for Hekron.

"For several years," Tera said, "Hekron focused on rooting out those who were part of the Radicals to eliminate them."

"Why?"

"Because they threatened to create a new world order. Most, myself included, assumed that is what happened to Rence after he turned on Garassia."

"Is Jati a Radical?"

"I'll let them answer that one." She raised an eyebrow.

"But Hekron didn't kill Tusolo?"

"No, apparently not. The other theory is that he fled to an outer star system to live with the collective thinkers, scientists, linguists, and others on the run, somewhere on the edge of civilized space. If it were true, then they'd be living under a form of anarchy, which by the way is called an 'eco-anarchic syndicate.' I'll tell you more about that next time." She placed the grinder back on the counter. "Whether or not that is the case... well, I guess we're going to find out."

Ailo stared at her.

"I know. It's confusing," Tera said. "And a lot to take in."

Ailo's mind went to Jati and the upcoming destination in the Cesix sector. So Tusolo was alive? What about the others, the new Radicals? And why did Jati want her to join them in their recruitment effort? What could she do to convince a hermit to return to the world and fight for the People's Army?

"So Firecracker, tell me about Rence Tusolo." Jati sat in the captain's seat and watched the blue FTL light crackle in the void outside the *Carmora*. The general spoke the words without moving, like a statue on a throne. Their lips curved upward in a subtle smile after they finished, breaking stone back into flesh.

"The pariah?" Ailo asked. Tera shifted in her navigator's seat.

"We don't refer to him that way. Not on the *Carmora*."

"Sorry."

"Not your fault. It's how he's been recorded by the chroniclers. There's still time to change that."

"But..." Ailo made sure Boar wasn't on the bridge before continuing. "His weapon destroyed the Hamut's entire world."

"*His* weapon?" Jati raised an eyebrow. "Rence wasn't in the weapon-making business. He was... still is, a researcher. A philosopher of discovery. Those who desired domination and power over tolerance and humility twisted his knowledge."

"I don't understand."

"How far did you get into his story?"

From her seat in front, Tera gave her a quick, clandestine nod indicating she hadn't said anything about their conversation.

"I'm not spying on you," Jati said. "But if you want to cover your tracks or keep your activities private, it's a good idea to shut things off when you leave a room."

*I left the search open on the holo. In the lounge.*

"*You do that all the time, Ai.*"

*Shut up Gerib.*

"I know he discovered Urios," Ailo said, "an element in the atmospheres of the planets where we can't live. And it makes Serek, the weapon that destroyed the human population on Xerteej... at the end of the Patent War. In response to the Hamuts gassing soldiers on Yaqit."

Jati nodded. "Where Solazi fought in the war. Their home planet, by the way." They raised an eyebrow. "And was that the right thing to do?" The general untied the half-up, half-down ponytail and shook out their long hair. Sitting in the captain's chair they became regal, like images of the rulers of old. Not that those ancient leaders looked like that, but on entertainment broadcasts they romanticized First Span politics and made their commanders out to be god-like.

*I'm not sure how to answer, Gerib. I don't know that*

*there's a right or wrong. Both sides seem wrong.*

*Jati is testing you, Ai.*

"I don't know," Ailo said.

"Excellent response." Jati slapped their hands down on the armrest. "Honesty will keep you free of regret. It's the best strategy because your tactics can't let you down."

"So do you know?" she asked.

"No one 'knows' the answer. It's a matter of position... and moral philosophy. But one way to reconsider the question is to step back. Remove yourself from a 'side' and do your best to view the situation anew. Is it ever right to use weapons like that?"

Ailo considered the question. "It depends."

"On?"

"Maybe how big the threat is or how desperate you are."

"Desperate?"

"Like if you will lose, otherwise."

Jati drew their paw-like hands off the armrests and placed them together in front of their mouth, elbows on their thighs. "Hmmm..." The general bounced their fingers against their lips like a pendulum.

Ailo's nerves jittered. Were they waiting for her to speak?

"It's always justified, then?" Jati asked.

"What? Violence?"

They nodded.

"You fight," she said, a bit quicker than she intended. "You were... are a soldier. And you're Legion."

"True."

"It's justified to use violence if people stand in your way," she said. "That's what you told Nisi at the meeting."

"I did. But I'm still working on that position."

"What do you mean?"

"You think I have it all worked out?" Jati rose from the chair and put their hands on their hips. "I'm as unsure as you. As anyone else *should* be. Be careful of people who are too confident in their views or ideas. It makes them believe they are the 'right' ones." Jati made air quotations around the word for emphasis.

"Like being 'weird'," Ailo said, mimicking the gesture.

Jati laughed. "Yes, like being 'weird' as opposed to 'normal'. Good memory." They shot her with a hand blaster and winked. "Being too sure of things is much more dangerous than any weapon in the hands of a soldier. Or the commands at the disposal of a general." Jati gestured at the command seat. "Sit."

Tera's head swung around.

"There?" Ailo pointed at the captain's chair.

Jati nodded. "Care to take us out of FTL? We're coming up on the Cesix sector."

"But I... I mean, I don't know what to do. I don't have any understanding of how to fly a ship."

Jati turned to the view out the bridge window. Fluctuating hues of blue and white shot past at an unfathomable speed. "Ailo has the con," they said to Pozix and Tera.

The two nodded, their confirmations abrupt.

Ailo slid into the captain's chair. She placed her hands on the armrests.

"How does it feel?" Jati asked, without turning from the view outside.

Ailo's stomach fluttered. Half of it was nerves and the other half was thrill.

"Let me guess... terrifying but thrilling?" The general turned, eyes alight.

She nodded. But the weight of responsibility daunted her confidence. She had more than herself to think about. And power lay at her fingertips.

*So this is what it's like for Jati.*

"What do you think, Ai?"

*I think it's hard.*

"Hard how?"

*You have to think about others. How to protect them and do what is right. And...*

"And what?"

Ailo shifted in the seat.

*And you have to think about the power of the ship and what you can do. And who you can command, like people 'under' you. Even an entire fleet... and an army.*

"Coming up on Cesix, Captain," Tera said.

Ailo's eyes went to Jati. They didn't respond or acknowledge her.

"Captain?" Tera turned.

"What do I do?" Ailo asked.

Jati kneeled next to her. "Let those who know how to do their jobs do them."

"Thank you, Tera," Ailo said.

Tera gave a thumbs-up, the same as she would do for Jati.

"Ask questions of those you respect and trust. Listen and evaluate. Then, make the best-informed decision you can." Jati gestured for Ailo to turn her attention to the bridge window. The *Carmora* dropped out of FTL. An empty cosmos surrounded the ship. One small star radiated yellow light in the distance. Other than one object, nothing but the usual starry blanket filled the view.

"All clear on the board," Tera said. "We're the only ones here."

Jati nodded to Ailo.

*"Go ahead, Ai. They're waiting."*

Ailo worked up her nerve. "Thank you, Tera."

"Shall I make a course for the programmed heading?" the navigator asked.

"Yes."

"Roger that, Captain." Tera turned and smiled at Ailo. The navigator worked with Poz to steer the ship to its destination.

"Do you want your seat back?"

"Not yet," Jati said and rose from their kneeling position. The general turned to the view out of the ship. Their lavender hair and chiseled features glowed with the yellow light of the approaching star. Ailo imagined a Cantinool sculpture of their head with Nushaba's rays bouncing off their carved face.

*Someday they'll make a statue of Jati on Heroon, Gerib.*

The yellow orb grew larger in the window. Something blipped into sight a short distance from the star. Sunlight flashed across a small object in space.

"Cesix station in view, Captain," Pozix said. "Looks like it's holding position well. From what you told me, I think the last section of sail made a difference." Ailo knew the latter words were meant for Jati. The object grew in size as they approached. One form became two. A small silver orb sat at the center of an immense square-shaped silver fabric, like a single drop of ink on a blank page.

"Sail looks good," Jati said, their eyes examining the approaching object.

"Sail?" Ailo asked.

"Yes, Captain," Jati said.

Ailo smiled at the way they addressed her.

"That's Rence's design. It's a statitite."

"You mean satellite?"

Jati shook their head. "Statitite. A 'static' satellite. The solar sail connects to the station sphere by extension legs. It's in equilibrium and remains stationary as it orbits. The star wants to draw it in through gravitational pull but its orbital velocity, size of the sail, and the station's distance from the sun keep it from falling inward."

"How?"

"Solar wind. Invisible to our eyes but a powerful cosmic force. Rence's little world is riding the stellar wind like a ship on a windy sea. The forces are equally matched and therefore it causes a stalemate."

"And we're here, outside the conflict," Ailo said. "Like moving beyond right and wrong."

Jati's face lit up. Tera swung around in her seat at her station. Ailo noticed the same expression on her face when they were in the exam room when she remarked about poetry and her 'gift'.

*"Ai, I'm impressed. I didn't think of it."*

*Thanks, Gerib.*

"Is Rence here to get away from it?" she asked.

"It?"

"Right and wrong."

"Yes." Jati said in a solemn tone. "As best he can."

The station neared. The star side of the silver sail glowed with yellow light. The other half lay in shadow, casting the illusion of a square incision in the void of space.

*Gerib, the station is tiny but the sail...*

Ailo couldn't gauge its size.

*It's immense.*

Ailo calculated the orb's scale to the sail. You could fit at least a hundred of the small spheres along its surface.

"So much sail for such as small living space," she said.

"It takes a lot of constant energy and effort to stay in one place, Captain. It's a never-ending battle to fight off change." Jati winked.

*Are they referring to Rence?*

"I think it's clever wordplay, Ai. It refers to both."

Ailo smiled. She enjoyed the power of words. Something about language made it as powerful as a physical weapon. She made a note to remember to ask Tera about it.

"What if Rence won't agree to help you?"

"I don't expect him to, Firecracker."

Ailo cocked her head and sought an explanation from Jati. Their crow's feet crunched the corner of the skin around their green eyes. The general watched Cesix station approach.

"But I believe he *will* help us."

# NINETEEN

The *Carmora's* bridge became a classroom. Jati's tests kept me on high alert, especially with Ailo's recent challenges to my advice. Tension grew between us, demonstrated by my obstinance towards a teenager ready to turn adult who wanted a looser rein. Ailo's vocal outbursts during our arguments drew the attention of others, Tera in particular. It wasn't necessarily a problem, so long as we resolved things soon and she didn't make a habit of it.

Jati spoke to Ailo about morality on the bridge as if we were inside the brain of the ship. But the general didn't code their intentions to convey or convince her of right or wrong, or good and bad. Rather, their lessons focused on how to construct a personal moral philosophy. That had my support. It demonstrated humility and a 'practice what they preach' attitude.

No one imposed a belief system on Ailo. Nor did Jati evoke ideology to persuade and convince her of a particular position on a moral spectrum. Instead, they guided her past the limit of her world experience. The general opened an extant space in the human mind, perhaps its greatest gift — the ability to see *beyond* the self. It activated a new epistemology in Ailo. Jati passed on a form of knowledge that had helped them become who they were. Did they get it through hard-won experience? Through trial and error? Or were they lucky enough to be brought into the world with it?

No matter how the leader of the People's Army obtained it, I noted an important distinction with how they wielded it. The wisdom Jati imparted wore a specific face and it wasn't morality. It was ethics.

It didn't take much coaxing for Ailo to engage and buy-in. She walked out of the room of objective illusion without hesitation. I told you she's fiercely determined when it comes to what she wants. That didactic exercise became the first step to what I know will be fully formed critical thought. To my surprise, Ai was listening. Closely. And paying attention. She'd absorbed the early conversation on Ffossk about 'normalcy' and used it to comparative effect. Poetically, I might add.

Boar said it in the nav room: Jati is one of a kind. I don't know if that's true but I started to believe it. I realized something else on the *Carmora's* bridge: Jati and I are more alike than I'd thought. My job is internal, managing a 'family' of subpersonalities comprising a psyche and its dynamics. Jati performs a similar task on the 'outside,' facilitating their team's idiosyncrasies. The distinction they'd made between strategy and tactics wasn't just about combat or war. Conduct and social relations were just as central.

When Jati sat in the chair on the bridge evoking a ruler of old, it came to me: the *Carmora* is a collective psyche. The crew, its internal dynamics.

Jati has their job cut out for them too. Nisi? Boar? I can relate. It's a matter of scale and context but we're in the same business. When those under our charge can't handle personal crises, real or imagined, emergency responders step in and make a mess for both of us to clean up. I work through internal monologue. Jati labors on the individual in face-to-face conversation and collectively as part of social relations. And perhaps most importantly, by example.

I experienced a humbling and thrilling realization as we glided towards Cesix station. I considered it an equivalent to sitting in the captain's seat on the *Carmora*. Those of us who are managers, like Jati and me, are more than facilitators tasked with keeping our charges safe and stable in the face of life's challenges. That's what our job looks like from within the objective 'room.' As part of Ailo, I stepped with her outside of that enclosure under Jati's hidden erudition. And the landscape changed.

We're more than managers. Jati and I are teachers, whether through wisdom (in their case) or practicality for survival and peace of mind (in mine). And teachers fail when they stop learning. Something told me that Jati was drawn to Ailo for a reason. They were gaining education from their relationship. But something else lurked, yet to show itself. It hovered over the edge of a fateful horizon, soon to rise. I wasn't able to see its light, but I had a sense of what it might be.

There was something else, too. It was a long time coming, but its imminence could no longer be denied. Call it the ironic fate of all teachers. Your part in someone's education was vital but brief in their lifelong learning. You knew it when your support system turned into their self-reliant foundation. Challenges were signs of an approaching time to let go and set the student free. Success meant accepting your role was finished. Ailo needed Jati for a more advanced degree, but I couldn't deny my own pedagogical and therapeutic fate: she was ready to graduate.

# TWENTY

The pod shot out of the docking bay with Boar at the controls. The thrust and the way Boar maneuvered caught Ailo off guard. She'd been on a few short rides up to the orbit port on T9 and those were public shuttles, not personal flyers. Boar's attitude towards passenger comfort when it came to piloting was less sympathetic. Good thing she strapped in or she would have toppled over.

Ailo pushed a finger into her thigh and traced a line around the edge of her lucky Rim wedge. The small token lay sealed inside the pocket of her spacesuit. Jati promised the outfit was a precaution but a necessary one when visiting a station without a docking bay.

"Extra-vehicular activity, 'EVA' for short, is something you have to be ready for at all times when transferring between ships and stations via pods," they said. "Just standard procedure, Firecracker."

Now, as Ailo sat in the passenger seat along the wall of the pod she hoped they were right.

At least she didn't need to put on the helmet. She'd never worn one, nor a full suit. All residents on T9 got certified on how to use them in case of an accidental leak or emergency evacuation, but she'd never done it. That's what you get for being a street kid. Most of the time avoiding mandated requirements liberated individuals from tedious and boring instruction. But this one? She wasn't so sure now.

The idea of being shut inside a body capsule gave her the jitters. Ironic, considering T9 was a glorified spacesuit for the small colony that lived there — a restrictive and claustrophobic living and working environment. But at least citizens had freedom of movement in an atmosphere, albeit a pathetic one.

They cleared the ship and Jati motioned her up to the cockpit. She unfastened the straps, walked up the aisle and stood in the narrow space between the two cockpit seats. An array of buttons, switches, and screens ran across the dashboard, up the sidewalls, and overhead. How someone kept track of all of it, she didn't know. Out the window, nothing but the twinkle of stars filled the view. Nisi and the others had remarked that Cesix was in the middle of nowhere. They were right. No planets or stations at all and the stars lay more distant than off T9 and Heroon.

Boar rotated the steering grips and banked the pod back towards the *Carmora*.

"This thing's got some serious pep, Jati. Let me guess, you scored some off-market parts from my old pal, Parnak-ta after the Patent War?" The Hamut raised an eyebrow and turned the pod in a graceful arc. The *Carmora's* stern appeared in the window, its massive boosters a series of soft, glowing honeycombs.

Jati didn't respond. They whistled and fiddled with a control overhead.

"That's what I thought," Boar said.

The two spent several minutes discussing a modification Jati had made on the thrusters at the P-Frigate's stern. They bantered enthusiastically, pointing at various components and growing excited like little kids with a new toy. With Jati and Boar absorbed in 'gear-talk,' Ailo forgot about the conflict at hand. She stared at the glowing embers of the ship's engines and thought back to the decision to flee the moon base. This had been the most exciting two months of her life. But something told her that soon it would get complicated. And more dangerous.

*"It's the risk for the reward, Ai."*
*Huh?*
*"It's a life choice."*

*Between what?*

"Staying home and living a life that might be smaller, safer, and more comfortable. Or going over a threshold and entering an unknown where risk can lead to unknown experiences, struggle, and danger but also a different set of rewards."

*Yeah, well I didn't have that choice. There was no home, no safety back there.*

"Maybe that's better."

*Leaving was the right choice?*

"Both choices are right. There is no wrong."

*You sound like Jati.*

"I'll take that as a compliment."

Ailo studied the PA general. They appeared happy despite the larger circumstances. Somehow even with Arira in danger and the threat of collapse for the PA's war effort, Jati still managed to live in the moment. Boar too appeared to be enjoying himself.

*It's funny Gerib.*

"What is, Ai?"

*How they can turn it on and off.*

"Look Ai, I know you're frustrated with me."

Ailo sighed. *It's not that, Gerib. We're fine. Just don't...*

"Yes, I know. Treat you like a kid. I think that's abundantly clear to everyone now."

Ailo laughed.

Jati turned. "What?"

Boar swung around as well.

"Nothing. You two are like kids." She waved them off so they would go back to talking.

"We're the kids now, huh?" Jati said.

"I didn't mean to interrupt."

Jati and Boar re-engaged their talk of turbo boosters.

"But Ai, what I was going to say is that it's important, healthy actually, to be able to forget things now and then and let go so you can find a way to recharge."

*You know I know how to live in the moment, Gerib.*

*"I do. But I'm not talking about a 'to heck with the future' attitude. That gets your ankle broken and puts you in stasis for three weeks. I'm talking about allowing yourself space to let go."*

*Of what?*

*"Just remember it, OK?"*

*Let go of what?*

*"Well, that's something for another time."*

*Good, because now you are getting annoying.* She smiled.

Boar brought the pod parallel with the *Carmora* and hit the thrusters. Out the left side of the window shone the lone star for which the system took its name. Cesix burned bright, casting golden beams onto the side of the P-Frigate as they passed. Yellow light gleamed off the ship's curves and corners. The memory of the *Carmora* docked off T9 flashed into Ailo's mind. How different the ship was now from when she first stowed away. Old, yet tough and experienced then — a menacing marauder with the battle scars to prove it. Now, it appeared like the protective leader of a pack, sheltering its crew and standing on the front line of an army kept safe from a world teetering between promise and catastrophe. For her, it had even began to feel like 'home.'

"Stay star-side until we're close," Jati said from the co-pilot seat.

"Roger that, Captain." Boar aimed the pod between the station and the star.

The silver sail and orb appeared in the upper right corner of the cockpit window.

"Can we take the heat?" Boar asked, scanning a readout on the board.

"We're good until about three miles out, then you'll need to turn to starboard and bring us in on the backside."

Boar nodded.

Ailo tracked over the sail until her eyes reached the half-orb in the center of the massive fabric. The sail material sparkled and shimmered in the golden rays of sunlight.

Solar reflections bounced off the curved surface of the small station.

"One minute to turn," Boar said. "I like the way this pod handles, Jati. It's got a lot of hours on it but it's still tight and responsive."

"It's my favorite of the three we've got." Jati turned Ailo. "You know Firecracker, Keen Draden sat in this very seat." They nodded at the co-pilot spot where they were sitting.

"Keen Draden was in this pod?" Boar asked.

Jati nodded. "Sure was."

Boar's orange eyes examined Jati in earnest. "She knows about Keen?"

"Ailo met him. And still has a Rim wedge he gave her."

"Really?" Boar said and turned. He nodded in a way that said, 'Interesting.'

"How old were you Ailo?" Jati asked.

"Seven, I think." She touched the Rim wedge's contour through the suit. The memory of the portly person with a mane of curly hair and goatee flashed into her mind.

"He stepped onto this pod as one person... went to T9," Jati's green eyes focused on Ailo, "met you, got a haircut," they laughed and shook their head at the memory, "and stepped back on board for the return ride a changed person."

"Have you ever been able to get word to Razor?" Boar asked.

Jati's expression shifted as if the mortar between the golden slabs of their face softened. They stared at the station looming ahead.

"No." Jati's voice came out at a whisper, barely audible over the hum of the pod's ventilation fans. "It's probably better this way."

*Who is Razor?*

*"I don't think now is the time, Ai."*

Jati perked back up. "Anyway... yes, this pod's sound as can be. We'll use it for the run through Kusk and down to Garassit."

"Good." Boar tapped the dashboard as if petting an

animal. "I like this one." He lifted his head to gaze out the window. "Station's in view now. Take a look Ailo, we'll be turning and then it'll be dark."

Ailo felt relief at the Hamut's softer, mentor-like tone, so different from the contentious and arrogant person that battled Nisi and spit out snide remarks. And as a Hamut, he was without a planet to return to and call home. Maybe he was more complicated than she'd realized? The ambiguity unnerved her. She hesitated.

"Go on," Jati said.

Ailo leaned forward.

"So you met Keen Draden?" Boar asked.

Ailo nodded.

Details on the orb rolled into view. Its surface spread out like a finished steel grey puzzle in three dimensions, comprised of hexagonal pieces. Opaque, no windows penetrated the shell. To be so close to a star and have to resort to artificial lights for illumination seemed a shame.

"I guess we're all here for a reason," the Hamut said.

*What does that mean?*

"All of us," Jati said and winked at Ailo.

In the aisle, Ailo rested her hands on the top of the two seats and peered to the left. Through the shaded shields, Cesix glowed with steady and determined radiance.

"Is that where we get in?" Boar pointed to a spot on the station's shell.

"Yep," Jati said and fiddled with something on the control board.

The station changed. A larger hexagon with a small black square entered into view.

"It's spinning," Ailo said.

Jati nodded.

"He's not working centrifugal gravity, is he?" Boar asked. The Hamut's orange eyes went to a readout tracking the station. "At that rate of spin, it'd be nominal."

Jati shook their head. "Has something to do with the water system at the bottom of the sphere. Some kind of whirlpooling related to space/time dynamics and his modified gravity engine. He's explained it to me a dozen times. After about two minutes he loses me… every time." Jati made a gesture with a hand like a ship passing over their head.

"There's no gravity?" Ailo asked.

"There's gravity," Jati said. "Although it's less than you're used to so get ready to be a bit lighter."

Ailo perked up. She'd watched people move about on broadcasts in lower gravity environments in adventure dramas, but she'd never experienced it. "How much less?"

"You won't be pushing off walls and floating around if that's what you're thinking," they said.

Boar laughed.

"What's so funny?" Ailo shot him a snarky look. *That's the other Boar back again.*

"Nothing." The Hamut banked the ship to the right and the station passed out of view at the left corner of the window.

"Rence built the vital components into the station's lower section. Things are a little funky down there. But the habitable areas have decent gee," Jati said.

So they'd been inside and done more than helped with the materials and setting up the construction. Were they and Rence friends?

"But…"

"What?" Jati swiveled in their seat to face her.

"How do we dock if it's spinning?"

"We'll line up in a synchronized position and spin with it. There's more space between the leg extensions from station to sail than you'd think from this distance. The station attaches to the sail network on the top and bottom with rotating pins. There's a web of support lines running through the fabric like inside the wings of a bat." Jati held up a hand and spread their fingers apart. "On the orb's sides a second set of pins attach, but those run on a rail system on the outside of the sphere. Those don't turn but they stabilize the structure. It's complicated. When we get closer it'll make sense."

"We have to fly in there?" she asked.

"No. It'd take some pretty crafty flying to pull that off..."

"Please," Boar said.

"Boar could do it," Jati said, thumbing at the Hamut. "But for the rest of us, getting in and back out isn't something you'd want to risk trying. If you screwed it up and hit a pin or the sails, you'd damage the ship and have who knows what to deal with. Not to mention if the components of the sails were affected it would offset the balance in orbit and screw up the heliostationary equilibrium. The station would fall into the sun."

Boar shook his head. "Gotta be crazy to design something like this."

"*Or...*" Jati's emphasis made clear the choice of wording was both a response and a counter to the accusation of madness. "You don't want any visitors."

"But he lets you visit," Ailo said.

"Well, let's hope so."

"What does that mean?" Boar asked.

Jati shrugged. "Hopefully he's in a good mood."

"Sake of the Arm, Jati! I should've known." Boar shook his head.

"What? This whole thing got thrown together in a week or less. You can't expect me to have everything worked out."

"Except maybe the most important aspect of the plan."

Jati did a 'shuffle' in their seat, making a dance-like arm and shoulder movement. "It's called strategy."

"Oh really?" Boar said. "And what kind of strategy is it?"

"Chance," Jati said and shrugged. They winked at Ailo.

*Jati...*

"Don't worry," they said. "I've got his water resupply. It's been a while since I've been out here. His system is efficient with recycling but it's not one-hundred percent. He'll be down significantly by now. The whirlpool can't get too low or Rence's little paradise away from the world will implode."

She'd almost forgotten about the issue at hand with

their lighthearted entertainment, but now it came back in crystal clarity. "So how are we getting in?" Ailo put her hands on her hips. "Is he doing it?" She nodded at Boar.

"Nope. Rence will do it. Well, if he's willing to see us. He's got a remote tracking and control system. It's one of his pet projects. Been working on remote flying tech systems for years. I bring him parts requests when I deliver water."

"Remote flying, huh?" Boar said.

Ailo caught a skepticism to the Hamut's response.

"Here we go," Jati shook their head. "Don't listen to Boar, Ailo. He'll tell you that you can't fly a ship from outside as well as you can from inside."

"It's an instinct thing," Boar said. "Can't replicate the actual experience."

Jati rolled their eyes. "*Anyway...* Rence will take over the nav controls on the pod from the station and a program will calculate an algorithm for the spin, orbital velocity, and whatnot. We sit back and enjoy the ride."

"Rather do it myself," Boar said.

"I'm sure you would, but Rence would never allow it." Jati's face turned serious. "He knows what he's doing, Firecracker. Don't you worry." They turned to Boar. "You as well."

Boar banked the pod back left. The non-star facing side of the sails and station appeared in the window. Behind the blocked light of the Cesix, she lost sight of the *Carmora*. The Hamut steered towards the sphere inside a cloak of darkness. Intense and narrow solar beams flooded through the open areas where the station legs attached to the sails.

The pod was like a mote of dust illuminated through the pinhole of a giant black box. With its sail and central body silhouetted by the sunlight, Cesix station hovered in a dark and fiery abyss like a strange, winged creature built of metal and fabric.

"How do we get inside?" Ailo asked.

"You have to go EVA," Boar said. "We spacewalk the last stretch."

*What?* Ailo stepped back as if retreating from the reality

of Boar's remark. Her boot caught on the edge of the passenger bench. She stumbled and bounced on the seat along the wall before falling to the floor.

Ailo stared at the ceiling of the pod. From her prone position, she read the red letters on the handle of the square emergency hatch.

*Caution: open space on the other side.*

Jati's head appeared in the view, followed by an extended hand.

She took it and they heaved her up.

"You good?"

She nodded. Her stubbed toe throbbed.

The PA general bent down to speak eye-to-eye. "Boar's joking. We're not going EVA. Rence has an extension tube. Connects directly to the ship."

A wave of relief rushed through her body.

"And it's pressurized. You can walk right down the tube and into the station. Rence is a techno-wiz."

"Do we wear our helmets?"

"Do you want to?" Jati asked.

Ailo shook her head.

"I think this time it'll be fine to go without. But make sure you bring it with you just in case. That's a rule."

Ailo smiled.

"It'll be nice to see Cantinools again," Jati said and went back to their seat. The general raised their arms and clasped their hands together behind their head, leaning back in the seat.

"What do you mean, Cantinools?" Ailo stepped forward and rested a hand on the edge of Jati's seat.

The station drew close. The Hamut switched on the pod's exterior lights. Out the window, the grey sphere looming large in front of them.

"Oh, didn't I tell you?" Jati said.

"Tell me what?"

They turned, their green eyes glowing. "Rence is something of a gardener."

"So now what?" Boar held the pod stationary a few hundred feet back from Cesix station. The dual sconces underneath the cockpit window shot beams of light onto the steel grey sphere.

The station rotated with the unwavering pace and precision common to space-based environments. Ailo found it hard to comprehend its presence. All alone in the emptiness of the Cesix system, the lone inhabitant cast an ominous and oddly *alive* aura. To be so close to something and yet be held safe inside an artificial atmosphere felt uncanny. Exploring space was much more visceral in a pod than a large ship like the *Carmora*. The distance and scale from the bridge of the P-Frigate made things detached. Like Jati's lectures, it made you think in terms of strategy. Here, so close and with the sense of the reality of what stood before you, the view triggered the tangibility of tactics.

A suspension of time, a quietness in the vastness of space hit you in the pod. It made you feel small and uncomfortable. The atmosphere held too little activity and too much stillness and silence for a species born of planetary origins amidst billions of other organisms.

Jati opened their mouth to respond to Boar but a message alert interrupted them. A small holographic of Cesix station popped up on the control panel in the center of the dashboard.

"That you, Jati?" a voice asked.

*Tusolo.*

Ailo knew the tone. She'd heard it during tense situations with other street kids on T9. Tusolo's voice carried the same defensive urgency as those from behind a portal door unsure it was a co-conspirator and not the patrollers she and her fellow street kids were running from.

"Indeed it is, Rence."

Jati's voice carried a light, almost playful tone.

"I'm reading three heat signatures," Rence said.

"I'm here with a few friends."

"One's smaller. You've got a kid with you?"

Jati put up their hand before Ailo could respond. She knew better than to say anything, understanding the delicacy of the exchange.

"No, more of a budding adult." They winked at Ailo. "It'll make sense when we speak. She's from Tarkassi 9. Now she's fighting the good fight."

"There are no good fights."

Jati winced at the retort and shut their eyes tight.

"Have to disagree with you there, Rence," Jati said, drawing their face into an awkward smile. The calm, lighthearted tone of their voice still led their remarks. "We've had this argument how many times now?"

There was no answer.

Boar held out his hands as if to ask, 'Now what?'

Jati waved him off. "Rence, this isn't a social call. We're straight with each other, you and me. It's the reason you've trusted me and also the reason why, I might add, you've been able to live out here in peace."

"While the rest of the world doesn't," Boar muttered.

"Is that who I think it is?"

Jati's eyes went wide with frustration. They glared at Boar for intruding on their conversation.

*Gerib, this isn't going well. And, I think Rence and Boar know each other.*

"Yes, I think you're right."

*Should I say something?*

"Be patient and let Jati do their job. Remember what they said on the bridge about that."

*But it worked at the Assembly Hall. When I spoke up, I mean.*

"Ai..."

"Darro-ti is with me, yes," Jati said.

Hearing Jati use Boar's proper first name sounded odd. What kind of relationship did Rence have with the Hamut?

It couldn't be a good one knowing the history of Rence's connection to the destruction of the Hamuts on Xerteej at the end of the Patent War.

"Rence, let's talk about this inside," Jati said. "I've got your water back on the *Carmora*. Plus, I'd like to see how the trees are coming." Jati held up their hand and crossed their fingers.

"Trees are fine."

"Well, Arira is not."

Ailo couldn't help but notice the patient way Jati conversed with Rence. But when an opportunity to turn the conversation to more serious arose, they pounced. Like in the training room as she had done with JeJeto and the clock. It reminded her of their discussion on the bridge — that words could be weapons. Rence wasn't the 'enemy,' but Jati's approach wasn't impulsive. It was calculated. Things were so much more complicated in the Arm than she'd realized on T9. And so much potential for how you could make your way through it.

*"Interesting observation, Ai."*

*Thanks, Gerib.*

*"Look at you, all grown up."*

*What?*

*"Nothing, reminiscing."*

"Arira?" Rence asked.

"Yes, Rence. She's on Ceron."

"Ceron?"

"This is why I'm here. I need to speak with you about something important." Jati edged up in their seat. "I need your help."

"My help?"

"Hekron has her, Rence. He abducted her during a stopover on Ffossk. On Aradus's orders, I suspect. I need your help to get her back. You're the only one with the skill to do what I need to be done. We're at a tipping point in the Tide War. If I don't get to her and stop a full-on assault, the resistance will fall."

"There is no more resistance, Jati. Just sides vying for power. And you're one of them."

"That's not true," Jati said.

Ailo picked up on the growing frustration in the general's voice.

"How many times have we talked about this?" Jati asked.

"Enough that you're not going to change my mind."

"Damn it, Rence!" Jati slammed their fist on the console.

Ailo jumped and Boar flinched in his seat. She'd never seen them angry.

"She's in a madman's hands," Jati exclaimed. "I'm scared for her, Rence."

Ailo's eyes went wide. Jati, scared? They'd never shown vulnerability in the form of fear.

*Arira really is in danger on Ceron.*

"I'm sorry about Arira," Tusolo said. "I am."

*But not sorry enough to help us.*

"It's terrible," Jati said. They glanced back at Ailo.

She shot her gaze down at the floor.

"Darro, why are you here?" Rence asked over the com. "If you expect an apology from me you can turn back now."

Ailo caught Jati shift their gaze to Boar. The diplomat gestured in a way that asked, 'do you want me to speak?'

They nodded.

So these two had discussed things beforehand, and more than one issue flowed through this conversation. She couldn't help but note how Rence also took an opportunity to turn the topic away from the opposing beliefs between him and Jati. She stood 'outside the box,' assessing things from a neutral position. It did make visible otherwise hidden layers of reality.

Ailo liked it. A portion of her intellect craved more of it. This small taste started what she knew would be an addiction.

"I'm here to apologize, Rence. Not to ask for one. It's

time to put the past behind us."

Ailo's eyes went wide in surprise. Boar apologizing?

Silence.

*Did Tusolo sign off?*

"Rence?" Jati checked the board to make sure the line remained still open.

"It's not to me that you should apologize."

Boar nodded. "I would if I knew where she was."

*Gerib, who is he talking about?*

"She's gone."

*Who does he mean?*

"No idea."

"They're all gone," Tusolo said. "All we can do is hope they're safe. All but Cin Quinti. She speaks from words on a page now."

Ailo gasped.

Jati glanced her way.

*Cin Quinti? Gerib... Cin Quinti. I know that name.*

"Yes, Ai. You do."

Neither Jati nor Boar responded to Rence but Ailo's mind rapid-fired neurons. The interest in critical thinking swept aside as she broke into a fury of memory, her thoughts like an idling engine flooded with gas.

*The books. The ones my parent wrote, by hand.*

"Yes, Rence. We know." Jati broke the silence.

*Gerib? Where are you?*

"It's time, Ai. I'm going to let you do this yourself. I won't hold you back. That's what you've been asking for... I'm here if you need me."

The past flooded into the present. Ailo watched her parent's hand perform the anachronistic action of writing with ink on a page. The words were strange, like symbols on broadcasts running Second Span historical dramas.

Where had these memories been hidden?

She sat on her parent's lap, an arm holding her close against a soft belly in the kitchen unit on T9. A vivid warmth and comfort spilled out from the past into the present and ran through her limbs.

*I don't understand.*

The view of the book on the table grew in clarity. That first page; five words set apart from the text at the top. The ones her parent taught her through endless repetition, her delicate tawny-skinned finger bouncing from one icon to the next as she pronounced them for her child. They sounded now inside her head, a parent's voice patient and dedicated to the lesson. As if back at the kitchen table, in a call and answer, Ailo recited aloud from memory:

"Dossnok fer te vot pontariam."

Boar and Jati both turned. Her gaze went from one to the other.

*Did I say that out loud?*

Boar's face expressed confusion. But Jati... their green eyes radiated wonder and satisfaction, like watching someone place the final nettlesome piece of a puzzle into the last remaining spot.

"I knew it," Jati said.

"What?" Ailo asked.

"You're her child. It all makes sense." They shook their head and smiled as if they should have known something sooner.

"What makes sense?" Ailo reared back. "Whose child?"

"Cin Quinti-té's."

Ailo shook her head. "That's not my parent. Her name was Tenuv-té."

"Yes." Jati nodded. "It doesn't matter."

"I don't understand," she said.

"Who is that with you, Jati?" Rence asked. "Who spoke the Fallen Words?"

Jati's eyes went from Ailo to the spinning holographic of Cesix station and back to Ailo.

"Her name is Ailo-té" they said.

"Ailo?" Rence asked. "Did you say, Ailo?"

His tone mixed surprise and interest.

"She's the reason we're going to win this war." The

fortress walls on Jati's face tilted as the smile creased the wrinkles around their eyes.

Ailo remembered the line. Jati had said it in the training room back when she first mentioned Keen Draden. Her hand went to the wedge in her thigh pocket. She pushed down on it as if it were a talisman.

Boar's orange eyes narrowed, shifting his pale white skin around their corners. Deep in thought, the Hamut remained silent.

Jati gestured for her to speak. "Introduce yourself, Firecracker." They opened their palm and motioned towards the holographic station on the control panel.

*Gerib, what does this have to do with my parent?*

*"I know as much as you do. I'm not protecting you from anything, not any longer. That's the truth, Ai."*

"My name is Ailo Harrond-té," she said.

An awkward silence passed. Cesix station rotated on the dashboard.

*Gerib?*

*"You're doing fine on your own, Ai. You don't need me."*

The holograph vanished. The pod's electronics blipped off and the cabin went dark. The silence of space outside broke into the pod as the whir of the idling engines ceased.

"What's happening?" Boar tried to work the controls.

The lights came back on and the circulation fans restarted their soft hum. Ailo sensed motion. Out the cockpit window, the station neared. Boar's hands weren't on the controls.

Jati wiped a hand over their face and exhaled.

"Easy," Boar said, speaking to the pod.

Ailo snapped out of her internal confusion. The station approached.

"Easy... we're too close." The Hamut reared back in his seat. "Jati, he's taking us too close."

"It's all good," Jati said, their green eyes turning to Ailo. The usual legibility of their expressions fell away. This one wasn't in her gestural inventory.

*Why is Jati looking at me like that?*

"They're shocked, I think. Working some things out."

*About my parent?*

"Probably."

*Who is she? I don't understand.*

"I get the feeling you'll find out soon, Ai."

The pod banked right. Boar let out a sigh of relief. They ran parallel to the station about fifty feet above the mid-line where the track system for the extension legs connected to the sails. Ahead, emerging on the curving edge appeared a black, accordion-like square. It sat on the surface like a geometric mole on an otherwise smooth-skinned circle. The pod slowed.

"We're synchronizing the rotation of the sphere," Boar said.

The raised retracted black accordion disappeared on their left. The pod halted.

Ailo leaned forward to peer through the window. The station no longer spun, but the sail and an extension leg crept by out the right side.

"Welcome to the wonderful world of relativity," Jati said.

"He barely pulled that off," Boar said. "I'm impressed. And look," he nodded ahead. We're going sun-side." The sail system passed to their right and the approaching light of Cesix cast a soft glow on the arcing horizon of the station.

A creaking noise like a rusty old machine coming to life broke through the silence. Ailo stumbled right and grabbed onto Jati's headrest as a slight bump jostled the pod. The cockpit shield lowered taking the light of the approaching star with it. The control board shut down.

"I'll put on some Cantinool tea," Rence said over the com.

# TWENTY-ONE

Something wasn't right. Space stations weren't supposed to smell like this. And they weren't meant to look like this, either.

Ailo walked the corridor from the pod's docking tube, confused. Her senses had to be playing tricks on her because everything existed in the opposite of what it should be. Space stations were cold, with stale air smelling of five gens of recycled use. Yet, this had a perfumed scent like the rainforest on Heroon. Rich and savory aromas lingered in the corridor... some even earthy. Warm, humid air filled her nostrils.

Stations didn't sound like this, either. Transition spaces like the ones off T9 were silent and socially awkward or overwhelming with broadcast streams bombarding you with visual fireworks and aggressive advertising. This one? A soft ambient soundtrack lingered at the edge of her hearing like the first hint of a far-off waterfall or rushing river deep in the woods.

She turned and caught sight of Boar walking slowly about twenty feet behind her, his head went down to the floor in confusion.

Ailo gazed down to the floor, or what should have been a floor. Her steps took her over an ocean. Deep, rich, blue water filled the lower station about a foot below the transparent flooring material. No bottom was in sight. And there were fish... *schools* of fish. Ailo had never been in the water and she had no idea how to swim. Every time her feet took a step, swarms of fish underneath her responded with a small pulse in unison, moving as one in the watery world below.

"Welcome to Cesix Prime," Jati said.

Ailo pulled her head back up. In front of her, two worlds kept separate, planets and space stations, synthesized in a mesmerizing dreamscape.

A central atrium with curving walls of shimmering reflective glass three hundred feet across and at least five stories high came alive with plant life. Various species of small ground level flora, medium-sized shrubs and bushes, and even small trees filled a variety of tiered levels connected by a series of wooden staircases and bridge-like walkways. Railed platforms lay at intervals like scaffolding through the lush garden system.

Ailo recognized the wood: Cantinool. Her nostrils did too. And not only that; flowers bloomed somewhere. Marmish lingered, its scent dancing through the richness of fertile soil.

A buzzing whizzed around her ear. She swatted her hand at the sound to shoo it away. A small insect flitted about, circling her twice and hovering in front of her face. Its segmented body appeared... metallic. The arthropod shot away like a dart. Ailo tracked it across the interior and noticed what couldn't be missed. In taking in the entirety of the edges of the space, she'd neglected to look dead ahead to its center. When she did, it turned her marvel into wonder. "Wow," she said, eyeing the obvious.

"I'll second that," Boar said, appearing at her side.

In the center of the atrium, a towering formation of rocks and greenery rose for several hundred feet. Water cascaded down various ledges and moss-covered surfaces until it tumbled off a large horizontal ledge and splashed down into the mini-ocean ten feet or so lower than the floor level. Ailo tracked over the transparent surface above the water world below. A central circle cut out around the organic spire allowed for the cascading falls to return to the aqua system underneath the atrium.

Closer examination of the platforms and tiers of the gardens revealed water running underneath each level. High up, near the dome, she found the source: a system of clear pipes fed into the transparent rectangular sections under the decks. She followed one to the top, back to another pipe, to another platform, and on and on until it dropped back into the ocean below.

"That light," Boar said, tilting his head up to the top of the curving dome.

Ailo realized she hadn't even noticed. "It's like Nushaba," she said, closing her eyes and letting the illumination warm her face.

"Same intensity, but it's calibrated for distance and ozone. And a few other minor, but important safety details."

Ailo knew the voice from the broadcasts.

*Tusolo.*

She opened her eyes. Rence Tusolo descended a Cantinool staircase from one of the nearby lower decks. He wasn't much different than when she'd seen him on the broadcast feed. A bit grey in the goatee and above the ears, and a few more lines on his cheeks, but otherwise he hadn't changed. He still radiated a unique mix of intellect and physicality. As if in evidence of her statement, his outfit confirmed it. His tan jumpsuit ran with smears of turquoise, with hand and finger marks where he'd wiped them clean while working in the atrium. The tips of his fingers were blue from the material as well.

"Rence, thank you for seeing us," Jati said.

Tusolo nodded and shifted his gaze to Boar. "Darro."

"Been a long time, Rence. You look well."

Rence nodded.

"I'm impressed. This is spectacular," Boar said.

"Someone has to try and save the world before the rest of you destroy it."

"Rence," Jati said, stepping forward. "This is Ailo-té." Jati gestured for her to approach.

Ailo walked closer.

"She's your Contex orator."

*That was Contex...the dead language of the Second*

*Span.*

Rence's eyes scrutinized her. He took a step closer.

"Ailo. From Tarkassi 9?"

"That's right," Jati said.

"Nice to see you again."

*Again?*

"How long did you live there, Ailo?" Rence asked.

"My whole life. Until I left... on my own."

"She's joined up with me," Jati said. "And I believe we're all going to have a lot to talk about." The general turned their head up to the deck from which Rence had descended. "You said something about tea?"

Rence smirked, still eyeing Ailo.

*What is he staring at?*

"Jati's quite the strategist aren't they, Ailo?"

She nodded.

"A philosopher too," Tusolo said. "I imagine you're learning quite a bit?"

"Yes." *What is he getting at?*

"Well, I can tell you this, Ailo." Rence ran a hand through his goatee. "You weren't born on Tarkassi 9."

"What?"

Rence nodded. "You were born *en route* to Tarkassi 9, while your parent was on the run."

"On the run?"

Jati put a hand on Rence's arm. "I think we should have some tea and talk this over."

"You knew my parent?" Ailo asked.

Jati nodded at Rence, encouraging him to head up to the deck.

"Come. Jati's right, let us have tea and talk." Rence shot his eyes to Boar. "And I sense this is going to take a while."

"I'd rather get something done now," Boar said. "Before tea." He stepped forward.

"Very well, Darro." Rence turned his hand, gesturing for him to begin.

"The world has moved on, Rence. We must move on too. I do not ask for forgiveness. Nor do I ask it back from you. Instead, I offer an apology for taking too long to have this conversation. And for holding on to the past."

Ailo watched Rence. His face remained stoic. Was it shock? Or did Boar's words mean nothing?

"I'm a diplomat now, Rence," Boar continued.

"Are you?"

"On Heroon. I'm working to repair the past and prepare for the future. Some of us take longer than others to realize their limits and embrace a new road."

Ailo turned to the Hamut. She'd never expected words like this from him. How could he be so obnoxious to her when he arrived and yet act so apologetic now? Was this a game he and Jati were playing? Was he pretending to change and forgive? What was this about the war? Xerteej and Boar's homeworld? Or was it something personal between them?

"Go up and have some tea," Rence said.

*He's dodging.*

"I need to do one or two things to the Cantinools and then I will join you. We can finish this conversation and have the other one." He turned to Jati. "I'll help how I can with any equipment and advice in your attempt to bring Arira back safely, but if you're asking me to leave Cesix, my answer is no."

He walked past Jati and Boar and headed towards the far side of the atrium.

"Can I come with you?" Ailo took a step in his direction.

Rence stopped but didn't turn.

"Have you seen Cantinools before?"

"On Heroon, yes."

"Well, these may disappoint you then." He turned. "But yes, you may come along."

Jati raised a finger. She followed before they could intervene.

"How does the waterfall work?" she asked, catching up. They walked around the central pillar of cascading water. It danced gracefully level to level. The sound had a refreshing and invigorating, playful quality.

"It contains algae that purify the water. And it converts $CO_2$ to oxygen. The plants and trees feed on the nutrients discharged from the fish in the water."

Ailo stopped to observe the tank running underneath the floor. Schools of fish darted through the spiraling water. "I meant where does it come from?"

Rence halted. "You mean, how does it pump up and down?"

She nodded.

"Gravity takes care of the latter. The former is done through a simple propulsion pump system. It runs off solar energy, as does all of the technology at the station."

"From the sails?"

"You ask a lot of questions."

"Sorry."

"On the contrary, thank you. They are the *right* questions. Each builds on the last one, extending understanding."

She smiled at the compliment. Rence wasn't as the broadcasts suggested, at least not from what she'd seen of his innovations here on the station.

"To answer your question: from the sails, yes. And I think I can guess what you are going to ask next."

"About heliostationary orbit?" Ailo beamed inside. She'd marked the word in her inventory after Jati'd used it on the bridge.

"Yes."

"I already know about that."

Rence nodded and eyed her.

"What?"

"You remind me of your parent."

"So you did know her?"

"Yes." He began walking. "What do you think of the sound of the falls?"

*Now he is strategizing. He doesn't want to answer more.*

"It's soothing."

Rence nodded. "It's also calibrated. I've spent years experimenting with sonic waves and plant response. The equation is the most productive."

"The plants can hear it?"

"The plants hear everything. But they only listen to what pleases them."

Ailo paused and faced the towering rocks and multi-level waterfall. She closed her eyes.

*One... two... three...*

Alike to the geysers on Ffossk. Not quite the same, but similar musical repetition.

"There's three of them," she said, eyes closed.

"Three?" Rence asked.

"Phrases repeating a cycle. Five, seven, nine." She smiled at the pleasing percussive melody.

"I'm impressed."

Ailo opened her eyes. Rence scrutinized her in earnest.

His eyes were different than Jati's. They shared a vibrant green hue but were speckled with flecks of black as if an onyx crystal had shattered inside the irises. The fragments left behind were like the exploded ruins of an internal tragedy.

He stared at her.

"What?"

"Nothing. I was thinking back on a memory. You are correct... about the pattern." His gaze tracked up the cascading tower to its peak. "The ears of your mind are listening."

*That phrase...*

The aphorism from the Ran Cycle on Heroon. Tera spoke it on the tarmac when they first arrived.

"Silence reminds me how to listen," she said, reciting the second portion.

Despite its persistent and unyielding stubbornness, Rence's face broke into a wide smile. He nodded acknowledgment but did not speak. Without a word he turned and walked on.

Ailo lingered, listening to the sonic orchestra. Her eyes

tracked around the atrium, taking in the lush and abundant plant life. She peered down at the water and schools of fish through the floor. A harmony existed to all of it — an odd one, at that. Rence had managed to take two opposing worlds and find a beautiful compromise between them.

Her thoughts went to her parent and the mysterious identity, 'Cin Quinti.' Was she also part of this closeness to the world around them? Including this unusual way of thinking? Somehow she'd been less shocked than she'd expected at learning of this strange connection, as if a seed has been planted long ago and sat dormant inside of her, waiting to germinate.

"Ailo."

She made her way further on past lush vegetation towards Rence's voice. The thick shrubs and bushes petered out, and a low section of planting opened with no scaffolding or decks above it to the top of the atrium. Running in rows, about knee height, were small saplings. She recognized them at once. Cantinools.

Rence knelt in a row, tending to one of the young trees.

"How old are they?" The signature violet bark of maturity sprinkled the narrow trunks. All were thickly leafed and some even had small flower cups in bloom.

"Twelve. But more like twenty-four if you are strict in interpretation. They are on an accelerated growth cycle with constant light and hyper nutrients."

"Constant light?"

Rence nodded and adjusted a turquoise sponge-like material around the base of the tree he tended. It contained no soil, just a small amount of the sponge to keep the trees upright. Roots dangled in the water underneath the floor.

Rence wiped his hands on his jumper, smearing more blue stain onto the tan fabric, and turned. "I have transmitters running from outside the station." He pointed to the curved wall. "The light of the star is brought in through an optic cable network. It's filtered and re-projected inside. The station rotates to help with the gravity engine and tidal simulation in the water system but the light is captured from circumnavigational parts on top. Technically, the sun doesn't rise or set so I keep the light on to accelerate the growing process. Although I am conflicted."

"About what?"

"About whether or not it is right to impose this on them."

"Them?"

"The flora. As Cin Quinti states in the Book of..." Rence paused.

Ailo read the awkward reference on his face. He'd quoted her parent instinctually without realizing the present coincidence.

"Do you have a copy?"

"I have the one remaining copy," Rence said, turning from tending the small tree.

"But I remember more than one. A stack of them. All written by hand."

Rence nodded. "Yes, most were written in Neo-Contex to be as widely read as possible. One copy she made in Contex, the Origin Tongue from the Second Span, in honor of Cin Tuinti." He paused in his work. "The loss of that copy, I lament most." Tusolo sighed. "Others were translated, with the help of allies aligned with our cause, into the indigenous languages of planets where we could spread the word."

"Spread the word?"

"You don't know much about our history."

"Only a little, from broadcasts."

"Bah," Rence waved his hand dismissively. "Lies."

"But it was a People's Army broadcast."

"Misinformed nonsense, even that." His attention turned to the platform with the mention of the PA.

Jati and Boar sat across the atrium, sipping tea.

"Our beliefs were shared by mouth. For both safety and protection of content and because we believed in the importance of the spoken word."

"Because it has a presence," Ailo guessed. "And a heart behind it."

Rence stared at her. Obsidian flecks in his eyes sparkled against the filtered light of Cesix.

"You impress me, Ailo. This is an odd meeting."

"Are the books valuable?"

Rence's eyes narrowed. "They are blasphemy to many, especially the Garassians. And blasphemy is a dangerous weapon when exposed as truth. The power of the words your parent crafted threatened their rule in the Arm. None were more frightened by her than the Council. Confiscating and destroying the books ended your parent's challenge to their arrogance and domination."

"I want to know about her. Please."

"You wish for me to tell you about Tenuv?"

She nodded.

"You must have been quite young when they took her."

*Gerib?*

*"I'm here. You want to know, don't you?"*

*Yes. But I'm scared.*

*"I know. Anyone would be."*

*What will happen?*

*"You won't know until you confront it. But if you do, you may not need me any longer, or you may need me more than you do now."*

*And you are O.K. with that?*

*"I am you, Ai. I am O.K. with whatever choice you make."*

*Show me.*

A wave of memory surged up from the deep. A person in the apartment. Unwelcome. Her parent's surprise. Tenuv resisting. The intruder's anger. Her defiance. Their anticipation of punishing her spoken in a grin of bloodlust. The tear of a sleeve as she struggled. A pattern of dots on the person's arm. Red laser tattoos in strict linear sequence. Three rows. Two long, the other with two dots at the bottom near the wrist.

All seen from inside a vent. She'd been shoved in there by her parent and told to be quiet and not come out. *No matter what.* Never did the person search for her, nor ask about her. Why?

Scared that she would make a sound but wanting to scream. Watching them take her and catching her parent's eyes flash toward the vent. One last look.

Ailo broke internally but filled with new strength. "I was very young. I don't know how old."

"You were three… four at most." He knelt and pushed a thumb into the aqua-colored sponge around the base of the trunk. "We had done our best to hide her. And to hide you."

"From what?"

"Don't you know?" Rence's eyes bounced once towards the others on the far side of the atrium.

She shook her head.

"This is something to be done in Jati's presence."

"Are you friends, you and Jati?"

"Yes," Rence said. "But don't tell them." He smiled. "They're good enough at strategy already."

Ailo smiled. "Why do you call my parent 'Cin Quinti'?"

"She is Cin Quinti. *Was* Cin Quinti… the voice of our age. Of our movement. The revival of the Arm."

"I don't understand."

"But you know the book, yes? You quoted it."

Ailo nodded. "She taught me the phrase."

Rence's eyes scanned the grove of young Cantinools. "For a time, I believed it might happen."

"What?"

"Change. Our group, your parent's group. We were the hope for a different road."

"The Radicals?"

"So you do know?"

"Only a little bit."

"Well, you know everything if you know the Fallen Words."

Ailo cocked her head.

Rence caught her reaction and stood. "*Dossnok fer te vot pontariam.* 'Of them, we are One'."

"Of them, we are One?"

"The words of Cin Tuinti, the Second Span prophet on whose teachings we based our own. Your parent led the revival."

"And were you right?"

"We were fools," Rence said and bent back down to continue tending the small trees.

Ailo gazed out over the bed. The saplings made it appear like she soared over the dense rainforests on Heroon at low altitude. She walked over and kneeled next to Rence and ran a finger over the smooth violet bark of a trunk. A wisp of Marmish wafted into her nose.

The Cantinool grove in the interior of Heroon flashed into her mind. The world of the cantina, and Nisi's rage, blown away by the forest's quiet. The memory of Jati leading her deep into the heart of Heroon returned in vivid clarity. That intimate touch to the smooth-skinned bark had pulled her back through time, tapping an ageless link between the living wood and human hands.

Here, in Cesix Station, it sparked a different connection. Now she was the towering and massive one. The saplings around her, their lanky and fragile stems so vulnerable, needed protection and care. Was this majestic species meant to come along on this future, hand in hand with humanity? Or had their time come to pass? Was Rence, and her parent, and all the rest who'd chosen an alternative view, fools?

The last gasp of a passing age meant one world would fall, replaced by another. Is that what was happening here? A species at the end of its aeonic lifespan. Withering and sacrificed on the altar of history. Its decomposing leaves metamorphosing into an archival document, passing the centuries as a thin gravestone made of paper. A eulogy inked by humans on mummified Cantinool skin. Her parent had been right to speak with her hand, ink scratched across pressed, dried vegetative flesh — words written across the body of another. *Of them, we are One.*

Maybe it was a fool's errand to think it possible to stop history or turn it around. Nothing more than a romantic hope, like those sappy endings on the free broadcasts that made her want to gag.

*No.*

Ailo followed the small army of saplings to the curving wall of the atrium. The Cantinools were too noble, too strong to be allowed to fall to change. A surge of responsibility rushed through her — not the weight of obligation, but dedication. She wanted this. And not just for her parent. She'd left the sheltered struggles of T9 and crossed the Arm on the *Carmora* to stand in a grove of ancient trees on a mysterious planet. To gaze over them in a surrogate home on an isolated space station.

Jati's cause made sense now. They weren't an idealist, far from it. They were a servant, a gracious facilitator who penetrated the veil of human progress. Maybe it was idealism. And even if it was, why did that matter? From what she gathered from Rence, her parent was one too. And so she would be as well.

She turned to Rence, kneeling at the level of the Cantinool leaves. "I don't think you were fools."

Rence fiddled with a sapling. "And why is that?"

"Fools never call themselves fools."


"Rence!" Jati leaned on a rail across the atrium, waving.

"What?" Rence stood and wiped his hands "I'm trying to…"

"The *Carmora*'s taking fire."

Ailo rose.

*Fire?*

"Fire?" Rence started back towards them in haste.

Ailo stood frozen.

*Under attack? It's not possible. No one knows we're…*

"Ailo, hurry!" Jati waved at her to hustle. Their voice bounced off the curved atrium's walls, competing with the rush of falling water.

Ailo ran after Rence, her eyes on Jati.

The general's attention went to their wrist com and then back towards her and Rence. "It's an ambush," they yelled. "Dropped out of FTL on the far side of Cesix. Move!"

"Who?" Ailo yelled and bolted to the stairs, taking them two at a time. She passed Rence who did his best to hurry.

Jati turned the wrist-com so Ailo could view the small holo.

The same insignia from the nav room spun in a three-dimensional projection, sent from Nisi on the *Carmora*.

"Rogues for hire," Jati said. "Doing someone's dirty work."

*Bastard.*

"Grab your helmet and go with Boar." Jati pointed to her equipment on the bench.

Ailo snatched it up. Boar ran down the hallway back towards the pod.

"Come on, Rence," Jati said and pulled him by the shirt sleeve.

"I'm not going anywhere." Rence resisted Jati's hold.

Ailo stopped and turned.

"They don't want me," he said pulling against their forceful grip. "No one even knows I'm out here."

"Two more dropped in," Nisi said over Jati's wrist com. "They're coming around the far side of Cesix. I can't maneuver over the... turn us to port!"

Jati's expression shifted as they listened to Nisi fight off the attack ships from the *Carmora*. A calm washed over the general. Their green eyes simmered.

"Well, they do now," Jati said to Rence.

"I can't get to them, Cap," Nisi said. "You've got three minutes to range for intercept. I'll be there in four, once I take care of the ones on our tail. It's the best I can do."

"Got it, show them what the *Carmora's* got."

"We make for the pod, double-time," Boar said.

"They're going to destroy it," Rence said, his attention consumed with his creation. Elegiac surrender filled his eyes.

"All this work..." Rence glared at Jati. "You brought this with you," he said and pointed a harsh finger, fury extinguishing the futility.

The PA general turned away, ignoring the accusation. They spoke in a commanding voice that hit Ailo with the force of a battle horn. "Get to the pod now!"

Boar's hand grabbed her shoulder and dragged her away.

"Rence, I have an idea," Jati said. "It may save the station. If we hurry."

Ailo turned and hustled down the hallway after Boar. His strides bounced over the transparent floor like a person running on water. A good ten feet ahead, he turned into the accordion tube leading to the pod.

"Boar, wait!" Jati called from behind them.

Ailo stopped and turned. Jati approached.

"Come back, this way."

"But the pod?" Boar stopped at the corner.

"Follow Rence, the other way." They waved him back. "Trust me." Jati ran by Ailo, lavender hair flowing and bouncing with each massive stride. "I'll be there in a minute. Go!"

"Come on, Ailo," Boar said and motioned her back towards the atrium.

"What's happening?" she asked. "We won't get out of here in time!"

"Come on," Boar said again. "Trust Jati."

She moved, for that reason and that reason alone. They wouldn't do this unless they had a plan and a good one.

Ailo reached the deck down to the atrium and spotted Rence crossing in front of the Cantinool saplings making for a door on the lower level. He turned and waved for them to follow him around the central tower. She ran behind Boar down the stairs and around the open gardens. As they passed the Cantinool grove she slowed. Something told her this might be the last time she'd see them.

"Down here," Rence said from a portal leading out of the atrium. He motioned to a set of stairs.

A massive shudder rattled the curving walls. Ailo lost her footing and fell. Her helmet flew out of her hands and rolled ahead towards the portal.

*What was that?*

"Station's hit," Jati said behind her. They barreled to her and helped her up. "We're about to launch," the general spoke the words into their wrist com. "I thought we might make it off before it took fire but..."

A rumble ran through the sphere.

"Maybe we can still make it before they hit it again. Call you from the pod," Jati said.

"Got it," Nisi said.

"But the pod's the other way?" Ailo said. Jati pushed her ahead to the stairs. A second impact sent them both slamming to the floor. It felt different from the others, like a lever pulling the station, rotating its position in space.

*The sail.*

"Here." Jati handed her the helmet she'd dropped. "Go." They motioned towards Boar running behind Rence through the portal.

Ailo took off after them. She bounced down the flight of steps and ran at a tilt as if an unknown force pulled her to the side of the hallway. Her equilibrium went askew as the station leaned to the side.

"It's up ahead," Jati said behind her. "Focus on the corner."

The station gurgled and belched. Sparks exploded from the ceiling and glittered the passage in blue fireworks. The lights flickered and went out. Emergency lamps, red and ominous, replaced them.

Time slowed. Her heart raced and her limbs were like jelly. She'd never experienced anything like this before.

*This is bad, Gerib!*

As if to confirm her concern, like a giant waking and yawning after centuries of slumber, a deep and guttural groan resounded through the sphere's architecture. The floor heaved to the side.

*What was that?*

"They're hitting the sail on their way in... targeting the extensions. Get out of there fast!" Nisi's voice screamed over Jati's wrist com.

Ailo turned. Jati had taken a knee, their hand gripping the fabric on their chest. "We're out in... thirty seconds," they grunted. "We'll make it. You focus on knocking them out as they drop in. Give us some cover when you see our pod."

"Are you alright?" Ailo yelled.

"Fine." Jati said and rose to their feet, their breathing labored. "Go, Ailo. Don't wait for me."

Ailo started off and passed an open room. She caught sight of something that made her look twice. Books. The image of the volumes stacked on the walls and those fallen onto the floor lingered as she ran around the corner. At the end of the hallway, Boar guided Rence through a hatch.

To another pod. Rence had an escape vehicle.

*The book, Gerib.*

She slowed.

*"No, Ai."*

*Rence said he has it. The last one.*

*"Don't."*

Ailo swung around and reversed direction. She bolted past Jati back towards the room. The station rolled and pitched, most likely from another shot hitting the sail.

"Ailo!" Jati's voice barreled down the corridor after her.

Her shoulder hit the wall as the station rolled right. Using her arm as leverage, she rounded the corner and leaned her way down the hall and into the room, managing to get through the portal. She fell onto the floor inside the small library. Her hands shoved and tossed the fallen books around in a desperate search.

"Ailo, let's go!" Jati grabbed her by the arm.

"No!" She yanked away, expecting Jati's strength to hold her tight. Instead, they'd let go and she rolled across the room and slid into a bookshelf. Stacks of volumes crashed down on her. She pushed them off and grabbed her helmet from the floor. Jati stood at Rence's desk. In one motion they flipped a thick tome on an ornate reading stand shut and into their hand.

The general grabbed her arm and shoved her into the hallway. Jati's strength shocked her almost equal to the attack on the station. Like a graceful avalanche, its power hit with accuracy and precision yet remained mighty beyond measure. Ailo turned to head for the pod.

The world crashed down on them.

The upper layers of the station came alive with the cacophony of collapse. Booms and shudders rang down through the levels.

The hallway swayed. The temperature dropped. A breeze picked up. The air thinned. It reminded her of T9, but worse.

An object slammed into her belly. The book. She grabbed it with her free hand from Jati's grip. They stood, helmet on (when had they put it on?) and snatched hers out of her hand before fitting it on her head. The general twisted it shut and pushed a set of square buttons on her chest. A series of readouts appeared on a small holo on one side of her visor's interior; all green.

Jati gave her a thumb's up.

The atmospheric restriction and cold both dissipated. She nodded.

"Fast now. Go." Their voice came through a commlink inside her suit. Jati threw her in the direction of Rence's pod. She jumped over a fallen beam, with too much ease. Stride by stride, her movements grew lighter.

*Gravity loss. The station's atmosphere is leaking into space.*

She turned the corner and slowed. The shock caught up with her. A push on her back sent her lurching forward to the chute hatch down to the pod. There was no handle. No way to open it. Before she could turn to Jati, the unthinkable became real. The seal broke on the tunnel and the pod moved away. Air rushed out. The vacuum pulled on her like a demon trying to suck her into the void. She gripped the book and set her boots on the edges of the square to keep from being dragged into space.

"They're leaving us!" she screamed. A strong hand turned her around.

Jati held a safety bar and clipped a carabiner on her suit. The rush of air diminished as the vacuum took over. She noticed massive cracks and damage in the hallway exposing the station's upper levels. In one fissure the view out into space broke through. The bright light of Cesix blazed.

"I guess Boar was right." Jati had that look in their eye she'd seen in the training room on the ship — playful with a dash of their wild side.

"What?"

"Gonna do a little spacewalk, Firecracker." Jati winked through their visor. "Boar and Rence had to close the hatch and break off or we'd have lost the pod in the station's collapse. They saved us." Jati hit a switch on the wall and the entire portal with the hatch connect detached and floated away. A hallway size opening and ledge led into the void of space. "Hold on, kiddo." They grabbed her and jumped off.

The station fell away. Nothing lay underneath them, no bottom to allow her to make sense of how far 'up' they were. It went on forever.

"Keep your attention ahead in front of you, not down." Jati's voice remained calm and instructive.

She followed their instructions and raised her head. Rence's pod hovered a short way off, stationary but rotating towards them. At a distance to her right, the *Carmora* engaged in combat with three smaller vessels. The fighters swirled around the much larger ship like insects around bright light. Laser fire shot out from the P-Frigate at the enemy targets. To the far left, one side of the sail stretched out, riddled with holes and bent like a broken limb. The scale of the structure even when damaged remained sublimely terrifying.

Her chest tightened.

"I can't breathe... Jati."

"Relax. Rence is coming to get us."

Tusolo sat at the controls through the cockpit window. Boar flanked him playing with a box with various sticks and buttons, wearing a set of white goggles.

A pod from the *Carmora* went whizzing past a few hundred yards farther back with two enemy fighters on its tail.

*Who is that?*

She gasped for air, her lungs struggling.

"Relax. Almost there," Jati said.

The lights on her visor flashed red alerts.

"Something's wrong," she said.

"You're fine, kiddo. I have you."

"You're aligned. Get in," Rence said. Through the cockpit window, Ailo watched him rise adjust something above Boar's seat. The Hamut frantically worked what appeared to be a set of controls on the box.

"Jati, I can't..."

Rence's expression changed.

"Jati, her suit. The boot's leaking."

Ailo looked down. A steady stream of gas poured out of her boot where she'd stubbed her toe and fell in the pod.

"Get her in now!" Jati said. "Rence, the emergency airline."

"I released it."

"Ailo, take a breath and hold it," Jati said.

She gasped but barely sucked anything in. Jati pushed her forward. The pod hatchway opened.

"Grab the edge, Ailo," Rence said on her com. "Take the air snake. Twist it onto your suit. On the front. Do that first. Then pull yourself in."

The lip was close. A white tube rose like a serpent from a basket out of the entrance and drifted about. She went for the edge of the opening with her free hand, her left holding onto the book.

"Grab it!" Jati said. "Get the snake."

"She's going to miss it," Rence said.

*"Let the book go, Ai. Please. You have to."*

*No, Gerib. I won't.*

*"If you don't, we'll die."*

*Then we die.*

In the distance, the *Carmora* blazed away in combat.

Ailo thought of Nisi in the captain's seat, and Tera working the nav board, maneuvering to fight off the attack ships. And Arira, who saved her life, now a prisoner in the Garassian palace. And Jati, who'd done so much work.

*I can't lose it, Gerib.*

"I understand, Ai."

"I'm sorry," she said.

"Ailo!" Jati's voice screamed through the comm.

"I'm sorry," she repeated, this time for her parent, and let the book go. Her two fingers reached for the pod and caught the far corner of the hatch. Her chest burned. She had nothing left. She'd never had anything anyway. This was the story of her life. It wouldn't be enough.

But she was raised on T9. And that meant she was tough.

And fierce.

She pulled.

Because she owed it to all of them. And being weightless, two fingers was enough.

She reached the opening and grabbed the dangling hose, fit it to her suit, and twisted it secure. Oxygen swelled inside like a balloon filling. She gasped for breath, gulping. Rich, rushing air brought her back from the brink.

The book spiraled gracefully away through the emptiness of space, end over end, open somewhere near the middle.

Ailo watched it go.

Jati's gloved hand touched her shoulder. "Now you write your own."

# TWENTY-TWO

Jati undid Ailo's helmet and tossed it on the floor of the airlock. "You good?"

She nodded, panting.

They held out a hand. "Give me some muscle," they said, indicating she should clasp it.

Ailo lifted her arm. It took all her energy to get it up from her side. She reached for Jati's elbow and gripped the white suit. Their forearms met in the universal soldier gesture.

Jati gave her a nod, their green eyes burning into her own. They pulled her in tight against their chest and held her head. "You're a brave one. Stubborn too."

She reached around with her other hand and dug her two fingers and thumb into the back of Jati's suit.

"That'll serve you well," they whispered into her ear. "You learned about 'the line' out there."

Ailo nodded, her breathing almost normal. She couldn't think of anything to say.

The airlock opened. "We're not out of this yet," Rence said, standing in the pod's corridor. "Jati, you better get up here." Rence nodded towards the cockpit.

Jati smacked Ailo on the shoulder, and followed Rence out of the airlock.

She sunk to the floor.

Voices of the three in conversation echoed from the cockpit. Boar talked at a feverish pitch. Rence argued back. Jati's voice interrupted them on occasion. None of it meant anything; just noise in her ears.

The pod leaned and shifted. They were moving.

Nisi's voice came over the com, urgent.

White sparkles danced around the airlock, like reflections of Nushaba's rays on the Lantoon Ocean. Ailo's head grew light. The room narrowed. Cold sweat made her skin stick to the interior of the suit. She wretched, vomiting onto the floor of the airlock.

And burst into tears.

If this was what it was like to be a soldier, she wanted none of it.

Ailo walked to the cockpit, as if in a dream. Jati sat at the controls. Rence stood behind them, hand on the seat. Boar was in the co-pilot chair, still wearing goggles and playing with a joystick on a small box on his lap. Blackness filled the view out the window, with faint hints of glitter as if someone had turned out the lights in space.

Her mind sensed a subtle sensation of motion. Where were they?

Rence turned and put his finger to his lips, indicating she shouldn't speak.

"Turning to starboard on the far side of the sail!" Boar's voice shocked her, frantic and mismatched with the atmosphere in the pod.

"You've got two on your tail!" Nisi said over the comm from the *Carmora.*

"I know, damn it!" Boar leaned left and right in the seat, his head twisting around and his hands working the controls on the box.

*What is he doing?*

"Watch out, watch out!" Nisi yelled.

"I see them!" Boar leaned hard to the left.

The explosion nearby in space shook their pod as Nisi screamed through the com line.

Jati threw a switch on the board. "Clear," they said.

Boar tossed off the visor and wiped the sweat from his

brow, panting. The Hamut turned to Rence, exhaustion on his face. He nodded and Rence returned the gesture.

"How was my timing?" Boar asked Jati.

The general gave him a thumbs-up. "Fighters are heading away from the station. Nisi's on their tail."

"She'll tear them to shreds," Boar said. "They can't get away fast enough now that their job is done."

A holo of the sector around Cesix appeared on the pod's dashboard. The *Carmora* fired on a set of fighters. A red circle flashed around a sphere of what was left of the station.

"Hate doing this to her. And the rest of the crew," Jati said.

"It's a brilliant idea," Rence said. "Although difficult." He put a hand on Jati's shoulder. The general nodded.

The fighters blipped away one by one, jumping into hyperspace. All except one that exploded, taking fire from the *Carmora*.

"What's going on?" Ailo couldn't hold back any longer.

They all turned.

"A diversion," Rence said. "The only way out. But it meant fooling everyone." The scientist's irises glistened, their obsidian shards sparkling.

An alarm went off on the control panel. "*Alert*," the ship's computer announced. "*Reaching minimum secure distance on heat shields. Destruction imminent.*"

"O.K. everyone, this is where the fun starts," Jati fired up the engine boosters.

"Starts?" Boar said.

"You don't like my plan?" Jati said, smirking.

"Is this what you'd call a Plan C?"

"You know it," Jati said and pushed the throttle.

Ailo stumbled into Rence as the pod surged backward. She regained her footing and watched as the darkness receded. A stream of intense light hit the port window. The more they reversed, the smaller it got. Ailo put it all together. They'd been in the collapsing sail, descending towards the sun inside the remaining ruins of the station.

The broken wings of the mortally wounded bird that was Cesix station fell towards the burning ball of light. The battered and ruined sphere entered the view inside the mangled wings. Debris floated and swirled around the structure. A large mass of water and plants spiraled within the half-destroyed station.

Rence stared in silence.

Ailo couldn't imagine what it must be like for him to witness this, to accept the reality before him.

"*Carmora*, this is Cesix Minor 1." Jati's words were official in tone. Ailo's respect for them welled up inside. It wasn't about Jati and their brilliant plan or about the response they were about to get when those on the *Carmora* realized they were alive. This was about loss. And not just one person's dream or hard work. A symbol falling away, the last manifestation of a belief system sacrificed in a blazing stellar funeral.

"Jati?" Nisi's voice said over the com.

"Roger that. It's us."

"Sake of the... Sake of..."

Cheers roared on the open line from the *Carmora's* bridge.

"Are you kidding me? If I weren't so happy to hear your voice, I'd knock your head off."

Jati nodded. "That's about right."

The memory of their arrival at the cantina on Heroon to meet Nisi flashed into Ailo's mind; same words.

"We're here still," Jati said. "But not all of us."

Boar turned to Ailo and made the same gesture as Rence, urging her to remain silent.

"Oh no, not the kid?" Nisi asked.

"No, Ailo is here. Although we almost lost her."

The muffled sound of Nisi relaying the news to the crew came over the com. "You split up. Between pods?"

"Yes, we had to make a choice," Jati said.

An uncomfortable silence from the *Carmora* passed as they waited for Jati to continue.

"Our pod... how many?" Nisi asked.

"Just Boar."

Jati decelerated Rence's pod. The docking bay doors on the *Carmora* pulled apart about a half-mile out the cockpit window. "Alright Boar, you ready?"

"I guess so," the Hamut said and rose from the co-pilot seat.

"It won't be as cramped as you think," Rence said. "The sleeping tube isn't isolated. I had it rebuilt so it's open plan, connected with the small living area."

"Got any media?" Boar asked and walked past Ailo to follow the scientist aft.

"Books," Rence said.

"Why did I know you were going to say that?"

Ailo turned to Jati. "He's hiding?"

"He has to, otherwise this won't work." Jati turned the angular steering column and maneuvered the pod into the docking bay. "This pod's got a nice feel. Sake of the Arm, too because we're going to need it now."

"What won't work?"

Jati steered them to an open lane to the right between a set of rectangular containers. Red and blue flashing floor lights illuminated the landing zone. They brought the pod to a halt and lowered it down onto the floor of the bay. Nisi ran towards them across the tarmac as the craft settled, Tera at her heels.

Jati pointed. "And that right there is why I had Boar go back before we flew inside the ship." They turned to Ailo. She watched their green eyes grow intense and earnest. "I don't have time to go over it now, but you'll get the gist when we have a team meeting. Right now, I need you to take on your second mission as a secret agent."

"What about the first one?"

Nisi and Tera approached through the cockpit window. Nisi's hands were splayed wide in a 'What the heck?' gesture. Tera's face expressed solemnity. The general sighed. "The mission's done now, and it didn't go the way I'd hoped." They turned to Ailo. "You did a real good job on that one, Firecracker. Keep a tight hold on this new one too and we may make this work, O.K.?"

Of course, she would do what Jati asked. But it didn't mean she wasn't conflicted and confused — conflicted about how this 'plan' separated the team into those with privileged information and those without. And confused as to why Boar lay hidden in Rence's pod, his death faked in the escape from Cesix station.

She noticed the PA general's gaze on her. "Soon." Jati winked and flipped the switch to open the pod. Rence came back up from aft as the ramp unfolded with a whoosh and came to rest on the tarmac. He nodded to Jati that they were good.

Nisi started up the stairs. Jati raised their hand. "Whoa, Nisi."

"What happened?" The soldier stopped and rested one muscular leg on the bottom step; her tan, veined arm gripping the rail. "He's gone?" Thigh muscles danced like seismic tremors across a planet's surface on her bent leg.

Something about Nisi's voice told Ailo she was more upset than she let on.

"Yes." Jati rose and lumbered down the stairs. "The arrogance of our operation has gotten a good slap in the face." Ailo peered down the steps. Behind the soldier, Tera put a hand over her mouth.

Nisi shook her head. "Let me guess, he went and did something noble?"

"Indeed," Jati said.

Nisi's remark wouldn't settle. Ailo didn't know what meaning to assign it. She sensed it had two sides in the soldier's conscience: resentment and bitterness. The bitterness Ailo understood. She'd observed that as a daily experience between the two since they'd boarded the ship. But why resentment? Was it because she would now be forced to admire Boar's 'humility' and 'sacrifice' on behalf of others? Or, because now she wouldn't be able to be happy to see him dead and gone?

"Tera," Jati said, peering to the side of (rather than *over*) Nisi's head. The navigator shook off her emotions and focused on her captain. "This is Rence's pod." Jati thumbed back behind them. "He's asked that it be left alone by the crew. No one in and out. He won't abide any disturbance or intrusion into his space. We need to honor this, Tera. It's part of the deal I've made with him."

She nodded.

"Deal?" Nisi said.

"That's right." Rence said, and brushed past Ailo and descended the pod's steps. He stopped next to Jati.

"Rence Tusolo-ti," Jati said. "Welcome aboard the *Carmora*."

"Thank you."

"What happened, Captain?" Tera asked. She stepped up next to Nisi, her gaze on Tusolo. "Welcome aboard," she said to Rence. "My name is Tera Sirshet-ta-té, ship's navigator. I've followed your work... I mean after you left. Your later work."

*Is she nervous?*

"Despite this difficult moment," Tera stopped to let the weight of Boar's death pass, "it's an honor to meet you."

"Well, Tera," Rence said, "that's not a phrase I hear often. Thank you."

"From what I hear you don't hear human voices often at all... unless they're in your head." Nisi eyed him, but out of etiquette hand signed 'té.'

"Nisi, assemble the team in the nav room in thirty minutes."

Jati's stern expression reminded Ailo of when they broke up the fight between Nisi and Boar on departure from Heroon.

"I want to make an announcement about Kin-tuk. And I need to debrief you all on what's happened and where we go from here."

Ailo knew the tone. The general spoke and this was a direct order.

"Yes, Captain." Nisi walked away, but not before giving Tera a visible eye roll.

"In the meantime, you and I can go over a few things," Jati said to Rence. "We can head to my office."

The scientist nodded.

"Ailo, why don't you come with me," Tera said. "I imagine you'd like to get out of that suit and into some clean clothes. We can make a quick pass by your quarters before heading to the nav room."

The idea of hot water over bare skin pulled at her like a drug.

"Alright, thanks." Ailo hobbled down the steps and squeezed between Rence and Jati.

"We'll talk more later too, Ailo," Rence said as she passed.

Ailo didn't turn. She reached Tera and they started back across the hangar.

"Are you O.K.?" Tera put a hand on her shoulder as they walked.

She nodded.

"You'll be surprised what getting out of those clothes and washing off can do."

*Had Tera been through similar experiences?*

"I was a bit older than you my first time," Tera said, with a depth to her eyes that Ailo hadn't noticed before. It spoke of more than education and historical research. Trauma lurked behind her more recent professional exterior. "But shedding what you can, whether it's the clothes you wore or washing off the marks on your skin, helps. Trust me." The navigator ran her hand over Ailo's crimson hair. "Death is never easy. But the loss is harder when you're with them. And know them."

Ailo felt a fraud. Recovering from the shock and trauma of the surprise attack and catastrophic destruction of the station, not to mention the knowledge of learning her parent represented some kind of prophet in disguise hurt. Forget about choking to death in space. Watching the one token, the one lifeline back to her, spiral away was almost too much to bear. That was all legitimate. But deceiving Tera into revealing her vulnerability out of empathy and for sympathy? She didn't approve.

"I'm fine," Ailo said. "Boar was no one to me."

# TWENTY-THREE

A shower and a set of clean clothes helped. It washed away the visible and superficial associations of the traumatic events, like taking off make-up at the end of a day to let go of the professional self. But the lasting memory and impact of what transpired at Cesix station still hadn't settled inside. It fell like a feather swinging back and forth, slow and unsure of where to land and what to call itself.

"We should get going, Ailo," Tera said from outside the changing station. "Otherwise, we might be late. Don't want to have a repeat of last time."

Ailo observed her reflection in the mirror as she towel-dried her hair. The shaved side of her head had a good two inches of growth. She pushed it back behind her ear. The crimson bangs on the other side fell to her chin. She needed a trim, or to cut it all the way back to match the other side. The constant need to brush hair out of her face annoyed her. And it hid the scar on her forehead, the one from the K-speeder crash. If she'd be fighting alongside the others she liked the idea of a visible battle scar.

She felt like a different person now from when she and Gerib decided to flee T9. A new look might be in order. Maybe she'd even change her color. Bright yellow?

Maybe this is what it's like for Tera, shifting and changing her self-expression.

She scoffed at her reflection.

"Are you actually feeling good now?"

"Ailo," Tera said, from the other room.

"Yeah, I'm coming."

She finished up and dressed.

"O.K. let's go," Tera said and turned to leave.

"Tera?" Ailo stopped while they were still in her quarters.

She turned. "Yes?"

"Is Jati okay?"

"What do you mean?"

"Are they sick?"

The navigator walked back to her and gestured for them to sit together on the bunk.

"Why are you asking me that?"

"I've seen them chewing on something, and usually when it's stressful," Ailo said. "And... on Cesix station, there was a moment..." She looked up at Tera.

The navigator's head went up and down. "I understand what you mean. Jati's been through a lot. They're not invincible, you know. They have a body like everyone else. Things catch up with you later in life. The Patent War was hard on them. Very hard." Tera's eyes softened. "Jati's carries the weight of many people. It makes others' lives easier, but theirs harder." Tera smiled. "It's just a medication that helps ease that stress on their body. Lightens the load."

"So they'll be okay, then?" Ailo asked.

"Should be, yes. But remember, at some point we all move on. Not that I think you have to worry about that with Jati. Not yet. They've got too many things left to do. Like mold some youngsters into tough soldiers." She gave Ailo a soft punch on the shoulder. "Or, maybe even warriors." She raised an eyebrow. "And ship captains."

Ailo looked at the floor and nodded. Her eyes were going watery. "Do we have time for me to ask you one more thing?" She chanced a glance at Tera.

The navigator's wrist came up and she checked her readout. "I think so, yes."

She wanted to ask her something personal but couldn't decide about its appropriateness.

"What is it, Ailo?"

"Why did you self-express as 'ta-ti' in Gontook?"

Tera's head cocked to one side. "Because that's how I'd been feeling all morning. Even the day before we arrived I sensed myself shifting."

"How do you decide?"

"It's not a 'decision' so much as a feeling." She ran a hand through her green and blue hair, holding a swath of the cerulean portion and looking at it." Tera titled her head to one side. "Or, you might say that it's 'cyclical'?" The navigator raised an eyebrow. "It's always gradual for me. I can't speak for anyone else, of course. But when I sense it, I wait until it feels more like 'me' than what I've been feeling and I adjust and adapt whatever parts of me on the inside and outside that I want to feel in 'synch' with myself. That could be the way I talk, or walk, or look... many things. Some of them are internal and not easy to put into words. It's all a matter of being the way I 'feel'. Does that make sense to you?"

"I think so, yes."

"And luckily for us, we can present ourselves when and where we want in the Arm. It wasn't always like that, you know."

"But it has been for a long time, right?" Ailo pulled a cherry-red strand of hair off her thigh and released it to fall to the floor.

Tera nodded. "Since the Second Span."

Ailo thought back to when she'd first self-expressed as 'té' on T9. She'd known that was where she was comfortable. But she'd never given thought to the fact that she might not always feel that way. It just seemed to fit, like the jumpers she'd worn until they frayed and fell apart. She'd never felt conflicted or confined by presenting that way.

"And so, whenever we aren't on the *Carmora* you're 'ti'?"

"Not necessarily."

Ailo cocked her head. "So just Heroon?"

Tera laughed. "You are full of questions, aren't you?" She grabbed one side of her long hair and started running her fingers through the green strands.

"I'm just curious... and confused." Ailo turned away.

Fingers turned her chin back. Tera's gold eyes looked into her own. The navigator smiled. "It's good you are curious, and that you want to solve your confusion. And it's fine to ask me. We've gotten close, and I am also here to teach you what I can."

"So then just on Heroon?"

Tera laughed.

"What's so funny?"

"My answer is going to make it more complicated, rather than clearer. You're thinking about places and my relationship with them as something fixed. But it's more about my relationship with myself, and also where I am and how I want to self-express. But it isn't fixed. It may be the case that next time I step foot in Gontook I'm 'té' because that's how *I've* been feeling."

Ailo fiddled with her hair by her ear. "I think I understand."

Tera smiled and raised a hand to Ailo's cheek. The navigator grazed the back of her fingers down her skin. "You've got a whole life in front of you. Just don't box yourself in. If you feel secure now, that's what matters. But be open to change. It doesn't change you to change."

"That sounds like a 'Jati-ism'."

"Ha!" Tera swung her hair off her shoulder and rose. "Indeed it does. Now, we should get going." She nodded to the portal.

"Can I ask you one more thing?"

"Ailo, you can ask me anything." The navigator started fiddling with the blue side of her hair.

"Will you teach me to sign?"

Tera cocked her head. "You already know how to do it. I saw you at the café."

"No, I mean to sign Neo-Contex. I want to communicate with everyone as best I can."

Tera smiled. "Come here." The navigator held out her arms in front of Ailo.

Why did she want her to come to her?

"I don't understand," Ailo said.

"Just come here, will you?" Tera motioned for her to get up and take her hands.

Ailo rose from the bunk and reached out her hands. Tera clutched them. The navigator's grips were warm, the skin soft. She squeezed Ailo's fingers. "I would gladly do this for you, Ailo." Tera's gold eyes were watering.

"What's the matter?"

*Gerib, did I say something wrong?*

"No, Ai. I think you said something just right."

Tera released her hands. "I'm proud of you." The navigator wiped a tear from her cheek.

"I'm sorry, Tera."

"For what?"

"Making you cry."

"Hah! It's a good thing, Ailo." She flittered her eyelids and ran a finger under an eye to wipe the remaining moisture. "How many languages are we learning now?"

Ailo laughed, but she couldn't get all of herself into the humor of the moment.

"Tera?"

"Yes?"

Ailo held out her hand. "What about my fingers? Can I still do it?"

"Of course," Tera whispered and stroked a hand over her head.

# TWENTY-FOUR

The two walked to the nav room in silence. Tera stopped outside the portal. The navigator turned to Ailo and opened her mouth but froze.

"What?"

Tera closed her mouth and smiled. "Nothing." She turned and opened the portal.

What would the mood be like among the crew? Boar wasn't a crowd favorite, or so Ailo thought.

She made for a vacant chair next to Nisi.

"Ailo." Jati wore their blue official PA jumper and stood, muscles bulging, at the front of the room. "Up here." They gestured at a seat next to the one Tera headed for.

Did Jati want her to speak?

Ailo scanned the room and found only Nisi and JeJeto. Without Boar, and with General Hirok with his armada heading to Ceron, the team thinned. The confidence amongst the experts assembled a few days ago had turned to sullen apathy. Nisi sat, head bowed between her legs, elbows resting on her knees. JeJeto's violet eyes stared out the panorama window. Tera sat and fiddled with something on her wrist comm. Were they still going through with this?

"Rence," Jati gazed past Ailo, "thank you for joining us." The general invited the hermetic scientist, whose sheltered existence had been shattered, to come forward and sit at the front. Tusolo walked up and took the chair next to Ailo. He still wore the tan jumper smeared with turquoise stains. Caked lines of the fertilizer had settled in the creases of his neck, running like rivers over his weathered skin.

Jati walked over to where they sat. "Tera, when we finish please show Rence to the showers so he can clean up. And we'll get you something to eat as well," they said, turning to him. Tusolo nodded. "I can put you in quarters aft, to port, if you like. Next to the docking bay. Unless you'd rather sleep in the pod?"

*With Boar?*

"Port aft would be fine. Thank you. I've got some work I'd like to do on the pod while we're in FTL."

Jati nodded. "Tera will see that you're not disturbed." The general took a step back and switched on the holo for the starfield. The entire Arm blipped into virtual three-dimensional existence.

From this close distance more details were legible. Star systems, asteroid belts, and large portions of space were so well rendered they appeared almost physical. Ailo imagined a version of the *Carmora*, like a tiny dot of light, tracking through the cosmic field. It brought back a memory of approaching Cesix station from behind the sail wall in the pod, minute and insignificant. She pushed it aside, not ready to revisit what had followed their arrival at the station.

"JeJeto," Jati said.

"Cap?" The mechanic ran a hand over their spiky yellow hair.

"You and Rence have met."

"We have." JeJeto nodded at Rence, and out of courtesy for the years since they last interacted, signed 'tō' to the Garassian.

"That's everyone." Jati clasped their hands together. "Look at how our group has changed." The general's green eyes went from person to person. "We're down a person. An important one. Complicated, talented, and born into life as random as any other. He did his best to navigate the road he was put on."

A long sigh cut the silence behind her. Nisi, head down at the floor, made a small back and forth motion indicating disappointment.

"Boar volunteered to run a diversion with our pod so the rest of us could get out clean. He didn't expect *not* to make it. The Hamut was one of the best flyers in the Arm. But he was also a former soldier and knew the score. And as it happened, his ruse worked. But because of it, he got outgunned and trapped by debris." Jati focused on Nisi, who had raised her head. "Let that be a lesson for all of us. We're good, but it doesn't mean that the world, or a roll of the dice, can't beat us now and then."

JeJeto nodded and pumped his fist.

"We'll send an empty body capsule out in the direction of the Beyond tomorrow. I'll do the eulogy. Full dress uniforms for those in the service." Everyone but Rence nodded.

Tera leaned over. "You'll wear your blue interns. You're PA too."

Ailo nodded, remembering the word from the earlier conversation.

*Does she know, Gerib? About Boar?*

*"I don't know."*

"We're at war. Kin-tuk wasn't, but he was on our side." Jati turned their attention to Rence. "And he was on this team, so as far as I'm concerned that's as good as PA." They folded their massive arms across their chest. "Anyone have a problem with that?" Jati's eyes were on Nisi.

Ailo stole a peek at the soldier. Were her eyes watering? Nisi bit her lip and fought back emotion.

"And," Jati's tone shifted. It carried more of the usual sanguine air Ailo had come to know and enjoy. "Tonight I'm drinking kartan. A lot of it. If you want to join me, I'll be in the mess at 21:00 Standard Arm."

Heads nodded around the room. But not Rence.

"I'm going to make Patreli. It was his favorite dish," Tera said, her voice fragile.

"That's a great idea," Jati said. "He would be honored."

"Good call," JeJeto added humbly and nodded.

"Now, let's turn our attention to the future," Jati said. They swiped a hand. An unfamiliar solar system appeared on the holo. Ailo recognized one detail. Ffossk, identified in blue letters, rotated off a star labelled 'Jarken.' It moved in a wide orbit, the fifth of seven planets. "You all need to know what's happened and get up to speed." They shifted from team member to member. "At least the three of you." Jati's eyes went from Tera, across the room to Nisi and JeJeto. "And some details are withstanding for all of us about the plan from here."

They walked over to the zoomed-in section of the holo displaying Ffossk. "Our mole is out of the hole. And exposed."

"What?" Nisi perked up.

"That's right," Jati said. "We know who it is now. And some of us knew before we left for Cesix station. But we never expected them to follow us there and try that stunt."

"Who is it, Cap? It wasn't Boar was it?" Nisi's eyes were alive with anger.

Jati shook their head. "It was someone much more entrenched in the history of this struggle, someone whose tipping point came when I chose to detour from the ambush on Guinde-4."

"Hirok." JeJeto pronounced the general's name long and slow.

Jati nodded.

"What?" Tera said.

"Yes. I get it." Nisi's head bobbed up and down. "No one else knew we were going to Cesix."

"But Cap says they knew earlier," JeJeto remarked.

"We did," Jati said.

"Who's 'we'?" Nisi's eyes went to Tera.

"Not me," the navigator said, shaking her head.

"Secret agent?" Jati said to Ailo. "Care to enlighten the rest of the team?"

"You knew?" Nisi said, turning to Ailo.

Ailo nodded.

"Come on up here, Firecracker." Jati motioned for her to join them at the front of the room.

Ailo stood and walked over. She turned to the team.

JeJeto's brows scrunched in confusion. Nisi appeared... well, Ailo wasn't sure how Nisi appeared. Angry? Stunned? Surprised? Maybe all three together.

Rence acted neutral. That made sense. He was new to the game.

And Tera? How to describe it?

"Parently."

*So you are still there?*

"Yes, enjoying some downtime, Ai. Now that you're 'grown-up' and all..."

*Ailo smiled internally.*

"Don't let me interrupt you. Wouldn't want you to blurt out something now."

Ailo laughed aloud. From the looks around the room they all mistook her outburst as an expression of as pride.

"Come on, then. Spill it 'Secret Agent'," Nisi said.

*"Looks like you're one of the team now, Ai."*

"Floor is yours. Take us through it," Jati said.

"Do you have a copy of the message that General Hirok showed us?" Ailo asked.

Jati nodded to Tera. The navigator went over to the board below the window and pulled up a holo of the parchment with the threatening message to Jati.

"We were on Heroon," Ailo said. "After I'd gone to the Assembly Hall. The two generals were making plans. We drank some Cantinool tea on the street, and General Hirok went to the restroom. Jati asked me to do something... to describe the insignia from the message Hekron left on Ffossk when they took Arira."

Nisi, JeJeto and Tera stared intently.

"So I did."

"And did a darn good job of it too, I might add. Under pressure. With quick thinking," Jati said.

"What am I missing here?" Nisi asked, arms wide.

"Jati went to the restroom next." Ailo pointed at them. "And I told General Hirok about the insignia. When he came here, to this room for the meeting and showed us the letter from Garassit, it had the same insignia. And so did the one that Nisi sent us when we were under attack at Cesix station."

"O.K..." Nisi said, "it's Hekron's new insignia. So?"

"Wait for it." Jati smiled and did a little dance.

Was she supposed to say it now?

"Go ahead," the general said. "You're the star of the show."

"It's not Hekron's insignia."

"What?" Tera said. Her eyes went to Nisi and JeJeto. Both their mouths were open wide.

"It's not the same as the one from Ffossk," Ailo said. "I added an element. A dot at the bottom."

"I'll be a Gor hunter!" Nisi said. "You crafty lot, you..."

Jati winked.

"So when General Hirok showed up here," Ailo said, "and displayed that message..."

"You knew it wasn't from Garassit," Nisi said. "Hirok wrote it to cover the ambush on Cesix... to make it look like they were hired by the Garassians."

Ailo nodded.

"It doesn't rule out their collaboration," Jati said. "In fact, I am certain this is a team effort between them. But that message, whether sanctioned by Aradus and Hekron or not, originated from Hirok."

"And you two knew at the time?" Nisi asked.

"Yes," Jati said, their tone solemn.

"And you managed to play it off through the rest of the meeting?"

Jati indicated that Ailo should respond. "Yes, we both did."

"Cool as Cantinool on ice," JeJeto said and whistled.

"Why didn't we laser burn his ass then and there?" Nisi asked.

"Because we need him to get Arira. Which means we need him to think we don't know... even though we do."

Nisi leaned back in her chair and gazed at the ceiling.

She sighed for all to hear.

"Also, I need proof, hard proof to convince General Galank and the others to call off the attack. An insignia that he did or didn't make — that would be Galank's counter — isn't enough. I want him red-handed."

"So now what?" Tera asked.

"First, we thank Ailo," Jati said.

Everyone nodded around the room. Even Rence gave her a subtle tilt of the head, his lips curving into a small smile.

"Thanks, Firecracker." Jati indicated she could sit.

She went and sat back down next to Tera. The navigator put her hand on Ailo's shoulder. "Nice job."

"Thanks." She tried to hide the smile on her face.

"How could he do this?" Nisi asked. "He's been on our side for decades."

Jati nodded, "We went through the Legion academy together, before the Patent War."

"So why?" Tera asked.

"That question has a long answer. I can tell you all more about it over kartan afterward. *If* we make it out of this in one piece. But for now, remember that we were still on the Garassian's side when we joined up. We fought for them until the Patent War treaty shifted the allegiance and moral position of the Council away from the Legion. I pulled Hirok back into the fight against the monopolies a decade or so later, as part of the rogue underground network. But his heart wasn't ever really in it... it was more in his wallet."

"Credits," Nisi shook her head. "It's always about credits."

"Money is power," Jati said and shrugged. "And in Hirok's case, he'd fought the good fight for a long time. When we were young he did it because he believed in it. Call it youthful idealism."

"Yours hasn't faded," Nisi said.

Jati bowed. "I'll take that as a compliment, thank you. But by the time I had him back in the game after the Patent

War, running weapons with me, skimming off the top through the Hamut Alliance, Hirok had more interest in the profits at the end of the road than the justice driving the ship."

"But he stormed the Temple of the Rising Wind on Heroon? He helped you take down Reynaria," Tera said.

Ailo turned at the mention of Reynaria. So Hirok was a part of that story? The one including Keen Draden.

Jati nodded. "He did. Essential to it. And he reluctantly followed me into a leadership position at the general's table afterward. There was power there. And power is...?" Jati raised an eyebrow at Nisi.

Her head down staring at the floor, she lifted a veined arm and rubbed her index finger and thumb together for all to see.

"And Hirok was never quite convinced that the Council did wrong with the treaty and the Alliance. He fought for us, but not so much against Garassia as for those who needed help. And for the money." Jati shook their head. "He wants to retire. And he wants to do so with power, to convince himself it's all been worth it."

"It doesn't seem like enough to kill one of his own? His Legion brethren?"

"You're right," Jati said, nodding. "I think Guinde-4 was the tipping point. That was going to end the war, potentially. The thing about that ambush was, it meant getting to take down the central leadership of the Garassian army and fleet, including Hekron, and it would have been a credit mountain. There was enough glory and money there to set Hirok up for life. And my decision to call it off, and pull back my portion of the fleet, took it all away."

*This is about me.* Ailo didn't know what to say. She felt guilty. And responsible.

"This is *not* about you." Jati's response came as if she'd spoken the words aloud. "What I mean is, this was about ethics." They walked over close and knelt. "I know what you're thinking. And many of you may be thinking this too." Jati's gaze went around the room. "One life worth saving, at the expense of all those that might not make it without the end of the war?"

No one spoke. Ailo knew she wasn't the only one thinking it.

"Remember I told you I was new to this 'general' thing?" She nodded.

"Well, I've made lots of decisions on the fly. Some I've regretted, some I've realized were mistakes. But not this one. It was the right thing to do. And I stand by it." Their green eyes, closer than they'd ever been before, displayed new details. Obsidian shards, deeper and further entrenched than Rence's, lay like shrapnel floating in suspension from a past tragedy. "I'll die by it. And don't you forget it." They rose and puffed up their chest. "I'm Legion. To the end. That means I aim true, always."

"Right on, Cap," Nisi said and pumped her fist. JeJeto nodded in agreement.

Jati gave them both a hand-blaster gesture.

"So what's Garassit offering him?" JeJeto asked. "What's worth throwing it all away, and trying to kill your close ally and oldest friend?"

"I don't know JJ," Jati said. "But we're going to find out."

"How's that?"

"Welcome to the 'plan inside the plan' people," Jati said and walked over to the holo-field. They swiped a hand and opened the area around Ceron. The planet, its moon Yelo, and the meteors of the Kusk shower were all in view. Farther out sat Hirok's fleet.

"Right now, Hirok thinks I'm dead. Blown up with whoever else was in the pod."

"You think he planned on hitting you at Cesix?" Nisi asked.

Jati shook their head. "That was an opportunity strike. He didn't know about it until our meeting in this room. My guess is it was worth the chance. Hire some rogue pirates to take us out in the middle of nowhere, where no one will know and nothing destroyed will be missed." Jati turned to Tusolo. "Sorry Rence."

The scientist waved a hand, dismissing the remark. "Makes sense to me, Jati. If anything, Hirok could brag about it once this was over and he was on Ceron. 'Removing' a remaining 'threat' to the Council in the form of an 'old, insane renegade who's lost his mind.'" Rence turned back towards the others. "Who talks to people in his head."

Nisi lowered her head in embarrassment.

"With me out of the picture," Jati said, "he was guaranteed to know the PA siege wouldn't last. My guess is he had it set up so that he could make a weakening move in their attack veiled as a 'bad' strategic decision, exposing the PA forces and making them vulnerable while Garassit got going and came in to finish the job. I'm sure he has a deal waiting with the Council."

"And now?" Tera asked.

"We force his hand," Jati said. "I'm going to put a call into him before we jump. That should give him quite a surprise."

Nisi and JeJeto nodded in unison.

"I'll relay to him that Boar took off on us at Cesix when we were ambushed. He left us for dead in the collapsing station but we got out in a backup pod that Rence had. I'll play up that I'm convinced Boar was connected to the mole and that I suspect it to be someone in the PA administration back on Heroon selling information to a Hamut diplomat. That's a solid link to the Council."

"But how can you account for the pod? And them taking out Boar?" Tera asked.

"I'll tell Hirok that Boar's mistake was thinking he'd be safe from the conspiracy when in fact, whoever was betraying us was more than willing to get rid of their source at this point to clean the trail back to them. Nisi 'heard' Boar radio to the attacking ships, identifying himself over the pod's frequency, but they ignored it and took him out. This should lower Hirok's guard in terms of suspicion. But it means he'll have no choice but to play dumb and follow through with our original plan and go with us on the Dodger to Yelo. My guess is, he had that set up as Plan B anyway."

"So we're still going in?" Nisi asked. "But what about the A-Dodger? And the pod through Kusk?"

Jati raised an eyebrow in earnest.

Nisi poked one of her fingers into her thick pectoral muscle.

Jati nodded.

"I'm flying us in?"

"Can you?"

"Well…" Nisi gazed around.

Uncertainty spoke on the faces of JeJeto and Tera.

"I'm going to ask you an important question. The one I asked Boar in this very room."

Nisi's eyes grew wide. She rose from her chair and strode to the window. Her head of black curls bent down, presumably to observe at the A-Dodger in the bay below.

"I don't know, Cap. If it was just me, I wouldn't blink."

"But?"

"But it'd be you and JJ. And Tusolo."

"And Ailo."

Nisi turned. "What?"

"I'm going too?" Ailo's attention perked.

Jati nodded. "If we do this, we're going to need you now. Tera's been unable to get the diorite to block the chips."

"Sorry, everyone," Tera said.

"Not your fault, Tera," Jati said. "There's a reason no one's been able to get around scanners in the Arm for the entire Third Span. No one expected you to figure it out in a week."

"How does Ailo relate to this?" Nisi asked, leaning back on the control board.

"I'm not chipped," Ailo said. It all made sense. Every time she'd ever gone through a station she'd either ignored it, used it to her advantage, or had to explain her way out of it. She was untraceable, a ghost.

"Everyone's chipped," Nisi said.

"She's not," Tera said. "I've done a full sweep and scan. There's nothing there. I have no idea how."

"I do."

Everyone turned, including Ailo, to the source of the voice.

"Your parent gave birth to you on a freighter when we were on the run," Rence said. We'd set up several drop points for ourselves on various nondescript planets and moon bases with false identities. We needed to disappear or the Garassians hunting us would slit our throats. Hekron was relentless. Your parent, being Cin Quinti, was target number one."

"Cin Quinti?" Tera said.

"Wait, what?" Nisi added.

"Yes," Rence said. "Ailo is the child of Cin Quinti. Whose real name is Teluv Harrond-té."

"Sake of the Arm!" Tera whispered.

Ailo flushed, her cheeks going hot, but her interest in listening to Rence wouldn't allow embarrassment to overpower her.

"We bribed our way onto T9," he said. "It wasn't easy. It worked because I was able to project a small jamming frequency through immigration that presented a secondary body scan of your parent on the machines. That's how we got you through undetected. I don't think it's ever been done before or since."

"Why?" Ailo asked.

"To protect you. Teluv knew people would try and come for her. You were a potential liability as her child. You could be taken, used as a bargaining chip, or worse, made an example of."

"Sake, this is deeper than the pit at Parshoo marsh," Nisi said and shook her head.

"You got that right," JeJeto said.

"So this is now a set-up/frame job and a rescue?" Nisi asked.

Jati nodded.

"And you need me to fly us to Yelo through Kusk?"

"And take the pod down through the shower and drop us in the Lorassian Sea," Jati said.

"What happens to Hirok?" Tera asked.

"Oh, we leave him in the Dodger on the moon. He'll be stuck there until the storm passes. And Rence is going to help get something ready while we FTL to Ceron to make sure we get all the evidence we need. He's going to do some modifications to the Dodger."

Rence nodded.

So he and Jati had spent that half-hour before the meeting talking. Ailo couldn't put it all together.

*How had Jati convinced him to help? And what about Boar?*

"Sake of the Arm, all this spy-level intelligence stuff. Ain't my style," Nisi said. "I don't like loose ends. We should nail the bastard when we have him in the Dodger."

"It's strategy," Ailo said.

"Ooooo," JeJeto said and clapped their hands. "She got you, Nisi." They grinned at Ailo, revealing their signature smile. "You're big time now, Ailo. Watch out, Cap. Might have another general soon."

"Indeed," Jati said and winked at Ailo. "So Nisi... I hate to put this on you. But it's on you. Can you fly us in? I told Boar and I'm telling you. There's no shame if you can't."

Nisi turned back to the window. "The Dodger doesn't worry me, Cap. I can get us to Yelo." She lowered her head. "As Boar said, might be a few dings, but I can get us in."

Why was she so upset about Boar? They did nothing but fight.

"And the pod?" Jati asked. They walked over and put their arm around her shoulder. The soldier stood a good foot taller and Jati leaned up to reach around.

"Fifty-fifty. I'm sorry, Jati."

Ailo noted the use of their first name. Nisi always deferred to them as 'Captain' on the ship, at least she had since they departed Heroon.

Jati nodded.

"What if you had guidance?" Rence asked.

"On the pod?" Nisi's response made it sound beyond the realm of technological reality.

"Yes." Rence's voice carried confident.

"Well, I mean..." She turned back to the team members. "Seventy-five percent, yeah. Sake... maybe even eighty if the odds are in our favor."

"Music to my ears," Jati said. They walked back over to the holo-field of the Arm. "I'll take that wager."

# TWENTY-FIVE

"I can't wait to see this," Nisi said and took a seat next to Ailo. On the front wall of the nav room, where the starfield normally hovered, a life-size holo-version of Jati appeared. They sat in a small com room off the cargo bay.

On Jati's orders, Tera had set up a remote link for the team to listen in on the call.

This would be delicate. The navigator told Ailo that while Nisi and the others were interested in watching Hirok's reaction to confronting an alive and kicking Jati, she should use the opportunity to observe their rhetorical strategy and tactics. Always the teacher.

JeJeto entered and took a seat on the other side of Nisi, a bottle of booster juice in their hand. They took a slug and nodded at Ailo.

Tera sat in her usual spot at the front. Rence leaned against the back wall, his fingers peeling a piece of Goolit fruit. He tossed the orange and white-striped rinds in a nearby bin, one by one with a *ping* as he ate the interior flesh. The sucking of his lips pulling juice from the orange fruit made Ailo uncomfortable.

*He is so strange.*

*"I think he's happy to have that Goolit."*

"Let's get this party started," Jati said and triggered the link to General Hirok's ship.

Ailo shook her head at Rence and turned her attention to the front of the room.

"General's assistant Firde Eji-ti. *Carmora*, is that you?" A low and deep voice said. "Tera, I'm so sorry about..." The visual popped up. Firde sat, one hand twirling bone-white hair that fell straight to his shoulders. Broad and heavily muscled, with skin the color of onyx, his deep red eyes punctuated his appearance. A strong jawline, high cheekbones, and the way his bicep bulged as he twirled his hair, gave him an intimidating aura.

The assistant's gaze avoided the capture lens, uncomfortable with the situation of Jati's 'death'. When he raised his eyes, they went wide. "Jati… I mean, General… excuse me. It can't… but we got word that…" Firde shoved back his seat so fast the chair crashed behind him. "Just a minute, I…" A palm came up. "Hold please, General." He dashed off.

Jati turned to the team and winked.

"Do they know?" Ailo whispered to Nisi.

"That Jati was 'dead'? Yeah, obviously. We sent out a PA-wide announcement after Cesix."

"No, that Hirok set it up."

"Of course not. I doubt anyone else knows," the soldier said.

"What is it?" Hirok's voice came from outside the holo-field. "This is highly irregular, Firde. What…" The general perked up and sat in the assistant's seat. His face froze, lips parted and mouth opened wide.

"We all set for Phase 2? I got Rence."

"You… but… Jati?" Hirok smacked his hands down on the desk. "Jati! Sake of the arm, we thought you were dead."

"Kick my teeno," Nisi said and shook her head. "He's worse than the second-rate entertainment broadcasts." She pointed. "His fingers are shaking."

"What can I say?" They folded their arms and leaned back. "I've got a habit of getting out of jams."

"What happened?"

"Yeah, I'll bet you wanna know," JeJeto said.

"Rence is with us," they said. "Cesix is gone. Destroyed."

"Who was it, Jati?"

"You mean the ambush?"

Hirok nodded.

"Pirates. They sent Hekron's insignia over the com to the *Carmora*. Nisi got it while at the helm. Did some fine flying."

Nisi elbowed JeJeto and smiled.

"Someone tipped them off," Jati said.

Hirok shook his head and leaned back. "But that means they had to know *before* Kusk blocked communications from the planet?"

"Or, someone else made contact after that."

"Ooooooo" JeJeto's voice rose. "Smackdown!"

Ailo noticed Jati's subtle rhetoric, their spurious strategy. They didn't confront Hirok. They let his comments lead to their own conclusion. She read the insecurity on Hirok's face.

"You have an idea who it was?"

Jati nodded. "And it's no longer a problem. It was Boar."

"The Hamut?"

Nisi pointed. "He can't hide the relief. Slip and slide, Cap!" She high-fived JeJeto.

"You have him?" Hirok asked. "He confessed?"

The elation in the nav room fizzled. The reality of the fake news about Boar returned to everyone else but Ailo and Rence. What was Jati's plan with Boar? And where was he? In Rence's pod? Ailo turned to Tusolo. He tossed the last of the Goolit fruit in the bin and wiped his mouth.

"He's gone," Jati said. "Boar was in the pod. He left us high and dry on Cesix station, like Gor trapped in Parshoo mud. We got out because Rence had an escape pod. But it was close, Hirok. Too close..."

"I don't understand."

"He learned a hard lesson about betrayal."

A weighted silence hung in the air.

"You could put a star system inside that silence," JeJeto whispered.

"But we're here and ready to go."

"We're still on?"

"Of course we're on. My child is down there, Hirok. Nisi's going to fly the Dodger. She'll take us down in the pod through Kusk instead of Boar. Rence is almost finished installing custom guidance on it. We can do this, Hirok."

The general nodded. Ailo had known of his betrayal since the first message with the insignia in this very room. Now, when she watched him everything appeared as a performance.

"From there, it's all the same," Jati said. "Except it's going to be more of a smash and grab job now to get Arira. Without Boar we're going to get in, hit hard, and take that shield down."

"Right on, Cap. Just how I like it," Nisi said.

"Let's hope she's there," Jati said.

"Oh, she's there," Hirok said.

"Gor scum!" JeJeto muttered. "Cap caught him. Watch how subtle Jati plays this, Ailo."

Ailo leaned forward. She'd picked up on the areas of uncertainty Jati presented in their theory. She had to admit, they were as dangerous and effective with words as they were with a blaster. Or, a P-Frigate's lasers.

"You think so? I'm worried, Hirok. She's all I've got."

"Well... I mean. Hold on, I think some intel came in." The general's gaze went to the panel below the holo-field and he fiddled with the controls. "Firde!" Hirok's eyes shifted off-screen. "Hold on, Jati." He got up and stepped out of view. "Can you pull up those images of the palace for me?"

"What images?" Firde's deep voice asked. "We don't have any recent ones?"

"Ouch," JeJeto said. Nisi laughed.

"They're in my personal file. Ping it here. I'll open it on a retinal scan." Hirok sat.

The two generals waited. Ailo shifted in her seat.

*How can Jati be so calm and collected?*

"Thank you," Hirok said in Firde's direction. He leaned forward. A beam shot into his eyes from somewhere below the screen capture in front of him. "I thought I sent you these?"

A shoreline appeared with a chpppy sea splashing up

against high stone walls.

"Is that the palace?" Ailo asked.

"Yeah," JeJeto said.

Ailo had seen similar structures on the historical broadcasts. This one shared its qualities with ancient models from the First Span — grand, with emphasis on strength and protection over aesthetics and ornamentation. The fortress lay in tiers of gray stone, rectangular with wide domes rising at each level. A prominent, larger central dome rose at the top. Four towers, with many openings for defense, punctuated the corners.

Withered and old, yet permanent, it stood as if it would never crumble. In front of Jati, it cast a surreal image, small in scale with shifting water like the mental projection of a dream.

"How big is it?" Ailo asked.

"This is just one side," JeJeto said. "It opens and runs..."

"Look," Nisi smacked JeJeto on the arm.

The holo switched to a security scanner above a processional road. A few hundred feet ahead, the massive portal embedded in the bottom level of the palace announced its grand entranceway. They were now viewing the front of the palace.

By the scale and proportions, Ailo calculated that the opening would fit a small spaceship. No wonder the place was impossible to conquer. Water on two sides, composed of stone, and open space in front? It left nowhere to hide. And with a shield wall to protect the entire city? The reality of what lay ahead made her stomach turn.

"Where is the shield wall?" she asked Nisi.

"Not up yet, this was taken pre-Kusk. If it was you'd see a massive, faint, and translucent dome with a hint of emerald." The soldier placed both hands up, together, and made a wide arc down to her waist.

"Our person inside sent these out before the shower hit." Hirok swept forward in virtual space. The holo view shot down the open road at a near blur. Marshland, grasses, and small shrubbery whizzed by on either side of the processional way. The portal approached. Hirok aimed the view up and soared past several palace levels. Ailo lost count of how many. At the fourth or fifth tier, the image halted. They were now in front of a balcony running around the last and highest dome.

Ailo thought the architecture of the dome odd. Arched windows along its base were divided by thin columns. It gave off the illusion of hovering on a chain from the sky, suspended, without any weight falling onto the tier where it sat.

To the right, far below, the Lorassian Sea crashed into the walls of the palace.

*That water is rough, Gerib.*

"Now might be a good time to pull out the 'that's too far in the future' philosophy."

*You're no help.*

A hint of the city of Garassit fell away out of view on the left. The urban landscape ran in a contradiction to the topography and design of Gontook. Tall buildings with spires made the cityscape appear like a bed of nails. Few structures had open decks, and the windows were much smaller than on Heroon.

"Is it cold there?" she asked.

"It's temperate," Tera said, turning around. "Not as hot as Heroon and it has four standard seasons."

Unlike Ffossk, puffy clouds dotted a blue sky. Patches of a late afternoon sun cast an orange glow over the gray stone.

"Look," JeJeto pointed.

"There she is," Hirok said and zoomed in. Off to the side of the balcony, under a small table with an umbrella made of green material sat Arira, alone, with a half-eaten plate of food. Two guards stood at their post a few yards away.

*Gerib, it's like she's entirely ignored.*

"Or not there at all, Ai."

Jati made no move. They stood like a stone.

Nisi reached over and placed a hand on Ailo's arm.

"Here we go."

"Show me the others, Hirok. Is it who I think it is?" Jati asked.

"Yes, they're both there." Zooming back, Hirok pulled the view up in front of the balcony, hovering about thirty feet in the air over the processional road. Two persons stood, gazing out over the waist-high ledge. The general moved the image closer.

The first, old, bald, and gaunt, had at least four inches over the other person. The other, Ailo identified as middle-aged and similar in appearance to Rence: long curly hair and a goatee.

"Who is that?" she whispered to Nisi.

'It's Hekron and Aradus," Rence said from the back.

The shadow killer? And his uncle, Aradus. The mastermind and Keen Draden's parent.

"Tera, get Jati to zoom in. I want to see how many," Nisi said.

"No, I don't want to know," Tera said.

"How many what?" Ailo asked.

"Tera, message them." Nisi's voice sounded urgent. And angry. "Show me the bastard's arm!"

"O.K.," the navigator said. She typed on her wrist com.

"Zoom in Hirok," Jati said before Tera got the text off.

*Jati wants to know, too.*

The holo surged forward to a close-up of the two men on the balcony. Hirok shifted the viewpoint to the side and Hekron's forearms entered the view, resting on the balcony's ledge. The person's shirt sleeves were rolled up. Four lines of red dots ran up one arm, with the fifth line with two dots starting another row.

*Gerib...*

"Gor hunter!" Nisi said. "That's at least another full line since the last intel on him... bastard. How many people has he killed?

*Gerib?*

Ailo's dam cracked. The flood of memory broke through

the long-held wall of internal protection. Past and present rushed together, colliding inside her psyche. Through the vent on T9, in that cramped kitchen, she watched the olive-skinned arm with the laser tattoos grab hold of her parent. This arm. Her eyes filled with water. She turned around.

"He killed my parent? Hekron murdered my parent?"

Rence didn't respond.

"Tell me!" she screamed.

Tera jumped in her seat. Nisi and JeJeto's eyes went wide.

"Are you saying you know Hekron?" Nisi asked.

"Yes." The waters inside Ailo settled. She gritted her teeth and glared a hole into Tusolo.

Rence shook his head. "I only knew she was taken from our sources on Urolo. Our network lost contact. Ailo was assumed to be abducted as well."

Why was she reacting this way? Her parent had been gone for almost ten years. She'd been without her so long the memory was more of a dream. No, that wasn't true. It was there the whole time, no mere psychic mirage.

*Gerib, why now?*

*"You did it to protect yourself, Ai. To survive, a child finding safety in avoidance and denial. It's nothing to be ashamed of. It's part of why I am here with you."*

This wasn't what she wanted when she fled T9. Or was it? Had she left to start a new life? Or had this been there the whole time? Had she gone off in search of answers?

Now she knew her parent's identity and who took her away.

"Maybe she's alive?" Ailo gripped the back of the seat with her two fingers and shifted to view the rest of the team.

No one responded. Tera's gold eyes softened and her lips pressed together. It wasn't an expression she'd seen the navigator make before.

*Why is no one answering me, Gerib?*

"He took her. I remember it," Ailo said. "She could be alive."

Rence raised an eyebrow, like a scientist concluding the assessment of evidence and data. His stare was cold truth.

A strong hand lay on her shoulder. "Hey," Nisi said, her face soft, the soldier's mask wiped away. The lamentation of a child without a parent filled her eyes. She knelt and wrapped her massive arms around Ailo. Any other time, Ailo would push away. Every time she'd been trapped at social services on T9 and they'd brought in a therapist who tried it, she'd lashed out. No one had touched her in comfort since... she couldn't remember how long.

*Yes, you can.*

She didn't shove Nisi away; she fell into her strong embrace. The soldier's warm and muscular body surrounded her like a blanket, a shield held up in front of the reality surrounding her.

"I lost my parent, too. I know what it's like."

Ailo clutched Nisi tight.

"I wasn't much older than you," Nisi said.

Ailo's mind refused to acquiesce. Blue eyes burned into the floor behind the soldier.

"It gets easier over time." Nisi's brawny hands pushed her back and she put them on Ailo's shoulders. "The one thing you can do now, for yourself, is learn to accept it. And let it go."

"You haven't."

Nisi shook her head and smiled. "No, I'm still working on it."

Ailo bit her lip.

"I'm sorry, Ailo. Give it time."

Time? It couldn't pass soon enough. She'd help Jati retrieve Arira and expose Hirok's treachery. They'd stop the Garassians and save the PA from certain defeat. But she wasn't leaving the palace until Hekron was dead.

# TWENTY-SIX

The dam burst. I let it flow.

Every light-year Ailo traveled from T9 brought her closer to the past and the truth about her childhood. Space/time works in ironic and contradictory ways, too complex and nuanced for our petty minds.

It began at Cesix station. Profound revelations spurred growth, awe, and a confrontation with a difficult, personal choice. One requiring loss. I got the sense its reward would reap major dividends down the road (I know Ai doesn't like to think too far ahead — still working on that one).

But the shocking revelation in the nav room opened a different gate. There are doors we rush through with reckless abandon, seeking answers. Others hide the ominous, and we push them with a delicate finger, ever so slowly. We peek through the crack and hope the hinges are well-greased and silent so we can turn and run if what we confront is so frightening and threatening it will undo us. But too often what we see on the other side are shadows and illusions.

A mirage lingered for years as a shield. Now it settled into poignant clarity letting crisp, undeniable memories come into focus. Hard memories. Angry memories.

None of this is proactive. I don't 'let anything out.' Each time a reference returns, I react. I regulate what and how much Ai is ready to confront. Or, I *try* and regulate by suggesting alternatives, predicting outcomes, and when necessary, employing misdirection.

But now? Everything was out. A flood of memories ran their course. The waters eased. Past and present melted together.

What form it takes when it cools and hardens is yet to be seen. And you know what? I don't care. That's not my job. Ai is an adult, or close enough to it. She can confront the sobriety of maturity. I'm responsible for her mental well-being. What she does with her life and the choices she makes aren't up to me. Maybe I was too heavy-handed, maybe not. When we stowed away on the *Carmora* off T9, neither of us expected this result or our current circumstance.

From now on it will be different. She'll grapple with her issues like everyone else and make the best-informed decisions she can with a fully restored memory (is a memory ever full?). Some will work out and some won't. That's life. I'm confident she'll do well.

Jati is a great mentor. They couldn't have come into her life at a better time.

Ailo's vengeance towards Hekron boiled up in the nav room despite the compassionate empathy expressed by Nisi. It didn't bother me. If she exacts revenge at the palace in Garassit, then so be it. Why shouldn't she? After what she was put through?

Leave the ethics and morality of that choice to Jati. They can work it through with her.

But let's not dwell on pejoratives. There's something else at work in Ailo that is promising and exciting. A set of hidden, dormant talents is surfacing, and those on the crew are shaping and developing them.

Ai is proving to be a skilled linguist, knowledgeable in rhetorical strategy and tactics. Her time in the training room is improving her physical confidence and sanding a gruff street-wise scrapper into a refined and sophisticated martial artist. JeJeto joked about her leadership potential. I'm not certain it was facetious.

I can't shake off something Jati said during the Cesix debacle. As Ailo hovered on the brink of asphyxiation in space, her parent's tome spiraling from her hand into the void, Jati spoke five words: "Now you write your own." Did they mean the written word? Or was it a metaphor, a loose use of the term? It certainly wasn't facetious. What did they know, or hope for, in a young adult finding answers to her past that stung but healed into wisdom?

# TWENTY-SEVEN

*Leave your shit outside.*

The words, burned into the Cantinool plaque in handwritten script, flanked the entrance to the *Carmora's* training room. Ailo had read the sign many times, but now something told her the advice would be important.

Jati had requested they meet here for a special session. Tera relayed the invitation, adding that it would be the two of them.

She waved her hand to open the portal and stepped inside.

Jati danced with the Talon Caster. On the raised wooden platform, their pronged weapon swung high and low, striking out and sweeping back. At one end of the staff, a red laser blade's sparkling beam buzzed and crackled as it cut through ions in the air.

Jati's wrists loosened and the Talon Caster spiraled. They shifted stances and fought imaginary opponents. Each movement punctuated by an abrupt contraction of breath and rooted feet. An occasional slow, drawn-out exhalation hissed as a concentrated maneuver interrupted the fast-paced dance.

Ailo removed her shoes and placed them on the rack. Her feet crossed the cold tiles to the edge of the wooden platform. She stood, waiting for them to finish.

Jati lunged forward. Their ponytail rose off their back and into the air as they surged, sending the Caster's talons into an imaginary opponent.

"Ya!"

Ailo gasped and jumped back. The voice accompanying the final strike bounced off the walls of the training room with the ferocity of a mighty beast, wild and savage, yet controlled by the reins of its master. She'd known Jati as a wise commander, but she'd glimpsed the Legion side of them once on Ffossk in a futile attempt to intervene that came too late.

Their voice alone, even without the strike of the weapon, would intimidate a lesser opponent into submission. Did they want her to face them now, on the training floor?

Jati returned to a standing position, Caster in one hand. They pressed a button shutting off the laser blade and planted that end on the floor. The weapon flanked them in one hand like a staff. The general's chest swelled against their tight-fit tank top like the wooden strips of a barrel held back from bursting by a metal cross band. Words, spoken in a whisper, passed from their lips. She couldn't make them out.

"Sit," Jati motioned to the floor in front of them, chest rising and falling. Perspiration dotted their face and dripped from the tip of their nose and chin. The general walked to the wall and placed the Talon Caster back in the prongs above Keen Draden's plaque.

"What was that you were doing?" Ailo stepped up onto the platform and sat.

"Stone Fall," Jati said but didn't turn around. "An advanced form used in the Legion. It's very old. And, therefore good for old warriors. Like me." Their hand went to Keen Draden's plaque. "It's one of several series. They have different purposes and advantages." The general turned and came over to sit across from her in the middle of the training floor. They pulled their legs up into a lotus position.

Her eyes widened.

"What?"

"I... it's... you're flexible. That looks hard."

"Nonsense. You're young and limber. You can do it. Give it a try. Like this." Jati undid the bind of their legs and began again, one limb at a time, walking her through it.

Ailo pulled one leg up and then the other. Both fit into place, although one took a bit of coaxing.

"Is that the one you hurt on the K-speeder?" Jati pointed at the leg.

She nodded.

"That's a weak point. First lesson for today: learn to recognize and acknowledge your limits, but don't let them deter you. Instead, work twice as hard on those areas to bring them up to the same level as your other skills and abilities."

"How?"

"JeJeto will start you on a stretching routine. Whatever you do on the other leg, do two times as many on that one. Got it?"

She ran a hand over her ankle where the synthetic surgical implants had replaced her bones.

"Got it?" Jati asked again.

"Yes."

"Second lesson: when we're on the training floor, be efficient. If you're with an instructor, don't waste time. It's respectful to them and of benefit to you. Get everything you can, while you can. Do that and train hard, and one day you might be sitting where I am. If someone else doesn't best you first.

*What?* She wouldn't be bested. *Why did they think...*

"Ahhh, there's that fire," Jati winked. "Good. Final lesson for today..."

"We're done?"

Jati raised an eyebrow.

"What?"

Their green eyes narrowed, intensifying with a burning gaze. Jati exuded an authority she hadn't sensed before. Were they waiting for her to speak?

The eyebrow stayed up.

She reviewed the conversation. Standing 'outside,' their exchange revealed the obvious. "I was wasting time, wasn't I?"

A smile edged onto the corners of the general's lips.

"And, I interrupted."

They nodded. "Listen first. Then ask questions. It's respectful. But it's also efficient in another way. If you wait until I'm finished, the answer to your question may already be there."

Ailo understood. She liked this dynamic. It reminded her of the strategy discussion on the bridge when she sat in the captain's chair. This kind of knowledge was... *different*. And alluring. It attracted her more than a book or a broadcast. Or a history lecture by Tera. It wasn't only 'knowing' something. It was a style of living. Or...

"The Way," Jati said. "That is what I am teaching you here."

"Of a soldier?"

"No. Of the warrior."

"What's the difference?"

"A soldier is trained to fight. To carry out a task and work as part of a team. It's their job and duty to serve and protect others and defend. They follow orders, or give them, and they form part of a social group."

"Like an army?"

"Yes."

"And a warrior?"

"Let me answer with an example. I will use someone who sparked what became the Tide War. A warrior who helped Keen Draden. And who was, for a time, an ally."

Ailo focused on the memorial plaque behind Jati.

"Her name was Razor-té."

Ailo smiled. She remembered the name. It carried power and allure.

Boar had brought up Razor's name in the pod on the ride to Cesix station. Jati reacted with sadness, remarking they hadn't spoken to her and thought it better left that way.

"Was she a friend of yours?"

"For a time, yes. Razor was an important person in my life. She was from Kol 2."

"She was a Targitian?"

"No. She was a Mote."

"What's a Mote?"

"*Were Motes*. They've all disappeared. Feared extinct. They were rebels, cast out from their lands by a portion of their brethren who accepted support and political allies from elsewhere in the Arm, compromising their integrity and culture for money and power. In return, their planet transformed into a source of energy through eco-shaping."

"Desert," Ailo said. "With Wind Tides."

"Yes, so you've heard of Kol 2?"

"Tera told me about it. And the Targitians."

"Did she now? Good. Well, the Motes lived in the dunes, refusing to submit to foreign rule or to compromise their cultural heritage. They adapted to the new ecosystem, hiding in remote regions, surviving under a colonial, oppressive regime. Until a day came when they could no longer bide their time and they made a choice. That decision was to confront the Targitians and attempt to take back their planet and rebuild their indigenous culture."

"What does it mean? 'Mote'?"

"It depends on who you ask. If you ask a Targitian or a Garassian, they'll tell you it means someone small and insignificant. A nobody." Jati held up a hand and blew. "Like a speck of dust floating in the air, so small you'd struggle to see it."

She remembered the approach to Cesix station. Inside the dark curtain of the sail, the pod stood like a mote. The expanse of the cosmos, overwhelming in its grandeur and scale made her, and even the entire situation they were in, meaningless in comparison.

"But if you were to ask a Mote, like Razor, she'd tell you it means someone who is small but resists. Someone that no one cares about and may have forgotten, or don't take seriously."

"I don't understand," Ailo said. "So they knew it was a bad meaning, but they still used it?"

"Many examples exist in the history of the Arm of groups

like the Motes. All labeled with negative terms that were, in turn, embraced and worn proudly like a badge of honor in defiance of their enemies and oppressors. Appropriating those terms is both a critical act and a form of resistance that turns things around, or often can. How do you think your parent's group came by their name?"

"The Radicals?"

"Indeed. That negative designation was put on them. It wasn't chosen. They turned it back as a weapon against those who tried to demean and marginalize them."

"Are you a Radical?" She'd wanted to ask the question since it came up in her conversation with Tera. Now seemed like the best and most appropriate time.

"Me?" Jati pointed a finger at their chest. "No. But I share many of their beliefs."

"Like?"

"I live to defend and promote freedom. The Radicals believed in a form of anarchy touting a philosophy of freedom. We shared common ideas, but we're still different. I learned many important things from them that shaped my warrior philosophy."

Ailo wanted to ask another question. Her stomach turned at the idea of saying it out loud. She didn't know if she'd want to hear the answer.

"Ask me," Jati said.

Ailo averted their gaze, observing the wooden planks on the floor. She ran a finger across the Cantinool grain.

"Did you know my parent?"

"I met her once," Jati said. A small smile curved against their strong stony cheeks. "I sought her out. Having known Rence and being in league with him, and working to help save him from persecution, he was able to arrange a meeting."

"And? What was she like?"

Jati leaned forward. "A lot like you."

*Is that why they said, "of course" in the pod when they realized who she was, and who I was to her?*

"Your parent was..."

"You think she's dead too?"

Jati placed a paw on her thigh. "I'm sorry, Ailo. Your parent was a victim of those we are now fighting. She is gone."

"You know this for sure?"

Jati sighed. "Nothing is certain. But I have it from good sources that your parent was taken by Hekron. And killed." They withdrew their hand. "I am sorry."

Could she describe her reaction as shock? Each time the fact presented itself, it'd chipped away at the small amount of hope left in her heart. It got easier each time, like more arrows piercing a victim one after another. The first one stung worst and caused the most intense pain. After that? They diminished. But the anger remained. Hekron would pay. With his life.

"My parent was? You didn't finish."

"A warrior. Like Razor, but unique and different. A warrior fighting to change a world."

"And both are now dead."

"No," Jati shook their head. "Razor is not dead."

Again, they wore the expression from the pod. Sadness blended with quiet acceptance.

"As far as I know Razor is alive, back on Kol 2. She's in a prison cell, under the city of Targite. But that is a tale for another day. Razor was a skilled soldier, but she didn't fight solely for her people's cause. She fought for a philosophy, a personal one. It was built on the back of her Mote heritage and history, but it was hers alone. Forged and crafted from her own experience and circumstances. And it wasn't without its flaws. We all have qualities to our personalities that can serve us or work against us. And in her case, it meant making choices unpopular with her people." Jati nodded to emphasize the significance of their words. "Razor is a free spirit who sought to achieve a personal goal, one she considered virtuous and worthy because it would make her life and those she cared for better and safe. That made her a warrior. And she did it through all of her actions. *Not only in combat.*"

The general's final sentence took time to settle. So a

warrior performed outside the field of battle? "This is a way of life?"

Jati nodded. "And here is the beginning of an understanding of the Way."

"But..."

Jati raised an eyebrow.

"I interrupted. Sorry."

They waved a hand, indicating she should continue.

"But that means you can be a warrior but never fight. I mean... not be a soldier in combat."

"Ideally, or philosophically, a warrior or a soldier that is skilled enough and knows themselves — and therefore can know their enemy — shouldn't have to fight. Or, if they must, it often takes the form of an action before the confrontation."

"Like?"

"Like, rhetoric. Or a strategy that achieves an end without a need to engage the enemy." They raised an eyebrow. "Like, say... to reference something more closer to home, a pre-emptive plan that ends with the same accomplishment as a battle." They winked.

"Then what does it mean to 'win'?"

"Achieve the goal before you need to fight."

Her head swirled in confusion.

"Well? Thoughts?" Jati asked.

"It sounds a lot like... like strategy."

"Indeed. That is one important aspect. Another is to train your mind and your body. And to learn about your enemies. You can be a warrior and never engage in physical combat. Your parent, for example."

*My parent was a warrior?*

"Many of those are among the strongest and wisest warriors of all."

Ailo's cocked her head.

"What?"

"Nisi would call that a 'Jati-ism'."

Jati laughed. "Indeed, she would."

"Was Razor, sorry... *is* Razor one of the wisest?"

"Razor trod, and still treads in her prison cell, her own path. The same was the case for Keen Draden. We are all on the warrior's path, those of us who choose to walk that road. There is no destination, only the journey. Or, if there is an end, just a select few have reached it. Rare and legendary those warriors are, in tales of old." Jati said. "Razor and Keen were opposites in many ways. Their coming together was both good and bad. It exacerbated their faults, causing them to confront obstacles towards their goals. But it revealed shortcomings, and they learned to understand them."

"To 'know their limits'."

Jati nodded. "To know their limits, yes. And from that, each progressed on their personal paths. In the end, it pushed them apart, but it caused them to learn something important."

"What was that?"

"Can't say. I'm not them. But they reached common ground and had something to show for it. Some would say too late. But perhaps just in time because they both made peace within themselves. It was a tragedy in the truest sense of the word."

"I don't understand tragedy."

Jati's cheeks rose, golden stone slabs crushing the corners of their eyes into wrinkles. "Let's hope you never experience it, Firecracker. But you should know what it is and how it works. Ask Tera. She's the historian. She'll tell you what the recipe is and how it tastes."

Ailo watched Jati's eyes observe her in earnest. "What?"

"You two aren't that different."

"Who, Tera and me?"

"No," Jati laughed. "You and Razor. She left a remote world and set out into the Arm to learn she was part of a larger system of oppression, with others like her who shared her experience. And she was feisty, scrappy, and strong."

Ailo warmed inside, smitten with the compliment.

"A bit boar-headed too."

Ailo frowned. That wasn't so good.

"Which can be a good thing. Razor had an iron will and her morality was like a compass needle." Jati extended an arm straight like an arrow. "There was always a line with her. Her foot drew it in the blue sands of Kol 2. She never crossed it, no matter how many light-years away she was from her home. Or, no matter how much it pierced her heart."

"Was she right to make her choice? To end up where she did?"

"Only she knows. It was hers to make. And keep. Now it's blown away by the Tide. But that doesn't mean it's forgotten." Jati's eyes welled up. They wiped a tear with one of their paw-like hands. "Such is the Way of the Warrior."

A fire ignited in Ailo's belly. The Way called her, but no path to tread revealed itself.

*Where's my path, Gerib?*

*"You have to find it, Ai. I think that's the first step."*

"Remember that, Firecracker." Jati undid their legs from the bind and shook them out.

"Remember what?"

They stood and stretched, touching their hands to their toes. They bent back up and put their hands on their hips. "A time will come when you will find your path. And when you do it will be time to draw that line. It might be in Heroonese dirt or Garassian ground. Or on another world, yet to be trodden." Jati walked over to Keen's plaque and touched it. "Or perhaps deep in the blue sands of Kol 2." They turned, their green eyes alive with earnestness. "This entire conflict started on Kol 2. Something tells me it may end there as well."

# TWENTY-EIGHT

Ailo wasn't thrilled to be back in a spacesuit. Squeezed in the small seating section behind the A-Dodger's cockpit, she sat between Rence and a makeshift wall. The man's stout frame trespassed the unspoken line between them, his thigh pushing her own through the suit.

The awkward intimacy couldn't be avoided. After they loaded the cargo, the room left didn't amount to much. Jati managed to pack the team's equipment and the refitted pod into the ship's main hold by tearing out rows of asteroid miner transport seats. Once they were through Kusk and down on Yelo, planetside, at least she'd be able to switch to the pod. Hopefully, there would be more room in there.

The pod on the other side of the wall, with its new diorite exterior and Rence's tech adjustments to the nav system, would get them through Ceron's atmosphere and down to the planet. Without incident, Ailo hoped. The pressure to succeed fell on Nisi's shoulders, at least until they made it down and floated on the surface of the Lorassian Sea. After that? Ailo didn't want to think about it. She couldn't swim. The sooner her feet were on the dry land of the palace's shores, the happier she'd be. Talk about irony.

The A-Dodger wasn't a small vessel. That meant a lot of cargo stuffed inside the makeshift hold to aft. Walking across the loading bay before departure, Ailo guessed the ship to be a hundred feet from bow to stern, and that wasn't including the stems extending back to the flex-burners. Those added at least thirty to forty feet to that number.

Her eyes went from floor to ceiling and from the dashboard in the cockpit to the wall to her right. The entire space where they all sat couldn't be more than twenty feet long and almost the same across. That calculated to about sixty to eighty feet of length at twenty feet wide behind the abutting wall. For the number of people on the op, six in total, it amounted to a good deal of cargo. Whatever else they'd packed back there with the pod had to be important.

Jati knew what they were doing. So far, they'd managed to keep the fight alive, despite some major setbacks. If something came with them, it would be needed.

She inhaled and her side pushed into Rence. Tusolo, in what was becoming a daily habit, sat peeling and sucking on a Goolit. His slurps on the fleshy fruit added an audible accent of annoyance to the anxiety of her claustrophobic situation. Even worse was her view. General Hirok sat across the aisle, next to JeJeto. He'd arrived on the *Carmora* thirty minutes after they dropped out of FTL behind the fleet an hour ago. Now she'd have to sit for the duration across from a traitor.

Ailo half-expected to find Boar in the pilot's seat when she boarded, but the Hamut was nowhere to be found. Did he intend to stay on the *Carmora*? Or meet them on the planet by other means?

The downtime and waiting over the last two days whipped into a frenzy of activity on arrival in the Garassian system. Ailo sat sipping afternoon tea in the mess with Nisi when the announcement about the drop out of FTL sounded over the ship's com. The soldier came alive like a droid's power switch flipped on. A few fist pumps, punctuated by expletives, erupted and she barreled out of her chair and out of the cafeteria. Hooting and hollering bounced down the hallway as she ran to get her gear.

Why wasn't Nisi worried about flying the pod instead of Boar? The conversation in the nav room during the revised op meeting after Cesix pointed to concern. But now? She acted like a child getting a surprise treat from a parent to enliven a boring day.

Tera materialized at the door to Ailo's sleeping pod while she grabbed her things to head to the pre-flight room.

"Good luck," the navigator said. "We're grateful you're joining us to get this done."

"Thanks." Ailo shoved her things into a bag.

*I have my reasons, too.*

"Here." Tera held out her hand, fist clenched. She nodded for Ailo to approach

The navigator took her arm and placed something in her hand. She closed Ailo's two fingers around it.

It felt small and thin. But something else, looser and delicate, lay in there with it.

"Go ahead," Tera said. "Look."

She opened her two fingers. A perfectly edged circular chip of diorite lay threaded on a thin chain.

"A necklace?" Ailo held it up to inspect it. The diorite was extraordinary, full of glittering mini-stars and a multitude of layers and depth. Like a vast galaxy, an entire cosmos lay compacted and reduced into a thin object the size of a thumbnail.

"It's the best piece that I've ever seen," Tera said. "I couldn't resist."

She'd never owned a piece of jewelry. She'd never even worn a piece of jewelry.

"Go ahead. Put it on."

Ailo hung it over her head.

Tera stepped up. "Keep it under your shirt when you're out in the world. There's something special about wearing jewelry that isn't visible. You'll find it has extraordinary power." She smiled. "I gave you this to remember that you're unique, but you are also part of a community. And a vast universe. It's a tradition in the Radicals, going back to the Second Span and Cin Tuinti, to have something to remind you of this principle."

"'Of them, we are One?'" Ailo said, holding the pendant up to her eyes.

"'Of them, we are One,'" Tera said and put a hand on

her shoulder. "Come on, I'll walk you to the docking bay."

Ailo arrived at the loading bay to find Nisi standing with JeJeto. Her duffel bag, not as large as it'd been when she boarded on Gontook, hung over her shoulder. Ailo counted no fewer than three blasters holstered on her hips and one attached to her leg, as well as a series of knives and other devices clipped on a vest worn over an olive T-shirt. A steel line of cable gathered in a loop hooked to a clip on her belt. The laser tattoos on her arms were on full display.

"Ready to get this party started?" Nisi offered her a fist. Ailo bumped it.

"Let's get this one done, for Jati. And for the Arm," the soldier said.

"Don't forget," JeJeto said, "Cap said we're all smoking 'nool when we get back."

"I hear that," Nisi said, her eyes on the A-Dodger across the bay.

Ailo scanned Nisi up and down. All jitters, she was chomping at the bit to get out and accomplish this goal. *Jati's* goal.

The A-Dodger decelerated and a series of beeps sounding from the open cockpit brought Ailo back to the present. She shifted her arm next to Rence so it rested on her thigh, over the lucky Rim wedge.

"Edge of Kusk approaching, everyone," Nisi said from the pilot's seat. "Double-check your straps."

Music pumped through the speakers; a fast-beat, layered track with an aggressive static-charge melody. Nisi had played similar things while exercising on the *Carmora*.

JeJeto swirled a celebratory arm in the air and bobbed their head back and forth to the beats. Judging by General Hirok and Jati's tolerance, Ailo guessed it to be People's Army thing or a quirk of Nisi's that they both knew and allowed.

Ailo leaned forward. Out the window of the A-Dodger, not far ahead, a distinct line of space dust glimmered in the light of a distant star as a band of sparkling fog suspended in a black void.

"Pincori," Rence said.

Ailo pulled her head back. "What?"

"The name of the star in this system. The one that lights Ceron. It's strong, a G-Type star. Ceron has a wide orbit. We're about 150 million miles out."

Ailo nodded. Why he thought she was thinking about that, she didn't know. She wasn't. But it did present an opening. If she didn't ask now, there might not be another chance. It meant being prudent and careful. On Jati's orders, she'd been told not to mention her parent's identity in front of General Hirok.

The music helped and she should be able to speak low enough to avoid the others. She tugged on Tusolo's sleeve. He leaned over.

"Where was my parent from?" she whispered.

Rence tightened the clips on his chest straps. His eyes bounced to Hirok. The general was engaged in close conversation with JeJeto, poring over map data on his wrist com, pointing at areas of the palace. What a farce. JeJeto played along well.

"Do you mean where was she born, or where did she live?"

"Both, I guess."

"She was born on Vesto, a Garassian monopoly-controlled planet, near the Collanux Particularity. Because of her scholarly excellence, she managed to get a scholarship to the Academy on Ossihutu. So that tells you a lot." Rence pulled back and stroked his goatee.

"Tells me what?"

"The famous Center for Languages. I would think you'd have heard of it?"

"No."

"She stayed there for some time. After that, Teluv spent time on Heroon."

"Heroon?"

Rence double-checked the status across the aisle and leaned back in. "Yes. From there to Tarkassi 9 via freighter.

That was 3043. The year you were born."

Ailo computed the difference.

*It's 3058. Gerib, That means I'm fifteen, not sixteen.*

Fifteen? That was a *child*. Sixteen felt different. It sounded different too.

"It makes sense, Ai."

*What?*

"*I mean mathematically.*"

Ailo turned to Rence. "Are you…"

Tusolo nodded towards General Hirok, his eyes making clear the conversation would go no further.

She needed to ask one more question.

"Approaching the edge. Here we go," Nisi said. "Hold tight. Don't stress the whiplash, that's the flex-burners working their charm."

Ailo tugged his shoulder down and spoke in his ear.

"Who is my other parent?"

Rence pulled back. Obsidian flecks speckled the irises of his green eyes. Ailo recalled the first time she'd met him at Cesix station. She hadn't bothered to ask Tera about tragedy, but an answer lay in these eyes. It spoke not with words but through color and form.

"Anonymous," he whispered. "Chosen at random from the Arm fertility pool."

*Anonymous? That could be anyone.*

Rence leaned back in. "'Of them, we are One.'"

The A-Dodger swung right, sucking Ailo into the wall. It hurtled left and down at a wild pitch, sending her into Rence.

"Grab the holds!" JeJeto said, across the aisle. They nodded at their hands on the bars overhead.

Ailo reached up and clutched the handles, barely reaching them. General Hirok's hands gripped the runners over his seat, his face calm.

The A-Dodger surged right. A crescendo of engine rockets fought the music for control of the soundtrack.

"Flexers kicked on," JeJeto said. A wide grin stretched across their face.

*Why do they all enjoy this so much?*

The ship veered left. Ailo closed her eyes and held on tight. Nisi maneuvered the Dodger with serpentine precision.

*Anonymous? Gerib, why choose a random partner?*

"I don't know, Ai. How does it make you feel?"

*Confused. Disappointed.*

"Angry?"

*No, not angry... sad.*

The flex-burners whirred up again and the ship darted through and around a series of moving objects. How large or how numerous the Kusk meteors were, she had no idea.

*Crack!*

Ailo's body bounced up and down as if they'd hit a bump in the road. The Dodger's alarms went off. So, some of the meteors were big. Between the alarm and the music, and the maneuvering and impacts, the ride grew tense and chaotic.

"Sorry!" Nisi shouted.

"Why are we listening to this?" Ailo yelled at JeJeto.

"Chills her out, like the 'nool." JeJeto let go of the rail with one hand and made a gesture as if smoking.

The Dodger went vertical and spun in a spiral before inverting and looping down.

"Wooooo!" JeJeto cried out and smiled wide, almost losing his other grip.

Ailo's stomach swirled like a wash cycle full of dirty water. *He's having fun right now?*

"Fly it, Nisi!" Jejeto shouted.

"Trying," she said.

General Hirok, eyes closed, muttered across the aisle.

*Pang!* The A-Dodger veered left. Another alarm rang. Red lights flashed.

"Sake of the Arm!" Nisi shouted.

Jati pushed switches over their head. "Flex 1 damaged. I shut it down," they said. "Focus, Nisi. Yelo is ahead. It's not far."

The Dodger swung left and right, sweeping around a moving object. Small pattering on the exterior added a new instrument to the overture. Across the aisle, JeJeto's yellow head went up, tracking the source. "Micros!"

"On it," Jati said and spiraled a wheel on the dashboard. "Umbrella-filter at forty-eight degrees, adjusting for yaw."

"Aye, Cap," Nisi said.

"You got this?" Jati asked.

"Yeah."

Ailo didn't like her reply. Hesitancy usurped the usual bold and cocky tone in her voice. That didn't bode well. Out here, in the field on the op, Ailo wanted gutsy, overconfident Nisi. Not an unsure one.

"Yelo ahead!" Jati said.

Rence had shut down, his eyes closed as if his mind had powered off and left his body to endure the rest of the flight.

The Dodger went right and down, and back left. *Thump!* The ship swung hard to the right. Too hard. The interior lights flickered. An ominous gnawing like the scraping nails and an ear-grinding alarm, sounded in unison.

*What's that?*

"*Damage alert,*" an automated voice stated from the ship's system. "*Starboard fin. Forty percent compromised.*"

"Adjusting," Jati said and flipped a switch and ran some scans. "Flex 4 overheating. How far out are we?"

"I need three minutes!" Nisi steered them up and down, left and around.

*Thump!*

"Watch it!" Jati shouted. "You're going to get two minutes at this power level. If you need another hard maneuver it has to be now," they said and turned.

Ailo knew Jati read fear on her face. She grit her teeth. *I trust you, Jati.*

"Last turn," Nisi said. "Hold on everyone, I'm going to try and slip the loop."

"No, Nisi. The other way," Jati said. Their hands were waving for her to shift course.

"I got it, Cap. I got it."

"Flex is going to go. Don't do it!"

"I gottttttttttt..." Nisi's extended pronunciation paralleled a scraping and tearing somewhere behind Ailo's back.

She closed her eyes and waited for the inevitable. The necklace entered her mind. The external world retreated and an internal one called her. Equal in scale, a psychic expanse triggered by the mental image of the stone and its flat surface warmed the skin on her chest.

*Of them, we are One.*

"Flex 4 out!" Jati said.

"...it!" Nisi finished the sentence and the noise and vibration stopped. She banked hard left and decelerated. The whir of the flexers diminished like a symphony's final note in a decrescendo. The Dodger coasted in the clear space of the backside of the moon, music blasting and pumping out a fast beat.

"Sake of the Arm, Nisi. Shut that noise off," Jati said.

The music cut off. Ailo opened her eyes. JeJeto's arms were still up on the bars. They exhaled and let go of their grip. General Hirok did the same. Ailo pried her fingers from the bars and wiped her sweaty palms on the legs of her suit.

"Yelo ahead," Nisi said.

Out the cockpit window, shadowy dimples pocked the surface of a darkened stony sphere. A thin band of light from Pincori accented the edges of the craters on its right edge.

Jati turned to the four of them. "Well, that was fun. Phase One complete."

Rence opened his eyes.

"Nice job, Nisi," JeJeto said.

"That was crap. Sorry, everyone," she said. "Dodger's pretty banged up, General." Nisi turned to Hirok.

"I'll take it over being dead, thank you," he said.

Ailo didn't want to think about what the pod flight through Kusk would be like. This had almost killed them.

"We're flying *with* the storm going down to Garassit," Rence whispered in her ear. "Not against it. And the system

I've installed on that pod is way better than this one." He smiled. "It'll be much easier."

Ailo touched the lucky Rim wedge inside the pocket on her thigh. She hoped so.

"Alright, Nisi," Jati said. "Take us down."

# TWENTY-NINE

"Creepy," Nisi said.

Ailo leaned a hand on the dashboard and peered out.

Yelo looked like a graveyard for a lost space colony. She expected barren rock and dusty wasteland similar to T9. Instead, shadowy half-buried remains of human habitation projected from the moon's fissured surface. Portions of rusted equipment and debris littered the landscape like monuments to a tragic, abandoned history. The dim light beyond the lip of the horizon hid the details of the ghostly vista, and only around the Dodger's exterior lights did the view speak in legible vision. At the edge of the illuminated boundary, Ailo made out a bunker-style entrance to a sub-surface building.

"Check it out. Up there," Nisi pointed to the top of the window.

In the distance, Ceron was alive with fireworks. A myriad of intermittent sparkles dotted the planet as meteors struck the atmosphere and burned up on impact.

"Kusk's peaking," the soldier said. "Most of those don't get through. They incinerate on entry. But the bigger ones..." Nisi expelled a breath.

"O.K., let's move out," Jati said from the co-pilot seat. "Everyone gear up and we'll head back to the pod."

"How much longer for the Kusk shower?" Nisi asked.

"Forty hours," Hirok said. The general approached and stood behind Jati's chair.

"I hope you brought a book," Jati said.

"Very funny. I should be able to get up and out in a little under twenty-four hours, once the main surge passes."

Hirok peered out the cockpit window. "Can't say I am curious to go out there. I'll be happy to have some peace and quiet in the pod, and a bit of alone-time with what's coming next."

*I'll bet.*

"Ailo, go with Nisi and Rence back to the pod and get set up," Jati said. They leaned forward to address Nisi. "JJ and I are going to get the system linked and review one or two features with General Hirok."

"Can do, Cap."

Ailo turned. Rence opened the door for Ailo and Nisi.

"Good luck," Hirok said. "Fly well and aim true."

"Always," said Nisi as she rose from the pilot's seat and passed Ailo.

*Bastard.*

Ailo didn't move. She stared at the moonscape. Something wasn't right about leaving Hirok here all alone. Nisi grabbed her. "Come on, Ailo." She pulled her towards the doorway.

The hallway to the aft section of the Dodger followed the port side of the ship. Ailo knew from the preparations that the entire space to starboard was cargo.

"What's behind these walls?" Ailo rapped her knuckles on the gray surface.

"Beats me," the soldier said.

Rence, walking behind her, didn't respond.

"That's odd." Nisi stopped.

Ailo peeked around her husky frame. An airlock blocked the passage.

Nisi checked the system controls. "It's not active." She followed the seam from the ceiling to the floor, tracking the construction. "Rig job."

"It'll all make sense in a few minutes," Rence said. He pulled out a Goolit and peeled it. He caught Ailo's eye and smiled.

*More Goolits. That's all I need, on top of everything else.*

"Very funny, Ai."

"You know what this is all about?" Nisi flashed a suspicious eye at Rence.

"Head through, we need to move. Jati will explain."

Nisi clenched her fists. Veins rose like underwater rivers below the skin. "Better be a good explanation for all this," she said and opened the airlock.

The hallway continued another fifty feet, with everything on this side of the airlock secured for a zero-G environment.

"It's around the corner," Rence said.

Ailo followed Nisi. The soldier strode with determination toward the end of the hallway. Ailo had to double-time it to keep pace. Rence, not bothering to rush, peeled the Goolit and sucked on the fruit as he walked.

*Annoying.*

Ailo hit a wall of muscle, smacking into Nisi's backside as she came to a sudden halt.

"Miss me?"

Ailo knew that voice. She shifted around the brawny soldier and peered to the right. Boar leaned against a pod outfitted with a diorite shell in the cramped bay of the Dodger. The Hamut smirked.

"You didn't think I was going to let you fly us through Kusk, did you? After that performance getting us down here? You almost gave me a concussion."

"Did you find enlightenment in there?" Rence said through a mouthful of Goolit, reaching the corner.

"Enlightenment? No. Boredom, yes. I spent enough time with it for a lifetime. Call me crazy, but I'm looking forward to your company." The Hamut's eyes went to Nisi. "*Even yours.* It was *that* bad. The flight here, I mean."

The soldier's face battled between confusion and deduction.

"You going to speak, Nisi, or did you lose that function? Please tell me you lost that function." Boar smirked.

"Must be nice being the fall guy." She brushed past him and stomped up the steps into the pod.

Boar's mouth curled into an expression that said, 'As expected.'

"What's the plan?" Ailo asked.

Rence put a hand on her shoulder, encouraging her up the steps. "Inside."

Ailo did a double-take. "There's another pod?" An identical shuttle, strapped down securely, sat next to this one.

"Come on," Rence said and encouraged her to get on board.

Ailo walked up and into the black, sparkling shuttle. Nisi bustled about the passenger section, pulling out equipment and dividing it up into individual portions behind the cockpit, while muttering expletives under her breath.

"Take this." A muscled arm threw her a belt pack. "Open it up."

Ailo undid the fastener. A small metal cylinder with a mouthpiece lay secured in protective foam. A sleek, silver stem, sat snug in the soft material next to it. Narrow and long, it reminded her of a miniature tripod leg. Ailo pulled it free and examined it, twirling it in her hand.

"Know what that is?" Nisi asked.

"No."

"Tusolo," the soldier threw him an identical pack.

"These are aquatic kits. PA issue. The copper mini-canister with the mouthpiece is emergency O2. There's ten minutes in it. If you end up submerged or need to swim underwater you can use it. Stick that behind your lips, in front of your teeth. Exhale with force to break the seal to start it working."

"I can't swim," Ailo said.

"What?" Nisi stretched to her full height under the overhead compartment and banged her head. "Ouch! Sake of the..." She rubbed her crown through the black curls. "How are you going to get to shore when we're down?"

"Aren't we using the internal system on the Lorassian's surface?" Boar asked, entering the pod and walking to the cockpit. "I thought we were rowing to shore?"

"Yeah," Nisi said, "but when we get close we're gonna have to..."

Ailo's heart thumped. Her two fingers and thumb holding the metal tube shook.

Nisi's eyes went to her hand. "Hold on, Ailo." The soldier reached a tattooed arm up to the overhead compartment and pulled down a vest. "Put this on. Over your suit. It'll keep you afloat. No matter what, if you end up in the drink, you won't sink."

"The drink?"

"The water." Nisi knelt. "Listen, you keep cool if that happens. Chill, O.K.? You expend a lot of energy in water if you panic. I'll come to you and pull you with me."

Ailo slipped the vest over her shoulders and buckled it together on her chest. "What is this?" She held up the thin silver stick.

"That's a booster," Nisi said standing back up to grab something from the compartment. "Let's hope you don't need it. Put it back where it was."

"A booster?"

"Emergency chemical hit," Boar said from the cockpit, fiddling with pre-flight buttons. "The side with the green dot goes into your skin. Anywhere will work. Only use it if you feel like you'll die because when it wears off, you'll feel like you're going to die."

"You won't need it, Ailo. You're young and tough." Nisi's said. "Sibling soldiers, you and me. We're ass-kickers, right?" The soldier held out her fist.

Ailo smiled. Nisi's sibling? She bumped her fist to the soldier's large knuckles and sat down along the wall. She put away the booster and attached the kit to her suit at the waist.

"O.K. people let's roll." Jati barreled up and into the pod with JeJeto on their heels. "Let's hope there's a signal from here to the palace. I want hard evidence on top of whatever is waiting for us in Garassit." Jati clapped their hands to emphasize the need for haste. "JeJeto, help Nisi with the rest of the equipment. Rence, get the remote system for Boar set up. The sooner we get that airlock sealed and get out of this ship the better. If Hirok comes back here, we're made."

No one moved.

Jati turned around. JeJeto's sandy beige finger pointed at Boar.

"Oh, right. I forgot," Jati said and directed their attention to the Hamut. "Did you enjoy your silent retreat?"

"I was telling Nisi, I communed with the God of Boredom."

The general pulled JeJeto over to where Ailo, Rence, and Nisi stood in the passenger area. "I apologize to you two," they gestured at Nisi and JeJeto. "This was delicate. It had to be done thoroughly and with prudence. I wasn't sure if there was anyone else on the *Carmora* who might…"

"Us? You couldn't trust us? Are you serious?" Nisi could have been kicking teeno, or arguing over someone *not* kicking teeno, at the cantina on Heroon.

Jati waved a hand. "Lower your voice. The sooner we're on our way the better, well… the sooner the other pod is on its way…"

"Sake of the Arm, what are you talking about?" Nisi said. "And we sat through a eulogy? I cried for that Hamut bastard…." She shot a veined arm in Boar's direction without taking her eyes off of Jati.

"You cried?" Boar turned around in the pilot seat. He had on the same white goggles from when they'd escaped Cesix station. "I'm touched."

"You Gor Hunter! I'll…"

"Hey," Jati grabbed her arm. They pulled JeJeto over with the other. "We are on the job. It's op time. Now listen, and *be quiet*. Here's the score: there are two pods back here. The other one has the same diorite exterior."

"Two pods?" JeJeto remembered how to speak.

"Yes, two pods," Jati said. "We're going to use the same remote control system we used to get out of Cesix station." Jati pointed at Boar, who waved. Wearing the goggles, the Hamut held the box with the control stick up for everyone to see.

*Remote control...*

"Rence rigged the com system on the Dodger." Jati turned to Tusolo. "Nice job, by the way. I didn't get a chance to thank you for that."

Tusolo nodded.

"So far as Hirok is concerned, he'll be hearing 'us' in that pod. But we're staying *right here*." Jati pointed at the floor.

Nisi's eyes narrowed in a priceless grin.

"That's the million credit look I was waiting for," Jati said and winked.

Nisi punched the general's arm. "Nice, Cap. Real smooth." She turned to JeJeto. "You on it, JJ?"

JeJeto shook their head. "No clue."

"We're going remote with that pod," Nisi said. "He'll fly it," she pointed at Boar, "and we'll all be here. When it gets down, whatever trap Hirok's got planned is going to come up empty."

"And," Jati added, "I'm hoping once he thinks we're away from Yelo he'll try and make contact with the palace to confirm."

"We'll be recording in the Dodger cockpit if he does," Rence added. "I set up that as well."

"So that's what you were doing," JeJeto said. "I couldn't figure it out."

Rence nodded.

"If we are lucky enough to get a conversation on record, we're going to have an 'accident' and crash into the Lorassian." Jati's head swung to Boar, their ponytail flapped up and around. "Sorry, old tot. Your legendary flying skills may end in tragedy."

Boar raised his hand and gave a thumbs-up. "If we pull this off we can reverse that narrative. Nothing better than re-writing history."

"Either way, whether we 'crash,' they shoot us down, or intercept us on the Lorassian and open an empty pod, we're going to march back into the cockpit and confront Hirok,"

Jati said. "We restrain him and leave in this pod. If we get a recording, Rence will set it to ping to the fleet after Kusk clears. That should give the red light to Galank and the others. Hirok's armada will be dead in the water. Stunned. My hope is we get the shield down and end this. But if not, I'm sure enough that Galank will back off."

"Oooooooo," JeJeto whooped. "I get it now." They high-fived Nisi.

"And we can drop in with no one expecting us," Nisi said.

"They'll be focused on the fleet. *And* feeling quite overconfident." Jati did a little dance. Their green eyes sparkled at Ailo. "How's that for strategy?"

Ailo couldn't keep it all straight. "Well, um... I..."

Jati slapped her on the shoulder. "Watch, learn, and enjoy the ride, Firecracker."

It wasn't the ride she was worried about. Her stomach swirled, alive with jitters.

"What?" Jati asked, turning their head from Ailo to Nisi.

"She can't swim, Cap." Nisi raised an eyebrow and pointed at Ailo's vest.

"You can't swim?"

Ailo shook her head. Her eyes went to the floor.

"Weak point," Jati said. "Own it. We'll work on it when we're back on Heroon. Deal?"

Ailo smiled. "Deal."

The low hum of an engine filled the pod.

"Boar, not yet," Jati said. "We have to get the other pod up and out first."

"Wasn't me, boss."

Nisi pushed past Ailo to the stairs. She stuck out her head in the doorway. The tattoos on her biceps contorted, animating, as brawny arms held her weight. "It's not the other pod," she said. Her head popped back inside. "Those are flex-burners firing up. It's the Dodger."

Ailo's stomach dropped to her feet. Her body sensed it before her brain knew it. The Dodger lifted up and away from the moon. Jati, Boar, Nisi, and JeJeto all had enough military experience to react without delay. She and Rence were slower and stared, confused.

Processing the unexpected departure was different matter. Ailo got the sense that no one, especially Jati, understood the situation.

"What's he doing?" Boar said, pulling off the remote goggles.

"He's on to us," Jati said. "Beyond that, I'm not sure." Jati turned to Tusolo. "Rence, get us online. I want to talk to him."

The scientist sat down in the co-pilot seat and worked a set of controls. "I can pull up a two-way comm link with the cockpit."

The Dodger banked right. Ailo tipped toward the seats in the pod below the overhead compartment. She put an arm down to steady herself.

"Everyone strap in," Jati said. "Nisi and JeJeto, I want you to…"

"Airlock is venting! He's putting us in a vacuum." Boar pointed at an indicator light on the wall of the bay. "Close the door."

Nisi lunged past Ailo and dove for the door. Rence swiveled around from the co-pilot seat to reach it. The same *whoosh* she had heard on Cesix station echoed down the shuttle bay. Ailo's ears popped. Pressure increased over her entire body in the suit. She went for her helmet.

Nisi's fist smashed the door control shut before Rence got there. The pod's atmospheric system worked at maximum, restoring the lost pressure and O2. Ailo's suit expanded like a balloon, filling with air, as the ship's computer restored a comfortable equilibrium. She put the helmet down next to her on the seat, relieved.

"Jati, we're patched through to Hirok," Rence said.

"Whenever you're ready."

The engines hummed louder. The Dodger accelerated.

Ailo closed her eyes and leaned her head back against the wall. Where was Hirok taking them? To fly in the middle of a dangerous meteor shower meant madness. Was he as experienced a pilot as Boar? Or Nisi?

"He's going to kill us," JeJeto said. "Before he gets to carry out whatever it is he wants to do with us."

"Which is kill us, most likely. Or, get us thrown in a cell to rot in Garassit," Nisi said.

"What your plan, Jati?" Boar asked.

"Not there yet," they said, "but we can't get out of here until we have that door open," they pointed across the bay. "And we're second in line behind the other pod."

Ailo forgot about the twin shuttle. They couldn't get around it. That meant three steps before their escape: opening the door, sending the first pod out, and flying the one they were in through the bay doors. Which were, at present, closed and inaccessible. And they needed to survive long enough to make an exit.

"Open those doors, Boar," Jati said.

*Why don't we just switch pods?*

The Hamut flicked the switch. Nothing happened. He rattled it back and forth. "Nothing. He's locked them from up front."

"Sake of the Arm!" Jati wiped a hand down their face. "Get your helmets on, both of you," Jati instructed Nisi and JeJeto. "Get out there and try to manually open that cargo door." Jati stepped in between Boar and Rence in the cockpit. "No one talks to Hirok but me."

*Boom!* An impact to the Dodger threw everyone around the cabin. Jati tipped and fell onto Boar. Nisi and JeJeto crashed into each other. The soldier managed to keep them both from falling by hugging JeJeto and grabbing a bar on the ceiling.

"Needed some love?" JeJeto said, their faces close. They went to kiss her in jest.

"In your dreams." She shoved them away. "Get your helmet on."

Ailo watched the two longtime friends. *So this is work banter?*

"Wait," Jati said, pushing off Boar. "I'll be a Gor hunter, I'm not thinking straight."

Ailo noticed sweat dripping from their brow.

"Hirok's got us trapped," they said.

"How?" Rence asked, putting on the helmet and securing it.

"Cap's right," Nisi said, "We can't open the pod."

Ailo, and everyone for that matter, now understood. Pods have no airlock. They were meant for in-atmosphere and in-bay docking. You can't transfer passengers in vacuum.

Nisi took off her helmet. "We could all suit up? Strap in and fly out in zero-gee?"

Rence shook his head. "The internal system's not built for it. And I don't know what the custom mechanics I put in would do. Plus, the temp drop is too risky. Power might go out."

"We'd lose our communication line if that happened," Jati said. "Right now we need that more than anything."

The familiar hum of the flex-burners rose in a fiery crescendo. The Dodger pitched and rolled as Hirok avoided a myriad of dangers from Kusk like a snake weaving through the grass.

"Cap, the Dodger's banged up pretty good," Nisi said. "That front fin is at sixty percent and there's a flex out off the tail. JJ's right. He's going to kill us. We gotta roll."

"Rence, give Boar your seat," Jati said, grabbing a headrest to keep from stumbling. "Get him up and running on the remote pod." The general waved a hand at the pilot chair where Boar sat. "Nisi, have a seat. I've got an idea." They winked at Ailo. "Hang in there, Firecracker. Plan C in action."

Everyone did as they were told, shuffling around one

another into position.

Plan C. Ailo remembered the conversation from the nav room on the *Carmora*. "Improvise something," Jati had said. Nisi backed them up by emphasizing the importance of going with the flow. Ailo was all for it, so long as they had enough time and didn't crash into a meteor first.

"JJ," Jati waved them over. "I need you in Boar's ear. Quietly, so Hirok can't hear you. Run him through the Ortor five-out."

JeJeto pulled off their helmet and smiled. "The ol' Loose Edge?"

Jati gave him a hand blaster as confirmation. "But this time no casualties, got it?"

"Right, Cap."

*Casualties?* Ailo didn't like any of this. And she had nothing to do.

The Dodger dove. Everyone grabbed hold of something.

"Sake of the Arm!" Nisi said. "When did he make us? And what tipped him off?"

"I don't know, let's find out." Jati gestured for Rence to open a line to the Dodger's cockpit. "Can you record this?"

Rence nodded. "Audio and visual. I'll bounce it through the holo on the dash, there." Tusolo indicated the small projection field between the two seats. "We can't ping it to the fleet unless we take back the Dodger. But I can save it on a drive."

"Good, we may need it as evidence," Jati said.

JeJeto leaned to the side of Boar in the co-pilot seat and whispered instructions in his ear. Boar wore the goggles and fiddled with the box, nodding as JeJeto explained a 'five-out.'

Through the openings between Jati's frame and limbs, Ailo made out portions of the blank, square of the holo-comm blipping to life on the dashboard. She leaned forward, stretching the safety straps to get a better view. The feed from the camera relayed a shot of the Dodger's cramped cabin and cockpit. A wide-angle capture in the top corner of the makeshift wall displayed the entire space. Rence must have installed the system when they constructed the temporary interior.

"Hirok, old tot," Jati said, "want to explain what's happening here?"

The PA general sat, piloting the Dodger. His head shifted back and forth between a readout on the dashboard and the view out the window. The steering bars gripped tight in his hands, he rotated left and right to navigate through Kusk. Everything about the way he worked the controls suggested a desperate struggle.

"I think you know, Jati." Hirok rammed the flex-thrusters forward. The Dodger surged. He banked hard and pulled back, sending the ship up at a steep angle.

Jati put a hand on the ceiling to stabilize themselves. "About your betrayal, Hirok? Yes, I do. How could you do this to me and to your fellow soldiers?"

Hirok shook his head. "You don't know what you're talking about, Jati. You've got your head in the idealist clouds, always have. It's a great inspiration, but a tired narrative. People are exhausted with your righteousness and unwillingness to compromise."

"So you're throwing it all away?" Jati asked.

Ailo's attention turned to Boar. He fiddled with the contraption on his lap. Out the cockpit window, pod lights projected off a wall of the cargo hold as the other shuttle fired up.

"This little ruse of yours is over Jati. Don't think I don't know what's been going on." A miniature Hirok in holo-form jerked the steering controls around, avoiding obstructions from Kusk. "You and that vagabond youth working together to dupe me with your fake insignia. And your trap to leave me here. I'm smarter than you think."

*Insignia?* Hirok knew about their switch?

"What a shame. And after all these years." Jati waved at JeJeto, who whispered in Boar's ear. The Hamut nodded.

"Galank was right, Jati. You are a fool. So high in the sky that you miss the view on the ground."

*What does that mean?*

The other pod, covered in diorite like a glittering black ship of doom, broke into the view out the cockpit window. It hovered a few feet off the floor of the bay. Boar used the remote system to rotate it. The whir of its boosters sent a sonic wave against the shell of their pod.

Ailo's hand went to her chest. She pushed on the pendant under her suit. Diorite was such a...

*Smack!* The Dodger veered and pitched. *Pang!*

"Whoa," Boar leaned back and forth, stabilizing the other pod. He barely caught it before it hit their own.

The others were right. Hirok's limited experience would kill them. They'd taken more hits in these few minutes than the entire run to Yelo.

"Hirok, you don't have the skill to make it through this alive," Jati said.

Hirok laughed and shook his head.

"Where are we going?"

"To Garassit, of course."

Ailo watched Nisi. She sat like a fuse at the edge of the powder keg. Helpless and unable to scream was not a good look on the soldier.

"How could you turn on us, Hirok?"

"Turn on *you*? You're the one who turned on us, on *me*, when you veered from our cause to save a child! A nobody from the Outer Rim. You threw away victory on Guinde-4, a chance to end the Tide War, because of your moral high ground. You'll never win, Jati. You can't win and keep your ideals. It's why we're where we are, where we've been for *years*. I'm done with it!" Hirok jerked the steering column back and forth as he spoke. "We could have had glory, fame, and credits to last a lifetime. The Arm would've been free, with a new future on the horizon. But you threw it away for an orphan whose pity broke your heart. And where did it get you? Where did it get all of us? With our control eroding... Guinde-4 was our last chance."

Even through the holo, Ailo sensed Hirok's rage. She

wiped a tear from her eye. This *was* about her.

"You did enough damage before that, Hirok."

The general shook his head in disdain. "You preach like a philosopher from the First Span, standing proudly on a Cantinool pedestal, like some sage of old. You still can't clear the fog from your ethical glasses."

"You're right, Hirok. There's a greedy traitor clouding my vision."

"I'm just a soldier tired of fighting a losing battle." Hirok shook his head in disgust. "You care so much for the weak that the need for power is lost on you."

Jati turned. Ailo felt their eyes on her and tried to hide her shame and guilt. She wiped her cheek. The warrior approached. Kneeling so they were eye-to-eye, the general stroked a hand through her hair.

"You took my child, Hirok?" Jati's eyes narrowed.

Ailo dove inside the green sea of their irises. A landscape of shimmering obsidian shards danced around her floating body as she stood on the black plane of Jati's pupil. Emotions swirled around her as unseen currents. Ailo wasn't sure, but something told her this wasn't the first time Jati's heart had broken from familial loss.

"After what happened to my love?" Jati said. "You saw my pain, Hirok. You witnessed my anguish. And yet, still you could push the blade deeper into my already broken heart?"

Ailo returned to the pod and stared at the chiseled slabs of flaxen stone cheeks.

"You dare take away all I had left?" Jati said, their eyes pooling.

*Their love? Jati's partner is dead. They never spoke of anyone.*

"Arira is fine," Hirok said, watching the screen and flying.

Jati's eyes strengthened and they signaled to Nisi. She hit a button and the cockpit window vanished behind a heat shield. Jati double-checked Ailo's chest straps. They ran a hand over her cheek. Massive, course knuckles grazed her soft, skin. She grabbed their hand. They smiled.

"And you *are* right," the general stood to their full height. "I'm faulted to fail. By my code. By my oath. I will even fail at pride. But I don't make it this way; the world forces it on me."

Nisi swung around, fury in her eyes. Ailo's heart raged with her soldier sibling. How could Jati say that? The words were spoken as a warrior, that she knew. But there had to be a line. All warriors had one. They'd said so. Where was their line?

*Gerib, they must have a line. How can they say that?*
"Only Jati knows, Ai. As they said, it's their path alone."
*No, there's a line. This is over it.*
"Maybe it's so far from where we are that we can't see it."
*What does that mean?*
"Remember what Galank said? About idealists?"
'They never survive reality.'

Ailo closed her eyes to still the growing rage. She went back to the last moments at the Assembly meeting.

'They fall to save the innocent.'

That didn't make any sense.

"So long as Arira is safe when this is over." Jati signaled to JeJeto.

"Arira?" Hirok said, "I told you, she's fine. Your eyes are open but you still don't see, Jati. How ironic that..."

*Boom!* An explosion outside their shuttle sent them rocking to the left. The pod impacted the wall of the Dodger with a loud crash. Ailo held on for her life. Jati's hands were on the grip bars over their head. Their feet flew off the ground and swung out in the air before coming back to rest. Crackling, like a pot melting on a stove, crawled over the pod's exterior.

A whoosh blew Ailo's hair into her face. Anything not tied down whirled around in the cabin. Ailo knew the feeling: the cold vacuum of space. There was a hole in the pod.

"Breach! Aft!" Nisi screamed. The cockpit shield retracted. Ailo's mouth dropped open. JeJeto bolted past her, helmet in hand, toward the back as the venting system struggled to fight the rising vacuum.

"It's bad, Cap!" Nisi said.

The pod rested on a steep angle, tilting up against the wall of the bay. Out the angled window, a massive hole had been blown in the side of the Dodger where the retractable doors stood. Through the opening, the glitter of meteor dust whizzed past the ship.

The pressure slackened. Ailo's chest loosened.

"JJ's got us sealed!" Nisi said. "I don't know how but we're ninety-eight percent." Her eyes scanned a readout. "We can sustain a solid two hours with our passenger count." She pumped a fist. "Nice work JJ!"

"Com's out," Rence said. "We lost Hirok but I've still got a visual."

"Hit it, Boar," Jati said.

The Hamut moved the joystick. The other craft, streaked in soot with almost no more diorite veneer, shot out through the hole.

"Cross the bow so he'll catch sigh of the pod. That way he knows we're out."

*Out?* Then she remembered: two pods. Hirok didn't know about the remote piloting system.

Boar leaned and grunted, flying the remote ship. He shifted left and right, bobbing the seat. "There's too much debris. I can't hold it ..."

"Just a little longer," Jati said. "Get out in front."

"Yo JJ, Canti-ales on me," Nisi yelled to the back.

There was no response.

"I think they're outside," Rence said from behind Boar's seat.

"What?" Nisi stood up. She leaned forward and peered out the cockpit window towards the ship's stern. The whites of her eyes glowed as she strained to look back. "Oh no, we're wedged. They're out there. JJ's EVA."

"How?" Rence asked.

"They must have gone out the breach to plug it," Jati

said.

"Hirok's got me locked!" Boar said. The bursts of a laser weapon firing shook the ship. A shower of orange flame and sparks ran past the opening where the pod had exited.

Boar threw off the goggles. "We're gone."

"Nice work," Jati said.

The Dodger bucked and rattled. The hissing outside grew louder. "We have to get out of here," Rence said, his eye on the bay. "The Dodger is going to hold!" He pointed to the holo next to Boar. "I think Hirok knows it, too. Look!"

Hirok rose from the pilot's chair, pushing a series of controls on the cockpit dashboard.

"He's setting it to auto," Nisi said. She looked toward the window. "JJ's prying something loose."

"Hirok's sending a message out," Rence said, pointing at the holo.

"Good, he thinks we're dead," Jati said. "He's suiting up. There must be an emergency jettison unit."

"We gotta go, Cap" Nisi said.

"Help JJ. Hit the thrusters," Boar said. "Get us off it."

"But they're out there," Nisi said.

"Fire them up on low, they'll get the message," Jati said.

Nisi kicked on the pod's boosters. Ailo exhaled with relief at the buzz of the engines igniting. She loosened her straps and leaned forward to peer out the window. Out the blasted side of the wounded Dodger, Ceron stood through the meteor haze in the distance. The sphere was alight with flashes as Kusk's impacts hit the planet's atmosphere.

"Watch out, JJ," Nisi said and pushed the engines, knowing he couldn't hear her warning. The pod bucked and struggled but didn't budge. "Sake of the Arm, what's got us wedged?"

JeJeto appeared in front of them, moving in slow motion in the vacuum. They waved for Nisi to increase the thrust.

"Jati," Ailo tugged on their suit. They turned. "How is JeJeto going to get back in?"

Jati knelt. Their green eyes spoke volumes. They put

their hand on her shoulder and held her gaze in earnest.

"No." She shook her head.

Jati nodded.

She wiped tears from her cheeks. Did Nisi realize? She couldn't have, otherwise, she wouldn't be acting this way.

The general leaned into her ear.

"There comes a time for all who fight to face a choice, except for those lucky enough to live to retirement. For the rest, it either happens against your will, or your life is taken doing the job. But for those few given the privilege to have the choice, the honorable ones do what is right."

"Why?"

"Because their heart leads them. That's why I still believe in the world. Because of people like JeJeto."

The pod bucked and started. "Come on!" Nisi yelled at the pod, surging the thrusters. "Gor hunter, move!"

*Pang!* An impact tore into the side of the Dodger. It streaked along the wall next to the blown-out section, a trail of metal and sparks filled the bay with smoke. A thundering crack opened a fissure overhead. Debris fell around them.

"We're loose!" Nisi said. The pod rose off the tarmac and hovered a few feet off the ground, boosters revving.

"The Dodger's coming apart," Boar said. "And we've got a problem."

Ailo searched through the wafting smoke. A portion cleared and the problem appeared: a collapsed steel beam blocked the hole out into space.

JeJeto propelled themself across the bay, their jet pack burners firing. They aimed at the beam blocking the exit.

"JJ get back here!" Nisi brought the pod closer and aimed it out into space, ready to go. The fissure overhead split wider.

"We gotta go," Boar said.

"Not yet," Jati said. "We can't fit through there. It won't be heavy out there. So long as it's not stuck, JJ can move the beam and we can make it."

"We're dead in here in less than a minute," Boar said,

peering towards the bay's ceiling.

JeJeto strapped a cable around the beam and hooked it to their suit. They hit the thrusters. The wire tightened and bounced them back. It was no use. The beam wouldn't budge.

"There's no time," Boar said. "We have to blast it."

"No!" Nisi said.

"Nisi," Jati said and walked up. "Get up."

"No!"

"Look, kiddo," Jati said, pointing.

JeJeto hovered in front of the beam, blocking the exit. A smile grew on their face in the helmet. They pumped a gloved fist to their chest and made a gesture like they were smoking 'nool.

Nisi's hand hovered an inch over the firing button. Her fingers shook as if filled with an electric current. She fought a battle between a soldier and a friend.

"I can't..."

Ailo watched a familiar paw-like hand cover the soldier's.

"Together?" Jati whispered, their mouth buried in the dark curls by Nisi's ear.

Her head rose and fell. Once.

Ailo's eyes burned into the skin on Jati's palm. Every pore, every hatch of every scar, spoke of earlier wounds. This would be one more, but it wouldn't show on the veteran's outside. How many more internal scars did Jati hold, hidden from view?

With the grace and gentleness of an exhale, the general eased their hand down.

The laser fired. JeJeto and the beam incinerated. Jati's hand lay over Nisi's, flat on the button on the dashboard.

"Punch it, Boar," Jati said.

The Hamut slammed the throttle forward from the co-pilot seat. Debris and smoke flew past. They blew out the hole into space. Jati let go of Nisi's hand. She took control and banked left at a hard angle. The Dodger split in two next to them, spewing red and yellow sparks outward in a massive explosion. She veered back right to avoid the force.

"Look!" Boar pointed from the co-pilot seat.

Ailo followed his finger and caught a silver oblong craft no larger than a coffin track past them on a course toward Ceron's atmosphere.

"It's Hirok!" the Hamut said.

"Nisi don't..."

The soldier fired before Jati could finish their sentence. The single-person unit exploded in a mass of orange and green light.

"Put me in jeekoo stone, if you want." Nisi wiped a forearm across her eyes. "I don't care."

# THIRTY

Ailo had never lost a friend. She'd never had one to lose. The street kids on T9 were nothing more than a rogue band of desperados. They worked together and shared what they stole. But when it came down to it, they were all out for themselves. In a bind, if it was you or another street kid, they'd leave you behind and let you take the fall.

She didn't blame them. When someone got nipped, no one wept. No one lost sleep. They either got sloppy, greedy, or drew a bad card. You moved on. Someone else always came along to fill their spot. T9 had no shortage of underworld youths.

But this troupe wasn't forced together out of desperation and survival. They were here because they wanted to be here, for whatever reasons they each had. And that made them a team. Jati stood at the center of the circle, the glue binding them. And now a piece of the ring had snapped off.

Did JeJeto count as a friend? She'd like to think so. Regardless, the mechanic was part of their unit and their loss hurt. She couldn't imagine what it must be like for Nisi.

Ailo thought of the hug minutes earlier and their playful attempt to kiss their longtime friend and military buddy. The gap-toothed smile in the training room, ever-present in her mind.

A tear ran down her cheek. She brushed it away with the back of her hand. Kusk glittered out the window, threatening a second time. Grieving would have to wait.

"Nisi, switch seats with Boar," Jati said and placed a hand on the soldier's shoulder.

Ailo expected her to resist and put up a fight. It was Nisi's nature to let pride shine. Instead, she got up without a word. Boar, with solemnity, shifted over in silence. Nisi took the co-pilot seat.

Ailo turned and caught Rence's eyes on her. He sat, hands clasped together, hunched forward. He nodded to her in silent communication, his bushy hair and goatee bobbing up and down. It read as disaffected sympathy. Why was he here?

His hand stroked his beard.

What was in this for him? Did he owe a debt to Jati? Who was to say what Tusolo wanted, what the Radicals desired before they all disappeared? Jati claimed they shared a belief in freedom, but how far did that definition extend in the hands of a group that turned its back on everyone in the Arm?

Her eyes narrowed. Rence leaned back, retreating into himself as he had on the run to Yelo. The pod swerved hard right to avoid an object and she caught herself from tipping over with a hand on the seat.

"We've got an hour and fifty minutes of pressurization," Nisi said, from the co-pilot seat. Jati, who had gone aft, now returned.

"JJ did a quick seal job from the outside," they said. "It's solid work and saved us." The team chose silence as thanks and acknowledgment of their sacrifice. "My concern is if it will hold through the burn."

"Let's hope so," Boar said, fighting a way around an object. "Rence, get up here."

Tusolo opened his eyes and rose.

"I've got a course for entry." Boar worked the pod left and right, navigating around debris as they headed toward the planet.

Ailo leaned forward. Ceron loomed ahead. They were close enough that it filled half of the view out the window. One side of the sphere lay in darkness. As the night crept across the planet, she made out a massive landmass in the southern hemisphere. A short way over the equator, the continent met a sea that extended to a polar cap at the northern apex. Fireworks erupted across the atmospheric shell as Kusk slammed into the layers of gases at the exo-line.

"Jati," Boar indicated the holo-screen to his right, the one that minutes earlier had relayed the drama with Hirok. Three-dimensional diorite clusters marked Kusk's spread surrounding a small icon of their pod. "It's about to get hairy. And it'll stay dense through the burn."

"He's asking for the guidance system," Nisi said and leaned her head of black curls against the headrest, staring at the controls overhead. "Put it on so he doesn't have to grovel."

Rence reached up and pushed a button over the Hamut. A dropbox panel popped out with a set of buttons and a headset. Tusolo handed him the headgear. "Activating now," Tusolo said, programming a sequence on the mini-board above the pilot.

"Not seeing anything." Boar's head went left and right.

*Ping!* A small object bounced off the pod.

"Watch it!" Nisi said, gripping the dashboard. "Another one, starboard," she pointed.

"It's not on," Boar ripped off the goggles and veered the pod in an evasive maneuver.

Rence snatched the headgear from the Hamut and fiddled with its controls. Nisi turned to Jati, who waved her to calm down.

"Rence," Jati said, "Is it...?"

"I'm trying damn it!" Tusolo pushed a sequence of colored buttons. He leaned over Nisi and peered at the nose of the pod. "We've got a problem." He turned to Jati. "The sensor whiskers melted away when we blew the door."

"Boar, you have to do this yourself," Jati said. "It's all on you. Sorry."

"No," Nisi said. She ran her hands over her eyes to clear them of the memory of JeJeto. "We'll do it together. I'll spot you and call from the window, and the holo... cool?"

Jati's face shifted. Ailo caught a subtle twitch of the crow's feet around their eyes. Like a parent watching two children casting aside their usual bickering to work together, Jati acknowledged the rare moment of unity between the two team members. The general nodded and folded their arms.

"For JJ," Nisi added, her eyes blazing and focused out the pod window. Ailo had a flash of the cantina on Heroon. Nisi's temperament ranged to extremes, but whether raging in anger or lamenting in sorrow, the intensity never wavered. She was a force, no matter the particular emotional state.

Jati smiled and Boar nodded. "For JJ," the Hamut said.

A thought formed in Ailo's mind. Two separate links of a philosophical chain came together. The ring around Jati was recast, smaller but a full circle, once again.

*Gerib, I think I understand it.*

"Understand what?"

*The path. And the code...* Ailo stood on the edge of a paradox. Acceptance was close. Her resolution visible, but not yet within her grasp. The Way wasn't going to give her a path. It unrolled a map of others' trails, preparing her by example. But she would need to forge her own.

*There's a lesson here, Gerib. An important one.*

"What's our O2 status?" Jati asked.

"Hour and twenty," Nisi said, eyes on the readout.

"Time to the surface?"

"Without incident, forty minutes."

*Without incident.* That didn't sit well.

Rence sat back down and latched himself in across from Ailo.

"You better strap in soon too, Cap," Nisi said. "It's showtime."



"What is that?" Ailo pointed at the small case.

Rence had been inspecting it for the last few minutes as the pod barreled toward the planet. His hands kept it hidden from the rest of the crew and he handled it as if it were precious cargo.

Green eyes peered over the top of the small box. "A memento from Cesix station," he said and flipped the lid shut with a snap. "I intend to release it once we are on the planet."

So it was alive, whatever it was.

"To set it free?"

Rence shook his head. "To set *us* free. By taking back power taken from me."

"So it has to do with the Core?"

"Yes and no."

Tusolo's strangeness never ceased. At times, he was a historical well bubbling with information about Ailo's past and the beliefs of the Radicals. Others, such as now, he acted like he was scheming. Or was it that he knew more than the rest of the Arm?

*Maybe he does.*

"Don't worry about the Core. That'll be easy," Tusolo said. "Now that I have nothing else, it will be a pleasure to return to the world of disappointment and make my own contribution to those I despise." He leaned forward and spoke more softly. "If I find what else I'm hoping is there, you of all people will be pleased." The scientist smiled. "That's where this little treasure will be of help." He slid the small box into a pocket on his suit.

The Dodger bucked and bounced its way through Kusk. Nisi called out readings to Boar, her voice intense and urgent. The Hamut maneuvered the ship in response to her information, doing his best to keep them all alive.

Jati came aft and sat. Their hulking frame pushed into Ailo's side, but across the aisle, the space next to Tusolo was a screaming void. Ailo stared at the empty seat.

*Now we're five.*

"Watch it! Starboard, point eight," Nisi said.

"I'm trying, Sake of the Arm!" Boar answered.

*Pang!* The pod reeled to port from an impact.

"We can't take too many more of those. If something

hits the wrong spot, we're toast," Nisi said.

"I know. You think this is easy?"

Why didn't Jati intervene? The bickering rivaled their best arguments on the *Carmora*.

"There," Nisi pointed.

Boar shifted the pod, dexterously maneuvering it through a set of three objects barreling toward the planet. "That was nothing, you think I didn't see it?" he said, acting nonchalant.

Now Ailo understood: this dynamic worked. Jati let it be because Nisi and Boar were better off challenging and fighting one another to get this done. It was their language. If it kept them alive, Ailo would happily tolerate it. Boar's piloting skills had to be good if Nisi kept her envy in check.

Ailo's eyes shot to the empty seat next to Rence. She missed JeJeto. They were always around, taken for granted. They never presented themselves as essential to the mission, like Nisi or Boar, but they were. Teams had hierarchies like families, both in leadership and personality. JeJeto felt like the middle child who never got the spotlight but was the glue that kept the siblings together. Without them, polarities and extremes intensified. And lead to...

"Exo-line approaching, Cap." Nisi worked the grid, spotting visuals out the window. "Boar, there's a cluster..."

"I see it, I see it. Thinking down and left, ten degrees?"

"Try it," Nisi said.

The Hamut adjusted their trajectory. The view out the cockpit shifted from a barrage of meteors to a bursting curtain of orange lights as the debris from Kusk burned up in the approaching atmosphere.

"Here we go," Nisi said. "Sit tight, everyone."

"This was the worst part of being on the front lines in the Patent War," Jati said. "We'd come in low over the rainforest on Heroon..."

The world outside the pod shifted to a fiery rage as they hit the atmosphere line. The floor and seat rattled. Ailo's body bounced up and down with the steady rhythm of rain pattering a roof.

"When we crossed over into the war zone, the Hamuts would fire potshots."

"Getting hot," Boar said, pushing buttons and pulling handles.

"I'm watching it," Nisi said. "Temp is rising too fast."

"You could be the best Talon Caster fighter in the Arm. Or, the best shot with a Spirex Displacer. It didn't matter for those few minutes." Jati's warm breath filled her ear, the shaking of the pod giving it a staccato edge.

"How much more? We can't take this!" Nisi's veined arms stretched over the dashboard. She peered out into the atmospheric inferno.

The pod groaned. Ailo's ears popped. Pressure pushed on her chest.

"Thirty seconds," Boar said. "Come on, baby. Hold together!"

"You might be able to evade anyone on the ground in combat, but until you dropped in you were helpless. Like this," Jati said.

*Is this supposed to be helping?*

"So you had to let go," they said. "Go with the flow and bow before Fate."

Ailo turned to Jati. The general drew a deep breath and gestured, indicating that Ailo should do likewise. Nisi yelled at Boar. Boar shouted at Nisi. All background noise, like static on a cut broadcast. Her body sagged. The present turned vivid like a volume dial turned up to maximum. She expected it to fall away, that an exit from the crisis would be offered. On the contrary, she came *more alive*.

Where she was, what she was doing, and who she was with, registered with an intensity and lucidity more powerful than she had ever known. There was only the *now*. No past. No future.

"You feel it, don't you?" Jati smiled.

She nodded.

"Now you have your feet. All that remains is to find the

path," they said. "Then you will know where to step."

*I don't have any words for this. It's a new language, Gerib.*

She waited. Nothing.

*Gerib?*

Clarity faded. It slipped away and the mundane reality of the everyday returned. With it came the terror of the present.

"Central engine failure!" Nisi shouted, her arms pushing and pulling on mechanisms. "The shell burned out."

Boar pulled out a set of foot pedals and slipped his feet into the controls.

"Too fast Boar, we're coming in too fast," Nisi said.

"Shifting angle," Boar steered them on a hard turn. "We're going to try and cut some speed. Try the crank, give me some pressure."

Nisi's tattooed muscles flexed as she pulled against the circular metal wheel to the side of the copilot seat. It remained obstinate. "Gor scum!" She tugged. "Negative, it's burnt. It's all burnt." Her fist slammed into the wall above the wheel, denting it. Her head of curls spun around. Brown eyes, intense with concern, targeted Jati. "Engine failure, Cap. Hydraulics on manual."

"Cabin pressure and O2?" Jati asked.

"Holding."

Nothing but darkness in the view out the window. They had hundreds of miles to drop to reach the planet. In the first hours of the night, it would be like space but with the horror of gravity.

"We lost radar," Boar said. "We're like Gor running through a line of Heroonese spears. If anything makes it through the burn on our trajectory..." The Hamut turned to Jati. "We're flying blind."

"Sake of the Arm!" Nisi said.

"I'm cutting speed, we can do this. Just need to..." Boar's legs kicked and pulled and his hands turned the wheel, swerving the pod in the sky across invisible air currents.

"Where are we in relation to the shield wall?" Jati said from the seat next to Ailo.

"No idea," Boar said.

"Can you do anything, Rence?" Jati asked.

Tusolo shook his head across the aisle. "Not without..."

*Boom!* The pod careened and a flame shot out from the controls next to Nisi, showering her with sparks. The lights flickered. Alarms rang. The cabin went dark except for a set of dim blue emergency lights. The shuttle wobbled and descended at a greater pitch.

"Hit to starboard! To the nav system." Nisi unclipped and bolted aft.

A rush of air filled the cabin. The shuttle's wobbling increased, like a spinning top losing speed.

Ailo closed her eyes to fight the motion, her stomach unhappy with the whirlpool.

"Damage report," Jati said.

A hand touched Ailo's leg. Gentle and relaxed, yet large, she knew it to be Jati's. With her eyes closed, she imagined they were sitting on Heroon enjoying Cantinool tea at a Gontook café.

"Bad. We're going down," Boar said.

Ailo's ears picked up the squeaking of the foot controls as the Hamut struggled to fly the pod. "I can see the city. The shield wall is close. If I can just..." The pod dove. "Nisi!"

"I know!" The soldier's voice came from aft.

Ailo opened her eyes.

Nisi staggered into the cabin, holding the walls and seats for support in the chaos. Rushing air blew her black curls in a frenzy. "I was trying to fix the rudder. No go."

"One minute to impact," Boar said. "Lorassian in sight."

*The water.*

Jati's forceful grip turned Ailo's chin. "Remember," they said in earnest. "The aqua kit is here." They smacked the pack on her waist.

The impact sent a jolt from her side to her brain.

*On my waist.*

Jati yanked open a pocket of Ailo's suit and withdrew a glow stick attached by a cable. They shook the stick. It filled with a beaming light. "This will help us find you."

Green eyes and flaxen cheeks glowed in the stick's yellow light; they appeared like an explorer in a cave holding a candle, ready to crawl through a dark passage.

"I'm scared." She didn't decide to say it. Something inside her took over and spoke the words. Water welled in her eyes.

"I know you are, Firecracker." Jati squeezed her two fingers and thumb. "Boar is the best pilot I've ever known. He will get us down."

Rence muttered something, eyes shut tight. The noise of rushing air rose as they descended closer to the ocean's surface. A high-pitched whine somewhere to aft joined the chorus. She closed her eyes to block it all out.

"Thirty seconds," Boar said.

"I got you, Ailo." She knew that voice. Ailo opened her eyes. Nisi knelt in the aisle. The soldier's brown eyes were inches from her own. "Don't panic. Relax and wait for me after we're down. The vest will keep you afloat." Nisi's high cheekbones and brow line spoke of a hidden nobility. She could be on a Cantinool column with that gaze. "I told you, we're sibling soldiers. I won't let you down." The soldier's fist gently punched her shoulder. She leaped forward and fastened into the co-pilot seat.

"Brace for impact," Boar said.

*I don't want to die, Gerib. It's not fair. I haven't had enough time. I'm starting to understand.*

*"It's not up to you. Like Jati said, let go."*

"Inhale and hold. Now!" Nisi said.

Ailo breathed in and filled her lungs. Rence mouthed the words, 'Of them, we are One.'

Splashing. A rush of bubbles. Silence.

Ailo opened her eyes to flashing red lights. The image that repeated between curtains of darkness showed the pod's cabin, split in half like a cracked eggshell. Debris floated, flickering into existence with each burst of crimson light in an underwater night. Her lungs burned, crying out for air. She reached her hand to her waist, groping for the aqua kit. It hit something solid. A wall?

Her fingers touched a cable. Two digits threaded its length and found the glow stick. She held it up to her face and screamed, sending bubbles to the surface.

Rence's face stared at her, nor more than a foot away, his brown hair waving in strands like the tentacles of an octopus.

Tusolo shoved a respirator canister into her mouth.

Air. It was all she wanted. She gulped it down. The harsh chill burned her throat but she didn't care. She wanted more.

Tusolo pulled it back and sucked on it. Taking the glow stick from her hand, he gave her the air tube again and lowered himself down towards her legs. She knew why. Something had her pinched along her belt line, wedging her in.

The remains of the cabin hovered sideways underwater. Every time the red lights flashed, the equilibrium in her mind confronted an alternative tilting scene. She and Rence were on the lower side of the pod, aiming into the deep. The cockpit appeared over and over as the red light flashed. The repetitive haunting illumination made the underwater world visible, the two seats showed no one there. Boar and Nisi were gone. Jati, too.

A mirage of orange streaks glimmered about fifteen feet overhead. The surface of the Lorassian Sea reflected the fireworks of Kusk. Tusolo reappeared, rising in front of her. He took a hit of air and made a hand signal that he would swim around and underneath the outside of the pod to come up and push her free. She nodded.

The scientist inhaled several deep breaths on the canister, his hair waving hypnotically in the current. He pulled the respirator from his lips and pushed it into her mouth. With a nod, he vanished into the darkness below.

If he pried her loose, then what? Would the life vest bring her to the surface? Ailo's hands went to her chest. Fingers touched the suit. She flitted them about, padding on her upper torso. Nothing. Same with her shoulders. Just a torn section of the vest remained on one side, wrapped around her left arm.

The light from Kusk dimmed. Before her eyes processed it, her body confirmed it. The pod was sinking into the Lorassian's black abyss.

Had Rence left her? She tugged and kicked her legs. One hit something that grabbed back.

*He's down there.*

A strong hand ripped into her shoulder. Nisi stared her in the face. Her breathing tube sent bubbles rising toward the fading surface.

One tug was all it took for Nisi to understand that she was stuck. Rence's hands worked on her trapped legs, out of sight below. She felt him pull and push over and over. Ailo strained her leg muscles to support his effort.

Nisi tightened her grip and tugged upwards towards the surface. A muffled grunt came through the water. Whatever was stuck at Ailo's waist broke off. She was free.

She went for the aquatic kit at her hip. Nothing. It must have torn off.

Nisi made for the surface, pulling her along.

*Rence.*

A hand latched onto her foot, desperation in the grip. It fought to hold Ailo back. Nisi turned, eyes wide, bubbles rising from her mouth. The soldier yanked harder. Rence climbed, hand by hand, up Ailo's leg like it was a rope. She had to get the canister to him. He needed air or he wouldn't make it!

Ailo pulled against Nisi and reached down with her hand. The solider vocalized through the respirator, angry, tugging against her.

*No! Wait!*

Ailo flailed against her hold.

Nisi tugged harder. Ailo put it together. The soldier thought Rence wanted to hold her down!

She shook her head at Nisi. *He needs air!* The respirator muffled the words.

The soldier's strength overpowered her resistance.

She had one option. *I'll have enough air to make it.* She took a deep, burning breath of O2, withdrew the respirator from her lips, and sent it sinking toward Rence. He struggled to climb up her leg, unaware.

*It's there!* She spoke in bubbles. Her finger jabbed down, over and over, pointing at the barely visible metal canister shimmering in the dark water. Rence followed her gesture. His eyes widened. He lunged for the small canister as it passed, releasing his grip on her leg. It danced past him, taunting his attempts to snatch it like a fish bobbing back and forth in a current.

Nisi pulled and Ailo rose through the water. Holding the remaining air in her lungs, she floated upward with dreaded grace.

The canister sank into the pitch. Rence, in a final gasp of desperation, reached a hand for Ailo's leg. He got her foot. His other arm stretched upward in an arc, his eyes wide with the last of his strength. It clasped onto her other leg.

He was going to make it!

The other arm swung out and up. She held out her hand for him as Nisi pulled her upward.

*Come on, grab it!*

Instead of clutching onto her, Tusolo's hand opened against hers. From palm to palm he passed something. She gripped it tight. Rence's fingers slipped away, the last set of pads dragging over the edge of her knuckles like a K-speeder sailing the contours of rolling hills. The small case.

Nisi, with a titanic effort, pulled her up toward the surface.

Ailo reversed her view as they rose. Through the blur

of dark water, Rence fell away into the Lorassian's depths. A hand, open and desperate, reached up. Darkness swallowed it, the deep closing its jaws around it. Tusolo vanished below.

Another lifeline to her mother, lost. Like the book that slipped from her fingers into the void of space, he drifted into oblivion.

Ailo broke the surface. Rolling swells splashed her face in the dark of night. Cool air, many degrees lower than the water, chilled her wet skin.

"Jati!" Nisi swung her head around. She spat water and wiped wet curls out of her face. Her strong arms held Ailo tight. "You good?" The soldier had her in a close hug.

Ailo drew in deep breaths of the cool air. "He's gone. Nisi... he's...."

The movement of Nisi's brawny legs kicking about under the water sent repeated currents past Ailo's lower body. She followed suit, moving her legs back and forth. It helped her stay up and increased her buoyancy.

"That bastard," Nisi said and punched the water, sending up a splash. She clutched Ailo with one arm. "I knew we couldn't trust him! What a Gor hunter."

"No. He needed air. He saved me. He freed my legs with you."

Nisi's head reared back. "What?"

"He's gone. My mother... why does this happen?"

"Why does what happen?" Before she could respond, Nisi's eyes went to her one hand. "What is that?"

She held up the case. "He gave it to me. Instead of..."

"What is it?"

"I don't know." A wave splashed their faces. The rippling surface glimmered with the reflection of shooting stars. Nisi's eyebrows furled. "Are you sure he saved you?"

"Yes. That was his canister... the one I was using," Ailo nodded in the direction of the underwater realm. "Mine tore off when we crashed."

Nisi gazed off over the night sea. Her expression remained suspicious. "Jati! Boar!" She called out over the waves.

"Nisi, are they O.K.?"

The soldier nodded. "We came up together. They're here some…"

"Nisi!" Jati's voice carried over the water.

Over a wave, Ailo caught a glimpse of a glow stick bouncing light off the surface of the sea.

"This way," Nisi called, "we're here."

"Did you get them?" Boar's voice.

The two appeared treading water and glided over with the next swell to within a few feet of Ailo and Nisi.

"One of them," Nisi said.

"You hurt, Ailo?" Jati asked as they reached them. Boar had blood running down his cheek from a cut on his forehead.

She shook her head.

"You want me to take her?" Boar asked Nisi.

"No, I got her. Rence didn't make it."

Jati's head shifted to Ailo. "What happened?"

She didn't answer. Jati's expression made clear they sensed her shock and hurt.

"She says he saved her," Nisi said.

Ailo couldn't find words. What was wrong? She'd told Nisi about it moments ago. Her mouth opened and she paused. "I… he…."

Jati ran both hands over their loose lavender hair as they trod water, slicking it down the back of their head. "Relax, Firecracker. I get it."

"Without him, we've got no way to down the shield. That means no way to get out of here with Arira," Boar said.

Ailo held up the case. "He gave me this, before…"

Boar's orange eyes, visible from Kusk's glimmer, went to Jati. They shrugged.

"I asked him what it was on the pod," Ailo said. "He said he wanted to release it when we were down."

"And? Did it have to do with the Core?" Jati asked.

"I think…Yes and no, he said."

"That doesn't make sense," Nisi said. "Cap, I don't trust..."

"That's what he said!" Ailo interrupted. She wouldn't let Nisi override what Rence had done for her. "It has something to do with taking back power. That was what he said. It was part of the plan, I know it."

"What is it?" Boar asked, treading water.

"Something valuable enough for Rence to die getting it into Ailo's hands," Jati said. "You have a secure place for that?"

Ailo checked her torn suit. She had a breast pocket that would fit it.

"Hold on to it," Jati said. They started swishing their hand around their chest while treading water, patting various pockets.

"Cap, what's wrong?" Nisi asked.

"Nothing, I just can't find my..." Jati's hand went in and out of the pockets on their suit, searching. After a moment they stopped and looked at Nisi and Ailo. "It's fine. Let's go."

"How far to shore, Boar?" Nisi asked. The soldier's arm held her tight and her legs kicked under the water.

"About a half-hour in this current. We're a quarter-mile or so from the edge of the shield wall. The electromagnetic curtain halts about fifty feet from the surface of the sea. We can swim right under it."

A crash nearby doused them with water. Nisi held Ailo tighter. "Hang on, Ailo." A large swell hurled them up and down as the impact wave passed. At the crest, she caught the glimmer of the distant lights of Garassit.

"The sooner we do that the better," Jati said. They swam in the direction of the lights.

"Do you hear that?" Boar said, treading water.

Nisi swished around in the direction indicated. "Jati, we've got company."

A set of faint lights skimmed the surface of the Lorassian. The craft dove and swept down and up about a half-mile from them, ducking under the shield curtain.

"We've got nowhere to go. They've got us," Nisi said. "Bastards."

"I've got an idea." Boar pushed up on a swell to gain height. "There's a scrap of the pod's shell floating over there. That way." The Hamut pointed past Ailo and Jati. "There might be enough diorite left to block an aerial scan."

Nisi swiveled around and kicked to raise Ailo in the water. A scrap of wreckage floated nearby. "It's too small for all of us."

"You three might fit," Boar said.

"So we're back to the original plan," Jati said. "Are you sure, Boar?"

"I can use my diplomatic status as protection. Unless they pick me off right away on a pass with a laser shot, they can't touch me. At best, I'll get deported. At the worst, I'll end up in a cell. Guess it's time to roll the dice."

"You'll do this for us?" Nisi said.

The Hamut smiled. "Gladly. And for JeJeto, too."

"I..." Nisi paused. "I..."

Boar pulled a hand from underwater and held it out, palm facing Nisi in a gesture of peace. "Save it for kartan. And I'm our best shot for this. They won't risk killing a Hamut diplomat. Not now. It'll send a message that will tighten the loosening screw of our commitment to fight for the PA. Go, while there's still time." Boar turned and swam the other way, his bloodied head bobbing in and out of view with the passing swells. "And save me when you save Arira!"

"Come on," Jati said. "They're almost here."

Ailo did her best to help Nisi by kicking her feet. A jagged piece of wreckage floated about twenty feet away.

"It's not big enough for all three of us," Ailo said.

"It will have to be," Jati said. "We have to try."

The buzz of an engine rose and fell with the waves. Another meteor impact sent water exploding into the night sky. Water rained down on the three of them.

"They won't want to stay out here long," Jati said. "This is all about luck. I hope you saved some up from teeno, kiddo."

The aircraft banked in the direction of Boar. The scanner beam lit up the surface of the sea. Cresting swells appeared like icing on a pastry at the Gontook café. This was nothing like the gliding ride over the ocean on the moonlit approach to Heroon in the *Carmora*.

The beam hit Boar and homed in, narrowing its scope. He waved, drawing their attention.

Between swells Ailo caught sight of Boar rising on a cable to the hovering craft.

"Boar's on board. Here comes the flyby scan before they head back," Jati said.

Nisi passed Ailo off to Jati and grabbed hold of the wreckage. "Diorite is mostly gone. I don't think this is going to work."

"Can you lift it?" Jati said.

The soldier's arms flexed as she shoulder-pressed the scrap. The edge of the shell resisted, the suction of the Lorassian obstinate. "Gor hunt...!" The seal broke and the edge lifted. Jati pulled Ailo under, holding her tight. It left no room for Nisi.

"I can't hold this up much more," Nisi said through gritted teeth.

"They're turning and heading this way," Jati said. "Nisi you need to get under here."

"But we'll be underwater... Ailo can't..." The soldier's arms were shaking.

Ailo knew what to do.

*It's the only way Gerib.*

"It's your choice, Ai."

*I have to do it. JeJeto and Rence, they did it too. I'm on the team.*

Ailo grabbed the unlit glow stick on Jati's suit with one hand and smacked it against her arm, illuminating it.

"Get under here!" Jati said to Nisi.

Ailo yanked the cable loose from Jati's suit so the stick broke free. "You two will fit," she said. *I'm a ghost.*

She pushed off Jati and sank under the surface. Her arm went up, holding the glow stick above her like one of the heroes in works of art in a pose of glory.

The shell and their two legs kicking underneath it hovered above. It had shifted, leaving her descending under the surface within sight of the scanner.

The water grew colder as she descended, but the growing quiet brought tranquility.

*This is what the mind is like for a warrior. External physical chaos, but internal calm. The storm rages on the surface but the depths? They're like...*

The yellow light passed over her position. She watched it trail off, leaving a set of dancing, serpentine reflections as it went.

A hand fastened onto her arm holding the light stick. Her direction reversed. She knew that hand. Only one person had that kind of grip.

Ailo kicked her legs to help. She closed her eyes, concentrating to fight off the lack of oxygen. Her heart beat so fast it was going to...

Her head broke through the surface. She gasped for air and opened her eyes. The aircraft tracked away in the distance. Nisi let go of her. Ailo's legs and hands moved on their own. She didn't sink. Jati and Nisi trod water next to her. They grinned at one another.

"Impressive. And brave." Jati winked.

"That's my soldier sibling, right there," Nisi said.

# THIRTY-ONE

Death. It rolled in like a Tide Wave. Three lives lost. Two of them, team members.

Thrown between gain and loss, Ailo learned that with commitment and bonds came the potential for abandonment and hurt. So goes the Arm. As the saying went in the quadrants at the center of the system, push and pull between the ends makes the middle a dangerous place.

With the progress Ai made, I thought my role would diminish. I would relinquish agency to Jati. But what I didn't know was human minds are always in conflict. It didn't abate; it grew exponentially. With more knowledge came more doubt. Strengths revealed more weaknesses.

Unless you were a warrior. And wasn't that the lure for Ailo? You can't blame her for falling for the seduction. It offered her an answer to the pendulum of existence, the anomaly that halted the perpetual motion of psychological development. You had to get there first, though. And to do that meant walking the path. She'd found her feet.

Ai might be convinced of it, but I wasn't so sure. I hadn't forgotten the earlier soliloquies by Jati — the ones where they talked about "winging it" and not knowing what they were doing. The enlightenment of neutrality might be a cover for... dare I say it? Idealism in disguise.

The revelations couldn't be denied. A touch of mindfulness and attentiveness on the ride from Yelo before the crash. The profound realization made through metaphor as we fell into the Lorassian's depths. But I didn't care so much about that as much as I cared about what the decision meant for Ailo. She'd joined a team. She had a family. Some were distant but caring. Others, mentors. And some, protectors.

The monumental growth took the form of reciprocity. It would get her farther, from my position as manager, than the martial and philosophical revelations. If she wanted to walk the warrior path, that was fine by me. I wanted a stable mind and a stable life for her. And learning to give, as well as take. Understanding that there were people in the Arm who would hold to that commitment was the most rewarding aspect of her life since we left T9.

Now, with a portion of the mystery of her parent put to rest, that push/pull dynamic went into action. More information meant more questions. With a greater understanding of the players and what they'd done, came powerful responses... and desires. Some potentially dangerous to others and Ailo. And so, as the mission pushed us toward shore and the palace walls, I couldn't help but feel something pulling us back. As they say, so goes the Arm.

# THIRTY-TWO

Rising and falling over the swells, Ailo watched the night sky and listened to Nisi's heaving breathing and the splashing of water. Gliding on their backs together, the two cut a path without pause to the edge of the shoreline. Nisi's cradled Ailo as she kicked her legs. Not once did the soldier slow her steady pace.

The shield wall remained invisible overhead except for when a meteor struck it. Higher up, the dazzling display of Kusk continued unabated, casting thin lines of yellow across the sky like ice cracking and buckling.

"We lost some time," Jati said, swimming next to them. "We may not be able to wield Kusk as a threat much longer."

"But can we still lower the shield?" Nisi's words came in between breaths as she swam.

"If we can get to the Core, yes. And so long as Rence's gift proves valuable."

Ailo placed a hand over the small case in her chest pocket. Warm Lorassian water passed over her skin.

The haunting image of Tusolo falling into the dark depths returned. What had he taken with him in death that she needed to know? When he drifted into the darkness, the last direct link to her parent went with him. And the book… tumbling away into space as Cesix station collapsed. That image overrode Rence swallowed by the Lorassian's deep. If she had been able to read those words, what would she have learned?

"Shore's ahead," Jati said.

"Same plan?" Nisi slowed her strokes. "Look, scanner

lights on the towers."

Ailo's legs sank as the soldier halted. Her foot grazed something. "There's something under the water," she whispered. "It brushed my leg."

Jati and Nisi exchanged looks that Ailo read as concerned. The two weren't treading water, although they were submerged to their necks and standing on the bottom. Nisi pulled Ailo by the arm, drifting her a bit closer to shore. "You should be able to stand now. We're squatting a bit to stay out of sight in the water."

Ailo stopped kicking. The tips of her boots hit the bottom. She touched her feet down and kept her head above the surface. No more than fifty feet ahead the walls of the palace loomed. Waves splashed up against the fortress, the sound echoing towards them.

"If you feel anything again stand very still," Nisi said.

"What is it?"

"You don't want to know. Not until we're out of the water."

"Tell me," Ailo asked. Not knowing was worse, or so she thought.

Nisi shook her head, refusing to answer.

Ailo glanced up to an illuminated tower that rose at the palace boundary along the coastline. Beyond it, in the darkness, ran an open plain partially lit by the yellow lamps lining the processional road to the city proper. She tracked back past the spire and up the wall of the palace.

"Yes, same plan," Jati said. "We drifted a bit with the current. We need to go that way." They pointed right along wall away from the coastline.

The palace extended on a peninsula in the Lorassian. At its corner, a tower formed a harsh, angular stone edge. Beyond, the vast, rippling surface of the sea sparkled with the flickering reflections of Kusk. A beam of light highlighted the corner, casting a white glow up the side of the spire.

"What is that light?"

"Yelo rising," Nisi said, her eyes going from one tower

to the other. "I've got the scanner rhythm down. You ready?"

"The sooner, the better," Jati said. "Let's go. We walk from here. It's about five hundred feet to the right."

Ailo took a step, but found it too deep to make efficient progress. Nisi noticed and pulled her along.

Every minute or two they halted and adjusted their position by moving out and in as they made their way to the center of the wall, bypassing the scanners.

Jati, leading by about ten feet, took a step and disappeared under the water. They came back up, ran a hand over their head to push their lavender hair back, and swam a few feet back. "We're at the channel line."

"How wide is the stone barrier between the sea and the interior spring?" Nisi asked.

"From the plans we had, it's about twenty feet. If we can trust what Hirok provided."

Ailo didn't understand. A barrier to what? Nothing lay along the wall.

"O.K., Firecracker. Last water adventure," Jati said. "There is a channel under the palace. It's deep. We're going to swim up close and then go under to come up on the inside."

"Under?"

"I got you. This is easy, like kicking teeno against a rookie." Nisi winked, parodying Jati. "You don't need to do a thing. Got it?"

She nodded.

Nisi pulled her in, cradling her once more. The atmospheric fireworks had become less frequent now. Was Kusk past its peak as Jati suggested? And what was the plan once they were inside? An urge to retreat, to find a way off the planet undetected sent her heart pumping. They were down to three, what could they do? Boar was somewhere inside, in the hands of the Garassians, or so she hoped. JeJeto and Rence were dead.

Nisi spun Ailo around.

The stone walls showed their details for the first time — blocks, faded gray and worn by age and the sea. The Cantinool grove Jati led her through on Heroon evoked an epochal time, but it manifested in a forest alive and breathing that spoke of its ancient ancestry. The palace haunted the surface of the planet like a skeleton, or a tomb unburied. The palace architecture sat like a ruin that never had the chance to crumble.

Nisi gave her a thumbs-up and gestured for Ailo to hold her breath. She took in a massive gulp. Her hand went to the Rim wedge on her thigh and brushed over it once for luck.

Solazi's bar to here. This was Keen's territory. She'd closed a circle.

Nisi grabbed her and dove.


The air inside the palace was foul, to say the least. It rivaled that of T9's sewer level to Ailo's nose. Jati held up a lightstick and rats scattered from the slimy edges of the curved tunnel.

"Ah, the palace, just as I remember it." Jati slicked back their hair.

Nisi scoffed.

"Action time," Jati said.

The echoes of water and Jati's voice told Ailo a labyrinth of passageways spread in the darkness.

"How far do we have to swim in this rat hole?" Nisi asked.

"You know, usually that's a figure of speech," Jati said and swam ahead. "Two turns and we should be able to get into the complex."

Nisi pulled Ailo forward, following the general.

More rats. As the light spread in front of them, hundreds of rodents scattered. Ailo wanted out of the water and to be back on solid ground. Even the rock of Garassit would be better than the water.

Bursts of steam shot into the tunnel ahead on the edge of the visible light, the aroma rank. She gagged.

"Coolers," Jati said. "For the Core. So far so good. One

more turn and there should be a hatch."

So that was the source of the fumes and smell. At least it wasn't sewage.

Jati waited for them to catch up before rounding the bend.

"A bit late for a swim, don't you think?"

A blast of light hit. Ailo's vision went white. As it settled, ten Garassian sentinels appeared lining the walls of the tunnel, blasters out and aimed at the three of them. Next to a hatch stood an elderly person with a beaked nose. They wore a loose-fitting robe with deep crimson wrapped layers that surrounded olive skin. A large pendant hung from his neck, milky and green. By their stance and smirk, Ailo knew they were the vocal source of the welcome.

*Aradus-ti.*

"If you wanted to negotiate a surrender, the front gate was open," he said. "Your Hamut diplomat is an awful liar. He should stick to flying and shooting people. He's going to be a terrible politician."

"On the contrary, old tot." Jati swam up closer to the steps.

Ailo thought it amusing that the phrase worked, but with a reversal of irony.

A guard motioned with a blaster for Nisi and Ailo to follow suit and approach. Nisi lifted Ailo onto the first step. Her legs were like rubber. She'd been treading water and floating for hours. The muscles were like jelly and she could barely stand up. Nisi stepped up and out of the water and handed over her weapons. Ailo noticed the defensive posture of the guards. Her mere presence was intimidation.

"Kin-tuk-ti did exactly what I asked him to do," Jati said.

"Oh come now, Jati. Don't try your clever games with me. I'm no PA grunt or ambassadorial neophyte. The warrior philosophy routine might work on Heroon with those savages you rile into false hope, but not where it's civilized. Your words are unveiled, General."

Aradus's rhetorical artistry was concerning. He spoke with words of prejudicial and racist mastery. Jati faced a formidable opponent.

"Now what?" Jati asked, wiping off their soaked jumpsuit.

"I'd like to know why you have decided to infiltrate our palace. I assume it's to retrieve your child?"

"She better be well, Aradus."

That tone was new. Sparks flew from the words Jati spoke.

"She is fine. I may be ruthless, but I am not a savage."

*Again he uses that word. He's arrogant and thinks of himself and all Garassians as somehow better than others in the Arm.*

Aradus turned his attention to Ailo.

"Who is the child?"

"No one," Jati said.

"It's 'té' to you." Ailo's voice bounced off the water and rock walls. "I'm no child."

Aradus gazed into her eyes, probing. Her stubbornness and resentment for him and those he worked with held her fast. She stared back. *I don't like you.*

"Bold," he said and smirked.

*I don't like you.*

The old Garassian's eyes went to Jati. "I doubt that *she* would be here if not essential to whatever little ruse you had planned." The elder shifted to Nisi.

"Birevian," he nodded. "Still fighting, I see. I'm sure you're angry as ever."

*So he knows Nisi as well?*

Jati held up a hand to stay the soldier's explosive potential.

"Take those two to a cell." Aradus waved at the one set of guards. One of them shoved Ailo towards the hatch, which opened with a hiss of air.

"Come, General. You and I will dine. We have much to discuss."

Ailo turned her head as she was pushed through the portal. Aradus held up his wrist. "Look at the time. Kusk is almost over. You'll want to…"

The hatch shut before his sentence finished.

Four guards led Ailo and Nisi down the hallway. Even on this maintenance level, underneath the main floors, the palace architecture and interior design spoke of elegance and Garassit's earnest control of the Arm for centuries.

A contradictory aesthetic of discreet ornamentation grew from the walls' seams in the corridor. Black and gold tiles set in triangular formation ran across the floor. Sleek sconces, made of various metals, hung of the walls and spoke of advanced technology. The overall design sent a subtle message: wealth. If it were a person, Ailo would call them arrogant and overconfident in their position of privilege.

*I guess it works well.*

Yet the walls themselves, comprised of exposed rock, and the archways of stacked blocks sang of age on the edge of ruin.

How to put it into words? Tera came to mind. The navigator would appreciate Ailo's attempt at poetic description: Garassia was hurtling into a future on a bed of credits, but afraid to let go of the past. The linens on the mattress remained old and out of style, obstinate in the face of what lay ahead. Translation into plain Contex: *Garassit is powerful, but past its time. Or, at least, in need of new leadership.*

Nisi walked in front, flanked by two guards. Another crony strode alongside Ailo and the last kept pace behind her.

"You're a stupid little kid, you know that?" Nisi said.

Ailo slowed. The guard behind her shoved her forward.

*Why would Nisi say that?*

"Keep quiet," one of the guards next to Nisi said.

"You convinced us to come up through the channel,

you little…"

"I said, be quiet," the guard repeated.

*Got it.* Ailo had spent enough time on the streets of T9 to interpret the tone. She picked up on the hesitancy in the guard's voice. Nisi scared them. The soldier knew it and she was going to make a move. Ahead the passageway branched left and right. A portrait of someone Ailo assumed important based on their ostentatious attire and fancy headdress hung opposite them.

*O.K. here we go.*

"Shut up!" Ailo snapped back. "You think I care about any of this?" She used her best 'annoying teenager' voice.

Nisi shot around. "Gor scum! I'll…"

The two guards next to her flinched. One spoke. All they got out was a, "Hey, I—"

Nisi massive palms came right at Ailo. She didn't need to act it out. The force on her chest was so powerful it sent her flying back into the guard behind her. She fell on top of them. Nisi's arms, in perfect synch, drew back and elbowed both guards in the face. The two sentinels crumbled as a massive boot headed to the blaster held by the guard who, a moment earlier, stood next to Ailo. The weapon flew out of their hand so hard it hit the ceiling and broke into pieces.

Two legs wrapped around Ailo's torso like a crab. A hand crossed her chest, snaking its way to her throat. She knew this grappling move from the training floor. JeJeto loved to use it. When they got the three-point lock on her, she was finished.

Ailo drove her head back. She'd done this with the practice helmets on but never tried the escape maneuver skull-to-skull. Jati's words rang through her ears.

*Arch your neck. Retract in as you strike and you'll get the nose.*

Smack! The bridge of the guard's nose collapsed against the back of their skull. Out of the corner of her eye, she caught sight of Nisi's follow-up strike after the kick. A hard right cross made contact with the standing guard's chin. The sentinel crumpled to the ground.

The heavy *clunk* Ailo hoped to hear followed. A sickening shiver ran through her body. She'd got the 'double-trouble' option. Jati and JeJeto talked about it as a fifty-fifty chance. Her impact sent the guard's head back, hitting the floor. Hard. She slipped out of her opponent's grip and rolled over, three-fingered fist drawn back, ready to pound them in the face.

She did far worse damage than she'd expected. Blood ran in a thick, crimson trail like a ruby snake across the floor. The guard's open and lifeless eyes fixed on a distant, invisible spot overhead.

"Double-trouble, nice." It was Nisi. The soldier pulled her up to her feet. "First time?"

*What did she mean?*

"They're dead." Nisi nodded at her victim. "First kill?"

*I killed someone. Gerib... I killed...*

A smack crossed her cheek. "Sorry, you powered off. Had to do that." Nisi knelt so they were eye-to-eye. "We gotta move." The soldier snatched up the three remaining blasters from the guards. She shoved one in her thigh holster and kept the other at the ready. Ailo caught the one tossed to her.

"Safety is..."

"Got it," Ailo checked and cocked the trigger on the blaster, remembering how to do it from Jati's instruction on Ffossk.

Nisi nodded. "Come on. There's nowhere to put these chumps. We're going to have to leave them and hope for the best." She strode to the corner and edged up along the wall. "Finally," the soldier said, grinning. "We get to the fun stuff."

# THIRTY-THREE

Did a line between murder and justice exist? Could war excuse personal moral responsibility? Ailo's conscience lingered in an internal ethical purgatory.

*Gerib, was that murder?*

*"I think the answer is up to you, Ai."*

*And what about vengeance? Is that outside the circle of murder?*

Ailo slithered down the side of the hallway behind Nisi. Without an answer, Ceron tilted on its axis and with it her moral balance went off-center, her focus blurry.

"Hey," Nisi's eyes and thick eyebrows shifted through her muddled vision. "You going to be O.K.?"

"Yes, it's just…"

"Let it go, be in the present. The past and the future get you killed on an op. Like that chump back there."

Ailo inhaled and exhaled, as Jati had instructed on the pod. Her center returned. She nodded at Nisi, who turned her attention back to the corner.

Nisi had responded like a well-oiled machine during the confrontation. She didn't flinch at what had happened, literally or figuratively, afterward either.

*She's a soldier.*

Ailo continued along the wall, following Nisi. She ducked under and around a sconce.

*Am I?*

Nisi called her a soldier when they were on the pod, hurtling down toward the Lorassian Sea. Why?

"Because you are on the team. And this is a military op-

*eration, Ai. Jati defined it in the training room."*

But...

A part of her was here seeking answers. Another pushed on through an obligation to Jati. And the third?

Ailo didn't want to acknowledge what stared her in the face: an ugly portrait. Vengeance wore no mask; murder and malice lurked in the shadows and creases of its face, vital as the mouth that speaks and the eyes that see.

But what of its expressions? Were any of them just? If she killed the person who murdered her parent would that be justice served? She'd stop a killer. That couldn't be wrong. Or could it?

Jati stepped from the shadows in her mind, their sage face cast in soft light. She knew what they would say, but the words were suspect. After all, dare she say it? Jati was an... idealist.

Nisi gestured her to stop. The soldier peered around a corner. Across the corridor, a small icon lay on the keystone of an arched portal, confirming their position on lower level 2. That meant two floors below the ground level of the palace. Ailo remembered the layout from the pre-op meeting. The holding cells were on LL1.

"See the tile pattern?" Nisi pointed in front of the portal.

Five octagonal tiles, with repeating green and red mosaic patterns, stood out from the gold and black square flooring.

"That's the scanner. It's different in high-level Garassian security systems. More advanced. It resonates from the floor up to the ceiling, in a wavelength outside the optical range."

"What do I do?"

Nisi crossed her fingers. "You walk right through it and trigger the elevator. You're the ghost."

The controls lay in a small ornamental oval panel on the wall to the left of the arch. The icons for up and down glowed blue. At least those symbols were universal across the Arm.

"We're going up, right?"

"You want to swim some more?" Nisi's said, her expression deadpan.

That wry retort would normally be shot at JeJeto. Ailo was the op-buddy now. This was all a thrill for Nisi. From the physical combat to the banter, the soldier savored this entire experience. She'd had a chance to throw in the obligatory, snarky humor.

*I guess this means things are going well.*

Five guards lay on the floor down the hall. *One dead, by my hands.* She had to admit, there wasn't anyone else she'd rather be with right now in this predicament. Except, maybe Jati. They were on their way to 'dine' with Aradus. Did the arrogant ambassador mean it as a figure of speech, or a literal statement?

"Hey, we gotta move, Ai."

Ailo noticed the use of her shortened name. She smiled. A pang of guilt ran through her.

*"It's fine, Ai. It's good."*

*Yeah, she can use it.*

"We have to get close to the Core and let out that... whatever it is you're holding from the freak before someone finds out we're not on our way to the cells."

"He wasn't a freak."

Nisi sighed. "Alright, I'm sorry. Listen, you get us through that portal and we get this op done, and I'll buy you a Canti-ale and teach you how to ride the swamp box. Now get *over* there."

"And teach me how to fight? The way you did back there?"

"You did pretty well on your own."

Ailo frowned. True, but it had been defensive. Now that she thought about it, everything Jati focused on was defensive. Their offense functioned as a form of defense.

Nisi smiled. "I get it. You want to learn how to kick ass." A giant palm slapped Ailo's shoulder, sending her into the wall. "Oops, sorry."

Ailo teetered but managed not to fall over.

"Deal. But first, we have to make it out of here." She nodded her head toward the portal.

Ailo glanced in both directions. At this late hour, no one was down here. Other than the guards and Aradus, why would anyone pass by? There were probably standard guard stations at central points but for now, they were alone.

She stepped into the hall and chanced a toe onto the mosaic as if testing the temperature of the water before stepping in. Why was she worried? Everyone knew it, and she did too. She wasn't chipped. *As Nisi said, you're a ghost.* Her foot came to rest on the tesserae pattern. Nothing happened. No alarm. No response at all.

Nisi nodded and waved her hand to get moving.

Ailo stepped up and hit the portal door. Nisi practically leaped inside when it opened.

"Why doesn't it go off when you cross?"

"It blocks access. It's not an identity scanner. Those are all gold tiles." Nisi hit the up button. "Don't worry, we're going to deal with those too. Or, you are."

"You mean you won't be able to come with me?"

"Not a certain point. One step at a... no, no, no." Nisi pushed buttons at random.

The floor display went right past LL1. They were heading up. To Level 3.

"What's happening?"

"Someone triggered a request. It must be wonky since you didn't register on the scanner."

"What's up there?"

Nisi positioned herself so her arm with the blaster hid behind the side of the archway.

"We're about to find out."

The elevator hissed to a halt. The barrier vanished. Elaborate decorations and numerous floral and plant displays in a large ballroom spoke of a gala, one leaning toward extravagance. Several hover-droids and human supervisors broke down portions of the tables and chairs and carted off leftovers.

A few well-dressed attendees lingered. Ailo knew the type. They were either there to get as much as they could or, they were inebriated to the point that they refused to accept the event was over. She and the other kids on T9 would make their way into similar events, much less elegant and formal to forage for scraps.

"Oh! Kerlua!" A tipsy straggler from the gala, scavenging the last treats on a dessert table, called to another attendee gazing at a majestic painted mural. "Come dear, the elevator."

Their partner, a multi-colored hair tower soaring in an ostentatious braided column several feet high, continued to stare at the work of art.

"Next one," Nisi said, as inelegantly as Ailo expected. The soldier's finger went to the close button.

"Nonsense," they said tossing a pastry back onto the table. With their gown held up to scurry faster, they stumbled in ornate heels across the scanner tiles, triggering the elevator to hold before closing.

"Sake of the..." Nisi muttered.

Their companion turned from the artwork and danced their way towards the elevator, pirouetting and twirling in a black and white striped dress of multiple layers like a pastry. How they didn't fall over with the towering headdress, Ailo didn't know.

*These two won't remember a thing. And, luck willing, probably won't notice how out of place we look.*

"Thank you," the first one said and tripped into the elevator, catching themself on Nisi. "Oh, my you are tall," they said, recovering from their stumble. They laughed and turned to face the wall, playing bashful.

*They're trashed.*

The other slowed their dance performance and stepped inside, drink in hand. "Good evening." Their gaze passed from Ailo to Nisi.

"Birevians are attending the Kusk gala now?" They smiled and leaned over to whisper to their companion.

"What's the Arm coming to?"

Their partner raised a hand to their lips to cover a giggle.

*Oh no.*

The portal closed.


"A bit late to the party." Boar nodded at Nisi's outfit, amused at the wordplay.

"Not a word or you can stay in there," Nisi said.

"I'm speechless," Boar said and rose from the bench inside the cell.

Ailo was not comfortable, but she knew from Nisi's appearance and body language that she felt ridiculous. Not only was the outfit from the partygoer the antithesis of the soldier's personality, but it was also too small. Ailo didn't know much about fashion, but she did know about fit. There was small and then there was *small*. She knew the latter as a street kid. For almost a year, she had owned a jumper that made it no further than her mid-forearms and shins.

The elaborate gown Nisi wore barely made it past her kneecaps. The makeup, done by Ailo from the person's belongings, made her into more of an overexcited clown than someone made up for a ball. They'd had no choice when the elevator kept rising rather than going back down. After they crossed the tenth floor, it had refused to return. That's when they followed the two partygoers to their room. Now, the two attendees were barricaded inside their bathroom, quite less fashionable in their undergarments than they'd been earlier that evening.

Ailo had never worn a dress in her life. This black and white one felt like a straitjacket. She'd never worn one of those either, luckily, but she understood the general idea from broadcast dramas with scenes of hardened criminals detained before trial. In this outfit, she'd never be able to escape a chase by sentries and defending herself would mean tearing the seams of her armpits or fighting with the equivalent of tension bands holding back her blows.

At least Nisi's makeup job on her looked subtle and appropriate — the soldier whisked off her entire cosmetic decoration with deft hands. Surprising from what Ailo knew of her, but then again the more time went by and the farther she got from T9 the more she learned to hold back judgment of others. People's lives were turning out to be more complicated and layered than she'd realized.

The dress itself wasn't the worst part. Even now, standing at rest, she struggled for a full and deep inhalation. With her combat suit underneath the ornate and formal garment, and the corset squeezing her ribs, she could barely breathe. She'd never sustain herself in a prolonged scrap.

"At least give me three questions," Boar said rubbing his hands together.

Nisi ignored him and tried to work the cell controls.

"What's the plan? I mean after you two have your dancing lesson?"

Ailo laughed. Nisi shot her a look as hard as she punched. Ailo put her hands up defensively.

The two guards Nisi knocked out (that was something to watch in her outfit) lay with arms and legs spread on the floor across the cell block. Ailo had been able to get in without detection, but Nisi insisted the cameras had captured the footage. If they weren't made yet, they would be soon.

"Listen, there's something you need to know." Boar peeked through the laser bars. "It might change the plan." He gazed past Ailo searching behind her. "Where's Jati?"

"Dining with Aradus," Nisi said, concentrating on the controls. "Sake of the Arm, I can't get the card to work."

"Aradus?"

"Yeah, you're not a very good liar. He read right through whatever it was you told him."

"Well," Boar straightened his robe. "I thought I did a pretty good job, considering it's what Jati wanted me to do."

"What?" With a beep, the bars vanished.

Ailo noticed that Boar wore fresh, dry clothes and appeared ambassadorial.

"Not bad, huh?" he said to Ailo, gesturing at his outfit. "Diplomatic privileges. Thank the Arm I joined up. Where are your former revelers?"

"Sleeping off their highs." Nisi held out one of her two blasters to Boar.

He shook his head.

"What's wrong? Take it."

Boar shook his head.

"Where's Arira?" Nisi asked. "We'll get her first and then get up to the Core."

"She's not here." The Hamut's eyebrows rose. Ailo sensed a bomb about to drop.

"Where is she, then?" Nisi asked. "Lead the way."

"No, Nisi. She's *not* here. In the palace. She never was."

Nisi took a step back. Even in her combat boots (which paired with the formal attire made, Ailo thought, an excellent fashion), the soldier stumbled. "Sake of the Arm!"

*Even with all the betrayal, Hirok had a line.*

"Hirok only wanted to get Jati here," Boar said.

"How do you know this?" Nisi wiped the sweat from her cheek. Blush smeared and streaked with some purple mascara.

Boar pointed, "You've got some…"

"Sake of the Arm, I don't give a Ti-horn's ass, spit it out!"

"I had a brief conversation with Aradus on my 'arrival'. Arira was the bait. The old ambassador is sadistic and evil. He likes his enemies to know the full extent of their humiliation as part of their torture. Much of this was orchestrated between Hirok and Hekron. Aradus and his nephew wanted to lure Jati here to increase Galank's desire to attack."

"Why?" Nisi asked? "That makes no sense."

"I can't be certain, but Jati's hunch about an all-out attack being disastrous for the PA appears to legitimate. I think they *want* them to attack."

A flash of concern on Nisi's face told Ailo this was bad.

"Is she safe?" the soldier asked.

"Not sure. Hirok had her placed in a safe-house. He wouldn't allow her to be placed in the Garassian's hands."

"Do we know where?" Nisi asked.

Boar shook his head. "Aradus didn't say. And I'm not sure he knows."

"But we saw her here... with that Gor scum on the terrace. In the drone footage that Hirok..."

"Doctored," Boar said. "I should have picked up on it."

Nisi's head nodded slowly. "She didn't seem herself. Too..."

"Isolated," Ailo said. Nisi and Boar turned to her. "I picked up on it too." She held out her hands. "So now what?"

"We have to get to the Core," Nisi said, "and we have to do it fast. The PA is going to arrive ready to attack in a few hours. The clock is ticking against us. If we don't get that shut down somehow, Galank is going to show up ready for an all-out siege." Nisi stomped back and forth, her combat boots banging on the ground.

"Birevian thinking," Boar said to Ailo and nodded at Nisi.

"And we have to figure out how to get to Jati," she said, shifting the gown at her waist. "Sake of the... screw it." She tore an opening, pulled out a blaster holster and slid the weapon inside. It sat outside the frills of the dress.

"Very refined," Boar said, enjoying his share of op razzing. Ailo wasn't so sure this constituted 'fun stuff' for Nisi. Maybe when, and if, they made it out of this and they were all drinking at the cantina. More likely, it'd instigate another feud.

"I think Jati has their own plans," Boar said. "From what I was instructed, they wanted me to bait Aradus to you three, albeit subtly."

*Why would they do that?*

"Jati the strategist, working a Plan C," Nisi said, nodding. "They must know what they're doing. Alright. We go to the Core. That's our main objective. We leave the rest to them. Let's go."

"What about Arira?" Ailo asked. Jati's daughter got lost in the layers of problems.

"We can't focus on saving one person right now. Our attention has to be on the entire PA and everyone they're defending."

"But that's what Jati did for me," Ailo said. "They chose me over the PA last time. I can't leave their daughter in danger. We have to find where she is and get her."

"I hear you, Ailo," Nisi said. She approached and bent down so they were eye-to-eye. "My guess is Jati is on it, but if we're still in this mess when Kusk ends we'll find a way to get a signal up to the *Carmora*. Tera can contact Firde on Hirok's ship. Between the two of them they can go through tracking data on Hirok's communications and try and locate a lead to find her."

Ailo nodded. That had to be enough for now.

"I think you should lock me back up," Boar said.

"What?" Ailo and Nisi said at the same time and turned to the Hamut.

"Other than being a better shot than you, which would make getting through the palace easier, I'm more useful in my diplomatic role. Even locked up, I've got a level of immunity that gives me safety. Worst case scenario I can talk my way through potentially saving you depending on what goes down."

Boar did have a point. He'd been cleaned and put in detention, even though he'd shown up in a pod as part of a ruse to infiltrate an enemy facility.

"I hate to be 'Jati-esque,' but this is a 'brain over brawn' situation. Strategy dictates...."

"Yeah, yeah alright." Nisi shoved Boar back into the cell. He fell onto the cot and plopped onto the floor. She reset the laser bars.

"That was satisfying," Nisi muttered under her breath.

# THIRTY-FOUR

The outfits worked, at least enough to get them past a few more late-night revelers. Between the attendees' inebriation and distance, catching the quick flash of passing 'well-dressed' guests, even two whose combat boots slipped in and out of view with their strides, didn't expose them.

Now, she and Nisi stood inside the open portal to the hallway on the highest level of the palace: L17. They'd taken the elevator from the main level with one more encounter, a single drunken guest who rode with them to L12. Nisi managed to be chatty, and to Ailo's surprise, rather clever. By engaging them in conversation, she kept their gaze up for the ride to their floor.

"Clear," Nisi said, leaning out of the open portal at floor 17. "This way."

Ailo followed the well-dressed soldier to the next corner.

"Alright, you can ditch the dress," Nisi said. She made a motion for her to turn around.

Wave after wave of relief passed with each layer of straps that the soldier undid on her corset. When Nisi unlaced the final strap, she inhaled and exhaled loudly.

"Yeah, tell me about it," Nisi said. A strong hand patted her shoulder. "Put your arms up in the air."

"Is this a holdup?"

"Nice one."

Ailo smiled with satisfaction at her quick quip as the dress slid up and off. She turned and caught sight of Nisi scrunching it up into a ball and tucking it under an armpit.

"What about you?" Ailo asked.

"Not so lucky," Nisi said, peering around the corner. "Not until I get out of here."

"Now what?"

"This is on you now, Ailo. You have the case?"

She touched her pocket. "Yes."

"Well, let's hope that whatever Rence gave you will do the job." Nisi pulled back the sleeve on her dress. Ailo hadn't noticed it before with the tattoos, but the soldier had scratched a rough plan of the palace with some kind of ink onto her inner forearm.

"The Core runs up the center and tops off inside the central dome." She pointed at a spot on her arm. "You should be able to reach it by going this way." Nisi gestured down the hall to the right. "It's mostly meeting rooms and lounge areas for the elite family. You get to the Core through the worship chamber."

"Worship chamber?"

"It's got a unique entrance. They all do on this planet." Nisi rolled her eyes. "Don't get me started." The soldier's head shook in disgust. "Anyway, you can't miss it. Three lines like waves." She closed her thumb and pinky, leaving large fingers extended while motioning the hand in a gentle, horizontal curve. "It's the symbol for wind. It'll be somewhere on the portal, probably on the keystone at the top. Don't get lost. If you head back that way," she thumbed in the other direction, "by one of the other halls you'll be heading to the quarters of the highest members. That means guards and the people you want to avoid."

"Like Hekron?"

Nisi cocked her head. "Ailo, as much as I understand…"

"I want to know what I'm dealing with." True, if only in part, of why she asked.

"It's possible. Just get to the Core, O.K.?"

"Where are you going?"

"I hate to do it, but I'm getting out. I'm going back the way we came in, under the wall in the channel. I'll head to the shoreline and wait. I'm going to give Boar some time."

She lowered her head and muttered something. All Ailo saw were dark curls and she heard something about "regretting this" pass from the soldier's mouth. Nisi raised her head and looked at Ailo in earnest. "This way if something goes wrong inside the palace I can still get back in fast. As much as I want to find Hekron and slice his throat, I know that's not the right move. Jati has a plan. They must. Otherwise, they wouldn't have gone with Aradus so easily. I trust them. For now, this is our assignment. Cool?"

It did make sense. But she didn't like being alone.

"Hey, you got this," Nisi said. "You're an ass-kicking punk from T9. You and me, we're cut from the same cloth, and it isn't this." Nisi held up a piece of her dress.

Ailo laughed.

"You've done nothing but impress everyone on the team. Jati most of all."

"Really?"

"Sake, are you kidding me? I heard you took us out of FTL to Cesix. In the cap's chair."

Ailo's cheeks grew warm. Why did that always happen?

"You think they let anyone do that? The one other person I've ever known to get in that chair is me." Nisi raised her eyebrows and thumbed her dress. "Think about that."

Ailo nodded.

"Listen, I'm not one for all this 'meant to be' stuff. That's Jati's bag. I'm from Birevia. I believe in hard rock. We climb mountains using muscle not 'inspiration.' But, and don't you tell Jati I said this," she poked a finger into Ailo's chest, "or Tera for that matter. But you were meant to come along. And you were meant to be here, now. So *do your job*. Trust yourself. And remember, we're siblings. And not just as soldiers. We're family. Jati's adopted us both."

Nisi's eyes were stern. They shifted.

Ailo's chest felt...

"Now give me some." Nisi held out her giant arms.

Ailo hugged her tight.

*My sibling? Jati's adopted child?*

Nisi broke their embrace. "It feels good to do good, doesn't it?"

Ailo nodded, her eyes on Nisi's star tattoo. "Can I ask you something?"

"You're my sibling. You can ask me anything." Nisi held out a fist for her to pump.

Ailo raised her hand and tapped the soldier's large knuckles. "Why do you have that tattoo on your cheek?"

Nisi broke eye contact and glanced away. Her face shifted. She looked as if she'd gone somewhere far away from Garassit.

"Everyone thinks it's for my parent, Lexar," she said, coming back to the present and making eye contact. "In her honor and memory. It is, but not in the way people think. It's for me. When I look at my reflection, I'm always reminded to be better than I am." Nisi bit her bottom lip. "To try and let go of my anger and learn forgiveness. So I don't ever forget the lessons that Jati has taught me." She shook her head. "I am trying Ailo, but it is so hard." She wiped a tear. "I want to be bigger than it, to accept that anyone could have been on the other side of that war. I'm learning to face the fact that my anger is my own. I'm the problem. You feel me?"

Ailo nodded. She knew all too well what the soldier meant.

"So listen, it's fine to be a work in progress," Nisi said. "Anyone who isn't is a liar as far as I am concerned. What is important is that you don't give up trying. That you keep doing the work."

Ailo smiled. "You are so cool."

"Ha!" Nisi sniffled and thudded her fist on Ailo's chest. "I know." She winked.

Ailo's heart ached. Her chest filled with a newfound trust built from pathos. "I want to tell you something back. Something I've never told anyone else."

Nisi raised an eyebrow.

Ailo held out her hand with the three digits. It vibrated with nerves like a tuning fork.

"On T9, when they'd catch the street kids... sometimes they would do things to make an example of you. To scare the others and send a message. There was a Hamut enforcer who ran the district I squatted in... Gaktelo. He wasn't usually around but every few months he'd be on T9 for a few weeks." She took a deep breath. "He liked blades. And he liked convincing himself he had power. I got caught when he was there. Twice. The second time they brought me in for 'questioning', Gaktelo showed me my finger... from the first time. He'd kept it."

"Oh Ailo, I'm so sorry," Nisi said and hugged her.

Ailo burst into tears in the soldier's strong arms.

"I am too, Nisi. For you."

Nisi pulled back. "I'm glad we did this, you and me."

"Me too," Ailo whispered and wiped a tear from her cheek.

The chatter of a comm broke the intimacy. Nisi's eyes went wide. She peeked around the corner.

"Sentry patrol. It's showtime." The soldier reached into a pocket on her waist. "Here." She held out a small tube. "That's a flare. You get in trouble, get outside on any level. Set that off, if possible towards the eastern shore where we crashed. I'll be watching."

"Got it." Ailo tucked it away.

"Otherwise, make for the rocks outside the channel when you're done. The same way we came in. On my way out, I'm going to run this cable." She pulled the torn dress back from where the blaster rested revealing a looped silver line clipped to her waist. "It'll be attached on the inside and I'll wedge it into the stone on the outside. You take a deep breath and pull hand-over-hand. You'll get out in no time."

*Underwater? That whole way without knowing how to swim?*

Nisi held out her fist. Ailo bumped it. "Kick some ass." The soldier backed into the portal and closed the barrier.

The footsteps of the sentries grew louder. Ailo scurried down the hallway and around the corner.

*Time to become a ghost.*

Under the dim light of sconces, she slithered down the passageway, her fingers dragging over the coarse surface of the ancient stone. At the next corner, the tell-tale mosaic Nisi mentioned altered the floor pattern in front of the passage. Above the entrance, three wavy lines in the pattern of a wind icon decorated the archway.

Holding her arm out, she edged it over the invisible space above the tiles.

Nothing.

She moved on. So, she really had no chip.

A window broke the wall's rhythm of sconces ahead. She scurried to it. Out the arched opening, a small courtyard garden full of potted plants and a single tree rose one floor down. The majority of lights around the interior of the palace were out, but the looming tower glowed like a honeycomb inside the central dome's arched windows.

*The Core.*

Could she find a way over there? The dome dropped at least two floors below her position, but she couldn't locate any skywalks.

The sentries' footsteps bounced down a nearby hallway. She went to the next corner. Ahead, down the continuing hallway, a set of transparent doors led out to a small balcony. Close enough. This thing in her pocket had wings to fly so that meant it could cross to the Core. Or so she hoped. So long as there was open access on the dome. From what the team discussed back on the *Carmora*, there should be exhaust chambers to release the excess thermal discharge. And she could see smaller ventilators along the rim.

Her hand went to the small box in her pocket and withdrew it. Fingers shook from nerves.

She examined the latch. Her shaky fingers slipped against the tight clasp and the box dropped to the ground, clanging on the tiles.

*Sake of the Arm!*

The footsteps halted. Silence echoed down the corridor.

*Oh no.*

Footsteps. This time with haste. She snatched up the box. They'd be around the bend and within sight in seconds. If she chanced a dash to the balcony they might see her from the adjacent corridor and turn to follow. The alcove of the window along the hallway was the only safe option. She scrunched up and into the ledge.

*Please pass by. Please just pass by.*

The sound she feared hit her ears. The sentries turned into the hallway.

Attacking and trying to overpower them, even with the element of surprise, would never work. She tucked her face into her knees.

*Gerib, this isn't going to work. They're going to see me.*
"I know, Ai."

"Well, young one, looks like you've just been found," a deep voice said. "Get up and put those hands where we can see them. Call it in, Eron."

Ailo's hand facing the window slipped into her pocket. She brushed the Rim wedge once for luck and gripped the flare resting beside it. She tucked her head in tighter and thrust it in the direction of the sentries, finger hitting the switch. Even with her knees shielding the scene a burst of light flashed over her eyelids, sneaking between the small cracks in her clenched knees.

The sentries screamed. Two thuds sounded amidst a whir of sizzling.

She opened her eyes to smoke and a glowing red flare sizzling and cracking on the tile floor. Her combat boot stomped it out as she jumped down out of the alcove. Both guards had their hands over their eyes, writhing around, blinded by the flare's light burst and gagging on lingering smoke.

She bolted around the bend and backed up on the wall, panting. Her hand with Rence's box shook from the adrenaline surging through her veins.

*The balcony.*

She shot down the hall and opened the portal, stumbled over her feet, and fell on her face. The box tumbled toward the balcony's edge. Ailo dove for it and got to it before it fell. She rolled over on her back, panting. The cool night air sat quietly inside the stone atrium. No sound of the sea penetrated the castle's interior. The low hum from the Core broke the silence of the evening. Lying on her back, she pulled out the case and flipped it open.

*I hope you don't sting.*

Her fingers withdrew a shiny, metallic insect, like one of the predator bugs dancing around the tropical rainforest on Heroon. Its wings had a green iridescent tinge. Delicate golden metal bands mimicked the sectioned pattern of natural wings above a striated body. Two big eyes, bright blue, dominated the head.

*You are a marvelous thing.* She turned it around in her hand.

Rence, for all his mystery and reserve, designed things with extraordinary precision and beauty. She flipped the mechanical insect over. A small switch on the bottom of the body broke the smooth underbelly.

"Here goes." Her finger shifted the switch up toward the head. A dance of colored light shot through the creature. Against the backdrop of stars overhead, it stood out like a rainbowed shooting star flashing across the sky. The body's rear section lit up in yellow and blue, along with the eyes. Its delicate wings flapped open and, with a whir, fluttered rapidly. The AI machine struggled against her grip. It *wanted* to fly.

"O.K. little one." She launched it up and over her head in the direction of the dome. The bug took flight and zipped around in radiating spirals, increasing its range. It shot back toward Ailo, hovering a few feet from her face.

"No, that way," she pointed at the dome behind her head.

The insect buzzed past her and back out the portal into the corridor.

"No!" She got to her feet and ran in after it. It whisked down the hall and around the corner.

*Where is it going? The Core is the other way!*

She could hear the writhing moans and gagging of the sentries a hallway away. They were still recovering but she knew they'd called in back up by now. Through three long halls and around three corners, she followed the bug and ended up on the side of the floor that Nisi had warned her against. She rounded a bend and stopped short. The insect hovered at a portal, banging against it repeatedly.

She approached and read the letters on the keystone. *Royal Library.*

"Come here," she said to the bug and tried to snatch it. The insect danced around her with ease. Its agility and dexterity reminded her of the respirator that fell past Rence in the Lorassian Sea. Over and over, the bug banged against the entrance.

Voices and footsteps reached her ears, not close. Yet.

She needed to get out of the corridor but had no idea what waited inside the library.

*Plan C, Jati. I'm going with the flow.*

Ailo opened the portal. The insect bolted into the darkness. Blue and yellow light from the small mechanical creature left a trail like a ship leaving port at night.

She flipped on the light to an empty room with walls lined with books. Floor to ceiling in the mid-sized library, stacks of texts ran between dark wooden shelves. The bug beeped and flashed brightly, coming alive with new life. Ailo walked around a central table to the sidewall where the insect hovered, reacting to a large volume on a low shelf.

She gasped and froze. The letters on the binding, in Neo-Contex, ran in an elegant, recognizable script.

*Of Them, We are One. Cin Quinti.*

"Good evening."

Ailo turned and stumbled into a chair at the table.

"You're somewhere you shouldn't be, child."

*Hekron.*

"And who might you be?" The Garassian assassin stepped into the library, waving away the sentries with him.

Ailo didn't respond. Half of her wanted to lash out. The other half wanted to snatch the book and flee.

Like a protective parent, she had to make a choice: take out a threat at the risk of injury or death or prioritize the protection and survival of a child. The book was the last surrogate of her bloodline. Teluv's voice, her words scripted by hand, lay preserved in those pages. Ailo wanted it, but she also wanted vengeance. She chose to lash out.

Her hand reached for her blaster. When Ailo pointed it at the assassin, a blaster aimed back.

"Your draw needs some work," Hekron said. "I do love standoffs. They're so much more exciting and challenging than my usual line of work."

"You mean your cowardly strategy?" Ailo's hand with the blaster trembled. *Stop shaking.*

Hekron's eyes watched her blaster. He smirked.

This wasn't what she'd expected when she ran after Rence's bug. She'd never had a gun aimed at her face.

"What is that thing?" Hekron nodded to the buzzing insect flitting about the shelf.

"No idea."

"Lie." He stepped toward the bookshelf, his blaster staying true to its target. Ailo tracked him with her weapon.

"And what's this?" The Garassian indicated Cin Quinti's book. "Oh, now isn't this interesting?" Still aiming the blaster, Hekron bent down and pulled the thick tome out of the shelf. The insect followed buzzing and flashing.

She wanted to lunge but he remained out of reach.

"That's mine," she said.

Hekron tossed the book on the table and, with lightning speed, snatched the insect from the air. He investigated the mechanical device, rolling it around with probing fingers.

The bug pulled against his grip, seeking to fly toward the book. His thumb found the switch and shut it off. "This is much more sophisticated than you."

*You have no idea who I am.*

Hekron fiddled with the bug, twirling it around with nimble fingers. "You came to retrieve a book, with this as your guide?" He indicated Rence's device, keeping the hand with the blaster aimed at her face.

A pit dropped in Ailo's stomach, despite her anger. The seriousness of who she faced hit her with the quickness of the strike that had snatched the bug. Hekron wasn't just out of her league. He didn't even fit the T9 ranking system. He broke it.

That wasn't all he broke. The assassin squeezed the bug inside his fist. He grit his teeth as if to add strength to his hand before tossing the pieces to the ground.

*Gerib, I don't know what to do.*

*"Whatever you do, don't be rash. It will get you killed."*

"So, you wanted that?" Hekron gestured at the book on the table.

"And to kill you." Her hand with the blaster shook but she kept it aimed at him in earnest.

"Who are you?"

"You killed my parent."

"Ah," Hekron nodded. "I've killed many parents."

"Animal." Ailo's eyes flicked to the book. He'd placed it close enough for her to reach it in some kind of sadistic strategy.

"Tell me, child…"

"I'm not a child." She edged closer to the book.

*"Ai, be careful. Stay focused."*

*Shut up, Gerib.*

"Your someone's child. The question is *whose* child? My guess is one of the Radicals if you want that book." Hekron took a step closer.

*"Ai… careful."*

Ailo needed to make a choice. She decided to shoot.

If she hit him, her parent's killer died. If he fired too, she'd be dead. But not if she... Ailo dove to the ground, firing the blaster. She rolled to the bookcase and came up, weapon aimed toward her target.

Hekron had vanished.

She turned as the lights went out.

Her hand with the blaster twisted and the weapon disappeared from her grip.

The light flipped back on. Hekron stood by the panel near the door. He held his weapon and her blaster. And he had the book.

*How?*

"Bravery is bold. But its opposite isn't cowardice, child. It's prudence. And when you learn it, it screams victory through its silence."

"You're wrong," she said. "That wasn't bravery. It was desperation."

Hekron nodded. "So, I face a budding warrior. This explains a lot."

Ailo got to her feet.

"Sit." He motioned to a chair at the table with his blaster. "You've come with Jati. How interesting. Are you their protege?"

*"Don't answer, Ai."*

*I don't intend to.*

"Why do you want this book?" He held it up.

"It belongs to me."

Hekron laughed. "Wrong. Try again."

"It's rightfully mine."

"How so?"

"I don't owe you an explanation. And you don't deserve one." *I will kill you, you sadistic piece of Gor scum.* She glared at him.

The assassin's eyes widened. "Ah, yes. That look is familiar to me." He put the book down on a nearby shelf. "In my profession, I see it more often than I'd like." He walked closer, dismantled her blaster, and tossed it on the table in pieces.

At the open collar of his shirt, partially obscured by his goatee, a tattooed symbol lay under salt and pepper chest hair. Three arrows and a square, the same icon on the authentic note left on Ffossk.

*I remember, Gerib.*

Flickering images of the small kitchen unit on T9 returned. Her parent sat with another person, drinking tea at their small table. A memory flashed: her parent holding up a paper with that symbol.

*She was being hunted.*

"I don't know how it can be," Hekron said, "but it's written all over your face. And, I hear it in your voice... parentless child from Tarkassi 9."

*So she is dead.*

"Oh, you didn't know? Here," he rolled up a sleeve, "let me show you your parent."

"Get away from me." Ailo reared back in the chair.

The assassin grabbed her arm and drew her toward him. He shoved his forearm in her face, so close the black hair on his arm touched her nose. "It's right there," he said through gritted teeth. "Third row, third from the bottom."

She turned her head, eyes shut tight.

His face pushed against her head, mouth at her ear. "She died slowly. Long and painful."

"No!" She lashed and bucked about, fighting him with everything she had. "Let me go!" He pulled up on her arm, making her yelp in pain. "Let me go!"

"I don't think so."

Hekron's wrist comm blipped. His eyes, green and empty, without the obsidian of Jati and Rence, glared at her. "Yes, uncle?"

"Jati and I have finished."

Through the haze of trauma, the voice registered.

*Aradus.*

"The general has agreed to our terms. Or should I say, *your* terms," the old ambassador said. "I've sent them to meet their ship, which I cleared to enter the atmosphere and dock in Garassit at the municipal port. It's coming down now."

"Kusk is over, then?" Hekron dragged Ailo up from the chair and out onto the open balcony.

She'd shut down. The room passed as a blur. It wasn't supposed to be like this.

*The book. I... I'm sorry, parent.*

"Just ending. Safe enough for entry. The clock ran out on Jati's little ruse." Aradus said, his tone arrogant and smug. "Galank's ship, and the bulk of the PA fleet, is dropping out of FTL now."

"You think he'll still engage?" Hekron's head went skyward. Ailo, near-catatonic and bleary-eyed, followed his gaze, into the clear night sky over the Lorassian Sea. Through the haze, she made out the massive armada of ships. They littered the sky. Minute flashes indicated additional ships dropping out of FTL.

"Of course, there's no reason for him not to. He knows nothing. No communication has come in or gone out during Kusk. We've got them right where we want them. They're in for the strategic surprise of a generation. This so-called Tide War ends now."

*Surprise?* The old ambassador's tone bordered on hubris. She and Nisi had lost the window to shut down the shield as a forced negotiation.

"So Jati will meet me?" Hekron said.

"In the morning, yes." Aradus paused. "This is not my way of doing things. If it were up to me..."

"Yes, uncle. I know your ways."

"An entire empire now rests on your shoulders," Aradus said. "Do not fail us, nephew."

Ailo watched the assassin's face. It turned sinister. *Vengeance wore no mask.*

Hekron's eyes went to his free arm. "I've got just the spot for them."

"If things go as they should, Galank will strike with no quarter. I know him, he's more ruthless than he lets on," the old ambassador said. "Hirok turned out to be the perfect asset. Saved us the trouble of having to dispose of him."

"He was a fool," Hekron said, eyes up at the night sky as more PA ships dropped into orbit.

"Jati's friends made a small mess in the lower level," Aradus said. "Two of them are running about. It's just a matter of time before we round them up."

"Well, I've got one of them here."

"Not the Birevian?"

Hekron paused. "She's here?"

"Yes, and looking as ferocious as ever."

"Maniac... she'll be the death of me."

"Don't jest," Aradus said. "If she's caught she stays alive. Jati and I have an agreement. It must be honored or this all falls apart."

"Understood."

"Hekron, I mean it. This is delicate. Jati would not agree to my terms without my assurance. The other is a child and must under no circumstances be..."

"I've got that one."

"Is she hurt?"

The assassin stared into Ailo's eyes. His mouth curved into a sinister smile. "Not physically."

*Monster.*

"Excellent. I will send a message to the *Carmora* informing them."

Ailo's head cleared. All the moving parts of Aradus's plan didn't connect but she knew enough to understand that she needed to get to the *Carmora* and warn Jati. As the three of them had suspected, the entire PA was walking into a trap.

"Uncle, it gets better."

"Enlighten me," Aradus said.

"The child... Cin Quinti was their parent."

"What?" Aradus voiced surprise through the transmitter.

It was now or never. Ailo shot her boot at Hekron's shin. The assassin shifted his leg out of the way as if it were an afterthought.

To add to the humiliation, and his superiority, he didn't even grace her with a response.

"Hold on, uncle," Hekron switched frequencies and called for two guards on the comm.

Two guards entered the chamber. "Take this one down the hall and lock it in the guest room across from my quarters."

"Someone took out two elites on patrol down the hall. With a flare," one of the guards said.

Hekron's gaze went to Ailo.

She gave him nothing by way of a response.

"I want two of you outside that portal until morning," he said.

One of the Garassian sentinels nodded.

"I'm going to kill you," Ailo said as they took her away.

Hekron ignored her and waved the guards off. He went back to his conversation with Aradus.

Ailo struggled against the guards, kicking and pulling. She wanted to tear into him, to pull his body apart limb by limb.

"You're a feisty one," one of the guards said. Their grip tightened on her wrist.

"Let me go!" She fought their hold but with two of them, and her state of mental exhaustion, the effort was futile.

The library passed as the sentinels dragged her away. The vacant spot on the lower shelf where the book had sat, likely for her lifetime, stood out like a singularity in the preserved knowledge on the wall. In a way, the text had been a cosmic anomaly amidst the Garassian tomes.

Before she lost sight of Hekron, she caught a glimpse of the assassin laughing at the edge of the balcony.

# THIRTY-FIVE

Ailo woke disoriented. Her eyes stared at Garassian stone. Lying on her side, hands clasped under her head atop the bed's linens, she blinked to focus. The reality that returned did not bring comfort.

The night's events ran backward. Hekron's anticipatory delight on the balcony. The assassin's conversation with Aradus. His grip on her arm. The book, out of reach. Words about her parent.

She rolled over. In the waning darkness, the faint outline of a pitcher of water and plate of nuts and fruits stood like a charcoal sketch against gray stone. A small table and a single chair confirmed the palace aesthetics: prudent ornamentation.

*Too prudent.* It crossed a line, metamorphosing into restrained arrogance.

The offering on the table spoke volumes about her captors. Even with Hekron's blatant and willful cruelty and malice the Garassians put on airs and fed their enemies. They 'graciously' offered them beds. The whole culture of Garassian politics reeked of performance and feigned hospitality, courtesy in corrupted form and no more than an alluring trap.

Did the Garassians treat their victims the same?

Her eyes scanned the darkened room. Under the veneer, behind a pretentious surface, lay a prison. A window, too small to squeeze through offered little hope. The faint tidal rhythm of water through its hyperglass confirmed her suspicion. On high, the flat sea-side wall of the palace dropped in a sheer face. Even if she got through the opening, the fall would kill her. Not even the Lorassian's waters would buffer her plummeting body. If she cleared the rocks.

*The rocks.*

Nisi was still out there. Unless she'd been caught.

*Not a chance.*

The soldier either lay in wait or was dead. There was no taking her alive. Ailo had heard nothing to the contrary since the incident in the library. An image of the assassin surprising her as she discovered the copy of her parent's book flashed in her mind.

*Hekron.*

His malicious words, spoken into her ear through gritted teeth, surged from the depths. Ailo pushed down the returning horror.

*No, this isn't over. Not even close.*

The food and drink left by gracious hosts went down without a thought. She needed the energy for what lay ahead. No sooner had she placed the last nut into her mouth, than the portal opened. Two sentinels entered the guest chamber.

"You are to come with us," one said while motioning with a hand for her to exit the room.

---

The sun rose on Ceron. Rays like golden fingers reached across a topographic map. They shone across the processional road outside the palace with a stunning and surprising grandeur.

Ailo squinted. The guards had hold of each of her arms in gloved hands made of an unfamiliar, subtle armor. Soft and pliable, it added strength to their grips; their fingers worked like vices.

Ahead, a quarter-mile down the grand road, a small crowd had gathered. A quarter-mile further, at the city's edge, tiled buildings and spires decorated rolling hills. For the first time since arriving, Ailo noticed the sky alive with air traffic. Dozens of transport pods and larger shuttles crossed the urban vista, flowing in lanes at varying elevations. Judging by the obvious silence above, the boundary of the palace grounds remained restricted airspace.

She didn't need to look left to know the sea flanked the view. Its fresh, salty scent tinged the morning air. And, she didn't want to draw attention in the direction of the rocks where she hoped Nisi lay hidden.

The lives of lost souls from Three Spans of the Arm sang in her ears. People doing what they thought to be right, ending up in the clutches of their enemies. They too encountered worlds beyond their own as captives. Or worse, as prisoners sentenced to death. Her first opportunity to absorb the larger world of Garassia. How ironic that it came while bound as a prisoner with an entourage of sentinels. And on the way to what?

An unexpected and new experience washed over her at the question.

Her gaze went to the sea. It greeted land with gentle treaty. The palace, behind her, made by human hands, intruded, its rock jetty jutting with rude and brash intrusiveness out into the water.

Ailo scoffed at the poetry of it. She thought of Tera. Metaphors came so easily in a natural world shaped by human arrogance and greed.

The earnest pace of the sentinels didn't falter. Their feet hit the Garassian stone with the consistency of a metronome's steady beat. Every fourth or fifth step Ailo had to double-time it to keep her stride. Ahead, the uninviting and familiar face of Hekron appeared standing with a group of sentinels and other well-dressed Garassians.

A horn blared back at the palace. The sonorous call passed and bounced back off the city. Its blaring note reverberated and faded out over the Lorassian Sea.

Ailo swung her head back. A group of figures, tiny from this range, gathered on the top tier of the palace. Unless she was mistaken, the one dressed in a crimson robe was

Aradus. She turned back around and her stomach dropped. The assassin approached.

"Good morning," he said.

Ailo's eyes narrowed. She thought of Jati's lessons. This time she would follow their instructions.

"Silence?" Hekron folded his arms across his chest. "Not surprising. A lack of manners is to be expected from those raised without parents on the Outer Rim."

*You get nothing. Not even the satisfaction of a flinch.*

The assassin waited.

Ailo's temper sank below the sea, its temperature cooled by the Lorassian's depths.

"I admire your tenacity, child." Hekron brushed back his long brown hair and tied it, half-up, half-down. His green eyes passed to her left, gazing out over the water. "A day of days, this is." He shifted their emerald glint to her and took a step closer. "Your fate rests on today's outcome. And when it's done, I alone get to decide what happens to you. You're in a...."

A booming roar interrupted Hekron's gloating. It echoed away over the marshland and down the road.

The Garassian turned. Ailo peered toward the city.

A second thunderous boom rose and fell. An engine, rattling and clanging, like it wouldn't keep running and might stall, ricocheted off the palace walls.

The assassin disregarded Ailo and walked in the direction of the others.

*Vroom... vroom...*

Ailo's lips curved upward. *It's not? That would be too...*

Again the rattle and racket. A trail of smoke snaked behind the source back at the city line.

*It is.*

A figure on a K-speeder, a few feet over the road, zipped towards the crowd.

"Is that?" one of the sentinels holding her arm asked.

A thick exhaust trail ran behind the speeder, puffing up with each twist of the throttle. The unmistakable mane of lavender hair flowed free behind a chiseled face of flaxen skin.

"Jati," Ailo said. And with pride, added, "General. And warrior."

The sentinel's helmet shifted, their eyes on Ailo. She winked in delight.

"That thing sounds like a Swamp Boar with a sore throat," the other sentinel said.

Jati blew past the crowd, trailing black exhaust. Those who'd covered their ears moved their hands to their noses and mouths, coughing. The K-speeder bucked, almost stalling, as Jati arced it back.

*Nisi's bike from the cantina.*

The rattling of the engine ricocheted off the surroundings. Jati slowed the speeder and descended, bringing it down and to a halt in the dirt about fifty paces back from Hekron and the others on the city side of the plain. Ailo recognized the piece of equipment clipped-in along the side of the rattling speeder.

*Gerib...*

"What is it with you Dradens?" Jati said and cut the power. "You're always mixing family and state. It gets you nothing but trouble. Only your cousin learned better."

"And look where it left him," Hekron said. The assassin stood to Ailo's right, in the direction of the palace.

*"That was low, Ai."*

*And not a good idea.*

Jati sighed, a hand on the steering column. The other hand thumbed the belt at their waist. They had on a tight-fitting, deep red jumpsuit. Ailo recognized the Legion symbol tattooed on their arm sewn into the fabric on the chest.

"Yes, Hekron, unlike the rest of you, he's at peace." The PA general got off the speeder and tied their loose lavender hair into a ponytail. They aimed their chiseled, stone face at the rising sun over the Lorassian sea and inhaled. "Ah, you never forget the smell of Garassia in the morning."

"You know what your problem is, Jati?"

"Why don't you tell me, assassin."

"You care too much. It's your weakness."

"We Legion veterans have that flaw, Hekron. It keeps us noble." Jati crossed their hands on their chest. Ailo assumed the gesture to be the Legion salute.

"Like your friend, Hirok?" Hekron snarled. "That worked out well."

"Another tragedy. A lost promise."

"You think you're so righteous, don't you?"

"Think? No." Jati shook their head. "I know I am. There's a theme here, Hekron. Picking up on it yet?" Jati pulled the Talon Caster belonging to Keen Draden from the clips on the side of the K-speeder.

The assassin cocked his head.

"Didn't think so," Jati said, facing him across the plain. "That's what anger and hate do. They cloud the mind. Prevent you from *being* something and instead make you *think* you're something."

"Stop talking shit, Jati."

"Oh, I'm not, old tot. I left it back there." Jati thumbed behind them at the trail of fumes lingering in the speeder's wake.

Ailo smirked.

The general balanced the weapon across both palms, checking its weight. They ran a hand over the shaft.

The plaque on the wall in the *Carmora's* training room flashed in her mind: *Legion to the End.*

Hekron stood about thirty paces distant. The palace loomed behind him, jutting out of the rocky shoreline into the Lorassian's waters. In the light of the morning sun, the sea-side of the fortress gleamed pink.

"You can't win this fight, Jati."

"Never said I could." The general's eyes traveled up and down the Caster's shaft.

*Gerib, what do they mean?*

"It's got to be a metaphor, a warrior trick, Ai."

"So," Jati said. "About our agreement?"

Hekron turned to the small crowd. "The general and I come together in a Caster duel." Hekron's lips curled upward. "To the death."

*What?*

"By the terms," he continued, "if my opponent defeats me in fair competition they, and all other PA personnel present on Garassia will be released without harm. The location of their daughter will also be theirs. The coordinates are known to me alone and will be shared before we begin. Should the general call them out loud here, in..." Hekron paused for effect, "*desperation* before losing, I will change them and relocate their daughter."

Several in the crowd laughed in amusement.

"I will share the coordinates with my opponent now." Hekron started forward.

"What about them?" someone yelled.

Hekron halted and turned to face those gathered.

"What if they lose?" the voice added.

"What else?" Hekron replied. "Glory for Garassia!" He held up a fist to cheers. The sentinels next to Ailo hollered and stomped their feet.

Ailo watched as Jati lay the Talon Castor in the dirt and walked toward Hekron. The closer they got, the more disproportionate the two became. Jati had a good foot on the Garassian, and at least seventy-five pounds.

*And wisdom.*

Hekron muttered something inaudible to Jati from Ailo's distance. The Legion veteran nodded and turned their back on him, walking to their weapon.

Audible gasps erupted in the crowd. Hekron's face couldn't hide the insult. He strode in haste across the open dirt to a guard near Ailo and tore his Talon Caster from their hands, swirling the weapon in a fancy sequence.

Ailo tugged against the firm grip of the guard holding

her shoulders. "Let me go!"

"Don't worry, Firecracker," Jati said, picking up Keen Draden's weapon and acknowledging her for the first time.

She stopped resisting the guard.

"I don't lose, Jati," Hekron barked as he returned to his starting position.

"No, you don't," Jati said. "That's your weakness." They zapped the laser blade on the bottom end of the shaft to life. It ignited, sending off a wave of crackling electricity through the morning air.

Hekron shook his head and muttered something under his breath.

*I know what Jati's doing, Gerib.*

"You handle that weapon well." Jati nodded at the Caster in the assassin's hands.

"I was trained by Kartulu." Hekron spun the shaft in a series of arcs and lunges.

*An important piece of information. Now, Jati knows his instructor.*

"Are you not impressed, *old tot*?"

"With Kartulu? She's a great master." Jati's massive hands twirled their weapon with ease. They set their feet and shot a hard gaze at Hekron, the weapon's pronged end aimed at their opponent like a bird of prey's outstretched claw. "That says nothing about you."

Hekron's eyes narrowed. "Always you speak as if you were a warrior of old. You and your 'Legion' ways." Hekron spat in the dirt. "You polish an artifact to make it shine and serve as a talisman."

"Ooo, artfully said, Hekron. I may use that." Jati winked.

Ailo converted their conversational exchange into physical combat in her mind. Jati prodded Hekron. Nothing the Garassian said in response landed anywhere near the general, but every verbal parry hit back. And stung.

*They're winning before they fight.*

"Fool," Hekron said.

Ailo smiled. *Yes. His anger is rising. He's taking the bait.*

"So gracious with your compliments, too. Thank you," Jati said.

Hekron paced, like a lion in a cage, rage in their eyes.

"Your armor is thin, Hekron. You taunt too easily. I'll bet Kartulu tells you that all the time. You've probably got the scars from her Caster to remind you."

Hekron charged, striking with the fury of a venomous insect. The assassin lunged the Caster forward and back once, twice, three times. Each time Jati, almost magically, wasn't there.

Again and again, Hekron attacked.

Jati dodged but didn't parry. They simply danced.

Hekron's rage and anger drove him, again and again, to kill what stood right before him. Yet, no matter what he did, it failed to hit the target. Ailo's eyes went to Jati and observed grace and elegance. Even (dare she use this word in deadly combat?) beauty.

*They're not fighting. Hekron isn't an opponent. He wants to be but Jati won't allow it. This isn't combat. It's a denial of violence.*

Everything she'd known and thought about Jati made sense, as clear and crisp as the diorite pendant on her neck. All of their decisions since she'd met them, all the accusations placed on them, they were *all* accurate. Both sides were as right as they were wrong.

Jati *was* an idealist because they could be. They'd become one. The forces around them remained regressive. They were like a fist, ahead of the arm behind it, and she meant that both literally and metaphorically.

Hekron swirled his Talon Caster, the laser cutting blade heading towards Jati's torso. The general twirled the shaft of their weapon the way she'd seen in the training room. They caught Hekron's weapon and sent it soaring out of his hands. It landed twenty feet away in the dirt.

The crowd gasped.

Ailo scanned their faces. Up until now, they'd been flush with bloodlust at the entertainment.

"Hekron's dead," the sentinel said. "I don't believe it. So quick and easy."

Ailo watched Jati. They stood, weapon in their hands, pointed at their opponent.

*Why isn't Jati finishing him?*

"What're they doing?" the other sentinel asked.

"They're waiting," the one holding Ailo answered. "It's the ancient way."

"No one fights like that anymore," the other guard said.

"They do. They're old school," the sentinel responded. Ailo caught a tinge of newfound respect in their tone.

"I can wait," Jati said to Hekron and nodded at their weapon. "Take your time."

"Respect," the sentinel whispered.

*Jati. Legion... like the warriors of old.*

Hekron retrieved his weapon and put enough distance between the two of them to pause and recover from the exertion.

The assassin walked a circle, chest heaving.

Murmurs started in the crowd.

Jati shut off the cutting blade and rested the Caster down, holding it like the staff in the Assembly Hall. They looked at Ailo and winked.

Hekron charged. Jati activated the cutting blade and set their stance.

This time the older warrior danced to the side and drove Hekron back with their own attack.

*Here it comes...*

Jati lashed out with the Caster. A talon caught Hekron's side, slicing a cut in his flesh.

"Yes!" Ailo screamed.

Hekron yelped and fled.

Jati chased him, twirled the Caster, and tore a line in the Garassian's calf with the laser blade. Hekron cried in pain and stumbled.

*Jati has them!*

The general hands went high to come down with the

talons on Hekron. The weapon plunged toward the assassin. Jati faltered and went to one knee. The talons pierced dirt a foot from Hekron's position.

The crowd gasped and came alive.

Jati's hand went to their chest. They coughed and got back to their feet. Ailo noticed they staggered before steadying themselves.

Hekron paused, recovering from his near death at his opponent's hands.

Jati reset their stance. "Come on, Hekron! You going to run or fight?"

This wasn't their style. The general didn't taunt opponents into aggression. Something was wrong.

Then it hit her.

*Treading water after the crash in the Lorassian. They were searching for their medicine in their pockets.*

"Arrrggghh!" Hekron charged with a flurry of long extended strikes, lunging the staff's pronged end.

Jati dodged them all but dropped to a knee, chest heaving. The Talon Caster fell from their hand. They gasped for air and gripped the fabric of their uniform over their heart.

"I think they're having a medical issue," the sentinel holding Ailo said. "This should be stopped."

"No way," the other said. "It's no one's fault if you're old and agree to fight."

"Hold her," the sentinel passed Ailo to the other guard. They started towards the two fighters. Jati reached for their weapon with one hand and got back to their feet. Ailo could see the sweat running down their face and soaking the uniform on their chest. They were pale and struggling for air.

"Hekron," the sentinel called, "fair competition states…"

"Get back!" The assassin pointed the Caster at the guard. "Stay out of this!"

The sentinel backed away. Ailo scanned the crowd. The faces expressed confusion.

She looked at Jati. Their eyes connected. Green irises dazzled with obsidian. They looked up. Ailo followed their gaze. A multitude of ships of the PA fleet were visible as specks on the edge of the atmosphere.

"I was born here you know, Hekron," Jati said, struggling for breath. "On Ceron. In this city, before my parents moved to Ortor."

"I don't care," Hekron said.

"I always..." the general winced from pain as they drew in a breath but continued, "thought the view looking down on this plain from above to be the most moving."

"What?" The assassin shook his head in anger.

"Victory lingers here, Hekron," Jati said. "In the air." They drew in another breath, this time through their nose and glanced at Ailo. "And on the ground."

Hekron spit in the dirt and charged.

Jati parried the blow and shifted. They couldn't keep the weapon held up and the laser cut the dirt as they moved. Hekron came at them a second time. Jati batted away their weapon and struck back, narrowly missing Hekron's head, then fell to a knee, gasping.

"Stop this!" Ailo screamed. "Can't you see they're not well!"

Jati rose. Again their Caster's laser dragged in the dirt as they moved, deflecting another attack and shifting position. Hekron came back again, determined to finish them. One strike went high and Jati got the talon up in time. The assassin's follow-up went low to the ribs with the laser.

Jati made no sound as it cut them, spilling blood onto the yellow dirt.

"No!" Ailo screamed.

"No one stays silent when cut," the sentinel said in awe.

Jati spun and whacked Hekron in the knee, sending him tumbling down in pain.

The general stood, chest heaving and sweating.

Hekron smiled from the ground at the sight of red liquid coming from Jati's side. He rose and aimed the talons at Jati and charged.

With the aid of the weapon to deflect the strike, Jati

dragged the laser along the ground yet again. The general slowed and stumbled. Hekron pounced and slashed the laser blade across Jati's back.

The crowd gasped.

Ailo screamed.

Jati made no sound. They dropped to a knee, the Talon Caster flying from their hands.

Hekron laughed victoriously and held his Caster up over his head arrogantly.

The crowd stayed hushed. Hekron turned, confused by the lack of response.

"Please," Ailo begged the sentinel, her body hanging and tears running from her eyes. "Please stop this."

"I'm not done yet," Jati said on one knee. They picked up their weapon and pushed themselves up. Their hand slid off their thigh and they fell to the dirt.

"I'll wait," Hekron said, mockingly.

"Gor scum! Murderer!" Ailo screamed.

"Shame," the sentinel whispered at a hush.

Jati struggled and rose to their knees, yellow dirt dusting their Legion reds. They clutched the Talon Caster, stood, and turned. "I said, I'm not done yet. I'll tell you when I am."

Hekron twirled the weapon with anticipation. Jati held their Caster, talon up and laser burning the ground. The assassin pointed their Caster's talons at Jati. "I'm done with *you*, General." Hekron burst forward striking low and high. Jati shifted left, dragging the laser across the sand in a quarter circle. Then stopped.

Hekron's staff hit the back of Jati's knees and they dropped to all fours.

"No!" Ailo screamed and fought against the arms of her captor. "No! Jati!"

Jati grunted, chest heaving. They pushed off from the ground and balanced on their knees. Red blood poured from their side. It lay everywhere in splatters and splashes in the dirt.

Ailo scanned the track of the battle.

*So much blood...*

Jati's hand gripped their chest. Their face winced with pain as they gasped for air. Hekron strode in front of them, towering over them for the first time since they started.

Jati's green eyes glowed with sudden brightness. "Now, I'm done... You lose," they said.

Hekron's eyes filled with murderous delight. He raised the weapon and, with an arrogant roar, plunged the Talon Caster's prongs into Jati's chest. Mouth open wide, he screamed in fury into Jati's face, his eyes burning with anger. The assassin's rage echoed as murder triumphant across the plain and over the palace walls.

"No!" Ailo ripped at the arms of the guard.

Hekron left the weapon embedded in Jati's chest. Blood ran down over their thighs and onto the dirt. The assassin turned his back and walked away.

"Let me go!" She fought the hold of their armored grips.

Hekron waved for them to release her.

She bolted out of their grip, half her heart intent on snatching up the weapon and attacking while Hekron had his back turned. For Jati. For her parent. And for everyone memorialized in the sick and sadistic ritual markings on the assassin's arm. The other half pulled to Jati. It pulled with a force of compassion. Of ethics. And empathy.

Ailo knew it to be wrong, and a death sentence, but vengeance won. She went for the weapon on the ground.

A hand grabbed her before she could pick it up. A grievous groan accompanied tremendous strength that pulled her around and held her back.

"No, Ailo."

With their other hand, Jati withdrew the Caster out of their chest and tossed it aside. Blood pumped out of the three wounds and ran down their kneeling body.

They collapsed in the dirt.

# THIRTY-SIX

"Hekron!"

The assassin's name shattered the silence of tragedy. Ailo traced its source in the direction of the Lorassian Sea. His name echoed away, but an invisible rage lingered in the morning air.

"Hekron!"

Ailo scanned the rocky shoreline.

Blaster fire shot forth from the marshes. With expert precision, two shots clipped the sentinels who'd held Ailo. They collapsed on the ground.

"Hekron!"

The voice had no visible source, but Ailo knew it. Hekron's face answered for him. He knew it too.

*Nisi.*

Sentinels among the crowd fired blaster rounds into the wetlands. Their shots sent splashes up in the shallows and marshes in a futile attempt to hit whoever ambushed their companions.

Hekron strode in haste towards Ailo, the assassin's green eyes intent on his Talon Caster.

A round of blaster fire showered the crowd. The remaining sentinels dropped. Innocent Garassian officials who'd come to witness the duel scurried back and forth in panic, bumping into one another and confronting obstacles in their path in the form of dead soldiers.

A burst of fire tacked from one end of the crowd to the other. The officials fled, robes held up to run faster, towards the palace gates.

"Out of my way, child." Hekron backhanded Ailo. The blow sent her crashing to the ground. Over the searing pain of her cheek, she caught sight of Nisi barreling out of the shallows, her long strides flexing muscles of Birevian steel. Her tattooed arm came up and aimed the blaster.

*Pang!* The Talon Caster flew from Hekron's hands. The assassin went for Jati's weapon.

*How dare he touch that!*

Blaster fire flashed by Ailo's ear so close it crackled with heat. Nisi's shot split Jati's Talon Caster shaft in two. Hekron's hand froze, holding the lower end of the useless pole.

Nisi sprinted over the grass and shrub, the wrath in her brown eyes emboldened by the desire for revenge. With each stride, the soldier's muscles trembled, sending pulsing waves of fury through her limbs.

The soldier fired a single round. It hit Hekron's Talon Caster laying on the ground a few yards away from her first impact. The weapon shattered.

*Why isn't she shooting Hekron?*

Ailo looked toward the palace. A flurry of activity on the highest tier caught her eye.

Nisi tore past her in a rush of wind. "Get out of here." The soldier flung the blaster at Ailo without losing a step. "Get to the city, the *Carmora's* docked there."

Hekron set his legs, readying for her charge.

Ailo grabbed the weapon.

"Now!" Nisi yelled, eyes like a storm.

Ailo ran toward the shoreline. She reached the cover of the first line of rocks and tucked behind a boulder to watch.

Hekron, expecting a duel, positioned his stance.

Ailo watched the soldier continue without slowing down.

The Garassian's eyes widened as he realized her intentions, but it was too late.

Nisi tackled him. The two crashed to the ground. Nisi's arms spun like turbines; her fists impacted like meteors. It wasn't even a fight. Hekron's hands came up in defense, and his legs and knees worked to escape, but after about ten blows the signals in his brain stopped reaching his limbs.

Over and over, fists of fury slammed into his face like hammers to anvils.

Ailo's thrill turned to shock.

More blows rained down from the soldier.

A pit in Ailo's stomach opened as shock shifted to unease. The taste of vengeance soured into horror.

"Argggghhhhhhhh!" Nisi halted and leaned closer. She roared into what was left of Hekron's face. The violent and cathartic call echoed over the palatial grounds.

Her muscled legs lifted her off his inert body. She stood with fists dripping as if they'd been dipped in paint. Tattooed forearms, streaked and speckled with a decorative crimson glaze, told a tale of unrelenting rage.

Nisi tied Hekron's ankles with a cable and dragged him to the K-speeder.

*Oh no.*

To the right, a group of sentinels hurried from the palace gates.

Nisi kicked the speeder to life. Black exhaust belched from the engine, obscuring the bike and rider.

Hekron's body shifted on the ground and accelerated down the road, following the trail of smoke. The cadaver rose in the air.

The sentinels on their way from the palace slowed. Moving figures on the balcony halted. All of Garassit froze.

Nisi appeared from the black smoke, banking the bike right. She completed the turn and shot forward toward the palace. The K-speeder, and Hekron behind it, soared over the sentinels. Their helmets leaned back to watch it pass.

*Nisi, no.* Ailo's eyes went to Jati lying on the road. *They wouldn't want this.*

Nisi veered left of the complex, the K-speeder level with the highest tier. The distinct crimson robe of Aradus stood on the gray stone balcony. The soldier steered past the old ambassador, Hekron's body swinging close to the stone's edge. The speeder turned around the palace walls to its far side over the sea.

Nisi circled the palace to taunt them. Her bloody rage would be there for all to see.

The sentinels on the road resumed their forward push. They were coming for Jati's body.

The rattle of the K-speeder throttling up echoed over the Lorassian Sea. Nisi, trailing black and billowing exhaust, emerged on the palace's right side from behind the corner's stone tower. Hekron's cadaver swung around behind the K-speeder. She accelerated and the bike shot along the fortress face where they'd swam inside.

*That's it.*

The channel. The cable. Not a line of spite and death, or vulgar revenge, but a line to hope.

*Whooosh! Whoosh!* Two fighter Darts sailed overhead from the city toward the palace. Explosives dropped in their wake and tore up the landscape in sequential reports in a precise line from the city to the palace. Ailo was square in the path of the approaching demolitions. She bolted to the water. The ground erupted in surging red flames as the bomb chains detonated. Two more blasts and they'd reach and obliterate everything, including her.

Ailo dove into the estuary. Garassit shook. Cold water flashed as hot as Nushaba's rays. Even with her eyes closed, the dark world under the water went red. The reports continued beyond her position, diminishing in volume. She bolted upright, gasping for air. Pushing wet hair out of her eyes, she confronted a hazy world of ruin, tinged with a sulfurous scent.

The Garassians were finished negotiating and were wiping the slate clean.

Through the wafting clouds of smoke, a group of sentinels scurried back toward the palace, carrying Jati's body.

Nisi's speeder whizzed overhead with Hekron in tow, the two Dart fighters on its tail. The soldier banked back towards the palace. Why weren't the Garassians shooting at the bike?

The speeder belched smoked and swung around in front of the palace. Nisi aimed for the line of billowing clouds lingering from the explosions on the shoreline. She passed into it and vanished. The speeder's throttle echoed over the sea.

Ailo bolted to the rock where she'd watched Nisi massacre Hekron. A near impossible gambit, but her one shot.

*Well, two shots.*

Everyone, including Nisi, probably assumed she'd been vaporized.

She lay prone and rested the blaster's muzzle on a chipped edge of the rock facing back to the palace.

*Breathe.*

She aimed the weapon in the direction of the approaching chase.

*Relax.*

Something Jati said during a training session returned: *Nothing is difficult unless you make it so.*

Nisi whizzed overhead. Hekron followed in tow.

Ailo's finger pulled the trigger. Twice.

The first Dart fighter exploded. The second tipped left, smoke trailing from its wing. A whistling scream competed with the rattling K-speeder. The Dart bucked and stalled, arcing toward the sea. The craft smacked into the water at the shoreline and, with a flash, burst into flames.

The K-speeder's noisy engine fell away as it rode over the city, out of sight. At least Nisi would make it back to the *Carmora*.

Tired of death.

Exhausted and done with being wet and in positions that lacked control. If by some miracle she made it out of this mess, Ailo vowed that she'd learn to swim.

*After I mourn for Jati.*

She lifted an arm off the floating debris she'd scavenged

from a section of the ruined Dart shell and wiped seawater from her face.

The swells bobbed the flotsam up and down, cresting and splashing her with saltwater. The cable bolted into the rock with some kind of pin, lay a few yards away. Ailo appreciated Nisi's prudence in her mission preparation. The soldier brought everything she'd needed to carry out her tasks.

*Nisi...* Was that the glory of war? Did soldiers perform acts of violent brutality as revenge?

Hekron deserved death. But was there a line?

*There has to be a line.*

Nisi stepped in and delivered merciless revenge. Was it hers alone? Was it the PA's?

*Was it mine?*

Why Jati kept fighting didn't make sense.

*Or did it?*

Their words, whispered in Ailo's ear on the A-Dodger, returned:

"There comes a time for all who fight to face a choice... for those few given the privilege to have the choice, the honorable ones do what is right."

Ailo couldn't make sense of why Jati continued to battle Hekron as their body failed them. Was it a sacrifice similar to JeJeto's? If so, to what end? What made that 'right'?

*I don't understand.*

Jati had told Hirok they were destined to fail, that *"The world forced it on them."*

Something had to drive that determination. Some success must be hidden still, and it had to be more than a warrior's code.

The waves pushed her closer to the forbidding gray stone. Ailo kicked towards the cable. The floating debris bumped against the palace. She hated this wall and everything that lay on the other side. It had brought nothing but death and failure. But Jati wanted her to live. Every time she'd lost something, the general replaced lament and mourning with a call to action, like when she'd released her parent's book from her grip off Cesix Station.

*Now you write your own.* The words rang in her ears.

"Ai, they also said you were the reason the PA would win this war."

*I need help, Gerib. I don't know what to do.*

"Decide. That is what Jati gifted you. It's in your hands now."

Would it be a salvageable justification for the violence and sacrifice of this mission? She stared down the Garassian stone facade, treading water. How long would it take to pull under and through the channel? Nisi had guided her through last time. The soldier's strength made quick work of it, but even then Ailo's breath barely held as they'd emerged.

And what lay in wait on the other side?

She clutched the cable and released the fragment of the Dart's shell, shoving it away. Her gaze went to the Lorassian, as if to deny what lay in front of her vision only a few feet away. The water rippled in diminishing swells to the horizon. A beautiful sea devoid of human presence, the planet quiet and at peace.

*It's not the worlds in the Arm, but its inhabitants who corrupt.*

Back and forth, swinging like a pendulum. An endless cycle of reactionary violence, anger, and hate in perpetual motion. Jati broke it, if just for a moment and a future flickered through the cracks.

"No, Ailo." They'd said when she chose reaction.

A sea bird flew past. White and sleek, the graceful creature soared on the thermals over the water — a good image to hold in her mind of Jati's spirit. The gull grew smaller as it flew away over the sea.

*I understand, Gerib.*

Jati's last step as a warrior would be followed by her first.

*I'm getting that book.*

She took a breath and plunged into the deep.

Arm by arm, she pulled her way along the cable. The

water cooled as she dropped to the wall's lowest edge. Light cascaded through the depths behind her, illuminating gray stone. In the pitch below, the lower boundary approached.

Something brushed her leg.

"Ai, was that...?"

The cable ducked under and across the rock barrier. Ailo hovered and her legs rose. She passed underneath parallel to the stone's underside. Her breath held. The way up would be quicker. She reached an arm to the other side of the wall, seeking the cable. Once in her grip, she'd ascend to the surface with ease. Her fingers touched something other than rock.

*Ouch!*

A pang of pain hit her hand, followed by a serpentine form wrapping around her arm. Air shot out of her lungs in a silent scream, sending bubbles up to the surface. She twisted in fright and pain. Her head cracked on the bottom of the gray stone and her body flailed about, disoriented, arms groping for the cable.

The wall rose away. Whatever had a grip on her pulled her down.

Instinct kicked in and she pulled a fail-safe move from her days on T9. Her teeth sank into the creature wrapped around her arm.

Still, it pulled her down.

Her jaw forced through a scaly skin, teeth sinking into soft, fleshy muscle. Hot liquid filled her mouth as the creature bled, its contact stinging her inner cheeks and gums.

It unfurled from her arm.

Ailo kicked her legs as she'd done when Nisi dragged her to shore. The motion stayed her descent. Her mouth was on fire. She needed air!

*Use your arms.*

With a wide motion of both arms, she reversed the gravity of the sea. A second try sent her rising. The wall passed. It didn't matter what side she was on; she had to breathe. The pounding of her heart abated.

*It's no use. I don't have enough...*

"Relax, Ai. Your body will go as long as it can. Ignore it and swim."

*But Gerib, I don't have the...*

"Do it."

She trusted her heart to beat one more time and swung her arms in a last, desperate arc.

It was no use. The surface grew more distant.

*"Do it, Ai!"*

Gerib's voice ran like an electric shock through her brain, sending neurons firing. With her last breath, she reached in a wide arc.

The liquid world gave way to an empty hot void. Horrible, foul sulfurous air filled her lungs. She gasped, ravenous for oxygen. The stinging in her mouth had shifted to numbing swelling. Her tongue felt like it had doubled in size, making breathing difficult.

Holding onto a slimy ledge, Ailo raised her hand out of the black sea while she trod water. A small red mark ran over her finger pads, but no broken skin.

She'd never make it with the energy she had left.

Unless...

*"Ai, Boar said you'd regret it."*

She withdrew the booster and popped the top, inhaling.

A wave of power ran from her nose to her feet. "Woo hoo!"

Mission be damned, Ailo hollered. Even with her tongue numb she managed to call out in celebration. Her voice bounced and echoed down the narrow underground channels and sent rats scurrying. She felt ten feet tall and ready to run a race. The swelling in her mouth lessened. Her breathing eased too, most likely from something in the booster's concoction.

She was alive. And she could swim.

# THIRTY-SEVEN

Ailo never thought she would be thankful to be a street kid who hid and stole to survive. But the persistent irony since she'd crashed on Ceron continued to play strong.

She'd avoided notice from the lower levels up to the palace's main floor. Thanks to her expertise at stealth and being a technological ghost, her body passed unnoticed through every tile scanner.

Now, hidden in the shadows of the aisle in the first-floor basilica, she waited for an opportunity to make her way to the library.

She felt fantastic. The booster was a miracle.

"*Just remember what Boar said, Ai... about the crash afterwards.*"

*I know, Gerib. I know. You are such a downer! I've got this from here. Back off!*

You could cut the tension in the palace with a knife. High-ranking ambassadors and military leaders clustered in the spacious nave and spoke in hushed voices. Ailo knew how and when to pass groups of people unnoticed from her years on the streets of T9. She also understood how to read body language. What the Garassians demonstrated ran the gamut. Overt and even performative shock and outrage dominated. Hushed tones and furtive glances accompanied raised eyebrows and whispers acknowledging allies in what was sure to be opportunistic schemes and power plays in the destabilization of Garassit's leadership.

Jati and Hekron's deaths and the looming siege dominated the conversations bouncing off the vaults of the ceiling.

The scene passed before her eyes and ears in the shadows as she moved from column to column. Under the side aisle's barrel vault, she made her way to the grand corridor at the back. If she reached the elevator without notice, she'd be certain to make it up to the library on the top floor.

A hush fell over the basilica. Ailo stopped on instinct. All heads turned to the front doors. From her position hiding behind a column, she watched Aradus enter the building with a small entourage. As if following the direction of a conductor whose baton guided an orchestra into a rising crescendo, the voices of those in the majestic nave rekindled their gossipy fires.

The old Garassian, trailed by ambassadors and sentinels, aimed toward Ailo's side of the basilica.

She shifted to a safer spot behind a leaf-filled urn along the outer wall.

Aradus shuffled ahead of the others. What might the ambassador be thinking? His gait and distance from his entourage indicated he didn't want to speak with anyone.

"We will use the Hamut. He can talk with the Birevian and get her to stop this madness. This..." The ambassador trailing behind him shook their head, "...barbarity."

Aradus did not answer.

Ailo followed a few steps behind the group, using the columns and plant-filled urns in the aisle for cover.

Aradus shuffled on like a child being sent to his room. Despair and grief were written in his strides. The Garassian's frail body teetered. He caught himself with a hand on the wall.

*As old as the palace stone.*

"Aradus, are you alright?" The ambassador went to offer him aid.

He swiped his arm away and continued ahead.

"The Hamut can go," his companion said, following him. "It's too messy if we keep him after we defeat the PA."

"The PA is leaving, you fool."

"What?" The ambassador scurried up behind him.

*Leaving?*

Tension stirred everywhere. Hekron's death and desecration were felt by all. Ailo noticed it most in the sentinels stationed at points in the passage. As the old ambassador passed each post, the guards did their best to shrink into invisibility.

"We miscalculated, Morienda." Aradus walked and spoke the words without turning around. "Killing their moral leader did not enrage their army. Our message to them only tumbled it from within. It sent their Hamut support fleet packing. They don't believe in Galank. They *believed* in Jati."

"The Hamuts are no longer fighting with the PA?"

"Not today, Morienda." Aradus shuffled across the stone tiles as he spoke. "And if this makes the Hamuts reconsider their commitment to the PA, they may turn their backs on the Tide entirely."

"Isn't that a good thing?"

Aradus shook his head. "A scattered and dispersed set of opponents is much more difficult to conquer than a single concentrated one. Chaos in the Arm does not make for an easy victory."

"Chaos?"

"A stirred pot settles in surprising ways. Trust me, Morienda. I've seen it happen before."

Morienda scurried to keep pace behind the elder ambassador. "Perhaps the Hamuts will disengage entirely. We can hit the PA next time while they're weakened."

"Perhaps," Aradus said. "But unlikely. Your generation can deal with it."

Ailo watched Morienda's pace slow, the uncertainty of the old ambassador's words taxing their mind.

"And Hirok's armada?" they asked.

"What of it?"

"Have they, too, retreated?"

"I'm surrounded by fools," Aradus said as he walked.

"Ambassador?"

"Hirok's armada will be under the control of the Birevian shortly, I'm sure. And that presents an entirely new problem." He shook his head. "As I said, a scattered enemy... and one set on vengeance makes for a particularly dangerous foe."

Morienda shook their head in understanding, Nisi's reputation apparently well known among the Council.

"It doesn't matter at present," Aradus said. "What matters is that Galank can't lay siege to Garassit now. He doesn't have the numbers. Our trap has failed. It's a fitting irony."

*What goes around comes around.*

Their colleague slowed as Aradus decelerated, musing.

Ailo always imagined Keen's parent as fiery and viciously cruel. After today's events, his words sounded only surrender.

"You want to be attacked and you lay in wait," he said, "knowing you can destroy your opponent. Your trap is flawless. And then a martyr saves their own side *and yours* with their sacrifice. Stupendously ironic... and cunningly righteous."

"It's not over, Aradus. We still hold almost half the Arm."

"In whose grip?" He came to a halt in front of a portrait. A painting made up of deep and rich greens, browns, and dashes of reds depicted the face of Hekron.

"Without my nephew, what is left of our grip?" His hand reached up to the painted face. "I can't even bury him."

"I am sorry," Morienda said, examining the portrait and shaking their head. "We will make sure they pay for these egregious actions. We will crush them so they never forget the line they crossed."

Aradus turned. His gaze cut past his colleague to Ailo's position in the shadows.

She ducked back behind the urn. As if to bolster her invisibility, she squeezed her eyes shut.

The silence lingered too long. Aradus must have caught sight of her face.

"I'm going to the Royal Library."

Ailo chanced a peek in his direction. Aradus shuffled

down the hall.

"As you wish," the ambassador said, not following. "But Aradus, what about an exchange? If we can reach them before they jump... your nephew and, in return, the Birevian takes Jati's body back to Heroon."

"That savage will never set foot on Ceron again so long as I live. Not even to bring back my nephew."

"What about my idea to use the Hamut?"

Aradus halted mere steps from the portal but did not turn.

"Very well. And Morienda..."

"Yes, Ambassador?"

"I do not wish to be disturbed."

Ailo slid back into the shadow. *Believe me. I won't make a sound.*

---

The stones of the hallway outside the portal to the Royal Library were touched with the blush of the rising sun.

Ailo's nostrils picked up the salty signature of the Lorassian Sea through open windows along the passage. A warm breeze swept into the castle as if to blow out the corruption. She stepped to the edge of the portal like a child moving through a house with dubious intent and peered inside. Aradus sat at the room's far side, facing the balcony. The wall sconces glowed, their sensors not ready to accept the victory of the morning. Beyond the windows, a stone terrace projected outward into the warm sunlight.

Ailo tip-toed her way along the side of the room, making for a bookshelf. This time, there would be no hovering, flashing lights. No homing signals.

"So you *are* a ghost."

She halted mid-step, a foot in the air, frozen mid-action.

Aradus lifted a goblet from the armrest and sipped. He didn't turn.

"Don't bother, child. Your presence is known."

Ailo placed her foot down and scanned the room for a bodyguard. Aradus was alone. Her eye ran over the shelves of books to the spot the volume had occupied.

"It's on the table."

Spread open, as if he had been interrupted in the reading of it, the book lay on the table.

So she was playing a game. Or entering a trap. Did he want her to go to the book where some malignant and sadistic poison, literal or otherwise, waited to ensnare her?

"You're lucky,' he said.

"Why is that?" she asked, breaking her silence.

"Your opponent knows and values the power of their enemy."

*Is he speaking about himself?*

Ailo visualized the statement by Aradus as combat.

*Counterstrike.*

"So do all worthy foes," she said.

The old Garassian's head sank and rose once in agreement.

She got her answer. Knowing his penchant for rhetorical combat, it wasn't a game or trap. This would be a battle of words.

"What do you want?" she asked.

"There is nothing else to take."

*Dodge.*

A salty breeze blew in over the terrace. Pincori's rays dazzled the surface of the sea. Flocks of birds passed the balcony and harked. She found it difficult to imagine that a day earlier she'd crashed into the same water, amidst the chaos, struggle, and death. Now, it appeared so tranquil, even beautiful.

Ailo reviewed the old ambassador's words. *Was that a dodge?* She took a step in the direction of the table. *No, it was an admission. An opening.*

"Then all you have left is..." She didn't finish, but let it linger like Marmish in a Cantinool grove. Her eyes narrowed. *Heroon vs. Garassia.*

"There is nothing left. I have lost everything." The old Garassian sipped from the goblet.

"Do you expect me to pity you?" She edged closer to the table to get to the book, her fingers reaching.

"Oh no, child. I respect you more than that. I imagine you've managed to accrue enough compassion for your needs. And I am sure you know where and how to use it. There is none for me."

*Why wasn't he calling the guards on her?*

"You have an empire," she said. "That's all you've ever wanted or cared about."

He nodded.

"I kept my empire."

Another step toward the table.

"So you do have something?"

"My children and nephew are gone. My life partner is dead." The goblet rose again and settled on the armrest.

Ailo reached the table. Her fingers slid along the curved edge of the tabletop. Still no reaction from the elderly ambassador. The open page caught her eye. Illegible words, handwritten, ran across the bottom.

*Was it Contex? Was this the lost book?*

A map, a star system of some kind, covered the top portion of the page.

"You may take that. I never could make any sense of it."

Her fingers slid under the cover. With a motion as calm and practiced as a spiritual leader performing a sacrament, she closed the book.

"Did Jati speak to you of my children?"

Ailo's eyes picked up on the blade. It lay next to the book, the sheath ornate and decorated with an insignia. It matched the one on Jati's arm. Legion.

"One of them."

"Yes, my younger child. Keen." Aradus shifted in the chair. His bony hand, shaking and attached to a withering and wrinkled arm, ran over his hidden face. It appeared atop his crown, brushing back the few strands of hair that lay amidst pale skin speckled with age.

"Keen Draden was a hero," Ailo said. "His sacrifice sparked the Tide War."

*And saved my life.*

Aradus didn't respond.

Ailo's fingers walked across the velvet tablecloth like a dancer striding to their starting position on stage. With thumb and finger, she pried the hilt free from the edge of the sheath. A sliver of blade popped out from hiding. It matched the handle. Black steel.

"My elder child was less difficult. Reardon's heart was more easily... satisfied." He drank from the goblet. "But now, I have learned more about them both. Your mentor was there with them during the Patent War and knew what happened. They shared the truth with me when we dined together. Now I know, too. And I am..." Aradus didn't finish. A breeze carried off what would have been the final words of that sentence.

*I do not pity you.*

"My nephew, however." Aradus sighed. "There, I admit shame. That points back to me. For my hands molded Hekron into who he became."

She gripped the handle. Cool metal, dark as the night sky, met the heat of her skin. A constellation, etched in the blade, glowed to life as warm fingers altered the metal's composition.

"There were both Legion, my two children. Why I never understood."

*Because you have no virtue.*

Ailo left the book on the table and stepped closer to the back of the chair. "And do you know now?"

The sun's rays set the balcony aglow in warm yellow light, ending the tension of morning's imminence.

"Jati was wise. Idealists die without fear. And without... regret."

The ambassador's fingers stroked the goblet's stem. His caress shook with age. Or sadness? Repressed fear?

Ailo tightened her grip on the knife.

Two frail and bony legs protruded from underneath his ambassadorial robe. In his lap, Aradus cradled a picture of two young men in dark red uniforms, arm in arm, smiling. The one on the left appeared noticeably younger.

*Keen Draden.*

The old ambassador inhaled deeply through his nostrils. The lapping waves crashed against the palace walls below.

Her eyes watched the pulsing rhythm on his neck.

"Do it," he said.

Ailo plunged the blade into his neck.

# THIRTY-EIGHT

*That* was murder.

Ailo had no regrets. More than vengeance lay in the thrust of that knife. Her conscience refused to call it pity. That would be too forgiving and compassionate. But the faint glimmer of humanity that rose in Aradus's pathetic demise worked enough to numb the sting of immorality.

The dagger stayed behind, embedded to the hilt underneath aged folds of skin. A small, sadistic touch, a subtle scream of revenge. Jati might have been her mentor, but she spoke her own language.

The constellation etched into the blade, she hoped, glowed on with internal heat from the old Garassian's blood. If the ruse worked, whoever found him and withdrew the knife would confront a symbolic reminder of the Legion, and the lives of his children.

Ailo hurtled through the palace, book in hand, heading for the elevator. Her legs took the first corner so hard she bashed her shoulder against the opposite wall. The underwater cable remained the one way out. All exits would be guarded and watched in earnest after the morning chaos.

But she had the book! Her parent's words, the wisdom of Teluv's cause, and the ancient beliefs of their predecessors in the Second Span. She'd learn Contex. Tera could teach her the dead language. She would read every word scripted in her parent's hand and use her training to make sense of what she, Rence, and the others preached. Her origins would unfold as the pages turned. She just needed to find something to protect it while she went underwater and...

The book flew from her hand as she collided with an object at waist height. Her feet crossed and she face-planted on the ground. A child, no older than ten, lay on the floor. Ailo had plowed right into them.

She snatched up the book. "Are you alright? Here." Ailo offered a hand.

"I'm O.K." The youngster rolled over and got to one knee. They rubbed their side where they'd collided with Ailo.

She recognized the black robe, onyx skin, and flaming red hair shaved so close it glowed as a faint illumination against his crown. *They're from Kol 2.*

The child twisted and picked up a small text. Ice blue eyes went to her hand. "You have a book as well?"

"I do," Ailo pulled the volume tight against her chest. Their accent sounded unusual, the pronunciations of Neo-Contex words almost musical.

An obsidian finger pointed at her. "The sentinels are seeking you."

*Sake of...* would the child turn her in?

"Are you from Targite?"

"I am. We are here for the Kusk celebration. But they do not like us." Their face went somber. "I would rather be home in the Fins."

*They're a Targitian.*

"What is your book?" They asked and rubbed their side through the black robe.

Ailo sensed the child's interest was less on her identity as a fugitive and more as a fellow reader. She had to get moving. "My parent wrote it," she patted the cover. "I have to..."

"Your parent?" Blue eyes went to their book as if it would disappoint.

"It's the last copy," she said. "Don't tell anyone. It's a secret."

"Can *you* keep a secret?" They peered down the hall in both directions.

She nodded.

"I took this from the library." A finger gestured in the

direction where Aradus lay dead. "It is forbidden for me to read such books." They held out the small volume.

*Tales of the Legion and other Stories of Glory in War.*

"If my parents were to find out, they would not approve."

*I'm sure.*

"You like stories about heroes?"

"I do." The child smiled. "All I hear of are gods and our founders of old. I wish to learn about the Arm as it is now, of battles and the great warriors of the Third Span."

"There is one name not in that book that should, or will, be."

The Targitian's blue eyes lit up. "Who?"

"You will know their name soon enough, I think. And when you do, you will be able to talk about them first-hand. Because you were here and played a part in the story."

"I do not understand." They shook their fuzzy red head. "You speak in a language of shadows."

*Tera would be impressed. That's a poignant phrase.*

"I must return this book before my parents find out," they said.

No way would she let this child find Aradus. She would never let anyone else go through another version of what she had as a child.

"What is your name?" Ailo asked.

"The Wind has named me Lazro."

*Wind?*

She didn't have time to ask, but she knew it had something to do with Targitian religion. "I am Ailo-té."

"Why are they after you, Ailo?"

How to answer that question, and with the clock ticking? Her eyes went to the child's book. "Help me, Lazro, and you will be helping a Legion soldier who I follow... well, followed... in the cause of justice."

They stared without answering.

"Listen, you do not like the Garassians, yes?"

Lazro shook their head. "They are fake friends. That is what my parents say when they are alone."

Ailo held out the book. The child's eyes went wide. Speckles of blood dotted her arm. She wiped it across her suit with haste. "You and I are young, Lazro. We are the future of the Arm. Old enemies and fake friends are the past... the future is ours to change."

Voices bounced around the corner.

"Sentinels." Lazro gestured back behind her.

"Check the rooms. One by one," a guard said.

"You are in trouble, yes?" Lazro asked.

She nodded.

"I will not speak of you, Ailo. I do not like them. Helleuan says decisions must be made like the ebb and flow of the Wind Tide. If you are sought by them, then something you do is worth helping."

*There is hope for the Arm.* She reached under her top and pulled off the diorite pendant. "A gift, Lazro," she said and placed it around his neck. Against the child's black robe it melted into a vast void like a small galaxy alone in an empty cosmos.

The child held the chained stone up to his eyes.

"It's diorite," she said.

"It looks like stars."

"Yes. Remember... the Arm is a big place, but it's filled with people like you and me."

"We are forbidden to wear such things."

"Make your own choices, Lazro. That's how we can change the Arm." Ailo tucked the pendant under their robe. "Wear it inside. Or keep it somewhere else out of sight." She smiled, more to herself than Lazro at the words that followed, remembering they came from Tera. "Sometimes things that are hidden give us a special kind of power."

The sentinels barked at one another around the corner. They were close.

"I have to go." She took off in the direction of the library.

"Wait."

She turned.

"Will you?" Lazro held up the Legion text.

Ailo gestured for them to throw it.

The child tossed the book underhanded. She caught it and bolted down the hallway.

Ailo flung the book through the open portal to the Royal Library. It tumbled across the floor. Good enough. Consider it returned. No one would even blink when they confronted the tableaux at the balcony's edge.

She made for the elevator on the other side of the complex, the one where Nisi had sent her off to the Core. The voices of guards echoed down the stone corridors. Lazro hadn't slowed them down. Maybe that was good; they had ignored him as irrelevant and uninvolved.

She hit the call button and waited. And waited.

Too much time passed. She needed another way down.

Her eyes caught sight of the window from the previous night, the one where she'd been discovered by the guards.

*The balcony.*

It meant another jump, like the one from the staircase on the *Carmora*. She dashed around the corner. In a flash she stood on the edge, staring down at the garden. Another interior deck lay below it, a story further down. From there, a narrow skywalk ran across to the Core. If there was a way down inside the Core dome, she might descend to the lower level to the cable. And after that?

*Plan C.*

She pushed off the small ledge and aimed at a mid-sized fruit tree. Branches neared. Her free arm swept across the front of her body to protect her. Outer limbs scratched and scraped her face and arms. She managed to grab hold of an interior branch. With a snap, it broke and she fell to the balcony.

"Hey!"

Inside the apartment, a middle-aged person rose from a seat. "What are you...?"

Ailo sprung up and over the next ledge.

The stone floor neared. She steeled her body for the impact.

JeJeto saved her from a repeat of the disastrous drop on the *Carmora*. They'd taught her to fall. She pulled her legs together, inhaled, and relaxed.

Her toes hit first; heels followed. She bent into a near-squat and directed as much energy forward and to one side as possible, tumbling at a forty-five-degree angle into a roll over the shoulder with the book tucked tight against her chest. In a smooth motion, she rotated over and back up on her feet, heading for the skywalk.

Her feet rattled and clanged the bridge as she bound across in leaping strides. The archways on the lower rim of the dome ahead were open to the air. She bolted for the nearest one. Through the checkered mesh of steel, tiers of interior walkways descended to the ground level.

She raised her head and almost ran into a sentinel. They stood on the circular interior landing hugging the Core. The massive cylinder rose like a gleaming electric heart at the center of the castle. Black and cast of what she thought was diorite, scattered vertical lights, yellow and rectangular, blinked on its surface, like a colossal, technological hive.

The guard pointed a blaster in her face. "Don't move," they said.

A steady upward current of hot air blew through the grates at their feet from far below, strong enough to billow clothing and make talking more like yelling.

"I've got the child," they shouted into a wrist comm.

"So she'd not dead," a voice responded.

"Apparently not."

The blaster muzzle hovered a mere foot from her nose.

"We found an underwater escape line, though the channel," the voice over the comm said.

Ailo's eyes darted around the structure seeking a way out. Her chest heaved up and down.

"Belti, get over here," the guard said. "Need backup."

*Now or never.*

Ailo tossed the book down at the guard's feet. Like Je-Jeto glancing at the clock, they took the bait.

*Thanks, JJ.*

She spun inside his arm, controlling and re-directing the blaster. She slammed her elbow backward along her side into their kidney, fist following in a downward strike to their groin. The impact hunched the guard over and her hand reversed and came up into their mouth.

*Call and answer, for you Solazi.*

Ailo ripped the blaster from their grip, bending with the direction of the guard's digits. The fingers slid off the handle and out of the trigger with ease. She snatched up the book with her free hand and took off around the railing to the Core.

A blaster shot sent sparks flying to her right. Ailo fired off a volley of shots at the guard across the hive tower. She hugged the interior side, gambling on being careful enough to avoid damaging the Core.

Cool blue light bounced off the titanic cylinder, reflecting from the dome. An antenna at its peak released surges of cerulean lightning up a pole. Whatever it was, the Core held power and dangerous potential.

A burst of fire hit the floor to her right, narrowly missing her foot. The guard, hunkered down about thirty feet away behind a corner of a stairwell, rattling off rounds. She needed to get past this one and to those stairs.

More blaster fire.

*Sake of the Arm!*

There was no getting through. Ailo peered over the ledge to the interior capsule holding the Core. The strength of the rising current of hot air almost pushed her head back up. Garassit's central engine dove into a darkness of heat and wind. Across a ten-foot drop, a ladder ran on its shell. But to where?

Her underwater route out was no longer an option. They'd found Nisi's cable.

*This isn't over.*

She tucked the blaster into her waist and climbed over the rail. Fifteen stories of empty drop lingered underneath her toes. The rising current blew her crimson bangs up in the air.

*It's a leap of faith.*

But in what? The entire plan was a mess. What happened to the unwavering strategy laid out in the *Carmora's* nav room? Jati was gone. But Hekron was dead. The PA was leaving. But Aradus would no longer cause political mayhem. Where should she put her faith? She thought of the child, Lazro.

*In the future.*

She pushed off. Blaster fire sparked the rails. One arm stretched for the ladder's crossbar, the other clutched the book against her side. She fell in a failing arc. One, two, three handles passed. She reached for the next one. Grabbing it was going to be...

*Smack!* Ailo clasped the rail and face-planted into the bar below. Teeth shattered. Lips split. Warm liquid filled her mouth. The vertical railing collided with her hip and the blaster came loose and dropped. She smashed the leg against the ladder. The thigh caught the muzzle and the weapon dangled over the fifteen-story drop.

The guard would be in range in seconds. They'd pick her off with ease dangling from the ladder.

Ailo spit out blood and teeth and slid the leg holding the weapon up the railing. The blaster wobbled and slipped.

*Relax.*

She eased the leg higher. Her eyes shut to the pain in her mouth, Ailo instructed her mind to listen and relinquish control to the sights and sounds of the Core complex. With the same potency as the Ran Cycle on Heroon, an internal world opened and a mental architectural space took shape.

The rattling of the guard's steps told her their position on the railing. One side of her brain tracked the footfalls running around the Core while the other half worked to get the blaster within reach. She leaned to one side and hooked the arm with the book around the rail.

In a virtual simulation in her mind, the guard drew their blaster and aimed. Ailo's knee, slid like an amphibian's beyond her waist toward her shoulder. She let go of her grip on that side of the crossbar and withdrew her knee. Her body rotated to face the guard. The sentinel's blaster rose. Ailo's fell. The guard's shot hit the center of the ladder, but the punk kid turned strategist and tactician swung to the other side. Eyes closed, her fingers touched the handle of the blaster as gravity took it. She gripped it and returned to the visible world. The guard stood right where she expected. Her shot hit them square in the chest.

The arm with the book slipped. Ailo released the blaster and grabbed hold to save herself from falling. The weapon clanged off the rails into depths.

*"We're a long way from T9, Ai."*

Ailo laughed through busted teeth and stared down the ladder. The visible palace floors below blurred.

*Oh no...*

A throbbing drum rose inside her head as if someone hammered against the inside of her skull, trying to break out of a cranial prison. Her body weight doubled in her grip. Muscle strength halved. Fingers struggled to keep hold of the railing.

*The booster... it's the rebound.*

A foot slipped off the bar, forcing more strength into her hand gripping the railing.

"Not now," she grunted, putting all her energy into lifting the leg back on to a step. Any step she could find.

*Where is it?*

Was her foot moving as slow as she thought or was it her mind playing tricks?

The hammering in her head grew louder and the pain of exhaustion severe. She couldn't do it, not with so much strength needed to hold on with one arm. Her other boot wobbled, the updraft rushing past and adding to the confusion. Ridge by ridge the sole of her foot slid off the railing, like a clock's second hand.

*Need to pull up...*

With the toe of her boot, she pushed. It slipped off.

"Arggh!" The scream vanished in the torrent of passing air.

She dangled by one arm. In her other hand, two fingers and thumb gripped the spine of the book. Using her elbow, she tucked it close against her side.

*I'm not letting go of it. Not this time.*

Pad by pad each digit slid off the bar. She thought of Rence's hand dragging over her own in the Lorassian's deep until it lost contact and he vanished in the darkness.

It was the book or her body.

*I'm not letting...*

She fell.

# THIRTY-NINE

Ailo pulled the book into the center of her chest, crossing both arms and clutching it tight. Floor after floor passed as she faced upward, watching the dome recede. In flashes, the blue lightning released from the structure's apex revealed the interior as if in a dream.

Falling wasn't so bad. It got easier the further she descended, as the sensation of gravity lost the fight with the inevitable. Even the passing floors were moving slower. Maybe the impact would be painless.

*As long as it's quick.*

She hugged the book in tight. Flashes of blue stories above flickered.

The end had to be close now.

*Time to let go.*

She shut her eyes and waited.

Disorientation took over as she lost visible contact. She'd turned, or rolled over, because now she was being pushed down.

Her stomach did that strange thing like when they'd come out of FTL the first time. A little flutter, like banging a cup of liquid on a table.

*Did I hit water?*

She could still breathe. That didn't make sense, nor did it make sense that the air would be pushing on her back. Unless she was...

*Rising.*

The roar brought her back from the dream of death. Neither rising nor falling, she was...

*Hovering.*

Eyes still closed, as if dreaming, she'd returned to Ffossk and lay on the top of a geyser's plume. The big one outside the rehab center. Her favorite. The one that rumbled and spouted water off every five seconds. That would explain the roaring noise.

*Maybe I never left and I'm still in bed. Arira is here. We can start again.*

She leaned left and plummeted. Reality smacked her in the face. Her location came back in hard clarity:

*Ceron. Garassit. The Palace. In the Core.*

Ailo rotated back and felt a blast and push of forceful air as she rose a few feet and then halted, hovering.

Saved by the very thing she wished to destroy, she lay suspended in mid-air in an equilibrium. The force of the rising current and the weight of her body through gravity finding balance.

*Just like Cesix station.*

She opened her eyes. Over the near deafening sound of rushing wind, she released an arm outward and bent her legs. Her body tilted upward to a forty-five degree angle.

The railing along the second floor, marked in large letters in blue on a hallway, looked to be no more than twenty feet below and to her right. A circular railing ran around the edge of the floor, framing the open air and Core within the center of the palace interior.

She peeked down, adjusting her legs and arm against the updraft to maintain control in the blowing tunnel. The interior ladder on the Core she'd fallen from led to a crosswalk with an exit.

*Dance the wind.*

She twisted, reversing her position. The updraft blinded her with its strength, forcing her eyes shut. With as much strength as she could muster, she pried the book off her chest and held it down to block the current from her eyes. Ailo maneuvered her legs as a counterbalance. In a series of back and forth motions, she lowered herself through the air like a feather falling in a rocking motion.

A flashing image of the air tube passing by Rence in the Lorassian's depths came into her mind.

The causeway came within her reach. She released a hand from the book to grab it.

*Smack!*

The book pelted her in the face from the force of the updraft.

Her body straightened and dove underneath the railing. She danced herself horizontal and flew back up, slamming into the underside.

*Smack!*

Pain shot through her body. She screamed, the sound carried away in the updraft.

Ailo lay pinned underneath the causeway. Using the same rocking motion of a feather, she made her way to the edge of the second floor like a human body inflated with helium. Each time she moved, she slammed into the underside of the causeway.

Knees and elbows battered, but the book clutched tight, she made it to the edge.

*Here we go. One chance.*

She rotated. Her body shot up in the hot blowing air. A hand went for the railing.

*Got it!*

The first grasp she'd given away with the book in the desperate moment off a collapsing Cesix station, and the second one she couldn't keep with Rence in the Lorassian's deep. This time, her earlier losses returned and saved her.

With a little maneuvering, she made it to the causeway, fighting the rush of air through the open grating. Pulling along with her legs, bar-by-bar bar until she cleared the updraft, she collapsed onto the ground of the second floor.

Panting and prone, she took in her surroundings.

The second level did not match the palace aesthetic. Stark unadorned white walls lacked the usual designs and subtle ornamentation elsewhere in the complex, its look more in keeping with a military station than a castle.

That meant a better chance of a potential way out.

Exhausted, but alive, Ailo smiled, knowing that now she had the advantage.

*Time to be a ghost.*


Once again, Ailo haunted the halls and passageways of the Garassian palace. She snaked her way down the corridors looking for a sign of what direction to take.

"I don't want this getting out," a familiar voice said around a corner. "Not until we've decided how it should be messaged." Ailo put a face and name to the words: the ambassador who'd talked with Aradus, the one he'd called 'Morienda'.

"Yes, Minister," a stern, authoritative voice answered. She knew that tone.

*Military.*

Steps echoed off the cold floor, approaching. A steady, whirring hum accompanied the footfalls. Ailo slithered ahead to the next bend. A few feet short of the corner, an icon legible across the Arm glowed adjacent to an entrance: *Maintenance.*

Ailo put her back to the portal, elbow at the ready. She would wait until the last second before slipping inside.

"They're escorting the Hamut down now," Morienda said. "As soon as he gets here, get the body capsule loaded and get them away. I don't want that maniac Birevian changing her mind."

*Nisi.*

"What of Hekron's remains?" the other one asked.

"She's agreed to send a pod... with what's left him. In the end, perhaps it's best Aradus did not live to bear witness to the return of his nephew."

*They've found him and the word is out.*

"We'll find the youth," the one with the military voice said. "Last report is she's somewhere on the higher levels."

"Your sentinels better find her, Commander. She's managed to do more than evade capture. It's both a tragedy and an embarrassment."

*In your opinion.*

Ailo elbowed the button and backed inside the maintenance closet. The portal shut. Their muffled voices, and the steady whirring, passed as they walked on.

Nothing of use in the locker. Cleaning supplies, a few tools, and scrubbing devices couldn't replace the lost blaster. She opened the portal and peered out. Morienda and the commander strode around the corner. Ailo caught sight of the source of the whirring noise: the commander's locomotion aided by a prosthetic leg. She couldn't tell how much of the limb was mechanical, but the gait and fluttering fabric of the pant leg suggested higher than the knee.

Ailo scurried after them. At the turn, she leaned forward, clutching the book tight.

*There's my way out.*

Cold white lights in scalloped ceiling sconces illuminated a mid-sized interior docking bay. A transfer pod, of a make she didn't recognize rested on the tarmac. A short way back, like a sleek flattened egg, sat a large body capsule. Its aerodynamic shell reminded her of the ones on the *Carmora* used for cadavers sent into space.

*Oh, Jati.*

Ailo's stomach turned in sour lament. They were in there, resting, and she hoped, at peace. They must be; they'd always been since she met them.

*But not always.*

A new hand would write their story into Legion history or find another way to commemorate them.

Boar was right. In the end, leaving him in the cell turned out to yield an ironic and lucrative result. The Hamut, as a diplomat, had coaxed Nisi into returning Hekron's remains in exchange for Jati's body. Ailo couldn't imagine what that conversation must have been like. No matter. The important thing now was to get to that pod.

Morienda and the commander strode to the body capsule and stopped before it. The two spoke, nodding. Ailo scanned the bay. A control room hugged the interior wall to her right, adjacent to where she crouched. That helped. She could sneak up and under the window to get closer to the pod. But the question was: how to break across open ground without being spotted?

The Garassians moved to leave. Ailo sneaked along the wall to the control station, staying within earshot. Twenty feet ahead, the ramp to the com center cut across the tarmac, offering an enclosed crouching space. She dropped in and leaned up against its interior side.

"Are you staying?" Morienda asked as they walked past.

Ailo peeked up. The two Garassians headed for another portal on the opposite side of the bay.

"Yes," the commander said. "At least until the Hamut is on the pod. I will load the general's body with the others. It's only right."

They reached the exit.

Ailo needed a distraction, something to give her enough time to cross the open bay. The window of the control station ran around both visible sides.

*Screw it.* It was such a simple, stupid prank but it was all she had.

*Punk kid from T9 time...*

Crouching low, she scurried up close to the portal and reached up. Her knuckles wrapped on the frame.

She dashed across the bay.

Would it be enough to turn the controller's attention and reach the pod?

Ailo's sixth sense alarm went off, telling her she wouldn't make it. On instinct, she veered for the body capsule and slid around the far side, away from the control tower. Bent low, her eyes got a view of Boar and the Garassians walking into the bay. Her sixth sense was right; she would never have made it unseen.

The trio walked toward the capsule. Now she was

trapped.

*Jati. Help me.*

"I'm relieved we reached an agreement," Boar said.

She had a minute at most before they'd reach her position.

*Jati. Help me. You've always guided me. I was a stowaway, and you... that's it!*

She ran a finger along the capsule's edge and searched for the latch. With a flip, it rotated and the seal broke. The sleek coffin popped open. She'd need about a foot of space to slide inside. Her hand pushed the lid up. It extended a few inches and stuck.

*What's wrong?*

She pushed again but it wouldn't budge. Thirty seconds and they'd be at the capsule.

Her legs unbent far enough so her eyes were parallel with the rim. The hook on the mechanism lay millimeters from the release edge. Ailo groped inside with her fingers but they stopped short of the latch. Pushing in earnest, the tip of one grazed it. The nail caught on it.

*Come on...*

She pushed and the nail cracked, causing her to wince. Her hand flung out and landed on her thigh, coming to rest on a subtle contour protruding from her suit.

*The wedge.*

She withdrew the token and shoved her hand into the opening, the lucky wedge pinched between two fingers. The thin wafer covered the distance. With a flick of her wrist, the latch flipped open.

"Here we are," Morienda said approaching the capsule.

Up and inside she went, tumbling on top of Jati who lay prone in the darkness. Hands groping over their body, Ailo oriented herself in the small space next to them as the lid sank back down.

*Thank the Arm for the wedge.*

Her hand closed on nothing.

*The wedge!*

In the crack of light, Ailo caught sight of it resting on the edge, about to fall on the outside of the shell.

Morienda's voice grew louder. "I am glad you were able to negotiate this, Councilor. You are lucky, Kin-tuk. You should be heading for a life sentence."

"You have no intel on where Arira is being held?" Boar asked, ignoring Morienda's remark.

"No," the commander answered. "Unfortunately, none of us other than Hekron and Admiral Hirok were privy to that information."

Ailo groped a hand along the interior to pull the capsule's seal shut. Working blind, her fingers found a small recessed ledge. She pulled down with careful delicacy.

The coffin sealed.

The wedge clanged to the ground outside.

*Sake of the...!*

"You dropped something," the commander's deep voice said.

"Did I?" Boar asked.

*Yes, you stupid Hamut. Come on!*

"Isn't that yours?" Morienda said. "It looks like a Rim wedge."

Ailo put her arm across Jati's chest, their muscles soft and warm from recent life.

*The wedge, Jati. It started it all.*

Would it be the end?

"Oh, so it is," Boar said. "My lucky Rim wedge." A groan from the Hamut followed.

*He's picking it up.*

"It's a keepsake from the old days. Reminds me of a time when we were allies."

"Indeed," the commander said.

*Boar you brilliant diplomat. I'll never call you stupid again, I promise.*

"Unless you object, I'd like to get going," Boar said. "Before *someone* changes their mind. Birevians are quite unpredictable, as you know."

"I've ordered my personal guard to load the capsule in the pod," the commander said.

"Thank you. That's very diplomatic and gracious of you."

"We will, of course, run a scan of the pod to confirm identity before departure," Morienda said.

"Of course," Boar answered.

Ailo exhaled as the footsteps faded away.

Feet marching in time neared. Her stomach lurched as the capsule rose and wobbled in the sentinels' hands.

"There's a Legion soldier in there," the commander's deep voice came through the barrier. "They may be our enemy now, but they were once our ally. Be respectful."

The capsule swung left and right like two people carrying a sack. Ailo's feet lifted to a forty-five-degree angle and blood rushed to her head as the soldiers walked up the ship's ramp.

A pallbearer grunted.

"Yes, it's no easy task," the commander said. "Jati was big in both body and spirit."

With a thud, Ailo bounced once as the capsule came to rest.

"I'll be right there," the commander said. "Dismissed."

*What are they doing?*

Ailo held her breath.

*They know I'm in here.*

She froze.

"I've never seen anyone fight with greater skill, or demonstrate a degree of humility, determination, and sacrifice as you did today. I watched from the palace. If I had been on the plain I would have never..." An audible sigh reached Ailo's ears inside the capsule. "It's an honor to share a Legion heritage with you, sibling. I'm embarrassed to be part of those who opposed you today."

Ailo heard two thuds and knew the commander had crossed their arms on their chest in a Legion salute.

"Sides in this mess of an Arm, be damned," the Garassian said. "Rest in peace, fellow soldier. Aim true, wherever you are heading. To the end."

The commander's whirring steps fell away.

A tear ran down Ailo's cheek. The soldier's private eulogy confirmed everything she'd learned about the person lying next to her. And the words were spoken by someone on the other side of their war.

*"Are there really sides, Firecracker?"* It was as if Jati's voice whispered from their corpse.

She wiped the tear away.

The Arm would be forever changed by Jati's presence. If nothing else, for Ailo, there was hope. The PA hadn't run a military gambit ending in certain catastrophe. A friend-turned-traitor had been exposed and eliminated by their own impatience and greed. But a daughter remained captive and the Arm remained divided and threatened by abuse of power.

She'd gotten vengeance and her parent's book. It didn't turn out how anyone expected. Jati wagered everything on this, and on her, even their life.

What would become of the PA's war effort? How would the Assembly respond to Jati's brazen ignorance of their orders? To Nisi's actions?

*And mine...*

"Scan complete," a voice over the pod's com announced. "Two identities confirmed. The pilot and the deceased."

*And one ghost.*

"Clear for departure."

In the darkness, Ailo sensed the shift in gravity as Boar lifted the pod off the tarmac. With a surge of the thrusters, they shot out of the bay and away from the palace. Her feet tipped upward in the body capsule as the Hamut aimed for space and the protection and safety of the armada in orbit.

"PA main, this is Pod GR5," Boar said into the com. "Exit pattern: Garassian loop, requesting exo-docking algorithm."

"GR5 this is the *Carmora*."

*Tera!*

"Boar, is that you?" Nisi's voice cut into the line.

"Affirmative. I'm on my way up and request a docking track."

"Come to us. Tera, send him the coordinates. And go ahead and send down the other capsule."

*Hekron's remains. And Nisi is captain of the* Carmora *now.*

"What about Arira? Anything?" Boar asked.

Ailo waited. Nothing but silence over the com.

"Sorry," Nisi said. "Was working on your exo-route. Nothing. Firde couldn't dig anything up. The coordinates died with Jati. It's my fault, Boar. But we'll keep..."

"I have them!" Boar's voice broke in. "Son of a Gor...I have them, Nisi. Take down these numbers."

"Go," Tera said.

The pod banked hard to the right. "5... 79... wait... G..."

"Your off-course, Boar," Nisi said.

"I know. Hold on," he said. "G8. That's a sector in Garissit, right? That means..."

"It's a grid address," Tera said. "Coming through now... looks legit. I think that's where she is!"

"How?" Nisi added.

"It's scrawled on the ground," Boar said. "Big sweeping lines."

Ailo felt the pod bank left and start to climb.

"Burned into the open plaza, where Jati..."

Ailo gasped in the darkness. Jati's movements at the end of the duel. They were writing on the ground. The image of the Legion soldier dragging the Caster's laser blade across the dirt, with desperate pathos, flashed into her mind.

"I'm not done yet," they'd said defiantly between rasping breaths. A last desperate gesture before their heart failed them.

*But it didn't. It saved Arira. And the Arm.*

She hugged Jati's lifeless body in the dark.

*And me.*

Pride. Nobility. Honor. They were just words. Until now.

And there was one more. The one she'd asked Jati about.

*Tragedy.*

"I've got you on a track," Tera said over the comm, "should be on your board... now. I've got a pilot and one passenger for the log."

The lament in Tera's voice at the reference to Jati's body hung in the silence.

"Correction," Boar said, breaking it. "Pilot and *two* passengers."

*What?*

"Two?" Nisi asked, excited.

"Affirmative, *Captain.*"

Ailo couldn't hold back a smile at Boar's nod of respect. Raucous voices came over the open comm line to the *Carmora's* bridge.

"We'll meet you in the bay," Nisi said, over the rabble. An abrupt silence followed as she cut the *Carmora's* com line.

"Like I said," Boar's voice crackled over the pod's internal com, "you've got Outer Rim written all over you."

# FORTY

The path is laid.

A line is drawn.

And with a single step, a new journey begins.

Thanks to Jati, my work is done. No need to wax poetic here. Ailo no longer needs me. I don't expect our conversations to continue. Nor will she lean on me again, even when she's alone. From here, I'm a well-oiled and functioning internal manager. Or, to put it another way, now I'm the ghost.

The dam burst and Ai's flood passed. The waters settled. Her river flows steady and strong. Future obstacles can't block her life's direction or stop its flow. She'll redirect her course or glide the current with ease.

They'll be no more internal combat. With Jati's guidance, she's set herself free. Don't get me wrong, Ai will keep fighting. You haven't seen anything yet. Liberation unleashed is an unstoppable form of hope.

Wherever her river is heading, one thing is certain. The rudder is in the hands of a budding warrior.

\* \* \*

# CREDITS

Cover Design—Jessica Moon
Cover Layout—Chad Moon
Cover Art—Zishan Liu
Editing—Susan Floyd
Editing—Mandy Russell
Formatting—Mandy Russell

# ACKNOWLEDGEMENTS

First and foremost, I would like to thank my wife, Mallary, for her endless support and patience with my newfound love of fiction writing. To my mother, Nancy, thank you for playing the ever-willing first reader of my stories. You suffer through unfinished narratives with patience and offer vital early feedback, as well as important doses of enthusiasm when I am struggling and unsure of where a story is heading.

As with my debut novel, *Goodbye to the Sun*, a crew of trusted and reliable individuals shaped what became the final version of this book. Continuing their dedication and commitment to reading early drafts, beta readers Heath Mensher and Sharon Burke were invaluable assets. My critique partners, Lindsay and Michael Wells, went above and beyond for a second time in this series – providing layers of important critical observations and feedback as fellow writers. To all four of you: much of your influence sits in the pages of the book, implicit and explicit. As with *Goodbye to the Sun*, an early structural edit by Jonathan Oliver and a very important sensitivity reading by Catarina Nabais made the story, my writing, and the world building better and more appropriate for contemporary readers.

Mentorship from veteran authors can influence a writer's professionalism and outward facing identity. Two people have offered sage advice, guidance, and hard-to-hear but important "truths" about navigating the world of publishing. I would like to thank Michael Mammay and Dan Fitzgerald for providing valuable support and mentorship during the writing and revising of this book. It's a privilege to be able to learn from each of you. I am very thankful for your gracious generosity and support.

The general theory and psychological architecture for the role of Gerib in *Jati's Wager* is built from the very real work and theories of Richard Schwartz, Ph.D. Internal Family Systems, a popular method in the field of psychotherapy invented by Dr. Schwartz, was the basis for Gerib as manager, as well as the other "parts" within Ailo that formed her internal dynamic.

I would like to acknowledge Vladimir Stepanovich Korolev, Elena Nikoleavna Polyvakhova, and Irina Yurievna Pototskaya for their article discussing solar sail spacecraft in photogravitational fields (2020). That academic discussion helped spurn the idea for Cesix station. While the statitite in *Jati's Wager* is the stuff of soft science fiction, several of the general principles came from their serious scientific study and conclusions, as well as from other sources readily available to an amateur dreamer such as myself, who gleaned ideas from the Internet and turned them into half-baked speculative realities.

Lastly, my thanks to the editors, designers, and publishers at Shadow Spark. Jessica Moon, Mandy Russell, and Susan Floyd continue to make my books hit the shelves with exciting covers and well-tuned pages both in language and formatting. A thousand things happen behind the scenes on a book's journey to publication. I don't see or understand many of the parts, but I appreciate them nevertheless and all of you for your hard work and dedication. I look forward to working with you on the last book in this trilogy, *No Song, But Silence*.

## ABOUT THE AUTHOR

Jonathan Nevair is a science fiction writer and, as Dr. Jonathan Wallis, an art historian and Professor of Art History at Moore College of Art & Design, Philadelphia. After two decades of academic teaching and publishing, he finally got up the nerve to write fiction. Jonathan grew up on Long Island, NY but now resides in southeast Pennsylvania with his wife and rambunctious mountain feist, Cricket.

You can find him online at www.jonathannevair.com and on Twitter as @JNevair.

Printed in Great Britain
by Amazon